Suddenly

ALSO BY BARBARA DELINSKY

FICTION

The Secret Between Us

Family Tree

Looking for Peyton Place

The Summer I Dared

Flirting with Pete

An Accidental Woman

The Woman Next Door

The Vineyard

Lake News

Coast Road

Three Wishes

A Woman's Place

Shades of Grace

Together Alone

For My Daughters

More Than Friends

The Passions of Chelsea Kane

A Woman Betrayed

Within Reach

Variation on a Theme

Finger Prints

Moment to Moment

The Carpenter's Lady

Fast Courting

An Irresistible Impulse

Gemstone

Passion and Illusion

Search for a New Dawn

A Time to Love

Sensuous Burgundy

Sweet Ember

Rekindled

NONFICTION

Uplift: Secrets from the Sisterhood of
Breast Cancer Survivors

Does a Lobsterman Wear Pants?

Suddenly

Barbara Delinsky

An Imprint of HarperCollins*Publishers*

Mass market editions of this book were published in 1994 by Harper Paperbacks and in 2002 by HarperTorch, an imprint of HarperCollins Publishers.

FIRST HARPERLUXE EDITION

HarperLuxe™ is a registered trademark of HarperCollins Publishers

Library of Congress Cataloging-in-Publication Data has been applied for.

ISBN: 978-0-06-147055-4

08 09 10 11 12 ID/RRD 10 9 8 7 6 5 4 3 2 1

Acknowledgments

For the accuracy of many of the thoughts and facts included herein, I owe thanks to Judy Brice, pediatric nursepractitioner, without whom I would never have survived motherhood; to Mary Lou Eschelman of Wide Horizons for Children, which specializes in international adoptions; to Jonathan Epstein, who led me patiently through the morass of the mass casualty incident; and to Marilyn Brier, mental health consultant, fan, and friend.

For encouragement and guidance through both the writing of this book and the shaping of my career, I thank Karen Solem, my editor, and Amy Berkower, my literary agent.

And always, for the deep connect, I thank my lucky stars for my husband, Steve, and my sons Eric, Andrew, and Jeremy.

One

Paige Pfeiffer ran at the front of the pack, setting a pace that a less bold thirty-nine-year-old might not dare, but she had a point to prove and a bet to win. The bet involved dinner at Bernie's Béarnaise, central Vermont's most chichi restaurant. The point was that a woman her age who was in shape could easily beat a woman half her age who wasn't. At stake was the respect of the Mount Court Academy girls' varsity cross-country team, of which she was head coach for the fifth year in a row.

The race had become a tradition, albeit a predictable one. For the first of the three miles, the girls tossed cocky comments from one to the next. The comments waned during the second mile, which wove through a path in the woods and grew demanding of teenage bodies that had spent the summer indulging in the luxuries of the rich. Back on the road for the third mile, the pack thinned. Laboring runners fell behind. Only the stars of the team stayed with Paige.

There were six stars this year. Five of them had run for her the year before. The other was new to the school.

"How we doin'?" Paige asked of the group, and heard gasping complaints. Feeling wicked, she smiled. "Let's pick it up." She moved easily ahead of the others. Three moved with her. Minutes later, when she increased the pace again, only one remained. It was the new girl, so quiet up to that point that Paige knew little more than that her name was Sara Dickinson. Paige was surprised by her stamina. She was doubly surprised when, with a surge of speed, the girl took the lead.

Paige had to work to stay with her as they turned in under the wrought-iron arch that marked the school's entrance, and for a minute she wondered if indeed she were past her prime. When the thought of that rankled, she dug deep inside and found the wherewithal to draw even. Shoulder to shoulder they ran, down the long drive cordoned with tall oaks whose leaves were a ripe September green. Without missing a beat, they veered off onto the dirt path that cut to the field house.

"You're good," Paige breathed with a look at the girl beside her. She was tall for her age, had a lithe build, a comfortable stride, and a look of concentration that was nothing if not stern.

As Paige watched in darting glances, that concentration suddenly shifted, and in the space of seconds she was alone. Sara had reversed direction and was walking, winded but intent, toward the shrubbery edging the path. One by one, the others joined her there.

Paige made a wide turn and, slowing to a cool-down pace, headed back. In various stages of breathlessness, the girls were grouped around Sara, who was crouched beside a spreading yew. It was a minute before Paige saw what was beneath the bottommost branch.

"It's so tiny!"

"Whose *is* it?"

"How did it *get* here?"

Forgetting the race, Paige knelt down. She took the kitten, which was orange and gray and mewling piteously, in her hand and asked Sara, "How did you ever spot it hidden this way?"

"Something moved," Sara said, and the chorus resumed.

"It doesn't belong here. Mount Court only has dogs."

"Someone must have snuck it in—"

"Then abandoned it."

"It looks starved."

Paige was thinking the same and wondering what could be done, when all eyes turned her way.

"We can't *leave* it here."

"It'll die, it's so little."

"That'd be cruel."

"You'll have to take it, Dr. Pfeiffer."

Paige pictured her overstuffed home. "I don't have room for a pet. I don't have time for one."

"Cats are easy. They take care of themselves."

"*You* keep it," Paige countered.

"We can't."

"It's against dorm rules."

Paige had coached at Mount Court long enough to know that breaking the rules was a way of life, and while she certainly didn't condone it, she was amused. "Against dorm rules? What else is new?"

"The Head, that's what."

"He's an asshole."

"*Big* time."

"He expelled two guys on the second day of school."

"For what?" Paige asked, overlooking foul language for the sake of goodwill.

"Smoking pot."

"There was no warning, nothing."

"He's totally anal."

"We're talking crack-down city—"

"No-no-Noah—"

"Mount Court Penitentiary."

Paige hadn't met the new Head yet and was picturing something with horns when the pleading resumed.

"Take the kitten, Dr. Pfeiffer."

"It'll die if you don't."

"Do you want that on your conscience?"

Paige stroked the tiny creature, which was little more than a handful of fur and bones, and trembling at that. "I'm being manipulated."

"It's for a good cause," one of the girls said.

Paige shot her a chiding look. "It's for a good cause" was what she always said when she pushed the girls for an extra campus loop. "But I don't know where to *begin*," she protested, a mistake if ever there was one because the words were barely out of her mouth when she was barraged with advice on food, litter, and housing. Ten minutes later she found herself in her car with the kitten in a cardboard box on the seat beside her.

"Only until I find it a home," she warned out the window as she drove off and, determined to do just that, headed straight into town. She pulled up at the police station, intent on presenting the kitten to the animal officer, but he was gone for the day. So she left him a note and tried the General Store. The family who owned it had cats. They had lots of cats. She didn't figure another would make a difference, especially one so tiny.

"Can't do," Hollis Weebly said with a sad shake of his head. "Just had to put one of ours to sleep. Feline leukemia. It'll get the others, too. And yours, if I take it. You'd be best keeping it yourself. You're a doctor. You'll take good care."

Paige was feeling desperate as she followed him up and down the short aisles, making her case. "I'm a pediatrician. I don't know the first thing about cats."

"But you know the vet, and he does. So take it there in the morning, and he'll tell you what you have to know. Here." He thrust a large brown paper bag into her arms. "All you need 'til then." He guided her to the door. "Give it fresh water with the food, and a warm place to sleep."

"But I can't keep it."

"It'll love you, doc. Everyone loves you."

She was suddenly back in her car, with kitten supplies and the kitten, and Hollis had returned to his store.

"Swell," she told the tiny creature, which had fallen asleep snug in a corner of its box. "I am not a pet person, but does anyone listen?" She was a people person.

Between the hospital, the office, and the school, her days were a medley of interpersonal happenings, and she liked it that way. She lived to a smooth, steady rhythm.

Mara, now Mara was the one to take the kitten. She was a sucker for the defenseless, had a heart of gold, and between the loss of her last foster child and the baby from India who would be months yet in coming, she needed a distraction.

After arriving home, Paige tried phoning her friend and colleague, but there was no answer. So she carried the kitten box inside and went back for the supplies. By the time she had mashed food into a bowl, the kitten was awake and crying. It started eating the instant she placed it before the food.

She sat and watched, thinking that the kitten was a mere step from newborn, that it looked more like a mouse than a cat, that maybe it should be drinking milk. A human baby drank milk, if not breast milk, then formula, and if it had a lactose intolerance, there was a solution to that, too. Paige knew all the options for a human baby. A kitten was something else.

The kitten kept eating. After a minute, she wiped out an old plastic basin and filled it with litter. She set it down not far from the food and was about to plunk the kitten in it, as the girls had instructed, when the phone rang.

It was her answering service with an evening emergency. The victim was a five-year-old who, in the course of a backyard baseball game, had stepped up to the plate before his predecessor was done there. The bat—plastic, mercifully—had connected with his eyebrow.

Paige arranged to meet father and son at the Emergency Room of Tucker General in twenty minutes, which gave her just enough time to shower and get there herself.

The boy didn't appear to be concussed, but the gash was a deep one that would leave an unsightly scar if not stitched well. More immediate, he was terrified of the hospital and of Paige. So she sat for a bit before she began, telling him in the gentlest of terms what she would do, and even then it wasn't easy. Application of the anesthetic hurt, and no amount of compassion on Paige's part could prevent that. Once it had taken effect, though, the stitching was a breeze. She rewarded the boy's valor with a barley pop and a hug, then walked him and his dad to their car.

She was barely back inside when her beeper sounded. One of her newer patients, a nine-month-old who had been feverish during much of the day, had awoken from sleep hotter than ever and screaming. The parents were frantic. Paige, who was more worried about the parents than the child, directed them to bring her in.

"You wouldn't by chance want a kitten?" she asked the desk nurse, who quickly shook her head. "Know anyone who might?" When the nurse looked dubious, she volunteered, "I have one, if any possibilities come to mind."

She tried to call Mara again, again with no luck.

The baby had an ear infection. After instructing the parents on the fastest way to lower her temperature, giving them antibiotics enough to last until they could go to the pharmacy in the morning, and reassuring them that the child would be fine, Paige walked them to the parking lot. That was when an ambulance came screeching to the door.

In the hours that ensued, Paige knew why she had chosen to practice medicine in Tucker, Vermont, rather than in Boston, Chicago, or New York. In Tucker she came as close to being a general practitioner as most modern doctors got. While pediatrics was her specialty, the nature of the region and its medical community dictated an "all hands on deck in a storm" approach. In this case, the storm was a multicar accident, and though there were staff doctors on hand, her presence was put to good use. She stitched lacerations, set bones, even ran a fetal monitor on one of the victims, who was in her eighth month of pregnancy. Had the woman gone into labor, Paige would have handled that, too. Delivering babies was nearly as gratifying as seeing sick children get better, which was what her practice was about.

She had the occasional downer. Inevitably a child came by who was sick enough to need a specialist, and of that number there were the occasional grim prognoses. But these were the exceptions. For the most part, Paige's practice was about birth, growth, and healing.

It was one in the morning when she returned home, exhausted in a satisfied way. She might have passed through the dark house and been asleep in bed within minutes had she not tripped over the kitten's box on her way through the kitchen. In a rush, she remembered the baby. Apparently it remembered her, too, because the noise of her fall set off a distant meowing. She followed the sound through the living room and down the short hall to her bedroom. There, nestled between the patch-work pillows on her bed, was the tiny furball.

She picked it up. "What are you doing here, baby? You're supposed to be in the kitchen." The kitten began to purr. Paige stroked the fuzzy spot between its ears. Lulled by the fragile motoring sound, she sank onto the rattan love seat that bridged a corner of the room and relaxed against a second slew of patchwork pillows. She drew up her feet, which she had been on for eighteen hours straight, and might have purred right along with the kitten.

"Y'like this, huh?" she asked, feeling a vague pleasure. She knew she couldn't possibly keep the kitten, but for the moment it wasn't all bad.

She thought to try Mara again. Mara rarely slept before two in the morning, and then not for long. She was a brooder. She was also an activist, which meant that she had plenty to brood about. No doubt now it was Tanya John, the foster child who had run away. That one had hit Mara hard.

Then again, for that very reason and the fact that Mara had been looking tired of late, Paige didn't want to call on the off chance that she might indeed be asleep.

The kitten was curled in a ball, its nose tucked to its thigh, its eyes nearly closed. She carried it to the kitchen and carefully set it in its box, but she was barely back in the hall when it darted past. It was waiting on the bed when she arrived. Suddenly too tired to mind, she undressed and climbed in. She didn't have another thought until the phone jangled by her ear the next morning.

Ginny, the office receptionist, was calling to say that it was eight-thirty and Mara hadn't shown up. She was neither answering her phone nor responding to her beeper.

Paige grew concerned. She pulled the phone onto the bed and tried to call Mara herself, with no more success than she had had the night before. She couldn't imagine Mara had gone far, not with patients waiting to see her. Paige half imagined that she had been out driving the night before—she often did that when she was upset—and had pulled off the road when exhaustion had hit, and fallen asleep in her car.

Grateful for small-town familiarities, she punched out the number of the Tucker Police Department and explained the problem to the deputy chief, who promised to check the roads and Mara's house and sounded delighted to have something to do. The occasional automobile accident notwithstanding, Tucker, Vermont, was a sleepy community. Any excitement was welcome.

Paige set down the phone and made for the shower. Too few minutes' worth of hot spray later, she opened the door and reached for a towel, then made a sound of alarm when something small scampered through the steam.

She let out a breath. "You frightened me, kitty. I forgot you were here. Just looking around?" She dried herself off. "There isn't a lot to see. My place isn't what you'd call big."

She suddenly pictured her not-big place puddled with not-big gifts from the not-big kitten to which she hadn't shown the litter box. Fearing the worst, she returned to the bedroom and hurried into black overalls and a white T-shirt. After running a brush through hair that fell in waves just shy of her shoulders, she took the kitten to the kitchen and set it down where she should have set it the night before. "Okay. Do your thing." She noticed a bulge in the litter. "Ahhh, you've already done it. Good kitty." She also noticed that much of the food was gone, so she added more, refilled the water dish, then quickly drank a glass of orange juice and set the glass in the sink.

"I'm off to work," she told the kitten, who was studying her with tiny round eyes. "Don't look at me that way. I always go to work. That's why I can't have a pet." She knelt and gave the kitty a pat. "And if Mara won't take you, someone else will. I'll find you a home where they'll love you to bits."

She straightened and looked down at the kitten. It seemed so small and alone that she felt a tugging inside. "Which is precisely why I don't want a pet," she muttered, and forced herself on out the door.

The office was packed. She moved from one examining room to the next with neither a break nor a thought to Mara until the bulk of the patients had been seen. When she finally returned to her office, she found herself face to face with the chief of police.

Something was wrong. She knew it instantly. Norman Fitch was a large, normally ruddy-faced man, but he looked as if he'd been kicked in the gut.

"She ran out of gas, but not before it did her in," he mumbled. "Garage door was shut tight."

Paige drew a blank. "What?"

"Dr. O'Neill. She's dead."

That word echoed first in the room, then in Paige's head. She didn't like it. She had *never* liked it, which was largely why, after she had fallen hopelessly in love with the idea of being a doctor, she had gone into pediatrics. Of all the disciplines, it used that word the least.

"Mara, dead?" It wasn't possible.

"We've taken her to the morgue," Norman said. "You'll have to identify the body."

The body. Paige pressed a hand to her mouth. Mara wasn't a *body.* She was a doer, a fighter, a whirlwind. The idea of *the body* inert in a morgue was incongruous with the woman herself.

"Mara? Dead?"

"Coroner will do an autopsy," Norman said, "but there's no sign of violence."

It was a minute before Paige followed, and another before her horror allowed her to speak. "Then . . . then you think she committed *suicide?*"

"Looks that way."

Paige shook her head. "She wouldn't. Not suicide. It must have been something else." *Mara dead?* It *couldn't* be. Paige glanced at the door, half expecting the woman in question to barge through wanting to know why Norman was there.

But she didn't barge through. The door remained shut, and Norman was insisting, "It's the classic technique. Easy as pie and painless."

"Mara wouldn't commit suicide," Paige insisted. "Not with her practice thriving. Not with a baby on the way."

"She was pregnant?" Norman asked, seeming appalled by this in ways that talk of *the body* hadn't horrified him, which angered Paige into a sharper tone.

"She was adopting. From India. It's taken forever, but everything is fine. Mara told me so just the other day. She said that the authorities in India had approved her, and that the baby would arrive in a month or so. She has a room all ready, with clothes and furniture, baby equipment, and toys. She was so excited."

"Why a month?"

"Red tape."

"Did that depress her?"

"It frustrated her."

"Was she depressed about the John girl?"

"Not *that* depressed. I would have known if she was. We were best friends."

Norman nodded. He shifted his weight. "Maybe you'd rather someone else identify the body?"

The body. There it was again, a sudden stark image devoid of mind and spirit, the antithesis of

Mara O'Neill. Paige couldn't picture it. It was wrong, obscene, perverse. She felt another spark of anger, then one of dismay.

"Dr. Pfeiffer?"

"It's all right," she managed. "I'll do it." She struggled to think. "But I'll need someone here." She phoned Angie, mentioning nothing of Norman's claim. To say the words would make them real. Likewise, she insisted on following Norman in her own car. The more casually she behaved, she reasoned, the less of a fool she would feel when this turned out to be a joke.

But she was playing games with herself. She knew it the instant she entered the morgue. The whole town knew Mara, including Norman Fitch, his deputy, and the coroner. Paige's identifying the body was a formality.

Death was quiet and still. It was a faint blue tinge to skin that had always been rosy. It was an immediate, stabbing sense of fear and loss and sadness. It was also strangely and unexpectedly peaceful.

Paige recalled the Mara who had been her college roommate, the one who had skied the Canadian Rockies with her, who had baked birthday cakes, knitted sweaters, and practiced medicine beside her in Tucker, Vermont. She recalled the Mara who had prodded her into campaigning for more than one worthy cause over the years.

"Oh, Mara," she whispered, tearing up, "what *happened?*"

"You saw nothing?" the coroner asked from the side. "No sudden mood swings?"

Paige took a minute to compose herself. "Nothing to suggest she would harm herself. She was tired. She was upset about Tanya John. When I talked with her last—"

"When was that?" Norman asked.

"Yesterday morning in the office. She was on a tear because the lab messed up some tests, but that was typical Mara." The tests had involved blood drawn from Todd Fiske, one of Mara's favorite four-year-olds. Paige would have been angry, too. She hated drawing blood from a child. Now it would have to be drawn again.

She couldn't imagine telling Todd and his family that Mara was gone. She couldn't imagine telling *anyone.*

"Oh, Mara," she whispered again. She needed to be away from this horrible place but couldn't seem to leave. It wasn't right that Mara was staying, not when she had so much yet to do.

Mara's family back in Eugene, Oregon, greeted Paige's news with a silence that told none of their thoughts. Mara had been estranged from them for years. Paige was saddened, though not surprised, when they asked that she be buried in Tucker.

"She chose to live there," Thomas O'Neill said tersely. "She lived there longer than anywhere else."

"What kind of arrangements should I make?" Paige asked. She knew that the O'Neills were devoutly religious, and though Mara hadn't been, Paige would have respected any request they made, especially one that showed caring.

There was no request, just a short, "Use your judgment. You knew her better than we did." Which saddened Paige all the more.

"Will you come?" she asked, and held her breath.

There was a pause, during which she felt an incredible pain on Mara's behalf, then slowly, finally, a reluctant, "We'll come."

Angie looked dumbfounded. "What?"

Paige repeated herself, all the while reliving her own disbelief. Mara O'Neill was full of life and energy. The concept of death didn't fit her.

Angie's eyes begged her to take back the words, and Paige wished she could. But denial was absurd, given what she had seen in the morgue.

"My God," Angie murmured after an agonizingly long and helpless minute. "Dead?"

Paige took a shuddering breath. She had been the one to introduce Angie to Mara. They had become friends to the extent that rarely a weekend passed without Mara stopping at Angie's, if not for Sunday brunch then for an afternoon to argue politics with Ben or sneak hot-fudge sundaes to Dougie.

Dougie. Paige's heart went out to him. Angie shielded him from life's dark side, but there would be no shielding now. Death was absolute. There were no halfway measures, no reprieves.

Angie was on the same wavelength as Paige. "Dougie will be crushed. He adored Mara. Just last Sunday they went hiking on the mountain." She looked uncharacteristically rattled, but only for a minute, which was how long it took her to order her thoughts. Then she questioned Paige on the hows and wheres of Mara's death. Paige related what she knew, which was far too little for Angie's peace of mind.

"What about the whys?" she wanted to know. "Suicide is the first thing that comes to mind when a person is found dead in her car in a closed garage with the engine running, but suicide doesn't fit Mara any more than death does. It might have been an accident. Mara's been looking tired. She might have fallen asleep without realizing the engine was on. But suicide? Without a cry for help? Without letting any of us know that she was even *near* the breaking point?"

The absurdity of it frustrated Paige, too. She prided herself on being observant, but she hadn't seen a thing to suggest Mara was on the edge.

Angie barreled on. "What about her patients? They'll have to be told. Most will hear about it through the grapevine and call us for confirmation. Should we let Ginny handle it from the front desk?"

Ginny was an able receptionist, but juggling the appointment book was a far cry from grief counseling. Fortunately Paige didn't have to point that out. Angie was already shaking her head.

"We'll have to talk with them ourselves. Mara was their champion. They'll need help dealing with her death. Her death. My *God*, that's awful."

Leaning against the edge of Angie's desk, sharing the pain with someone competent enough to help with the decisions, Paige could be weak as she hadn't been since she had found Norman in her office earlier that morning. She touched her throat. The vividness of Mara's death was choking her.

Angie gave her a hug. "I'm sorry, Paige," she said softly. "You were closer to her than I was." She drew back. "Have you told Peter?"

Paige shook her head. She forced the words out. "He's next on my list. He'll be as stunned as we are.

He thought Mara was tough as nails." She made a self-deprecating sound. "So did I. Never in a million years did I imagine she would . . . she would . . ." She couldn't say it.

Angie hugged her again. "Maybe she didn't."

"Without violence, what else could it be?"

"I don't know. We'll have to wait and see."

"Wait and see" implied the future. Catching a glimpse of it, Paige felt a deep inner pang. "The practice won't be the same without Mara. It's been an incredible foursome. Each of us different, but meshing into a great team. The group worked."

Paige was its common denominator. She had known Mara from college, Angie from a year-long overlap as pediatric residents in Chicago. Angie had taken time off to have Dougie, was living in New York and ready to return to work, when Paige connected with Peter, a native of Tucker with the kind of leisurely small-town practice that appealed to the others. Given the promise of the small community hospital nearby and the fact that none of the four pediatricians was out for big bucks, they pooled their time, effort, and expertise in a way that enabled them to offer high-quality medical care while working reasonable hours. Angie's pragmatism was a foil for Mara's dynamism; Paige's business sense countered Peter's provinciality. They complemented each other and were friends.

"Mara was a good doctor," Angie said in tribute. "She loved kids, and they loved her because they knew she was on their side. Her shoes will be hard to fill."

Paige could only nod in agreement. The sense of loss she felt was devastating.

"Will you be making the funeral plans?" Angie asked.

She nodded again. "Not looking forward to it."

"Can I help?"

She shook her head. "I have to." She owed it to Mara.

"We'll close on that day," Angie said. "Ginny can reschedule appointments once the plans are firmed up. In the meanwhile, I'll see as many of Mara's patients as I can. Peter will see the rest. Want me to call him?"

"No, no. I'll do it." Paige was, after all, the hub of the wheel. Hard to believe a spoke had been taken out for good.

She woke Peter from a deep sleep. He sounded none too pleased. "This had better be good, Paige. I'm not due at work until one."

"It's not good," she said, too mentally taut to cushion the blow. "Mara is dead."

"Dammit to hell, so was I. I didn't get to bed until two—"

"*Dead.* I just came back from the morgue."

There was a pause, then a more cautious, "What are you talking about?"

"They found her in her car in the garage," Paige said. With each repetition, the story grew increasingly surreal. "They're guessing carbon monoxide poisoning."

There was another pause, a longer one, then a puzzled, "She killed herself?"

Paige heard a mumbling in the background. She waited until Peter impatiently hushed it before saying, "They don't know what happened. The autopsy might tell us something, but in the meantime we need you here. I have to make plans for the funeral, and Angie is already—"

"Was there a note?" he asked sharply.

"No, no note. Angie is already seeing patients. We have to contact Mara's patients and let them know—"

"No note *at all?*"

"Norman didn't mention one, and I'm sure they looked."

Peter's voice rose a notch. "The *police* are involved?"

Paige was the puzzled one now. "They were the ones who found her. Is that bad?"

"No," he said more quietly. "Not really. It just makes the whole thing seem sinister."

"In that it was untimely, it is sinister, and if it's upsetting for us, just think of what Mara's patients will feel. She was so involved with them."

"Too involved," he declared. "I've been telling her so for years."

Paige knew that all too well. Peter and Mara had spiced up more than one group meeting with their banter. But Mara was no longer there to argue her side, so Paige did it for her. "Mara's involvement was of the good-hearted sort. She felt a strong moral commitment to her patients. And they loved her."

"This has to be about Tanya John. She was depressed about that."

"Clinically depressed? Enough to do herself harm?" Paige couldn't imagine it. "Besides, her baby was coming. She had so much to look forward to." Paige was going to have to call the adoption agency with the news, but she figured it could wait until the funeral was done.

"Maybe the adoption fell through."

"No. She would have told me if it had, and she didn't say a word." Certainly not the morning before, which was the last time Paige had seen her. "When did you see her last?" she asked Peter.

"Yesterday afternoon around, say, four-thirty. We were on the last batch of appointments. She asked me to cover so she could leave early."

"Did she say where she was going?"

"No."

"Was she upset?"

"She was distracted. Very distracted, come to think of it. But nicely so. She's usually so *strident*."

Paige had to smile at the helpless way he said it. But he was right. If Mara wasn't fighting one war, she was fighting another. She was an advocate for those who couldn't speak for themselves. Now, suddenly, the advocate was silent.

Paige bowed her head. "I have to make calls, Peter. How soon can you be here?"

"Give me an hour."

She swept a handful of hair from her face and looked up. "An hour's too long. Angie needs help, and you're five minutes away. Look, I know that I've interrupted something"—the mumbling in the background had been female, no doubt Lacey, Peter's latest love—"but we need you. The group works because we all care about the practice, and the practice is at stake. Our patients depend on us. We owe it to them to minimize the trauma of Mara's death."

"I'll be there as soon as I can," he snapped, and hung up before Paige could press further.

Two

Paige planned the funeral for Friday, two days after Mara's body was found, time enough to allow for the O'Neills' journey east and her own acceptance of Mara's death. But the latter didn't even begin to happen. Not only did Paige feel guilty making funeral plans, as though she were rushing Mara into her grave, but she continued to resist the idea that the woman she had known to be a fighter had taken her own life.

She was haunted by the possibility that Mara's death had been a rash and impulsive thing. Tanya John's defection was only the latest of the little disappointments Mara seemed always to be suffering. In a single weak moment, a combination of them may have overwhelmed her until sanity was lost.

Paige couldn't begin to imagine Mara's pain, if that were true. All she could think was that the tragedy might have been prevented if she had been more attentive, more understanding, or more perceptive a friend.

Her doubts were echoed, it seemed, by every adult passing through the office. They wanted to know whether anyone had seen Mara's death coming, and while Paige knew that their questions reflected their own fears regarding the mental health of their children, spouses, or friends, she wallowed in guilt.

It didn't help when the coroner's report came through. "She was full of Valium," Paige related, stunned.

"Valium," Angie repeated dumbly.

"She *overdosed*?" Peter asked.

Paige was thinking the same word, but that wasn't one the coroner had used. "He said that the carbon monoxide did the killing, but that there was easily enough Valium in her body to have clouded her thought."

"Which means," Angie concluded in the concise way she had of going straight to the heart of the matter, "that we'll never know for sure whether she accidentally passed out at the wheel or deliberately sat there until she lost consciousness."

Paige was bewildered. "I didn't even know she took the stuff. And I was supposed to be her closest friend."

"*None* of us knew she took it," Angie argued. "She was vehemently against drug taking. Of the four of us, she issued the fewest prescriptions. I can't begin to count the number of discussions we've had on the subject, right here in this room."

From the start of their association ten years before, Paige's office had been the site of the weekly meetings at which they discussed new or problem patients, developments in the field, and office policy. Hers was no different from any of the other three offices, with the same light oak furniture, mauve-and-moss decor, and soft artwork on the walls, but Paige had been the one to put the group together and was their anchor. The others simply and naturally gravitated to her office.

She was feeling like a pretty poor anchor just then. Valium. She still couldn't believe it. "People take Valium when they are extremely nervous or upset. I had no idea Mara was either. She has always been passionate about things, but passionate doesn't mean nervous or upset. When I saw her last, she was racing off to fight the lab for having messed up the tests on the Fiske boy." She tried to remember the details of that encounter, but they had seemed insignificant at the time. "I could have stopped her. I could have talked with her, maybe calmed her down some, but I didn't try. I saw how tired she was—" She looked quickly up at the others. "That could have been the Valium. It didn't occur to me that it was anything but too much work and a lack of sleep. At the time, I didn't want to say anything that might get her going more than she already was. Cowardly of me, huh?"

"That was early in the morning," Angie consoled. "She may have been fine then."

"And reached overload in a matter of hours?" Paige shook her head. "If she was popping pills, things must have been wrong for a while. Why didn't I see it? Where was my mind?"

"It was on your own practice," Peter said, "where it had to be."

"But she was in need."

"Mara was always in need," he argued. "She was always going on about one thing or another. You weren't her keeper."

"I was her friend. So were you." Paige recalled dozens of times he and Mara had been together. Not only were they avid cross-country skiers, but they shared a fasci-nation with photography. "Aren't you asking yourself these same questions?" If so, he was remarkably calm. "You said that you saw her late in the day and that she was distracted. Was she tired then, too?"

"She looked like hell. I told her so."

"Peter."

"That was the kind of relationship we had, and she *did* look like hell, like she couldn't be bothered putting on makeup or anything. But what I said didn't bother her. I told you, her mind was somewhere else. I didn't know where."

"Did you ask?" Angie prodded.

He grew defensive. "It wasn't my business. She was in a hurry. When did *you* see her last?"

"Midday." She turned to Paige. "I stopped her in the hall to ask about the Barnes case. She's been fighting to clear coverage of an MRI with the insurance company, and they've been giving her a hard time. How was she? Tired, but not necessarily distracted. She knew just what I was talking about and gave me a perfectly good answer, and there was spirit in it, just not as much as usual. It was like she was running on fumes."

"Great analogy, Angie," Peter said.

Paige pictured Mara's garage, willed down the sick feeling that came with the image, and forced her mind on. She had a desperate need to reconstruct Mara's last day on the chance that might offer a clue. "Okay. Each of us saw her at different times. When I saw her in the morning she was fired up; when Angie saw her midday she was tired; when Peter saw her late in the afternoon she was distracted." She paused. "Did either of you sense depression?"

"Not me," said Peter.

Angie grappled with that one. "No. Not depression. I'm sure it was fatigue." She looked at Paige sadly. "When she turned away and went into her office, I let her go. There were patients to see. We were booked solid for the afternoon."

She was rationalizing. Paige knew they were all doing it, making excuses for their lack of insight, and it was fine up to a point. If Mara's death was accidental, they were in the clear. If not, well, that was something else.

The bitch of it was they would never know.

While Peter and Angie picked up the slack at the office, Paige worked out the details of the funeral. She gave intent thought to every choice, desperate to do the things Mara would have wanted for reasons that went beyond love and respect. The extra effort she gave was by way of apology for not having been a better friend.

She talked with the priest about what he would say. She arranged for a local a cappella group to sing. She picked out a simple casket. She wrote an eloquent obituary.

She also chose the clothes in which Mara would be buried. In that this entailed going through Mara's things, it was a more painful task than the others.

Mara's house was Mara through and through. Being there was to feel her presence and doubt once again that she was gone. Paige found herself searching for clues—a farewell note Mara might have left on the mantel, a cry for help tacked to the cluttered kitchen chalk board, a plea for salvation scrawled on the bathroom mirror—but the only things that could be remotely interpreted to reflect undue upset were the Valium in the medicine chest and the messiness of the house. And it was messy. If Paige had been the paranoid type, she might have suspected that someone had rifled the place. Then again, of Mara's strengths, housekeeping had never been one. Paige neatened as she went, on the chance—in the hope—that Mara's family might want to see her home.

The O'Neills arrived on Thursday. Paige had met them only once before, in their home in Eugene, at the tail end of a trip that had taken Paige and Mara so close to Eugene that Mara hadn't been able to find a good reason not to stop—not that she hadn't tried. Her family was unpleasant, she said. Her family was parochial, she said. Her family was large and opinionated and xenophobic, she said.

Paige hadn't found them to be half-bad, though, granted, her perspective was different from Mara's. Having been an only child, she liked the idea of having six brothers, their wives, and a slew of nieces and nephews, and compared with her own parents, who never stayed put for long, the fierce rootedness of the O'Neills was rather nice. Paige decided that they were simply old-fashioned, hardworking, devoutly religious people who couldn't, for the life of them, understand what Mara was doing.

That had been true when Mara was a child with an insatiable curiosity, a soft spot for the wounded, and a fascination with social causes. It was true when she decided to go to college and, faced with her parents' refusal to pay, raised every cent herself, and it was true again with medical school.

It was still true. The O'Neills never understood why Mara had settled in Vermont. Even now, viewing their surroundings from the security of Paige's car during the drive from the airport, one would have thought they were in a foreign country, and a hostile one at that.

Only five of them had come, Mara's parents and three of her brothers. Paige told herself that financial constraints kept the others at home. She hoped Mara believed it.

They pulled up to the funeral home in the same silence with which they'd made most of the drive. After guiding them inside, Paige left them alone to say their good-byes. Back on the front steps, she tried to remember the last time Mara had mentioned her family, but she couldn't. It was painfully sad. True, Paige didn't see her own parents often, but she regularly saw her grandmother, who lived in West Winter, a mere forty minutes away. Nonny was spritely and independent. She had been mother and father rolled into one when Paige had been young and was more than enough family for Paige now. Paige adored her.

"She looks pretty," came the tight voice of Mara's father. A tall, stocky man, he stood with his hands in the pockets of tired suit pants, and iron-hard eyes on the street. "Whoever set her out did a fine job."

"She always looked pretty," Paige said in defense of Mara. "Pale, sometimes. Hassled, sometimes. But pretty." Unable to leave it at that, she spoke with a certain urgency. "She was happy, Mr. O'Neill. She had a full life here."

"That why she killed herself?"

"We don't know she did. It may as well have been an accident as suicide."

He grunted. "Same difference." He stared straight ahead. "Not that it matters. She was lost to us long time ago. This never would've happened if she'd done what we said. She'd be alive if she'd stayed back home."

"But then she wouldn't have been a doctor," Paige said, because much as she realized that the man was in pain, she couldn't let his declaration stand. "She was a wonderful pediatrician. She loved children, and they loved her. She fought for them. She fought for their parents. They'll all be here tomorrow. You'll see."

He looked at her for the first time. "Were you the one told her to go to medical school?"

"Oh, no. She wanted that long before I did."

"But you got her up here."

"She got herself up here. All I did was tell her about the opportunity."

He grunted and stared at the street again. After a minute he said, "You look like her, y'know. Maybe that was why she liked you. Same dark hair, same size, you could be sisters. Are you married?"

"No."

"Have you ever been?"

"No."

"Have you ever had children?"

"No."

"Then you're missing as much in life as she was. She tried with that fellow Daniel, but he couldn't take his wife being gone all the time, don't know what man could, and then when she didn't get pregnant, well, what good's a woman like that?"

Paige was beginning to get a drift of what had driven Mara from Eugene. "Mara wasn't to blame for

Daniel's problems. He had a drug habit well before she met him. She thought she could help, but it just didn't work. Same with getting pregnant. Maybe if they'd had more time—"

"Time wouldn't have mattered. It was the abortion that did it."

"Abortion?" Paige knew nothing about an abortion.

"She didn't tell you? I can understand why. It isn't every girl who gets pregnant when she's sixteen and then runs off to get rid of the child before her parents have a say in the matter. What she did was murder. Her punishment was not being able to get pregnant again." He made a sputtering sound. "Sad thing is, having babies would have been her salvation. If she'd stayed back home and got married and had kids, she'd have been alive today and we wouldn't have had to spend half our savings flying to her funeral."

At that moment Paige wished they hadn't come. She wished she had never spoken with Thomas O'Neill. Mostly she wished she had never learned about the abortion. It wasn't that she condemned Mara for it—she could understand the fear a sixteen-year-old must have felt in as intolerant a house as hers—but she wished Mara had told her, herself.

Paige had thought they were best of friends, yet in all the talks they had had about Mara's marriage and its lack of children, about the foster children she had taken in over the years, and the child she would have adopted had she lived, never once had she mentioned an abortion. Nor had she mentioned it in any one of the many, *many* discussions they had had on the issue as it related to the teenage girls in their care.

Paige was heartbroken to think that there were important things she didn't know about someone she had called a close friend.

Friday morning dawned warm and gray, the air heavy as though with Mara's secrets. Paige found some solace in the fact that the church was packed to overflowing. If ever there was proof of the number of lives Mara had touched and the esteem in which she was held, this was it. Particularly in light of the presence of the family that had never recognized her achievements, Paige felt vindicated on Mara's behalf.

But that small, victorious kernel came and went quickly, buried as deeply in the grief of the day as Mara in the dark hole in the ground on the hillside overlooking town, and before Paige could quite catch her breath, the cemetery was left behind, the lunch at the Tucker Inn for all who cared to come was consumed, and the O'Neills of Eugene, Oregon, were delivered to the airport.

Paige returned to Mara's house, a Victorian with high ceilings, a winding staircase, and a wraparound porch. She wandered from room to room, thinking that Mara had loved lighting the narrow fireplace, putting a Christmas tree in the parlor window, having lemonade on the back porch on a warm summer night. The O'Neills had told Paige to sell the house and give the proceeds to charity, and she planned to do that, but not yet. She couldn't pack up and dispose of Mara's life in a day. She needed time to grieve. She needed time to get used to Mara's absence. She needed time to say good-bye.

She also needed time to find a buyer who would love the place as Mara had. She owed Mara that.

She left the kitchen through a bowed screen door that slapped shut behind her and sank onto the back porch swing, watching the birds dart from tree to tree and feeder to feeder. There were five feeders that she could see. She suspected others were hidden in the trees. Mara had enjoyed nothing more than to sit on that very swing, holding whatever child was in her custody at the moment, whispering tidbits about each bird that flew by.

I'll feed them for you, Paige promised. I'll make sure that whoever buys the house feeds them. They won't be abandoned. It's the least I can do.

Mara would have taken Paige's kitty, no doubt about it. She had loved wild things, weak things, little things. And Paige? Paige wasn't as adventurous. She loved needy things, too, but in a more controlled environment. She thrived on constancy, order, and predictability. Change unsettled her.

Leaving the swing, she wandered into the yard. The birds flew away. She stood very still, held her breath, and waited, but they didn't return. She was very much alone.

I'll miss you, Mara, she thought, and started back toward the house, feeling empty and old. The house suddenly seemed it, too. It needed a painting. I'll have it done. The door needed new screening. Easy enough. A shutter had to be replaced by the upper left bedroom window. No sweat. And by the upper right bedroom—the upper right bedroom—Oh, God . . .

The doorbell rang, distant but distinct. Grateful for the reprieve, Paige returned to the house. She guessed that a friend might have seen her car and stopped, or that one of the townsfolk who hadn't made the funeral wanted to offer condolences.

The wavy glass panel of the front door revealed a shape that was bulky but not tall. She opened the door to find that the shape wasn't a single body at all, but a woman holding a child. Neither were locals; she had never seen them before.

"May I help you?" she asked.

"I'm looking for Mara O'Neill," the woman said worriedly. "I've been trying to reach her. Are you a friend?"

Paige nodded.

"She was supposed to meet me in Boston earlier today," the woman hurried on, "but we must have crossed signals. I've been stopping along the highway at intervals to call, but she doesn't answer her phone."

"No," Paige said, studying the woman. She was middle-aged and Caucasian, clearly not the biological mother of the child, who had skin the color of pecans and the largest, most soulful eyes Paige had ever seen. She assumed the two were part of the adoption network with which Mara had become involved.

"Is Mara here?" the woman asked.

Paige swallowed. "No."

"Oh, dear. Do you know where she is or how soon she'll be back? This is dreadful. We had everything arranged. She was so excited."

The child was looking at Paige, who found she couldn't look away. It was a little girl. Her size said she wasn't yet a year old, but the look in her eyes said she was older.

Paige had seen that look before, in a photograph Mara had shown her. Her heart skipped a beat, rendering the hand that touched the child's cheek unsteady. "How do you know Mara?" she asked the woman.

"I'm with the adoption agency. Among other things, it's my job to be on hand at the airport when adoptive children arrive from other countries. This little one came from a tiny town a distance from Calcutta. She had an escort from the agency in Bombay. Poor thing has been at it for better than three days. Mara must have mistaken the day or the time. Is the office closed? The answering service is taking her calls."

"Sameera," Paige breathed. *Mara's baby.* "But I thought she wasn't coming for weeks!" She reached for the child.

"We often advise our parents not to speak of dates. Political unrest can delay things."

Paige thought of that upper right bedroom with its bright yellow walls and the large, lopsided navy stars that had just now been visible from the yard. Her eyes filled with tears as she cradled the child. "Sami."

The child didn't make a sound. Paige was the one who cried softly, mourning for the mother Mara would have been and the happiness she would have known. The child's arrival made Mara's death that much more of a mystery. Mara wouldn't commit suicide with Sami three days away.

Still hugging the child, Paige wiped her eyes on her arm. It was a minute before she was composed enough to look at the woman and say, "Mara died Wednesday. We buried her this morning."

The woman gasped. "Died?"

"A terrible accident."

"*Died?* Oh, my." She paused. "Poor Mara. She waited so long for this child. And Sameera—she's come so far."

"That's all right," Paige said with an odd calm. "I'll keep her." It made sense, the one thing she could do to make up for all she hadn't done before. "My name is Paige Pfeiffer. I was Mara's best friend, a pediatrician also. We practiced together. I was interviewed as a character reference during her home study. If you check your files, you'll see that my name is listed as the one to call in case of emergency, which is pretty much what you've done." She looked down at the child. The little girl's thin legs straddled her waist, tiny fingers clutched her sweater. Her head lay on Paige's chest, eyes wide and frightened. She felt light as a feather, but warm in a pleasant sort of way.

I'll take care of her for you, Mara. I can do that.

"I'm afraid it doesn't work that way," the woman said quickly.

"Why not?"

"Because there are rules, procedures, red tape." The words ran together. The woman was clearly flustered. "International adoptions are complicated. Mara worked her way through it, and even then she was going to have to wait another six months for the adoption to be final. In the meantime, technically, Sameera is in the agency's care. I can't leave her here."

"But where else can she go?"

"I don't know. Nothing like this has ever happened before. I guess she'll have to come home with me until we decide what to do."

"You can't send her back to India."

"No. We'll have to look for another adoptive family."

"And in the meantime she'll be put into foster care. Why can't I be it?"

"Because you haven't been approved."

"But I'm a pediatrician. I love kids. I know how to handle them. I own a house and earn good money. I'm a totally reputable person, and if you don't want to take my word for it, ask anyone in town."

"Unfortunately, that takes time." She reached for Sami, but Paige wasn't giving her up so fast.

"I want her," she said, "which puts me up at the top of the list. I want to take her home with me now, and keep her until a better home is found, but you won't find a better home than mine, I can promise you that." Mara would be so *pleased.* "There has to be a way I can keep her."

The woman looked pulled in every which direction. "There is, I suppose. Assuming the head of the agency agrees, we could do a quick foster care home study."

"Do it." The impulsiveness was pure Mara, and it felt good.

"Now?"

"If that's what's necessary for me to keep her tonight. She needs love. I can give her that. I can give her an instant, stable environment. It makes perfect sense."

The woman from the adoption agency couldn't argue with that. After making several calls and getting a preliminary okay, she put Paige through an initial battery of questions. They were basic identity ones, just a start in the study the woman promised, and all the while Paige was answering, she was toting Sami up and down the stairs on her hip, transferring baby supplies from the nursery to her car. She stopped only when the car was full.

The agency representative, who had followed her up and down, looked exhausted. After giving her a list of phone numbers and the promise that she would be in touch the next day, she drove off.

Paige shifted Sami so that she could see the child's face. Large brown eyes met hers. "Not a peep from you through all this? Not hungry or wet?" The child stared up at her silently. "Wouldn't like supper?" The child didn't blink. "Maybe a bath?" Paige knew that she couldn't understand English but was hoping that her tone would inspire some tiny sound. "Yes?" She paused again. When no sound came, she sighed. "I could use both. Let's go home."

She rounded the car and was about to open the passenger's door when the sight of Mara's house gave her pause. Mara hadn't owned it long; she had spent her first three years in Tucker paying back education loans and her next two saving for a down payment. The house wasn't showy in any sense of the word, but buying it had been a triumph.

Now it was empty, and Mara was buried on the hillside overlooking town. Paige felt a chill. Mara had been a vital part of her life for twenty years. Now she was gone.

Paige closed her eyes. She held Sami closer, then closer still. The child was warm, silent but alive, and, in that, a comfort—but only until Paige began to think forward rather than back. Then, slowly, with dawning awareness, she opened her eyes and looked at the child, and in that instant, with the house locked, the agency representative gone, and Mara's baby in her care, the reality of what she had done hit home. On as sorrowful a day as ever there was, it wasn't sorrow she felt. It was a sheer and profound terror.

Three

Paige wasn't one to panic, but she came close to it during the drive from Mara's house to hers. She kept thinking of all the things she didn't know—like what the child ate, if she had allergies, whether she slept through the night. The answers, along with detailed medical records, were in the pack of papers she had brought from Mara's, but Mara had had weeks to peruse them. Paige did not.

Anxiously she pictured her house. It had three bedrooms, the one on the first floor that she used herself and two upstairs. The larger of the two was stuffed with furniture that Nonny hadn't been able to keep when she had sold her house several years before; the smaller of the two was cluttered with sewing goods, knitting goods, and all manner of medical journals that Paige had glanced through and stacked for later reading.

The smaller room would be easier to clear out, but the larger one would be better for a child. Then again, Paige didn't like the idea of Sami being alone on the second floor. For the time being, she could sleep in Paige's room.

Between Paige, Sami, and the kitten, the bedroom was filling up fast. What have I done? she wondered, and, gripping the steering wheel, tried to stay calm, which meant absolutely, positively, *not* thinking about what she was going to do come morning, when she had to be at work. She darted quick looks at Sami, who was sitting in the brand-new car seat Mara had bought, sending that long, soulful stare right back at her.

"We'll work everything out," she assured the child and herself in what she thought was a very mommy voice. "You're flexible. All children are flexible." It was what she had told many a parent on the verge of panic over a new baby. "Well, I'm flexible, too, so we'll be fine. What you need most is love, and I can give you that, yes I can. Beyond that, you'll just have to let me know what you like and what you don't."

Sami didn't make a sound, simply stared at her with those huge eyes that had seen too much in too short a time.

It struck Paige that maybe the child *couldn't* make a sound, that maybe she had been punished for crying or had simply given up when crying had gotten her nowhere, in which case Paige was going to have to teach her that crying was healthy and, indeed, one of the few ways babies had of making their wants and needs known. The teaching would involve lots of cuddling and attention, even some spoiling. It might take time.

Time. Oh, Lord. She couldn't think far ahead. Not yet. "I really can do this," she told the child as she pulled into her driveway and sprang from the car. "I'm level-headed. I'm easygoing. I'm a whiz with children." She ran to the passenger's side and tugged at Sami's seat belt. "Women have instincts," she quoted her own advice to new mothers, tugging harder when the seat belt wouldn't come free. "They do things with and for their children that they never imagined they could do." She put both hands to the task, pushing, tugging, twisting. "It comes from deep inside. A primordial nurturing." She was about to go for scissors when the buckle came free with a *whoosh.* "See?" She breathed in relief. "We'll do just fine."

For the next few minutes, while Sami watched from the safety of her car seat on the front porch, Paige ran back and forth carting baby goods into the house. When she was done, she brought Sami inside, set baby and car seat on the floor, and scooped up the kitten, which had been scampering around underfoot.

"Sami, meet kitty."

The two stared at one another unblinkingly.

Paige rubbed the kitten's cheek to hers, then offered the tiny creature to Sami. "Kitty's even younger than you are. She's alone, too"—the vet had declared it a female—"so we'll take care of her until we can find her a home. Isn't she soft?" She touched the kitten to Sami's hand. The little girl pulled it back. Her chin began to tremble.

Paige immediately set the kitten down and took Sami in her arms. "It's okay, sweetie. She won't hurt you. She's probably as frightened of you as you are of her." While she talked, she sorted through the food she had brought from Mara's. Assuming that Mara had stocked only what Sami could eat, she put a nipple on one of the bottles of formula. Her own hunger had faded. There didn't seem room for food in her stomach, what with all the nervous jangles there.

Sami drank every drop of the milk, looking up at her all the while. Buoyed by that, Paige mixed up a dish of cereal, sweetened it with peaches, and spooned it up, and again, Sami ate. Given how small and thin she was, Paige might have given her more had she not known the danger of pushing too much food into an untried stomach. So, after changing into a T-shirt and jeans, she bathed her, rubbed Mara's baby lotion over her, diapered her, and dressed her in a pair of stretchy pink pajamas that Mara had bought. Then she held her up.

"You look so pretty, sweetie." Pretty and soft and sleepy. "Mara would be loving you to bits."

But Mara was no more. Paige felt a sharp pang of grief, followed by a sudden fierce fatigue. She drew Sami close and closed her eyes, but she had no sooner tucked her head against the baby's dark hair when the phone rang.

It was Deirdre Frechette, one of Paige's Mount Court runners. "We need help," she said in a broken voice. "We spent the whole of dinner talking about Dr. O'Neill. One of the guys says she OD'd on heroine. Is it true?"

Paige's fatigue faded. "Definitely not."

"Another one says she was done in by the Devil Brothers."

"Not Devil," Paige corrected. "DeVille." George and Harold DeVille had been the butt of local tales for years. Huge and menacing, they were mentally slow and harmless. "The DeVilles wouldn't hurt a fly."

"Julie Engel says she killed herself. Julie's mother did that three years ago, and now she's going into all the details. She's getting slightly hysterical. We all are."

Paige could picture it. Teenage minds were fertile, all the more so in a group. She shuddered to think of where, if unguided, the conversation would lead. Suicide had the potential for being a contagious disease when the proper preventive measures weren't taken.

If ever there was a time these teenagers needed their parents, it was now. But their parents weren't around.

"Where are you?" she asked.

"In MacKenzie Lounge."

"Stay there. I'll be over in fifteen minutes."

It wasn't until she hung up the phone that she remembered Sami, and for a split second she didn't know what to do. But the second passed. The little girl was curled in her arms, fast asleep. One-handedly she sifted through the piles of baby paraphernalia and retrieved the baby carrier. A short time later she had the sleeping child strapped snugly to her chest.

One of the most important pieces of equipment you can buy, she heard herself instructing parents at prenatal meetings, *is a car seat. The baby should be secured in the seat and the seat secured in the car.*

"This is definitely not smart," she hummed softly as she slid in behind the wheel with Sami hugging her chest, "but you're tiny, and I drive safely, and I just think it's more important that you snuggle up to a body you know than sit in that hard baby seat, which I doubt

I could strap back in here again tonight anyway. So I won't tell anyone if you don't."

The baby slept through the drive.

MacKenzie was the largest of the girls' dorms. Like the others, it was three floors' worth of red brick, over which ivy had climbed unchecked for so long that large patches of the brick were obscured. Tall, multipaned windows were open in deference to the September warmth; electric fans whirred in many of them.

There were eight girls in the lounge, eight shades of uniformly long hair, eight oversize T-shirts and shorts. Some of the girls were runners, some not, but Paige knew them all. So had Mara.

They were subdued. Several looked as though they had been crying. Paige was glad she'd come.

She sank down on the wide arm of a chair.

"What have you got?" one of the girls asked.

"Duhhh," another mocked.

"It's a baby," someone said.

"Whose is it?"

Paige wasn't sure how to answer. "Uh, mine for now."

"Where did it come from?"

"How did you get it?"

"Is it a boy or a girl?"

"How old is it?"

Several of the girls had come to take a closer look at Sami. Paige eased aside the headrest so they could see.

"Her name is Sameera, Sami for short. She was born in a tiny town on the east coast of India, about a day's ride from Calcutta." Mara's excited words came back clear as a bell. "She was abandoned soon after birth—girls are considered the kiss of death to many in her homeland. She's fourteen months old, but small for her age and physically delayed. That's because she's spent her life being shifted from one orphanage to another. She hasn't had the encouragement to do much more than lie on a cot waiting for someone to feed her."

"She doesn't walk?"

"Not yet."

"Does she sit?"

"Only with support." Mara had told her this, too. Paige had seen it herself while she'd been bathing the child, when she'd done a cursory physical exam. She hadn't seen any sign of illness or physical deformity. "Given proper nourishment and attention, she'll catch right up. By the time she's ready for school, she'll be doing everything she should."

"So whose *is* she?"

There it was again, that loaded question. "I'm taking care of her for now."

"Are you adopting her?"

"No, no. She'll be with me until the agency finds her a proper home."

"Then you're her foster mother. She's lucky. I was sent to live with an aunt when I was eight. She wasn't *anything* like you." This, from Alicia Donnelly. She had started Mount Court in the seventh grade and was now miraculously a senior. Along the way, she had had every sort of illness imaginable, from bronchitis to strep throat to mononucleosis. Peter, as the doctor of record for Mount Court, had treated her for those. When she developed a yeast infection in her junior year, Mara had taken over her case.

Alicia had been a behavior problem as a child, so difficult for her socially prominent parents to handle at one point that removal from her immediate family had been the only alternative to hospitalization. Years of therapy had set her on her feet, and although she was far from a model student, she was extremely bright. Mount Court was more of a home to her than her own.

"You'll be a good foster mother," she was telling Paige. "You know everything there is to know about kids. You're patient. You have a sense of humor. That's important, a sense of humor." Her voice caught. "Dr. O'Neill had one, too."

Yes, Paige thought. A subtle one that could be dry or gentle but was always a delightful counterpoint to her intensity. Paige would miss both the intensity and the wit.

Sobered, the girls retreated to their places, some on chairs, others on the floor, and were still.

"Dr. O'Neill was a good person," Paige said quietly. "She was a dedicated doctor and a crusader. We should all take a lesson from her life. She gave of herself in ways that not many people do."

"She also took of herself," Julie Engel said in a high-pitched voice.

"You don't know it was suicide," Deirdre argued.

Julie turned to Paige. "I heard that she was found in her garage. Is it true?"

Paige nodded.

"And that she died of carbon monoxide poisoning?"

She nodded again.

"Then it was suicide," Julie told Deirdre. "What else would it be?"

"It could have been an accident," Paige answered gently. "She was very tired. She was taking medication. She could have passed out at the wheel."

"Not Dr. O'Neill," another of the girls, Tia Faraday, insisted. "She was careful about things. When I was sick last year, she wrote out every last instruction of what I was supposed to do. She didn't leave anything to chance. And then she called the next day to make sure I was doing exactly what she had written down."

"She would have turned off the engine before she passed out," Alicia concluded.

Paige sighed. "Unfortunately, passing out isn't something you can always control."

A bell sounded. The girls didn't move.

"Did she leave a note?" Tia asked.

Paige hesitated, then shook her head.

"Neither did my mother," Julie said, "but we knew it was suicide. She had been threatening to kill herself for a long time. We never thought she'd go through with it, but when a person climbs all the way to the thirty-third floor—"

"Don't say it again, Julie," Deirdre begged as girls from the floors above began to pass through the lounge and out the door.

"It was a deliberate act," Julie insisted.

"It's depressing."

"Life is depressing."

"Life is lonely."

"Was Dr. O'Neill lonely?" Tia asked.

Paige hadn't been aware of it. "She was always busy. She was always with people."

"So are we. Still, there are lots of times I'm lonely."

"Same here," came another voice.

And another. "It's the worst at night."

"Or after phone calls from home."

"Or out in the woods after ten."

"Which," Paige injected lightly, "is one of the reasons why going out in the woods after ten is against school rules. Everything seems ominous. Every little fear is magnified." Still, the girls had a point. Mara's days might have been full, but not her nights. She had more than enough time to think about the distance between herself and her family, the failure of her marriage, the child she had aborted years before. Paige hated to think it—Mara had never *said* anything—but she might well have been lonely.

"I can't imagine Dr. O'Neill being afraid of anything," Alicia said. "She was always so strong."

"But she *killed* herself," Julie cried, "so *something* was awful in her life."

"What was it, Dr. Pfeiffer?"

Paige chose her words with care. Although she wasn't about to betray Mara's secrets—didn't know some, she wagered—she wanted the girls to know that suicides, if that was indeed what Mara had committed, weren't frivolous happenings. There were reasons for them and ways to prevent them.

"Dr. O'Neill had disappointments. We all do. None of us makes it through life without some. If she did commit suicide, it was because those disappointments got the best of her, such that she lost her ability to cope."

From behind came a quiet, "So what makes one person able to cope and another not?"

Paige turned to face her runner, Sara Dickinson. She had a backpack slung over a shoulder and was among the last of the girls passing through the lounge. "I can't give you a definitive answer to that. The person who copes may have an inner strength, or a distinct reason for coping, or a support system that helps her cope when she has trouble doing it herself."

"Didn't Dr. O'Neill have those things?"

Paige was asking herself that. She struggled to understand and explain. "She may not have put them to use."

"What do you mean?"

"She was independent. Too much so, sometimes. She didn't ask for help."

Another girl spoke up, Annie Miller, a junior, sounding frightened. "My brother swallowed a whole handful of aspirin last year." There were gasps from the group. "They pumped his stomach. He was okay. It wasn't enough to kill him anyway. My dad said it was a cry for help."

"Probably," Paige said, terrified that one of the girls listening might contemplate a similar stunt, "but that's a tough way to get it. Overdoses of drugs can cause physical damage that the person who survives then has to live with for the rest of his life. It's a foolish way to get help. A *dangerous* way." She went from face to face. "The thing is that when something like Dr. O'Neill's death happens, we have to learn from it—the lesson being to speak up when we're upset."

"To who?" Sara asked from behind.

Paige looked back. "A family member or a friend. A teacher, a coach, a doctor."

"That's the support system you mentioned?"

"That's it."

"What if you can't talk to people?"

"Everyone here can talk to people."

"I mean, what if you can't *trust* people?"

"There's always someone you can trust." But Sara remained doubtful, so Paige added, "If not the people I mentioned, then a minister. There's always someone. You just have to open your eyes and look around."

Sara looked past her, her expression suddenly stony. Everything about her spoke of resentment, though she didn't say a word.

There were murmurs from several of the other girls. Paige followed their gaze to the door, through which was striding a man she had never seen before. He was tall and lean, wore gray slacks and a pale blue shirt that was open at the neck and rolled at the sleeves. His skin was tanned, his jaw square. His hair, which was long enough to hit the back of his collar, was the color of sand and either sun-streaked or shot with gray, Paige couldn't tell which. Round, wire-rimmed glasses sat on the bridge of his nose.

He was a spectacular-looking man.

She glanced at the girls. If they were struck by his looks, they didn't show it. They were sitting straighter, with nothing remotely akin to the adoration she might have expected to see on their impressionable teenaged faces. Oh, they knew him, no doubt about that, or about the fact that they didn't like him.

"Study hall?" he prompted in a way that was at the same time soft-spoken and steely.

The girls remained silent, but Paige sensed in them defiance rather than meekness. A confrontation was imminent. Given Mara's death and the upset they were all feeling, she wished to avoid that.

Leaving the arm of the chair, she approached the man. "We blew it, huh?"

"Slightly," he said in that same deceptively soft voice.

"Study hall?"

"Seven to nine, Sunday through Thursday."

"Something new?"

"Very."

"Ahhhh." She bowed her head, thinking. When she looked back up, he hadn't budged. Quietly she said, "The girls are upset over Dr. O'Neill's death. So am I. I had hoped we could talk it out."

"The girls have free times, but this isn't one. They were supposed to be in study hall ten minutes ago."

"Study hall can wait a few more minutes, can't it?"

He shook his head slowly.

She lowered her voice even more. "That's a rigid stance, given the circumstances."

He didn't blink.

In little more than a whisper, but one tinged with anger, she said, "Mara O'Neill meant a lot to these girls. They need time to grieve."

"What they need," he said in nearly as low and angry a voice, "is the assurance that there is some sort of order in their lives. They need routine. That's one of the things the evening study hall is about. The other is about incredibly poor grades."

Paige was getting nowhere. The man might be gorgeous, but he was as sensitive as a stone. She could imagine him a math professor or a dorm parent from hell. Mara would be incensed to find such a creature on the Mount Court payroll.

"What these girls need," she said with a steeliness of her own, "is understanding. Clearly you aren't in a position to give it. Hopefully the new Head will be."

"I am the new Head."

He was Noah Perrine? Paige had trouble believing that. She had known two Heads in the five years that she had been affiliated with Mount Court. The first had retired after twenty-three years, which was twenty-two years more than the second had survived. Both had been stuffy, white-haired, and preoccupied in the way ivory-tower minds could be.

This one was nothing like that. He was too focused to be the new Head. He was too young. He was too *attractive.*

But the girls weren't denying it, and then Paige remembered what they had said during practice earlier that week about the new Head being a stickler for rules. And it fit. Which meant that continuing the argument would be futile, even harmful if it was done in front of the girls. The last thing Paige wanted was to make a bad situation worse.

She returned to the girls, putting a hand on Deirdre's shoulder. "We've been preempted. But this talk is important. Why don't I come back tomorrow afternoon"—she would have preferred the morning, but it was her turn to do the Saturday shift—"let's say one o'clock, same place?"

Their voices were low and resentful.

"This is absurd."

"Like we'll really be able to study."

"It'll be a total waste of time."

Paige said, "Try. For me. Better still, if you don't want to do assigned work, write me a letter about what Dr. O'Neill meant to you. That would help me a lot. I'm having trouble with her death, too." Just when she thought she was in control, her eyes filled with tears. She wrapped her arms around Sami.

Tia wrapped her arms around them both. Several of the others came close and joined in. Paige was touched by their warmth, and grateful.

But the new Head was standing there, watching and waiting. One by one, with more than a few bitter looks shot his way, the girls left.

Paige recomposed herself. She was tired—exhausted, if the truth were told—and feeling hollow inside. She was also beginning to ache. It had been a tense day, a *few* tense days. Though Sami weighed next to nothing, Paige could feel the straps of the baby carrier pressing her T-shirt into her shoulders. She curled an arm under the child's bottom to ease the weight.

Assuming that the new Head had left with the girls, she herself turned to leave, only to find that she hadn't escaped after all. He stood there studying her, making her feel suddenly ugly and pale.

"Are you sure you don't want to escort them?" she asked tartly. "They may walk right past the study hall."

He allowed his mouth a tiny twist. "That's the most perceptive thing you've said yet. The kids at this school will do just about anything to test the limits we set, and they've been able to get away with it, until now. I may not be the most popular guy on campus—"

"To put it mildly."

"—but I'll be damned if I'll be run ramshod over."

Paige marveled at the man's coldness. "My partner *died.* If ever there's a time to be flexible, this is it, don't you think?"

"What I think," he said, "is that *you're* very much affected by your partner's death, and that while some of these girls may be saddened, they're using the situation to their own ends."

"If you'd known Mara, you wouldn't say that. She was a dynamic person. The girls adored her."

"At least one of those girls never even met the woman. This is her first year here, and the term is barely five days old."

Paige gave a quick shake of her head. "The discussion may have started with Mara, but it had broadened. We were talking about loneliness and the remedies for it, which is something girls this age obsess about. From the questions Sara asked, I'd say she has genuine concerns about the people around her. If she's new here, she's probably feeling alone and frightened, and she will, until she settles in with a group of friends. If, on top of that, she has parents who could care less—"

"Her parents care."

"Well, she sure doesn't know who to trust, or who to talk to if something's bothering her, and that scares the living daylights out of me. If *I* had a daughter—"

"What's that?" he interrupted with the jut of his chin.

The baby chose that moment to move against Paige, who drew the heavy corduroy aside. Sami's eyes were closed. One small fist was by her mouth. Paige gently unfurled the tiny fingers and put her thumb inside. "This," she said with a sigh, "is the baby Mara was to have adopted. She arrived a few hours ago."

"The woman killed herself right before *that?*"

It didn't make sense to Paige, either. Then again, she thought with great reluctance, maybe it did. Mara had been foster mother to five children over the years. Tanya John had been the latest. Taken from abusive parents, she had lived with Mara for nearly a year, during which Mara had believed she was happy, coming out of her shell, growing more confident. Then, out of the blue, she'd run away. When found, she had been placed in another foster home. Mara had been heartsick.

Paige wondered if Tanya's running away had been such a blow to Mara's confidence that she had doubted her ability to mother Sami.

But you didn't say anything, Mara. Right up to the end, you talked with enthusiasm about adopting the baby. You went through all the preparatory work, bought everything you needed, decorated the baby's room. You were on the verge of bliss.

Could she have gotten cold feet? It didn't seem possible.

Wearily Paige said, "Something happened. I'm going to have to find out what."

"And the baby? What happens to her?"

"She's mine until better parents are found."

"Are you married?"

She looked him in the eye. "Nope."

"And you're a practicing pediatrician?"

She felt suddenly lightheaded. "Yup."

"What'll you do with her while you work?"

Her voice went higher. "Beats me."

"You must have plans."

"Actually"—her lightheartedness rose to vague hysteria—"this has all happened so fast, I haven't had time to make any."

He looked away in disgust. "You're some role model for these kids." His eyes recaptured hers. "Do you always do things so haphazardly?"

"I *never* do things haphazardly," she cried. "I didn't ask for this. It just happened. I lead an orderly life.

I *like* leading an orderly life. But what was I supposed to do, send the baby *back?*"

"Of course not, but you can't just haul her around wherever you go."

"Why not?" Paige asked with a flash of belligerence.

"Because it isn't good for the kid, for one thing, and for another, it isn't appropriate. If you're going to be coaching cross-country—"

"Then you do know who I am?"

"Damn right," he said. "It's my business to know. But I didn't know you had a baby, and now that I do, I question the wisdom of your bringing her on campus. These kids have problems enough of their own. They need the full attention of everyone who works with them."

"I can give them my full attention."

He sighed. "It's a matter of discipline, don't you see? For years life at Mount Court was totally unstructured. Classes were held some days and not others; attendance was rarely taken; curfews were ignored; dorm behavior was unruly. These kids know nothing about delayed gratification or, God forbid, abstention. What they want, they get. What they can't have, they sneak. They were brought up that way, and the school did nothing to set them straight. So there have been scandals galore—incidents of alcohol poisoning, drug abuse, near warfare with the townies—and I'm supposed to clean it all up."

He thrust a handful of fingers through his hair. "For that, I need to establish discipline. We're talking rules here."

Paige waited for him to go on.

He looked pained, almost uncomfortable with what he was saying, and for a minute she wondered if indeed there was kindness in the man. In the next breath he dashed the possibility. "Rules can't apply to some people and not others. People leave their children home when they come to work."

"I'm not here for work. I came to talk to the girls as a friend."

"Then when you come as their coach."

"That's not work, either," she argued because she believed she was in the right. "It's fun, which is why I do it gratis. I love being with these kids. I care for them. I would have thought that if you're in this field, you did, too, which is why I'm amazed you wouldn't let me talk with them tonight. They needed someone to ground their thinking. They needed an adult. Before I got here, they were working themselves into a frenzy, or doesn't that bother you? Are grades all that count? Are you simply here as a paper pusher?"

He made a sound of disgust, cocked his hands on his hips, and looked out the window at the campus. "The damn place is in ruins. Our endowment is next to nothing, we can barely make ends meet, and that's without a single one of the physical improvements that are years overdue. The Board of Trustees is terrified that we're going down the tubes, and just when we need to raise money, our alumni are deserting us in droves—so, yeah"—he looked back—"to some extent, I'll have to be a paper pusher, but that isn't to say I don't care about kids. Of *course* I care about kids. I wouldn't be in this godforsaken town if I didn't. Hell, I was a teacher myself for years."

She liked him better when he was worked up. He was more human that way. "Really."

"You don't believe me? I taught science."

"I had pegged you for math. That's always struck me as the most rigid of the disciplines."

"I am not rigid."

"You sure sound it to me. But, hey, if you want a rash of suicides at this school, kids who think it'll be just fine to follow along in Dr. O'Neill's footsteps, that's your responsibility." A tiny cry came from the baby carrier, erasing whatever satisfaction she had found in roughing up Noah Perrine. "Oh, my. She speaks." Sami's eyes were only half-open. She was crying in her sleep.

"Maybe she's wet," Noah suggested.

"Thank you. I might not have guessed." She rocked the baby, with little effect.

"More likely she's tired of being in that carrier. How'd you like to be squished against another person for hours?"

"At one time in my life, I'd have given anything for it." She rubbed Sami's back, but the small, broken whimpers only sped up.

"She needs to be put to bed in a proper crib."

"I don't have a proper crib."

"And you're telling me what to do with *my* kids?"

She didn't need this. Not from Noah Perrine. She was too tired, too tense, too unsettled. "You're right. The baby needs to be put to bed." She started toward the door, calling out over Sami's crying as she went, "But I do know something about your kids, and that something tells me they need help. I'd suggest you either bring in a professional grief counselor or let me and my partners talk with the kids who are upset. These kids are at risk. You and I can argue for hours, but nothing will change that fact." She passed through the door and strode straight across the grass, which might have been against one of his precious rules but was the fastest way to reach her car.

"All right," came a call from behind, then abreast, "you can come talk with them tomorrow. You already told them you would."

She strode on. "Fine. But the baby will be with me. Where I go, she goes." She swung open the car door and slid inside.

"You aren't going to drive with her like that, are you?" he asked through the open window.

"The alternative," Paige said dryly, "is to strap her onto the passenger's seat. Since she has about as much muscle control as a sack of potatoes—and since she isn't particularly happy right now—I don't think that's a good idea. She's safer like this." She started the car, shifted into gear, and pulled away from the curb.

"You need a car seat," he yelled.

Ignoring him, she smoothly negotiated the curved campus road until she reached the iron arch. By then Noah Perrine was out of sight and Sami had stopped crying.

At the stop sign, she looked both ways, pulled out onto the main street, straightened the wheel, and headed home. She drove slowly, increasingly numb, as though her brain had finally hit overload and was temporarily ceasing to perform all but the most urgent of functions.

She might have liked it to stay that way a while, but she wasn't so lucky. By the time she had laid Sami carefully in the middle of her own king-size bed and set about assembling the playpen, which was as close

as she would come to having a crib until she had someone move the large one from Mara's house to hers, her
hands were trembling.

Somehow she managed to change Sami, give her half
of another bottle, and put her down in the playpen to
sleep. By that time her own advice was echoing in her
ears.

*The thing is that when something like Dr. O'Neill's
death happens, we have to learn from it—the lesson
being to speak up when we're upset.*

Seconds later she was on the phone to Angie.

Four

Angie Bigelow liked to say that she had spent the nine months of her earliest existence reading *Time* magazine through her mother's navel, and though her mother claimed it was *Newsweek*, the detail was moot. Angie was a knowledgeable woman. She had a photographic memory and an overview of the human experience that enabled her to understand and apply every fact she read. All this gave her more than her share of self-confidence.

Her patients loved her because she was rarely wrong. When she diagnosed something as a virus that would run its course and be gone in two weeks, that was just what it did. If she determined that a limb was bruised rather than broken, it was bruised rather than broken. She read voraciously in the field and was familiar with every medical study that had been done, which meant that she knew what tests were worthwhile and what medicines appropriate. Her instincts were unrivaled when it came to reading between the lines of a patient's concerns. She came closer to making medicine a science than many another doctor.

She ran her home in much the same way. She was organized, efficient, and thorough. Everything had its time and place—grocery shopping on Thursday afternoon, a load of laundry every night after dinner, house cleaning on Sunday afternoons. It wasn't that she couldn't have asked Ben to help with those things—he worked at home and had the time—just that she did them better herself. She liked the idea of being wife, mother, and career woman and prided herself on doing all three well.

That was why she went to the extra effort of making a full dinner—lentil soup, scrod, rice, and salad and the first of the Macoun apples from the local orchard, baked with honey and served à la mode—for Ben and Dougie that Friday night. Burying Mara had been the culmination of three long and emotionally draining days for all three of them. A pall lingered in the air. She was hoping to dispel it by reestablishing the norm.

Having finished washing pots and pans, she was wiping down the kitchen counter when the phone rang.

She reached for it before Dougie could, half expecting it to be his little friend from Mount Court, who had already called twice, three times yesterday, and twice the day before. Young love was obsessive. It was also worrisome for the mother of a fourteen-year-old boy, who knew how advanced fourteen-year-old girls could be. Dougie wasn't ready for this one. He wasn't ready for *any* one.

But it wasn't Melissa. It was Paige, sounding upset as easygoing Paige rarely was. There were high-pitched words, mention of Mara, a crib, and baby-sitters. Angie slowed her down, made her start again. When her meaning finally got through, Angie didn't know whether to laugh or cry.

"Mara's baby from India? You have to be kidding."

"She's lying right here beside me, big as a peanut but very real. And she's mine for now, Angie. I'm all she's got, and I have office hours tomorrow and double hours next week to fill in for Mara, and that's not to mention five practices and a cross-country race at Mount Court, and that's only *next* week. *What am I going to do?*"

Angie was still trying to deal with the fact of the baby having arrived. "Mara must not have known she was coming so soon."

"She knew. The agency rep talked with her Monday."

"How could she have killed herself, then? She was so excited about adopting a child. She looked on it as her saving grace. What went wrong?"

"I don't know!" Paige cried.

"Why didn't she tell us the baby was on her way?"

"I don't *know*," Paige wailed.

But words were coming back to Angie, mentions Mara had made of bad luck and a curse, more than once, in counterpoint to talk of a saving grace. Angie had assumed she was being facetious. Perhaps not. "She may have been superstitious. She may have thought that if she said the words, something would go wrong."

"Damn it, if she'd said something, we might have been prepared."

"That's assuming she planned to kill herself."

"Even if she didn't. She should have told us, damn it. We were her friends. She should have told us when the baby was coming. She should have told us she was upset—she should have told us she was taking Valium—she should have told us she was losing it. Damn it, Angie. *Damn it.*"

"I'm coming over," Angie said without another thought. "Give me five minutes to get things set here, and I'll be on my way."

Paige took a broken breath. "I'm okay. You don't need to."

But Angie did. Attempts at normalcy notwithstanding, she was sick about Mara. She couldn't blot out the image of that deep, dark hole in the ground into which the casket had been lowered earlier that day. She kept asking herself what she might have seen or done to prevent it, and although she didn't seriously think that Paige was on the verge of suicide, she wasn't taking any chances.

She wanted to talk with Paige.

And she had to see the baby.

Ben was sprawled on the den sofa, flipping between CNN and C-Span. His sketch pad was beside him, at the ready should he see anything worthy of caricaturing, but Angie knew it was more habit than anything else. He wore a glazed look that said he wasn't concentrating. Mara's death had shaken him badly.

She broke into his distraction. "Hon? I'm running over to Paige's. Remember the little girl Mara was going to adopt from India? Well, she arrived today. *Today.* Paige has her."

Ben's eyes reflected his surprise, though he didn't move a muscle. "She wasn't due for weeks."

"So Mara said. But she's here, and from the sounds of it, Paige is on the verge of panic."

"Paige knows how to take care of kids. She's a pediatrician."

"Pediatricians are the worst, when it comes to their own."

"You weren't."

"I was the exception. I also didn't work for four years, so I could devote myself to Dougie. And I had the luxury of you. Paige doesn't have a husband to support her while she raises a child."

He came straighter. "She's *keeping* it?"

"I don't know. I'll find that out when I go over."

"Are you arguing for or against?"

"I'm not arguing anything. I'm listening to what Paige has to say."

He settled mutinously onto the sofa and looked at the television again. Angie knew he was angry about Mara's death. She was, too. It had been a senseless loss of life, not to mention the loss of a dedicated doctor and a good friend.

"I'll tell Dougie I'm going," she said softly. "Do me a favor and grab the phone if it rings. If it's the answering service, have them call me at Paige's. If it's Melissa, don't let Dougie stay on too long."

"Why not? The funeral was tough on him. He could use some cheering up. Besides, it's Friday. He doesn't have school tomorrow."

"It's the relationship. He's only fourteen."

"What's being fourteen without talking to girls on the phone?"

"And your tux," Angie reminded him. "You'd better dig it out of the attic and bring it down. If it doesn't fit, we'll take it to the tailor tomorrow."

Ben sank deeper into the couch. "The awards ceremony isn't for six weeks."

"True"—she pushed off from the door jamb—"but it's been six years since you last wore that tux. Even if it fits, it may look ancient, in which case we'll buy a new one. You're getting national recognition with this award." She was proud of Ben. He was a talented cartoonist. "I want you to look *great*."

She climbed the stairs to Dougie's room. The door was closed. She knocked, opened it, and poked her head inside. Dougie was sprawled on the bed, looking incredibly like Ben and aggrieved by the intrusion. He must have known the minute she had hung up with Paige, because he was on the phone himself.

He quickly covered the receiver. "You never give me a chance to say 'Come in.'"

She smiled. "I'm your mom. I don't need permission." She paused, thinking of Mara. "Are you okay?"

He shrugged. "I guess."

"Who're you talking with?"

"Kids from school."

Angie knew how that worked. There might be half a dozen kids crowding around the pay phone in the dorm. "Melissa, too?"

He shrugged again.

"Not long," she warned with what she thought was due indulgence, then added, "I'm running to Paige's for a little while. Remember Mara's baby? The little girl she was planning to adopt? Well, she came today."

Dougie's jaw dropped.

"Paige has her."

"What's she going to do with her?"

"That's what we have to discuss. I may be gone a few hours. Why don't you drag your father outside to shoot baskets? The floodlights are working again."

"I thought I'd go down to Reels."

Angie was immediately uneasy. The video store with the soda bar in back had been the hangout of choice for the Mount Court kids since VCRs had invaded the dorms. "Who'll be there?" she asked gently.

He shrugged. "A bunch of kids."

"Melissa?"

He shrugged again. "If she decides to go with the others. There won't be any problem, Mom. They have to be back by ten."

Angie sighed. "I'd rather you didn't go, Dougie. Not tonight."

"Mara wouldn't mind."

"Not tonight."

He covered the phone more completely. "Why not?"

"Because groups of kids have ways of getting into trouble. I seem to recall an incident last spring when a bunch of kids were picked up for pitching beer cans at the war memorial in the center of town. The pitching was disrespectful, the beer was newly drunk, and the kids were all underage and tipsy."

"But we're going to *Reels.*"

"Which is on the same block as the drugstore, the card store, and, coincidentally, the package store." All it took was a little cash slipped to a transient truck driver buying his own beer. "It makes me very uncomfortable, Dougie."

"Don't you trust me?"

"Of course I trust you. I just don't trust some of the others."

"They're good kids."

"I'm sure they are." All kids were. Some were confused and rebellious, but they were basically good kids who occasionally conspired to do foolish things.

"Mom," he complained, whispering now, "I'm fourteen. This is embarrassing."

It was also the first year she had to face this kind of decision. Seventh-graders at Mount Court had to be back on campus by eight for anything but a chaperoned event, which wasn't to say that there hadn't been a few cruisers among those innocent seventh-graders, simply that Dougie had never asked to be one.

She sighed. "Do it for me, Dougie? It's been a difficult few days, and I'm feeling it. The last thing I want is to be worrying about you, and I will, if you meet the kids at Reels. Another time, maybe."

"But—"

"Your dad could use some help. He's feeling a little down."

"But—"

She held up a hand, blew him a kiss, and left. Back downstairs, she put in a fast load of laundry, grabbed her car keys, called to Ben that she was leaving, and started for the door. But her mind was into organizing her thoughts, one of which was that life would be immeasurably easier for Paige if she didn't have to work in the morning.

Saturday office hours were nine to twelve. With the time reserved primarily for acutes, of which there were rarely more than a handful, only one doctor had to be there. Who that doctor would be was always the source of much good-natured bickering and bartering.

Angie thought it would be super of Peter to take Paige's turn for free. So she returned to the kitchen and gave him a call.

The Tavern had been the major watering hole in town for as long as Peter Grace could remember. His father had imbibed there, and his grandfather before that, and although rough-hewn benches and bare bulbs had been replaced by polished pine and Tiffany lamps, it was still rustic. To hear his three older brothers talk, a Tucker male wasn't a man until he had staked out his booth at the Tavern. By that definition, Peter hadn't achieved manhood until he was thirty years of age, which was when he returned to Tucker with medical school and a four-year residency in pediatrics under his belt. Only then had the onetime runt of the Grace litter had the courage to choose his booth.

It was the second one in from the front door and offered a visibility that the darker rear booths did not. Peter liked being seen. He was an important man, having been places and done things that few natives had, and he was a doctor. He was respected by the townsfolk, even loved by his patients. Their adoration was like a tonic. It was a sign of success that no amount of money could buy and went a long way toward compensating for the days when he had felt like a loser.

Likewise, there was something gratifying about watching his brothers file past to the obscurity of their booths farther back. Once upon a time, the three had been hometown stars, headlining the sports section of the *Tucker Tribune,* scoring touchdowns, swishing free throws, and hitting home runs, while Peter was fending off the taunts of his classmates. Small and uncoordinated, measured against unfairly high standards, he withdrew into a quiet world in which he read, studied, and dreamed of the day when his brothers' knees went bad and he would shine.

He was doing that now. While his brothers worked construction, he played God. In counterpoint to their callused hands, beer bellies, and, yes, bad knees, he was in prime shape. Once skinny, he was now tall and firm. Once unruly curls had mellowed into dark auburn waves that were professionally styled. He dressed like a man who had known the sophistication of metropolis and successfully adapted it to hicksville.

Tonight, he was celebrating. He didn't tell anyone that, of course. As far as the general populace of Tucker was concerned, he was nursing his beer in an attempt to lighten the sorrow he felt over Mara O'Neill's death.

In fact, the sorrow had lightened with each clod of dirt that the cemetery workers had shoveled into Mara's grave. Peter had stayed to watch long after the crowd of mourners had left. He had wanted to be sure that the job was done right, had wanted to see with his own two eyes that she was six feet under and gone.

Mara O'Neill had been a dangerous woman. She'd had the knack of befriending a man, drawing him close, then stabbing him in the back. She had done it to her husband and nearly done it to Peter. A dangerous woman, to say the least. He was lucky to have escaped.

He took a healthy swallow of his beer and was setting the glass down when several men from the steelworks entered the Tavern. They passed his booth en route to theirs at the rear.

"Too bad about Dr. O'Neill."

"Real loss for the town."

"She was a trooper."

Peter nodded, spared a response by the guise of grief, grateful when the men moved on. A trooper? Oh, yes, Mara was that. Once she set her mind on something, she didn't give up, and yes, this was a loss for the town. But another doctor could be found, and in the meantime, he, Paige, and Angie could service their patients just fine.

Susan Hawes, who owned the Tavern, slid in opposite him. She was a born hostess, a natural talker. "Beautiful eulogy the minister gave this morning," she remarked. "Makes it even harder to understand why a woman like Mara would take her own life. Of course, ministers don't always talk about the down side of folks." She grew reminiscent. "She wasn't a regular here by a long shot, but when she did come in, she could drink with the best of them. She used to sit with old Henry Mills and match him beer for beer until he felt so bad making her drunk that he stopped. He was always back the next day, drinking again, but for that one time, at least, he went home sober."

Peter cracked his knuckles. "She did have a different way about her."

"I heard she was stone drunk in that car."

He shook his head.

"Then what?"

He shrugged. Sure, he had known about the Valium. But he hadn't dreamed she was taking so much. "Since I wasn't with her, I can't really say."

"Was she seeing anyone local?"

"Nope."

"No man in her life?"

"Nope."

"Spud Harvey's gonna miss her. He used to watch her coming and going around town. Nearly drove him crazy when she had that little fling with his brother a while back. Spud was in love with her, but don't tell him I told you so."

Peter might have made a pithy comment to the extent that Mara had been worlds above the Harvey brothers, intellectually and in every other way, had his beeper not sounded just then. Susan pointed to the phone behind the bar and left him to it. He dialed the number of his answering service, thinking all the while about Mara. He knew about the thing with Spud's brother. It had been an impulsive weekend and had meant nothing. Mara had done things like that sometimes.

But death? Death was *final.* He still couldn't believe she had done *that.*

"Doctors' office."

"Trudie, it's Peter Grace."

"Oh, hi, Peter. Dr. Bigelow just left a message asking you to cover for Dr. Pfeiffer in the morning. She said to call her at home later if there's a problem."

Peter sighed. "Thanks." A problem? He supposed there wasn't. He had hoped to sleep late, but it was probably just as well this way. He hadn't slept late—hadn't slept *well*—since he had learned of Mara's death. Demons kept waking him up, reminding him of the last time he'd seen her.

It had been late Tuesday afternoon. Mara had sent the nurse to ask if he could see her last patients for her. Covering for each other was a way of life, one of the very purposes of a group practice; still, he had been tired enough himself to be annoyed. So he had stuck his head in at her door and found her standing by the desk.

"What's the problem, Mara?"

She had looked at him in confusion. "Uh . . ."

"Are you sick?" he remembered asking. "You look like shit."

She hadn't said a word, had simply stared at him in that same confused way for another few seconds. Then, as though some spark inside had given her sudden momentum, she had bolted forward, pushing past him, running down the hall toward the door.

"Jesus, Mara," he had said, but she hadn't heard that, any more than she'd heard the "Crazy bitch" he had muttered on his way back to work.

He kept seeing her running down the hall, kept seeing it over and over again. He wondered if she was haunting him.

Lacey arrived at the booth just as he returned. "Good timing," she said with a smile. "Have you been here long?"

"Ten minutes," he said, slipping a hand under his suspender as he settled down in the booth. He took a long drink, using the time to shift gears from Mara to Lacey.

Lacey was a looker. At twenty-eight she was thirteen years his junior, but the age difference didn't bother him one bit. He was the knowing one, the experienced one, the one who called the shots—all the more so since he was a native. She had come from a publishing house in Boston four months before to help edit the biography of Tucker's oldest citizen, who at the age of one hundred and two had put together a collection of stories about turn-of-the-century New England. Peter was showing her the local ropes. In return, she was an attractive and sophisticated feather in his cap. Squiring Lacey around, he was the envy of many a native, and he liked it that way.

"How was it?" she asked with a grimace.

Peter knew she was talking of the funeral. She hadn't gone, hadn't known Mara. He had worked hard to keep it that way. "Not bad."

"Sad?"

"All funerals are. The turnout was surprisingly good," he said, though in truth he hadn't been surprised at all. Mara had been active enough in town to have touched the lives of nearly everyone there. What had surprised him was the high level of emotion, particularly given the way she had died. He would have thought there would be resentment, even anger, at her desertion. Instead the damned place had reeked of love.

"How were her parents?" Lacey asked.

He released his suspender with a snap. "I told them the usual, how good Mara was with her patients. They nodded stoically. Then I thought I'd be a good guy and tell them how fiercely she fought for what she believed in. Bad move. They don't appreciate spunk. They wanted her to be a sweet little thing with a husband and babies." He laughed. "Can you imagine it? That's the *last* thing Mara could ever have been."

"Why so?"

"She couldn't sit still, for one thing, had to be always moving, always doing something. And she was bull-headed. No way should Mara have ever taken a marriage vow promising to love and obey. She couldn't obey *anyone*. It was against her nature."

"She was married?"

"Once. Before she came to Tucker. But she blew it. The guy OD'd. Lucky for her there weren't any kids. She would've had trouble with them, too. Mara was spread too thin. That's why the foster child thing blew up in her face. She was too involved with too many things to do any of them well. Hard to believe she was actually thinking of *adopting*."

Lacey ordered a glass of wine. The waitress had no sooner left than, curiously, she asked, "Why did you hate her?"

He was startled. "I didn't."

"Then, dislike her?"

"What makes you think that?"

"Your tone of voice. The way your jaw is clenched."

He stared. "Since when are you an expert on my moods?"

"No expert. Just an observer."

"I won't be psychoanalyzed, Lacey."

"I'm not psychoanalyzing you. I'm simply saying that it sounds like you had a problem with Mara O'Neill."

"And I'm saying I didn't," he insisted. Image was everything. Hatred didn't fit the one he had chosen for the town to see. "She was my partner for ten years. We were friends. But"—he couldn't help it, the words spilled out—"I refuse to call her a saint, the way everyone else seems to be doing today. She committed suicide, for Christ's sake. She took her own life, which was an ultimately selfish thing to do. If you'd been at the funeral, you'd have agreed. All those people came to pay tribute to her, after she let them down. She let us down, too, Paige and Angie and I. We relied on her to carry her weight in the practice. Now, by her *own hand*, she's out of the picture, without a word, no warning, nothing."

He stared gloomily at his beer. No matter that he had seen Mara's grave filled in, he couldn't believe she was gone. He would have thought her too feisty to have allowed death to take her on its very first try.

Then again, Mara wasn't always what she appeared to be. She had a softer, more vulnerable side. He had seen it. He wondered if any others had.

The Tavern door opened, this time to the town's major landlord. Jamie Cox owned two of the three blocks of stores that made up Tucker's center, nearly half of the shabby double-deckers in lower Tucker, and miscellaneous other pieces of real estate scattered through town. He was tall and skinny and wore his clothes too short and too tight in a way that made him look as miserly as he was.

"So she's gone, huh?" he said, stopping at Peter's booth. "Can't say I'll miss her. She was a royal pain in the butt."

Peter snorted. "She loved you, too."

"Didn't like what I was doing around town, that's for sure."

Peter didn't, either. A person didn't have to be a crusader like Mara to recognize decay. "You have to admit lower Tucker's looking pretty bad. Can't you do any cleaning up out there?"

"That's the job of the tenant. Says so right on the lease."

"The houses need painting. That's your job."

"And I'll do it soon as they clean up the yards. That's their job."

"Come on, Jamie. You're the one with the money."

Jamie scowled. "Jeeez, you're sounding just like her. If you're planning to pick up where she left off, don't bother. I don't care if you *were* born here, you won't have any more luck than she did. It's my money that keeps this town going. That gives me a certain say-so."

"But she was right." There was a nobility to admitting it on this one small score. "Especially about the movie house. It's a fire trap."

"It's a gold mine, what with films every weekend and a special event in between. The concerts coming up are all sold out. I saved a few tickets, if you want a pair."

Peter grunted. "No thanks. I'm not into suicide."

Jamie gave a thin laugh and swatted his shoulder as he walked on past. "Bet you didn't think she was either, huh?"

Left without the last word, Peter felt a new stab of anger toward Mara, because Jamie was right. Peter hadn't thought her capable of suicide, hadn't thought her a coward, but that was just what she was. If she'd had any guts, she wouldn't have killed herself. She would have faced her sorrows and dealt with them.

Not that he was sorry she hadn't, he thought as he took a long, cool, calming drink. She might have had those few soft moments when he had found her irresistible, and those few mellow moments when he had found her interesting, even those few lighthearted moments when he'd found her fun, but the rest of the time she was as difficult a woman as one could meet.

Mara O'Neill wasn't irreplaceable, either as a doctor or as a lover. The proof of that sat before him right now.

He glanced around the Tavern, then at Lacey, and suddenly he wasn't in the mood for a burger and beer, but for a filet mignon and fine red wine. "We can do better than this," he muttered. After dropping several bills on the table, he slid out of the booth and reached for her hand as he strode toward the door.

Five

The picture sat in its white wicker frame, in its customary place on the mantel. It was a black-and-white photo, a family portrait, with a youthful Nonny at its center and six-year-old Paige perched on her lap. Paige's parents, Chloe and Paul, flanked Nonny's shoulders, looking younger than their twenty-five years and trapped by the camera in the way of creatures of the wild, frozen one instant, only to flee in terror the next.

And flee they had. Paige recalled the day well. It had been her birthday, and she had had such high hopes. "We'll do whatever your heart desires," Chloe had written from Paris weeks before. "It will be your day." So Paige had planned a special breakfast, then a trip from suburban Oak Park to Chicago to shop for her birthday gift, then a movie, then a dinner at home that Nonny and she prepared. She had wanted her parents to see how grown-up she was, how able, how well mannered and pretty. She had been desperate to please, and she had, she thought. Everything had been perfect. More than once Chloe and Paul had told her how wonderful she was.

She had been on cloud nine when the picture was taken in Nonny's sitting room right before dinner. Right after dinner her parents had given her hugs and kisses, then, to her dismay, had left her standing at the parlor window while the car pulled away.

Always before, Nonny had made gentle excuses for her daughter and son-in-law, using vague references to business, friends, or vacations, then counting on Paige's brief attention span and similarly childlike perception of time to cover the lapses. This time she was more honest.

"Your parents have what's called wanderlust," she had explained to Paige, who thirty-three years later remembered every word of that conversation. "They like to be moving, doing different things. They can't be kept in any one place for long."

"Why not?"

"Because they have a curiosity about new things, and it won't go away. It keeps them traveling. Last year it was France. This year it will be Italy."

"But what about Chicago?" Paige had asked. Chicago seemed to her a huge place filled with plenty that was new and different. "If they were in Chicago, I could see them all the time."

Nonny had nodded sagely. "You're right. But they've already explored Chicago. They did that when they were growing up, just like you are now. Sometimes when people get bigger, they have to go farther to satisfy that curiosity."

"None of my friends' parents do that. They stay here. I want *my* parents here, too."

"I know you do, pumpkin," Nonny had said, giving her a hug and holding her close. "But your parents are different from the others."

"They hate me."

"No, they don't."

"They didn't want to have me at all."

"That's not true. You were their wedding gift to each other. They love you very much. But it's them, they're different."

"Why?"

"Because your father doesn't have to work, for one thing. His parents are very wealthy. He has all the money he needs, so he can buy you nice things and travel around with your mother."

"Why can't I travel with them?"

"Because you have to go to school. But they do take you places. Remember last year, when you all went to New York? You loved that."

Paige had nodded. "But I got tired. I was happy to come home. Don't they ever get tired?"

"No. That's one of the things that makes them different."

"What's another thing?"

"The curiosity I mentioned."

Paige's child mind grouped curiosity with chicken pox. "But when will they get better?"

Nonny had hugged her again. "They're not sick. Some people say they have a fairy-tale life."

"Are they happy?"

Only after a while, and with a reluctant smile, had Nonny said, "I suppose," and thereby given Paige her first, full dose of reality. She had thought about her parents' happiness long and hard, standing in the circle of Nonny's protective arms, and finally, when there didn't seem anything she could think of to soften the blow, she had simply started to cry.

"Oh, pumpkin," Nonny had crooned.

"But I tried *so hard*. I didn't spill anything, or bite my fingernails—and I took the littlest piece of cake and gave them the biggest—I thought I was so *good*."

"You were, you were. You're always good, pumpkin. You're the best little girl in all of Illinois, in all of the United States, in all of the *world*, but that has nothing to do with why your parents can't stay put. They have money and curiosity, and so much energy that they just keep going."

"But what about me?" Paige had wailed, at which point Nonny had swung her up on her lap, and held her tight.

"You are mine, is what you are," she had said with a fierceness Paige had never forgotten. "You're the one who won't get away."

"What does *that* mean?"

"It means that you're different from your mommy. She never let me hold her like this. She had too much energy even back then. She was always running around, getting into things, *always* curious. And I'm not saying that you aren't curious, just that you're more normal about it. You'll be happier in the long run, Paige. You'll be more peaceful, more content, and you'll do good things in your life."

"How do you know?"

"I know. You'll do good things. I promise."

For a long time Paige hadn't been sure. She did well in school, had lots of friends, and grew closer to Nonny every year, but she continued to blame herself for her parents' absence. She racked her brain when they were home—dressed differently, talked differently, behaved differently—but nothing was good enough to keep them there. They always left her standing at the parlor window while the car pulled away.

Inevitably people asked about Chloe and Paul, and for a time Paige simply repeated what Nonny had said. "Wanderlust" became a part of her vocabulary long before any of her friends knew the meaning of the word. "My parents? Oh, they're in Alaska. They have wanderlust," she would say with a nonchalance that hid her hurt.

Then came junior high, an exclusive private school, and a new circle of friends. Paige was an adolescent, old enough to understand what jet-setting was, worldly enough to have friends with jet-setting parents, rebellious enough to be angry. When asked, she took to saying that her parents were dead—until the horrendous day when they did indeed have a close call in a small plane. She never told the story again.

There were, over the years, several longer stretches when Chloe and Paul were home. Sometimes they stayed with Nonny, sometimes at Paul's family's estate, and in either case Paige was always beside herself with anticipation at the thought of their being around. It wasn't until the summer of her seventeenth year that she was able to admit to herself that anticipation always exceeded fact. Nonny was right. Her parents couldn't stay put. They grew restless, impatient, irascible when restrained.

At the end of that summer, when her parents left again, Paige didn't stand at the parlor window watching the car pull away. She kissed them each, then turned and, feeling something akin to relief that the normal order of her life would finally return, walked Nonny back to the house.

The lesson of her sixth birthday conversation had finally sunk in. Paige's need for her parents' love would never change—and birthdays would always be painful—but she could finally accept that their love would come only on their terms. To compensate, she had Nonny.

"I'll always be here for you," Nonny had promised when she tucked Paige into bed on that sixth birthday, and Paige had always known it was true. She'd left Nonny to go to college, then to medical school, and by the time she was doing her residency in Chicago, Nonny had moved back to her own childhood home in Vermont. Through it all, though, they were in constant touch, sharing their lives, being there for each other, and although Paige still loved her parents, Nonny was the one in whom she confided.

That was why Paige had risen early on Sunday, bathed and fed Sami, then packed up a proper diaper bag, strapped the baby seat into the car, and driven to Nonny's.

Turning away now from the white wicker-framed photograph, she took the deepest, steadiest breath she had taken since learning of Mara's death. Nonny was a balm, a reassuring presence even before she spoke, and her home was as cheery as the woman herself. It was a tiny garden apartment, done up in the red and white that Nonny had insisted upon when she had sold the larger Victorian.

"*Everything* red and white?" Paige had asked at the time.

"Everything. I adore red and white. I've always adored red and white, even when I was the littlest girl, only we didn't have the money to decorate then."

"But I thought you liked blue. Our house in Chicago was blue."

"That was for your mother, who was rarely there anyway, and when I moved back here and bought the Victorian, it was easiest to just use what I had. But now I want red and white—and don't tell me I'm too old. I may be moving into a retirement community, but I'll never be one of those old fogies. So," she had said, sighing, "I want red and white. At last."

Catching Nonny's excitement, Paige had helped furnish the little apartment, and although she had worried that the colors might grate in time, that hadn't happened. To the contrary, they had grown on Nonny, such that she had taken to wearing white—blouses and skirts or leggings, even warm-up suits—with red in a beaded necklace, earrings, or a hair ribbon. On this particular day she was wearing a flowing white caftan and tiny red slippers. Given that she was slender and petite—like Chloe, while Paige was long-legged like Paul—she looked elfin.

She sat on her favorite white wicker chair, holding Sami, who was studying her curiously. "A baby. My word, Paige. You should have called me the minute she arrived!"

"I was in a mild state of panic. I didn't want to burden you with that. Besides, this is the first breathing space I've had since I opened the door and found Sami there." Saturday had been devoted to moving the last and largest of the baby paraphernalia from Mara's, which she had accomplished with the help of a revolving contingent of excited neighbors. There had been a return trip to Mount Court, another round of questions from another representative from the adoption agency, then more moving.

"She's such a sweet little thing!" Nonny cooed.

Paige bent over, bracing her hands on her thighs, putting her eyes level with Sami's. The child met her gaze for a minute before looking back at Nonny. "She's good as gold, sleeps through the night, rarely cries. I think she's still hung over from her trip—she may not be sleeping so much once her body adjusts—but she's in good health. I had Angie examine her."

"Why Angie?" Nonny asked, adorably indignant. "Why not you?"

"Doctors should never treat their own. Not that Sami is mine," Paige added quickly. "I only have her until permanent parents are found. But I felt Angie would be more objective. She was a help Friday night, let me tell you." She suppressed a shiver. "I can't remember ever coming so close to losing it like that before."

Nonny darted her a worried look before taking Sami's tiny hands and clapping them together lightly. "What happened?"

Paige straightened, sighed, leaned against the chair. "It was a combination of everything, I guess—Mara's death, the funeral, having to deal with the O'Neills. Then Sami arrived and I insisted on taking her, then the girls from Mount Court called, so I ran over there." And had a run-in with the new Head. That had been the last straw. Fortunately, he had been out of sight when she had returned on Saturday. "It's like my immune system was down and then suddenly I found myself with this huge responsibility." She touched Sami's silky brown hair. "And you are a *huge* one, for such a little girl. Forget the amoeba infection you came with, and the inoculation program we've had to start from scratch, and the exercises to build up your muscles, and the language barrier. Even *aside* from all that, I've never been into mothering before."

"To my eternal sadness," Nonny said without remorse. "You mother everyone else's children but your own."

"Which is totally satisfying."

"Totally?" Nonny chided.

"Totally. Besides, what with all I'm doing, I don't have time to have a child of my own."

"So what are you doing with this one?"

Paige opened her mouth, then closed it again. "Beats me," she finally said in bewilderment. "I'm telling you, something was amiss. My common sense was on hold. I was mourning Mara, thinking that I'd finish up the things she started, and then Sami was at the door, and it seemed critical that I finish that up, too. It was," she said deliberately, "sheer impulse. I mean, it's fine and dandy to say that you can take care of a child and have a career at the same time; the reality of it is something else."

"If anyone can do it, you can."

"But can I do it well? Will I be able to give this little one what she needs? And she needs plenty. She needs to be touched and talked to and played with, and encouraged to sit and then stand and walk. She needs to be weaned onto regular milk and the kinds of foods that other fourteen-month-olds eat—"

"She's that old?" Nonny asked in surprise.

"That old," Paige replied. "That's what I'm telling you. She needs extra love and care if she's going to catch up, but I'm not sure I'm able to give it to her."

"Of course you are."

"What with everything else I have to do?"

"You're the one who talks about quality time."

Paige grunted. "Sounds good, huh? But does it work?"

"You'll know soon enough," Nonny advised, then brightened. "I can help. Let me baby-sit while you're at work."

"No way. Babies are hard work."

"So?"

"You've paid your dues twice, first with Chloe, then with me."

"So? Why can't I do it a third time? I'm only seventy-six. My friend Elisabeth is eighty-two, and she baby-sits her great-grandchildren all the time."

"This isn't your great-grandchild," Paige reminded her. "She's only here for a little while."

"All the more reason why I can help. My friend Sylvia works three days a week at the day care center in town, and she's eighty-one."

"I need someone *five* days a week. With Mara gone, my caseload will be heavier than ever."

"I can work five days a week. My friend Helen does it, works at the library five days a week, and she's seventy-eight."

"And then there's Gussie VonDamon," Paige teased.

Nonny scowled. "Don't even *mention* Gussie. She's an old biddy if ever there was one, gives senior citizens a bad name, driving around in that boat of a car at fifteen miles an hour, yelling out the window and honking all the time— Oooh, pumpkin"—she drew Sami close when the child puckered up—"I'm talking too sharp? You'd understand if you knew Gussie VonDamon, and you may well, one day. If she catches sight of Paige bringing you here, she'll be knocking down my door asking all kinds of questions. *Far* better if I drive over to see you."

"It's a long drive."

"It's only forty minutes."

"Nonny," Paige said, giving her grandmother's delicate shoulder a squeeze, "this is a moot point. I've already arranged to have Mrs. Busbee baby-sit. She lives two doors down. It's a perfect arrangement." Unfortunately, it was also temporary. In several more weeks Mrs. Busbee would be going south for the winter, and Paige would have to find someone else.

"Is she good with children?" Nonny asked.

"Very."

"As good as I would be?"

"No one's as good as you would be. Or Mara." Paige sighed. She stroked Sami's dark hair. "Mara would have loved this little one. She's a darling." Sami was staring at the strip of red leather that looped around Nonny's neck and through a papier-mâché strawberry. Paige lifted the strawberry and touched it to Sami's tiny hand. "I miss Mara. I keep reaching for the phone to call her, or thinking of things to tell her. She was such an important part of my life." She paused. "I let her down."

"Nonsense," Nonny said.

"I wasn't there when she needed me. I was too wrapped up in my own life to take the extra time and make sure she was okay. I knew she was going through a difficult time. I should have made the effort."

"It might not have made any difference."

"No, but at least I wouldn't feel so *guilty.*"

Nonny shot her a knowing look. "You probably would anyway. You have a thing for guilt, Paige. When you were little, you blamed yourself for your parents' wanderlust, but it wasn't right then, and it's not right now. You may be a wonderful doctor, but you aren't a mind reader. You had no way of knowing what Mara was feeling inside."

That didn't keep Paige from wondering. She had re-lived Mara's death in her imagination dozens of times. "It haunts me, thinking of that. The feelings have to be *awful* for a person to reach the point of contemplating suicide, and to go through with it—" The horror hadn't yet begun to fade.

"Have you ruled out an accident?"

"Oh, Nonny," she said with a sigh, "Mara O'Neill didn't do things accidentally. She was an all or nothing person—then again, she had so much to live for, not the least of which was Sami, that I can't imagine she would deliberately kill herself. It just doesn't make sense."

Nonny sent her an understanding look. "I guess it never will. If Mara had secrets, they've gone to her grave with her."

Paige wasn't ready to accept that. Although her first order of business was to restore an element of normalcy to her life, which meant returning to work Monday morning and immersing herself in her patients' lives as though everything were as it always had been, her second was to dig deeper into Mara's last day. Between diagnosing Danny Brody's poison ivy, removing a bead from Lisa Manner's nose, assuring a terrified Marilee Stiller that the spanking she had given her three-year-old that weekend hadn't injured him, and repairing a subluxation with a quick snap, she talked with everyone who, to her knowledge, had had contact with Mara that last day.

By lunchtime, when she caught Angie alone in the kitchenette at the back of the office, she had a large sheet of paper covered with notes. "From what I can figure, Mara came here first thing in the morning. She was writing up reports when Ginny arrived, but it was standard stuff, nothing to suggest she was tidying up before killing herself. She didn't even finish what she was doing, because the first of the emergencies arrived. She saw patients until ten."

"Feverishly?" Angie asked.

"Not particularly, according to Dottie"—the nurse-practitioner on duty that morning—"but Dottie wasn't looking for anything unusual, any more than the rest of us were. Whether her energy was unduly frenetic is anyone's guess."

She studied her notes while she absently ate the orange slice Angie handed her. "She was on the phone between patients—talked with the lab, with the desk at

Two-E"—the pediatric wing of Tucker General—"and with Larry Hills." Larry was the pharmacist at the local drugstore. "There were some outgoing calls, too, Ginny says, but unless they were long distance, we'll never know who they were to. At ten, she asked me to cover so that she could run over and confront the lab over Todd Fiske's tests. She was annoyed, but certainly not distraught, and she was back in forty-five minutes. There were more patients after that, more phone calls—a consult on the Webber child, several calls to parents. No one remembers whether she took time for lunch. You stopped her in the hall at about twelve-thirty. She was distracted then and for most of the afternoon, from what Dottie said. Peter was the last to see her. That was at four-thirty. The coroner said she died around midnight."

She sank back in her chair. "That leaves a big gap during which she took a large amount of Valium. What was happening to her all that time?"

The phone rang. Angie answered it, then passed it to Paige, who felt an instant's fright. She had called Mrs. Busbee twice during the morning and been told all was fine, but that could have changed. "Yes, Ginny?"

"Jill Stickley is here. She'd like to talk with you for a minute."

Not Sami. Jill Stickley. Paige felt relief on one score, concern on another. Jill's name hadn't been on the daily roster. She would have remembered. Seventeen years old and one of Paige's original Tucker patients, Jill held a special place in her heart, which was only one of the reasons Paige was alert. The other was that the Stickleys had been through more than their share of rough times of late. One more wouldn't do.

"Show her into my office," Paige said without pause. "I'll be right there." She rose from the table with an apology to Angie.

"Go," Angie urged. "I'll see if I can learn anything more about Mara's day. Something's missing."

That had been Paige's thought exactly, but it was gone from mind the minute she saw Jill Stickley's face. The girl was standing awkwardly in her office, looking exhausted, pale, and tense.

Paige imagined that Jill's father, a frustrated insurance salesman, had beaten her mother again, or that her mother, who had been unemployed for a year before landing a lower-paying job, had been laid off again, or that Jill's brother had stolen another car and been caught again ditching it at the Tucker landfill.

She put an arm around Jill's shoulder and said, "No matter what it is, it can't be that bad." After a while, nothing was. "Go on. Tell me."

"I think I'm pregnant," Jill said in a reed-thin voice while frightened eyes sought Paige's reaction.

Paige swallowed. "Pregnant?" It wasn't what she'd expected at all. "Uh, I thought we agreed on birth control pills."

"We did. Only I messed up, I guess."

"What makes you think so?"

"I'm late."

"How late?"

"A couple of months."

Paige glanced at her middle, which was covered with loose layers and revealed nothing. The hand she put there learned far more. Beneath it was a distinct bulge. "A couple of months? Oh, sweetie. This feels like four at the least."

Jill's eyes filled with tears. "I guess I lost count," she whispered.

Lost count? Paige cried silently. How could you lose count? We've been talking about sperm meeting egg since you started menstruating five years ago. I pushed abstinence until abstinence became a pipe dream, and then I pushed contraception.

But the arguments were moot. The deed was done. "And you're terrified."

The girl nodded.

Paige rubbed her back. "Does Joey know?" Joey was the longtime boyfriend, an automobile mechanic, six years older than Jill. "Of course he knows," Paige answered herself. "He's seen this bulge."

But Jill shook her head. "He thought I was getting fat. He's been razzing me about it. So I told him the truth last night. He said he didn't want any part of a fat girlfriend or a screaming baby, and that I could do what I wanted with it. I thought he'd get used to the idea overnight, so I went home and sat up all night praying for it, but when I stopped at his place this morning, he had packed up and gone."

Paige sighed. "Oh, sweetie."

"I can't tell my dad—he'll go apeshit—and if I tell Mom, he'll accuse her of keeping secrets from him. He'll hit her big time for that." She wiped her cheek with the heel of her hand. "I've really messed up this time, haven't I?"

Paige clicked her tongue. "Bringing new life into the world is never a mess-up. What gets hairy is the way we handle it." She guided Jill to the examining room. "Let's take a look and see what we're dealing with here."

Ten minutes later they were back in the office, sitting close on the small sofa, trying to "handle" the situation. Jill ruled out an abortion, for which Paige, who had fresh visions of Mara pregnant at the very same age, would have been grateful even if the timing had been right, though it wasn't. Paige estimated that Jill was indeed four to five months pregnant, and although physically an abortion might still have been safely performed, the emotional ramifications would be tougher. Then again, raising the baby was a hardship Jill could ill afford; the Stickleys had negative economic resources, and without a high school diploma, Jill had little chance of improving on it. Adoption seemed the wisest solution.

The immediate problem, given that Jill was still a minor, was breaking the news to her parents. Knowing that the longer they waited the worse it would be, Paige phoned each, arranged a meeting in her office at three-thirty that afternoon, then ordered Jill to take a nap on the sofa while she saw her afternoon patients.

Frank Stickley was furious. His wife, Jane, stood by in fearful silence while he cursed Jill's lack of brains, morals, and looks, none of which Paige found lacking in the least.

"Jill made a mistake," Paige pointed out calmly. "It isn't anything that has to spoil her life."

"Are you kidding?" Frank yelled. "She's having a *kid.*"

"Which she'll be giving up for adoption. The adoption agency will cover the cost of her medical care. There won't be any imposition on you."

"But I have to *look* at her all those months, look at that belly getting bigger and bigger, and know that the whole town knows and is laughing up a storm."

He faced Jill. "You're a slut. I told you this'd happen. That boyfriend of yours was no good. I said it. But did you listen? Naaaaah. You knew all the answers. Well, what's your answer about school? How you gonna finish school having a baby?"

"I'm dropping out. I'll finish after I have the baby."

"She'll carry the baby to term," Paige said in support, "give it up for adoption, then pick up her life right where she left off."

"Not in *my* house, she won't."

"Frank," his wife protested, then cowered when he aimed a finger her way. The finger was threat enough. He didn't have to say another word.

"You won't know I'm around, Daddy. Really," Jill promised.

"I'll know. So will every randy dandy in Tucker. You can bet that once that baby's gone, they'll be coming round, now that that stupid boyfriend of yours ran off. Well, I won't have it. You want to stay in town, you can find somewhere else to live. I don't want to see you." Without so much as a glance at either his wife or Paige, he stormed from the office.

Jill started to cry.

Jane looked tormented, torn between appeasing Frank by following him out and staying to comfort her daughter.

"Go with him," Paige urged softly, taking Jill's hand. "Jill's coming home with me."

Jane gave a convulsive head shake. "You can't—"

"I've just hired her. I need a live-in someone for a little while. It's perfect." She shooed Jane out. "Go. Make things as easy on yourself as you can. We'll talk later."

Looking dubious, Jane left, and in the quiet that ensued, Paige told Jill about Sami. "It's the perfect solution," she concluded. "If you're determined to drop out of school"—which she was, though Paige had done her best to dissuade her—"you'll need something to keep you busy. I need someone to watch Sami when I'm at work and when emergency calls come through at night." With Jill in one of the upstairs rooms, she wouldn't have a qualm about setting up Sami in the other. The fact that her little house was getting fuller and fuller seemed secondary. "It's an important job. Sami has special needs right now. Do you think you can do it?"

"Do *you* think I can?" Jill asked cautiously.

Paige smiled. "Without a doubt." Her smile faltered, then reappeared. "And you aren't allergic to cats." She glanced at her watch. "This is perfect timing. I have cross-country practice in an hour. I was going to take Sami with me to Mount Court." Though the Head would never have approved. She wondered if he would be on the lookout for her. "Now I won't have to. We'll send Mrs. Busbee home, put Sami in the carriage, and you can take her for a long walk while I run. It'll be good for you both. She's a little angel. You'll see." She was rising to clean up her desk when the phone rang.

"There's a fellow on the line asking for Mara," Ginny reported. "He's calling from New York. From Air India. Do you want to take it?"

Paige felt the nudge of an awful sixth sense. "Right now," she said, and pressed in the call. "This is Paige Pfeiffer. I'm Mara O'Neill's partner. May I help you?"

"Yes, please," said a voice with a British accent. He gave his name and identified himself as a supervisor. "I've been trying to reach Dr. O'Neill, but I can't seem to get an answer at the number she left. I understand that that was her home number and that this is her professional one, and I do apologize for disturbing her here, but I would very much like to speak with her."

"May I ask what this is about?"

The fellow cleared his throat. "It's a bit awkward. I have an apology to make, actually. Is Dr. O'Neill there?"

"No. But I'd be glad to take a message."

"Oh, dear. I had wanted to speak directly with her."

"That may be difficult. For the sake of expediency, perhaps I would do."

The man considered that. "Yes. I suppose." He took a breath. "You see, Dr. O'Neill phoned this office last Tuesday to check on the progress of a flight from Calcutta to Bombay. The agent who took her call is new with us and was a bit confused operating the computer system. I'm afraid he erroneously told her that the flight on which, I believe, she had a child, had crashed."

Paige closed her eyes.

The voice by her ear continued. "Indeed there was an accident on one of our aircraft that night, but it was not the one on which the child and her escort were traveling. Unfortunately, what with trying to handle the calls we were receiving from those who truly did have parties on the ill-fated plane, our agent did not realize his mistake until week's end. At that time, he verified that the child and her escort had landed safely in Boston, but he did relate to me what had happened, and responsibly so. We would like to apologize to Dr. O'Neill for any fright we may have caused. Air India does not make a practice of passing on misinformation. We sincerely regret having done so in this instance. I trust that Dr. O'Neill has custody of her child, and that all is well."

Paige wrapped an arm around her waist. In a small voice she said, "Can you tell me what time it was when Dr. O'Neill called you?"

"It was four twenty-five. We had received news of the accident a mere ten minutes before that and were still trying to get the details, so you can imagine the pandemonium. . . ."

Not pandemonium. Total despair. Mara had wanted Sami more than anything. She had shopped around for just the right adoption agency, had waded through the paperwork and the preadoptive sessions, laid bare her soul and her financial records, paid every appropriate fee, bought a crib, baby clothes, and food. She had regarded Sami's arrival as the start of a new phase of her life.

". . . again our sincere apologies," concluded the Air India supervisor.

Paige managed a feeble, "Thank you." She needed two tries to settle the phone in its cradle, unable to think of anything but the pain Mara must have felt.

"Dr. Pfeiffer? Is anything wrong?"

She looked up, startled to find Jill Stickley there, but only for the minute it took to return to the present. She recomposed herself and took a deep breath. "Nothing for you to worry about," she said lightly, and gestured Jill toward the door.

During the drive home, she avoided thinking about that phone call. She settled Jill in with Sami—who recognized Paige, she was sure of it, though all the coaxing in the world couldn't bring a smile—and headed for Mount Court, where she put the girls through a series of sprints, two warm-up loops around the campus, a three-mile run on the course, then more sprints. She ran with them, pushing them as fast as she could push herself, and when they grumbled all she said was, "It's for a good cause."

What she didn't need was Noah Perrine, monitoring the final sprints from the stoop of the distant administration building, but there he was with his arms crossed over his chest and his glasses glinting in the late afternoon sun. Annoyed, she stopped where she was, folded her arms over her heaving chest, and stared right back until the girls collected around her.

"He sees everything—"

"Just waiting for us to slip up."

"Sadist."

Paige dropped her arms. "I'll bet he isn't in half the shape we are."

"He runs, too," one of the girls advised.

"He does?"

"Every morning—"

"Ten loops around campus—"

"Like he's the lord of the manor policing his domain."

Paige blew out a breath. "Then we can all feel a bit safer. Come on"—she set off for the field house—"let's wrap this up."

Moments later she was headed home again, but while she was preoccupied thinking of Jill and yet another addition to the house that had been so quiet and peaceful and *all hers* such a short time before, her car took her to Mara's.

She sat in the driveway, trying not to look at the garage and think about the agony Mara must have been feeling when she had pulled the car inside. She slipped from her own car, let herself into the house, and closed the door behind her. The click of the latch was followed first by total silence, then by the sound of soft footsteps as Paige moved through the rooms. In time she climbed the stairs and found herself at the door to Mara's bedroom.

A large Windsor bed dominated the space. The rest of the furniture—night tables, a dresser, a rocking chair—had been bought at the same time as the bed and matched it in style, but that was as close to coordination as Mara had come. The comforter was teal blue, the cushion on the rocker orange, the rag rug at the foot of the bed a cacophony of dissonant colors that would never show dirt, Mara had sworn. Given her aversion to cleaning, that had mattered, as had the fact that since the rug was a sampler done by a student from the local crafts collaborative, it had been a steal. Mara loved steals when it came to things like rugs. When it came to children, no expenditure—be it of money, time, or love—was too great.

Paige looked around the room. Her heart broke to think of the dreams that had been nurtured here, the long, lonely, dark hours when night thoughts had painted pictures of a happier life, pictures that had been dashed because . . . because . . . because why? Because Mara had had an abortion when she was sixteen? Because she had taken Daniel under her wing and failed to cure him, because Tanya John had been abused into a distrust of all adults, because a confused employee at Air India had passed on tragically wrong information?

She sank down on the edge of the bed, fingered the nightstand, slowly opened the drawer. Inside were the remains of a pack of Life Savers, two pens and a pencil, several crochet hooks, and wads of scrap paper with jotted reminders. Some had to do with work, some with mundane errands, but the majority, certainly the most recent ones, related to Sami.

A spiral-bound crossword puzzle book lay beneath the scraps. Paige flipped through it. Nearly every puzzle had several words filled in, never more than seven or eight before the puzzle had been abandoned. A few of the puzzles had a line scrawled diagonally across, suggesting frustration. Paige could imagine Mara pulling the book out in the middle of the night in an attempt to distract herself from the voices in her head and growing annoyed when the voices prevailed.

Why didn't you say anything, Mara? I knew how much you wanted Sami. If I'd known she was coming so soon—if I'd known what the Air India fellow said—I might have helped.

But Mara had kept it all to herself—the excitement and the despair, along with the Valium, the abortion at sixteen, and God only knew what else.

"Damn it, Mara, that wasn't fair," Paige cried, shoving the puzzle book back into the drawer. When it wouldn't go, she pushed harder. "You had no business keeping secrets. We were supposed to be *friends!*" She swore again, this time tossing the puzzle book aside and reaching into the drawer to see what was blocking the way. Her fingers closed on something and pulled, then continued to pull when that something kept coming. Moments later she found herself staring dumbly at her hand, spilling around which were a pair of paisley suspenders.

She had seen them before, many a time, though not lately, she realized, searching for the label. It, too, was familiar, high profile for cosmopolitan types. Only one person in Tucker wore paisley suspenders; only one person in Tucker was vain enough to value that particular label.

That person was Peter Grace.

Six

Angie was late. Hurriedly she made several last minute notes of things for Dottie to see to first thing in the morning. Then she slipped into her blazer, took her purse from the bottommost drawer of her desk, and, with a quick look around to assure that all was in order, strode out the door and down the hall.

The office was silent, in stark contrast with the noise of the day. Angie thought Peter had left, too, until she passed his door and saw him inside. He was at his desk, pencil in hand, though the way he was slouching suggested he wasn't doing much writing.

"Everything okay?" she asked.

He looked up, dropped the pencil, and kicked back in his chair. His eyes were tired, his voice tight. "We need help. This is the first time I've sat down all day.

Something's going on in this town. Asthma's on the rampage. I know we're into that season, but it's never been as bad as this before."

Angie smiled sadly. "We've never been without Mara before. How many of those asthma patients were hers?"

"Better than half."

"Asthma attacks can be brought on as easily by emotion as by pollen. The patients of Mara's who I saw were upset at being without her, and the parents were worse than the kids. They needed reassurance that the nebulizer would be here with or without Mara. Don't worry, Peter. It'll quiet down."

He looked her in the eye. "This practice is designed for four doctors. Our caseload is based on four doctors."

Angie held up a hand. "Can't think of that yet. Too soon."

"Christ, Angie, it's six-thirty and we're both still here. You think Ben and Dougie are going to like that for long?"

"Ben and Dougie will be fine. They know things are going to be tight for a while. I have a new schedule posted on the kitchen board."

"If today was a preview of what's to come, we'll be here until six-thirty lots of nights. It's either that or start turning patients away, and we swore we'd never do that."

"We won't. We'll reorganize and be more efficient, and if that doesn't work, *then* we'll recruit a fourth. Relax, Peter. We'll work things out. We can't be functioning at full capacity right now, what with Mara's death so raw. I spent a good deal of my day talking about her. But it won't always be like that."

He made a noise. "How easily people forget."

"No. But after a while, when there aren't answers to some questions, they stop asking them. Life does go on." She caught sight of the clock. "I have to run. I'll see you tomorrow."

"Yeah."

"We'll work things out," she repeated, raising her voice as she went down the hall. If Peter answered, she didn't catch it, and then she was trotting down the stairs to the door that opened onto the parking lot.

Five minutes later she passed under Mount Court's wrought-iron arch, swung around the drive, and parked in front of the library. Students were sprawled in scattered groups on the lawn, but she didn't see Dougie among them. She glanced at her watch. It was six-forty.

Two minutes later he ran up, tossed his books onto the backseat, and slid onto the front. "Sorry, Mom. Have you been here long?"

"No. I was a little late myself." She knew enough not to lean over for a kiss. Fourteen-year-old boys didn't kiss their mothers while their schoolmates were looking on. Instead she started the car. "Did you have a good day?"

"Sure."

"Where were you coming from just now?" It hadn't been the library, where she had expected him to be.

"The dining hall. I had dinner with the kids. You don't mind, do you?"

"I do," she said with a stab of disappointment. "I'm making dinner at home."

"I know, but I was starved. Soccer practice stunk. We had to run around the field ten times, and then do it again when one of the guys said something the coach didn't like. I was beat. I needed something to get me going again."

"Oh, Dougie." She sighed. She viewed dinner as an important daily family event. "So what did you eat?"

"Something with chicken. It was pretty good."

Angie could imagine a sauce with the occasional piece of diced chicken, mashed potatoes, bread and butter, and cake. "Not quite the steak I was planning to broil at home."

"I was *starved*. I don't know if I can make it to seven for dinner every night. That's late, Mom."

"Only forty-five minutes later than usual," she informed him, and turned onto the main road. "It's just a question of getting used to it. Besides, I sent you with fruit." She shot him a glance. "What happened to that?"

He scowled out the window. "I'm not eating fruit in front of the guys. Maybe Coke, or candy, but not fruit." He turned to her and said with surprising force, "What's so awful about my having dinner with the kids once in a while? If the food here is okay for them, it's okay for me, and besides, it's fun eating here."

"It may well be, but you're not a boarder in part because I like being able to talk with you over dinner. You're one of the fun parts of my day." She knew that time was limited, that Dougie would be increasingly independent, that too soon he would be going off to college, and that that was the natural order of things, but for now she wasn't giving him up. "Dinner at home isn't the same without you. Besides, I thought we agreed that you'd spend the extra time at the end of the day at the library. That way you could get a head start on your homework, so I wouldn't be annoyed when the phone started to ring at night." She had thought it a fine compromise.

"I was hungry," he said. "It seemed like the right thing to do at the time."

She smiled. "No great harm done. Besides, I'm running a little late. By the time the steaks are broiled, you'll be hungry again. So, anyway, tell me what's new. How did the Spanish quiz go?"

Travel time was quality time. Angie prized it, those few minutes when she had her son all to herself in the car, when he might share the small details of his life. The details this day, once he passed off the Spanish quiz as a snap, had to do with the new Head's special project. "He's building a house."

"A house."

"For alums, so that they have a place to stay when they come to visit. The kids who don't do a sport have to work on the house."

"Interesting."

"It *sucks.* The kids are furious. Always before they could skip a term for sports, now they can't anymore. They're saying it's child labor."

"Sounds more like a community project to me."

"That's what he called it. He got an architect alum to donate the plans, and he got approval from the Board of Trustees for the cost of the wood and stuff, and he has a carpenter from town who'll supervise the whole thing in exchange for his son coming to the school for free."

"That's a nice deal."

"The kid's a jerk. A real townie. He'll never fit in."

"Seems to me you were a townie two years ago."

"You know what I mean, Mom. His dad's a carpenter."

"So?"

"So most of the kids' dads can buy and sell him ten times over."

"Most of those kids' dads can buy and sell us ten times over."

"There's a difference."

"Because your dad doesn't work with his hands? No, Dougie, there's no difference. This boy may be just as bright as any other child at Mount Court. He has a right to the same opportunity, and if his dad is clever enough to find a way to do it, I admire him. Who is it, by the way?"

"Jason Druart."

Angie grinned. "I like Jason. Good for him. And good for the other kids at Mount Court. Building a house will be educational. It'll give them an idea of what it takes to make something that they take for granted. You too. Will you help?"

"No way. I'm staying as far from the Head as I can. He's trouble."

"Funny, he looked nice enough to me." Angie had met him at a reception shortly after he was hired the spring before. He had struck her as being a leader, which was what the school needed.

She pulled up at the house. Dougie hauled his book bag from the back and was out the door in an instant. She followed and found Ben in the kitchen with a damp paper toweling wadded around his finger.

"Uh-oh." She set aside her purse and took a look.

"It was getting late," he said in the grumpy way men had of doing when they botched things up, "so I thought I'd fix the salad. I was slicing carrots and missed. Does it need stitching?"

"Nah. The bleeding has pretty much stopped. A Band-Aid will do the trick. Dougie? *Dougie?*" When he didn't answer, she stuck the paper toweling back on the cut, told Ben to press tight, and headed for the bathroom medicine chest. A minute later she had the cut neatly covered and the bloody paper toweling disposed of, and was finishing the salad Ben had begun.

"You didn't have to do this," she said with a fond glance at Ben. He was leaning against the counter, wearing his usual jeans and T-shirt, looking endearing, albeit distressed, in his quiet way. "I told you I'd be home."

"I was hungry."

"Poor baby. You and Dougie both. But we're not eating that much later than usual."

"It sure seems it. The extra time is like an eternity when you're tired and hungry."

"Did you have a good day?" she asked, setting aside the salad and going to the fridge for the steaks.

"I faxed off a couple things." He held the door open, closed it when she set the steaks on the counter. "I hate it when you're this late. When are you guys hiring another doctor?"

"When we get around to it. Things are too busy right now, and too emotional." Paige understood. Peter and Ben, typically male, putting business first, did not. "Mara's still warm in her grave. It feels wrong to rush into replacing her."

"Mara's stomach isn't the one that's grumbling," Ben said, and walked off.

Angie smiled and called after him, "You'll survive. I'll have dinner ready in ten minutes."

And it was. Ten minutes later Ben was seated at the table and she was calling up the stairs for Dougie.

"I had dinner at school," he called back.

"You had food there. This is dinner."

"But I'm not hungry."

"Come on, sweetheart. Just a little."

"Mom, I have homework to do."

"Five minutes with us, that's all, then I'll let you get back to work." To Ben, as she poured Dougie's milk, she said, "There were times when I worried because he was so agreeable. This sputtering is a relief. It's so typically adolescent." She bobbled a hot baked potato from the microwave to Dougie's plate, then did one for Ben, then for herself. "The Harkins stopped by the office with their youngest this afternoon," she told Ben. "Gerry was asking for you."

"Is his daughter sick?"

"She's having trouble in school, and apparently the teacher doesn't know what to do. It sounds to me like an attention deficit problem, which can be easily treated once it's diagnosed. I recommended that they have her tested—" She looked up. "There you are." She nudged Dougie's chair. "I even have sour cream for the potatoes."

But Dougie didn't sit. "I'm not hungry, Mom. I told you that."

She smiled. He was a good-looking boy, had been as a child and was even more so now as a teenager. Given the rate he was growing, no amount of food was apt to make him fat. "Tell me again, once you've eaten that steak."

"I'm not eating it. I had dinner at six. I was hungry then. I'm not hungry now."

She set down her fork. Something in his tone went beyond the sputtering she had found relief in moments before. She could have sworn she heard an accusation. But that wasn't possible. Dougie adored her. "Then have some potato. The skin is the best."

"I'm stuffed."

"But this is *dinner*. Come on, sweetheart. I told you this morning that we'd be eating at seven." She gestured toward the bulletin board. "It's right on the new schedule."

Dougie made a face she'd never seen before. "I don't like that schedule. It tells me to get up earlier in the morning and eat dinner later at night. It's a pain."

"It's new," Angie soothed. "That's all. Give it a week, and you'll forget we ever did anything different."

"I doubt it."

"Oh, sweetheart," she chided gently, and sat back in her chair, "you're upset with the change because you're upset about Mara. That's natural, and it's okay, but you have to give the new schedule a try. With Mara gone, things have been turned upside down at the office. This is the best I can do for now. Be patient—you'll adjust."

"I *always* adjust," he complained.

"Once things quiet down at the office, once we hire another doctor, we can go back to the way things were—"

"I don't want to go back to the way things were."

Angie didn't follow. "What do you want?"

He opened his mouth to talk, then shut it again.

She sat forward and urged, "It's all right. You can say what you want. I'll listen. I always listen. What *do* you want?"

"I want to spend more time at school," he blurted out. "It's lousy being a day student. Day students miss half the fun."

"That's the point," Angie said on a note of amusement. "You get to enjoy the other half, and still be with your family."

"But I want to be with the kids. I want to live in the dorm."

The suggestion was absurd. "Sorry, but that's out of the question."

"Why?"

"Because it's not what I want for you. I sent you to Mount Court because I felt that you would be more challenged academically there than at the middle school here in town. Boarding is something else entirely."

"Why can't I try it?"

"Because you're only fourteen. I don't mind if you sleep over in the dorm once in a while—you did that last year—but I don't think it's necessary for you to move away from home."

"It's five minutes down the road!"

She shook her head again. "College is soon enough to board. You don't need it now."

Dougie stared at her for a minute, then turned on his heel and left the room.

Startled by his persistence, Angie looked at Ben. "Where did that come from?"

Ben finished chewing a mouthful of steak. "It's been building."

"Building from what? He's never said he was unhappy living here before."

"And he isn't saying it now. He's just saying that it would be fun to board at Mount Court."

"Do *you* think it would be fun?"

"If I were fourteen, with the confidence that kid has, I probably would. Dougie's feeling his oats. He's listening to the stories his friends tell about dorm life, stories that are probably greatly embellished, and he thinks it sounds pretty neat."

But Angie had created a home that she thought was pretty neat, one the likes of which many children would die for. She couldn't imagine Dougie wanting to live in a dorm. "It has to do with Mara," she decided. "We've all been down since she died. He's missing her, wanting to go someplace where he won't be expecting her to turn up. He feels her presence in this house."

Ben tapped his fork to the plate. "He does not. Hell, Angie, don't go looking for metaphysical explanations. It's simple. The boy is growing up."

"I know he is."

"Then stop smothering him."

She was taken aback. "I'm not smothering him."

"Sure you are. You watch him all the time."

"That's not *smothering*. That's *mothering*."

He set down his fork and sent her a look that was almost as foreign as Dougie's had been. "It was mothering when the boy was four, seven, even ten. But he's fourteen, and you're still right there telling him what to do. You lay his clothes out at night, you proofread his homework, you keep track of his phone calls."

"Is that wrong?" she asked in astonishment. "Should I just stand back and let him talk on the phone all night to whomever he wants? If he did that, he'd never do any homework. What would happen then?"

"He might fail a test or two, but at least he'd learn what happens when he doesn't do his homework. At some point, the initiative has to come from him. At some point, he has to develop his own sense of responsibility. But you won't let him *near* that point. You're smothering him, Angie. Clear as day, you are."

I am not, Angie thought. She didn't understand what was happening. Ben never criticized her. He was always happy with what she did. "Is it Mara?"

"Is what Mara?"

"This—" She gestured.

"For God's sake, *no*. Why do you keep saying that?"

"Because I don't understand what else it could be," she reasoned. "The death of a friend is so upsetting that you begin to find fault with things that would otherwise be just fine."

Ben scowled at the remains of his dinner. In his silence Angie felt a wave of relief. She was right, after all. Mara's death had set them all on edge. Things would be fine once the ache of the loss eased.

Then Ben raised his eyes. His gaze was direct, his voice tight. "Mara's death may be the catalyst, may be the thing that's made us more sensitive and therefore more apt to speak out, but I meant what I said before. This has been building. It was only a matter of time before it came to a head. The fact is that you're smothering Doug. He's fourteen and needs to be meeting his friends at the local video store on a Friday night. Teenagers do things like that."

"Some do, some don't."

"Well, Doug wanted to, and given that he stood there with us through Mara's funeral and that nightmare of a lunch afterward, he could have used the release."

"I suggested that he play basketball."

"With me, but I'm his father. It's not the same. He needs to be with his friends more than you're allowing him to be."

There it was, another startling slap on the wrist. "I don't understand, Ben. Why the sudden criticism? You've always agreed with me before."

"No," he said slowly. There was an ominous pause. "I've always gone along. That doesn't necessarily mean I agreed."

She felt a flash of anger. "Why didn't you speak up?"

He seemed to grapple with the question himself, rising from the table, crossing to the sink, and staring out the window, finally wheeling around. "Because you were always in such control, damn it. From the time Dougie was a baby, you had all the answers." He threw up a hand. "Hell, it goes back before that. You've had all the answers since the day I met you. Right from the start, you knew you wanted to be a wife, a mother, *and* a doctor. You picked me out at the start of your senior year so that we could be married the minute you graduated—"

"Whoa," she protested. "You make it sound like a cold, calculated act, but you were the one who asked me out, not the other way around, and you *kept* asking me out. I was legitimately in love by the time you asked me to marry you."

"And it worked out well, didn't it? You graduated in time to be married, honeymooned in time to start medical school, finished medical school and your residency in time to have a baby, got him out of diapers and into school in time to move up here and start practicing with

Paige. You orchestrated it all, Angie, and the amazing thing is that it *worked.* You're a remarkably capable woman. You plot things out, and they're done, and you rarely allow for help. I'd have been a more active father when Dougie was little if I had felt I was needed, but you had everything done before I could do much more than offer."

"I was making things easier for you," she argued. "You had a career. You had deadlines to meet. You were supporting us at the time. It was my *job* to take care of Dougie."

"Even after you went back to work? Okay, he was in school by then. Still, I might have done something. I'm here during the day. I drive. I love the kid, too. But you arranged your schedule so that you could drop him at school on the way to work and pick him up on the way home, and spend weekends and vacations with him."

"We did *wonderful* things on weekends and vacations," she reminded him. There had been road trips, and airplane trips, and trips to Boston to visit historic sights and museums.

"That's not the point," Ben insisted. "The point is that you personally planned and executed Dougie's childhood. You didn't need my help. After a while, I didn't bother to offer. The message that I was superfluous came through loud and clear. I just sat back and watched, which is pretty much what I've been doing for years."

Angie swallowed. He kept hitting, kept hitting. She was totally confused. "Was I doing it wrong?"

"*No.* You were doing it *right.* You were *always* doing it right. Wife, mother, and doctor—you got everything done when it was supposed to be done, even if it meant that you were programmed from morning to night. But things are changing now. Dougie isn't a baby anymore. You can't program his life the way you have up until now. He's growing. He needs space."

"I give him space."

"Not nearly enough. You tell him what to do, when, and why. You don't let him make decisions for himself."

"I'm *helping.* Life is difficult."

"You emasculate him, Angie."

"How can I do *that?* He isn't a *man* yet."

"And he'll never get there, if you keep on the way you're going. You deny him things that would make him feel good about himself. Sure, he's self-confident now, but after a while, when he begins to feel that he can't make decisions on his own because you've always made them for him, he'll be in trouble. You're taking away his sense of power. You're making him feel impotent, and that's devastating. I know. You've been doing it to me for years."

She sucked in a breath. "Not true."

He nodded, slowly and conclusively. "You treat us like children, like we can't be trusted to think for ourselves. You arrange our lives to suit your needs."

"Ben, I don't!" she protested.

"You do, and when we dare object, you pat us on the heads and send us off like little kids too young to understand what life is about. It's insulting, Angie. It's demeaning. It's *infuriating*."

She could see that. His hands were white-knuckled on the edge of the counter. But it didn't make sense. Ben was soft-spoken. He went about his business without hassle, passive in a positive way. This lashing out was totally unlike him. She struggled to understand what was going on in his mind.

"I know you're not pleased that I'm working longer hours, but it's a temporary situation."

"It's not the hours, Angie. It's the way you go about it. It didn't once occur to you to sit down with me and discuss how you planned to handle Mara's death. You decided what you were going to do, based on what was best for you and the office, then you put up a new schedule for us to follow and assumed we'd go along. Well, the scheduling isn't working anymore. Not for Doug, and not for me."

Her stomach twisted. "It's working," she insisted, because that had always been one of the givens of her life. She prided herself on having a successful career, a well-adjusted son, and a solid marriage. "You're perfectly happy."

"*See?* Damn it, you're doing it now, telling me how I feel! Well, I'm telling you I'm *not* pefectly happy. I spend hour after hour alone in this house—"

"You're *working.*"

"Not all the time. I take breaks, and I don't spend more than five hours at the drawing board. So what do I do when I'm done? I walk through this godawful quiet house and feel lonely."

"That's absurd, Ben. Up until this week, I rarely worked more than six hours a day myself."

"And when you're home, you're fixated on Doug." She shook her head in denial, but he insisted, "It's true, Angie. Your career comes first, then your son, then me."

She was stunned by a thought. "You're *jealous?*"

"If I am, I have every right to be." He jabbed his chest. "I'm a man, and I'm human. I need companionship."

"You chose a solitary occupation."

"I chose an occupation I was good at, that just happened to be a solitary one, but it wasn't even so solitary when we lived in New York," he went on, seeming unable to stop now that he had started. "I could hand-deliver my stuff and have lunch with the guys at the paper. I could sit around the city room for as long as I wanted. So now I have cable TV for stimulation. There's no comparison, Angie."

It seemed he was finding fault with *everything*. She was being torn apart. "Now it's Vermont that you hate? But you went right along with the move. You didn't once say boo."

"Because the move made sense! You were looking to join a practice that wouldn't be cutthroat; we were looking to buy a house, which we couldn't do in New York; my work was portable; the quality of life here seemed right. I figured the positives outweighed the negatives, and if you were happy, that was half the battle. So we moved and you were happy."

"So were *you*," she insisted, because she remembered too many smiles and good times for it not to be so.

"On some levels I was. You were working, which you wanted. I was working. We had our house and the freedom to drive down Main Street without experiencing gridlock."

"It's been good," she said, trying for points, only to be knocked down again.

"It's been lonely. At first I kept in touch with the guys, but after a few years, even with trips back once in a while, it wasn't the same. There's a high turnover rate in the newspaper business. Before long, I didn't know who to call, and you were at work all day and then preoccupied with Dougie the minute you walked in the house. But I have needs, too, damn it."

"You should have said something."

He tipped up his chin. "I have, only you never hear. When I ask if you can take an hour off from work to go to lunch, you say you have patients booked straight through. When I suggest taking off for a weekend, you cite something or other that Dougie has doing here. When he goes to bed, so do you. Where does that leave me?"

"But I *do* things with you," she argued. She didn't understand his attack. "We go out to dinner. We have friends over."

"You decide, you invite, you plan."

"And we do go away. That's what the awards ceremony next month in New York is all about."

"That awards ceremony is about recognition and prestige. It isn't about me. I could care less about getting an award. You're the one who wants it."

"For *you.*"

"But it isn't what I *want,*" he repeated, and raced on. "But you don't know what I want, do you. You formed an idea of who I am and what I do, and you've woven that idea into your life. You may listen to my words, but you don't hear my thoughts. You don't hear my needs. You don't *see* me. You haven't seen me in years!"

She came out of her seat to face him. "That's not true. You're my husband. I may not be here all the time, but I'm aware of what you do."

He shook his head. "You're so wrapped up in your own life that you haven't got a clue."

"You're dead wrong."

"I don't think so," he said, leveling her a stare. "If you were aware of any of what I've been feeling, if you *heard* the things I asked you and looked at me, really looked at me, you'd know that there's something going on in my life. But you're so blind to anything but what's on your own schedule that you have no idea, no idea." He thrust a hand through his hair. "For Christ's sake, Angie, I've had a relationship with another woman for nearly eight years now, and you haven't the foggiest."

Angie felt as though her insides had slipped to another part of her body. She put a hand to her chest to try to anchor her heart. "What?" she asked in a shaky voice.

"You heard," he grumbled.

I've had a relationship with another woman for nearly eight years, he had said, but that couldn't be.

She knew her husband. He was loyal and devoted. He *loved* her.

"Are you saying that just to hurt me?" she asked, because it was the only thing she could think of, and even then it didn't make much sense. Ben wasn't a hurter. He was a kind, introspective, innocuous sort.

He looked away. "I'm saying it because it's the truth, and because I don't know how else to get through to you."

"Who is she?" Angie heard herself ask. It seemed important, the acquiring of as much information as possible.

He turned to the window and put his hands on his hips, and for a minute she thought he wouldn't answer. Finally, in a low voice, he said, "Nora Eaton."

Angie conjured up the image of a pleasant-looking woman, average in nearly every respect except for a headful of long, incredibly vibrant salt-and-pepper curls. She was Tucker's librarian and terrifyingly real.

"She's older than we are," was all Angie could think to say.

Ben shrugged. "I never really thought about it."

Her legs were shaking. She eased herself down onto the chair. "How often do you see her?"

"I don't know—once, twice a week sometimes. Look, Angie"—he turned back—"it's not some kind of sexual perversion. There are times when all we do is talk, like you and I used to do before we were married. I miss that. I miss having you around."

"You never told me that."

"I did. You just chose not to hear."

"But if you have her now, you're not missing anything," Angie said, feeling empty inside and alone.

"Not true. I'm still missing you. She's a stopgap measure, not a cure. She can't hold a candle to you, but, damn it," he said with a renewal of the anger that had spewed earlier, "I can't spend the rest of my life competing for your attention and coming in last." That said, he pushed away from the counter, went out the back door, and disappeared into the night, leaving Angie with the scattered shreds of her life.

Peter spent an hour searching through reams of negatives, looking for just the right one. He put that one into a carrier, put the carrier into the enlarger, and adjusted the enlarger head for the print size he wanted. He made a test exposure, slipped the print into each of the developing solutions in turn, then turned on the light and examined the print. Back in the dark, he made a second, darker print, then a third one with higher contrast. With succeeding prints he focused on detail.

He made no less than a dozen prints before he was satisfied. Then he returned to the reams of negatives, selected a second one, and started the process all over again.

It was well past midnight before he emptied out the solutions and left the darkroom, and by then he was too tired to do much of anything but fall into bed.

He was up at seven the next morning, back in the darkroom, examining the prints he had left to dry; but what had looked good to him the night before no longer seemed adequate. So he hastily gathered what he'd done, crammed the prints into the trash can, and vowed to do better that night.

His frustration followed him to the office, where the first of the morning's drop-ins were waiting. On the theory that the more he worked, the less he would think, he saw patients straight through until ten-thirty, when he stopped for a cup of coffee. That was when Paige cornered him.

Seven

Paige drew the paisley suspenders from the pocket of her lab coat. She held them forth and watched Peter's face. Though his expression didn't change, he lost enough color to answer the question she hadn't asked.

"I found them in Mara's night table," she said. "It seemed an odd place for them to be."

"I'll say." He cracked his knuckles. "In Mara's night table? Interesting."

"You didn't know they were there?"

"If I had, I'd have taken them back. They're my favorite ones. I thought I'd lost them at the health club. Thanks." He took the suspenders from her hand and stuffed them into his pocket. "Why were you looking in Mara's night table?"

It was a fair question. Theoretically, Mara's death could be explained away by Valium, fatigue, and a mistimed telephone call. But Paige wasn't satisfied. The more she learned, the more of a mystery Mara became—and the mystery nagged. Paige was driven to learn more. Mara, in death, had become her personal responsibility.

"I was sitting on her bed, trying to get a better understanding of what had happened," she said. "Bureaus can be enlightening. Night tables, too. So I opened the drawer to see what was inside. Why do you suppose these were there?"

He took a gulp of coffee, grimaced, added another spoonful of creamer, and stirred. "She liked them, I guess."

"So did you. You used to wear them all the time. How did she get them?"

"She was at my house a lot. She must have taken them."

"Without your knowing?"

"She had free run of the place. I didn't follow her around keeping track of what she touched."

"But why would she take your suspenders and then hide them in her night table drawer?"

He drank his coffee.

"Peter?"

He looked at her. "Because, damn it, Mara had a thing for me. Come on, Paige. You knew that."

Paige hadn't known any such thing. She made a face that told him so.

"Well, she did," he insisted.

"You were friends. You did things together sometimes. What do you mean, she had 'a thing' for you?"

"She *liked* me. She was *obsessed* with me."

Paige shook her head. "Obsessed? Forget it. Mara wasn't obsessed with you. I would have known."

"Like you knew about the Valium? Like you knew the little girl was en route from Bombay? Face it, Paige. Mara kept secrets. She was a little crazy that way." He paused, then asked the question she had been grappling with most of the night: "Why did *you* think they were there?"

"I thought," Paige began, but the truth was that despite all the grappling she hadn't known what to think. "I thought that maybe you had spent the night once and left them there."

"Why on earth would I have spent the night? Mara was enough for me to handle in the daytime. Why would I buy into trouble at night?"

"Because you liked her."

"Sure, to pal around with sometimes, but being with Mara for any length of time was like having a pebble in your shoe. So why would I have spent the night at her house?"

"Because you *liked* her."

"I did not."

"Sure you did. And she liked you. Okay, you hated each other sometimes, too—the two of you could drive us nuts with your bickering—but through it all you were friends."

"Friends," he insisted. "Not lovers. What ever gave you the idea we were lovers? It's a preposterous thought."

Paige hadn't said they were lovers. Not once had she used that word. She had imagined that Mara and Peter might have been out late doing something, or *in* late doing something, then fallen asleep. A pair of suspenders might easily have been discarded for comfort's sake, then left behind. Sure, the placement of them was odd, but it wasn't beyond the pale to imagine that Mara had found them lying around and stuffed them anywhere just to put them out of sight.

No, Paige hadn't said they were lovers. It was interesting that Peter had mentioned the word.

"Hi," Angie said, joining them with a fast look at each before turning to the coffee machine. "Am I interrupting something?"

Peter moved aside. "Nothing I can think of."

"Why do I sense you were talking about Mara?" She poured herself a cup.

"Maybe," Paige answered, "because she's still front and center in our minds. Want to know what I learned yesterday afternoon?" She told them about the talk she'd had with the Air India supervisor.

Angie gasped. "Poor Mara! That might have done it. She wanted a baby so badly. If she believed that after everything she'd gone through, Sameera's plane had crashed, she might have been distraught."

But Peter was shaking his head. "She's lost patients without going over the edge, and she knew those children. She didn't know Sameera."

"But Sami was going to be her daughter," Angie pointed out, "and there's a difference. If you had children of your own, Peter, you'd know. When it comes to parenthood the emotional involvement is far greater. Mara had her heart set on adopting that child."

Paige wasn't a parent any more than Peter was, yet she agreed. "She saw adopting Sami as her best shot at motherhood."

"That's what I don't understand," Peter argued. "Why was it so important to her?"

"Time, perhaps. She was thirty-nine. She heard the old clock ticking away."

"You're the same age. Are you getting desperate?"

Paige didn't have time to get desperate. "I never lie awake for hours the way Mara did. It's the night thoughts that do a person in. Besides, I'm coming from a different place." Her parents were flighty, not rooted to home. They had considered parenthood a chore. Mara, on the other hand, had come from a home where the bearing of children was revered.

She thought of the words Thomas O'Neill had spoken, standing on the front steps of the funeral parlor. "Having a baby was what her parents wanted."

"But she hated her parents. She rejected everything they stood for."

"Outwardly, perhaps. Inside, maybe not so."

"Did she ever say that?"

"No," Paige admitted. "But it makes sense. Mara loved children, and she was big on motherhood. Speaking of which"—she turned to Angie, who looked distracted but snapped back under her gaze—"Jill Stickley had good reason to see me yesterday. She's pregnant."

Peter touched his cup to his forehead. "Good God, when will these girls ever learn?" He made for the door.

"It takes two to tango," Paige called after him—sharply, since she hated sexist comments, even offered in jest—then returned to Angie and told her about Jill. "I talked with her mother this morning, and she'll tell the school that Jill won't be back until September. In the meantime, she'll be my au pair."

Angie nodded. "Sounds good."

"That is, until the adoption agency finds a permanent home for Sami. She's a sweetie, Angie. She deserves the best."

"Mara would want that. Then again"—Angie looked at the ceiling—"who am I to say what Mara would want? I thought I knew her, but it seems I didn't."

Paige had said the same to herself all too often in the days newly past, and the mystery went on. "Angie? Do you think that Mara and Peter were ever romantically involved?"

"Romantically?"

"Sexually."

Angie hesitated. "That's an interesting thought. Why do you ask?"

Paige told her about the suspenders. "If she was hung up on Peter, she never let on to me."

"Or me. Then again," Angie said, frowning at her coffee, "maybe she dropped hints that I didn't hear. If so, she wasn't the first." She took a drink, burying her face in the cup.

Paige felt a glimmer of unease. "What do you mean?" For all her competence, Angie had never been a braggart. Nor, though, had she ever been one for self-effacement.

She sighed tiredly. "Oh, I don't know." She fingered the rim of her cup, running her thumb back and forth, back and forth.

"Angie?"

She raised her eyes. They were filled with tears. "I think I've messed up," she said slowly.

Paige reached for her arm. "You? Mess up? No way."

"Yeah, that's what I've always thought," Angie said, "but I was wrong. Ben and I had a huge fight last night."

"I don't believe that, either. You and Ben don't fight. He's too peaceful and you're too right."

"Not last night." She pulled a tissue from a nearby box and pressed it to her eyes.

Paige was shaken. She had never seen Angie vulnerable before. "Okay, so you had a fight. It can't be that bad."

"He's having an affair," Angie said into her tissue.

Paige was astonished. *"Ben?"*

Angie nodded. Her voice shot up and went wobbly. "With the town librarian."

"Are you kidding?" But Paige knew Angie wouldn't have said it, wouldn't be crying, wouldn't be in the least bit vulnerable, if she were kidding. "Why in the world is he having an affair with *anyone?*"

It was a minute and several quiet sobs before Angie was composed enough to answer. "He says that I don't listen to him. That I don't *see* him. That he's lonely."

"So why didn't he tell you?"

"He said that he *did* tell me, but that I never took it seriously, and I might have thought he was wrong if it hadn't been for Mara. But here Mara commits suicide, and I'm her partner and friend, and I didn't see it coming. So maybe I didn't see what Ben was feeling, either. And when he names the woman, how can I argue? Nora Eaton. My God."

Paige would never have guessed Ben capable of infidelity, which made a sad statement about her own insightfulness. She hadn't been any more perceptive about Mara's state of mind than Angie had been, and she had supposedly been that much closer a friend.

Now she wrapped an arm around Angie and offered what comfort she could. "I'm sorry, Angie. What can I do?"

"Not much," Angie said through her tears. "The dirty deed is done."

"What happens now?"

Angie looked utterly bewildered. "I have no idea. I've never been in this situation before."

"But your instincts are good."

"Apparently not, if I missed this. My own husband has been having an affair—for eight years"—her voice tripped—"and I had no idea. I'm looking over my life with Ben the way I looked over my life with Mara and wondering where I slipped up. I'm looking for things I didn't see, but, so help me God, I keep coming up blank. There was no lipstick on his collar. There was no strange perfume on his clothes—or on him." She shivered.

Paige could imagine the direction of her thoughts. Gently she asked, "Was there any change in his behavior toward you?"

Angie shot her a self-conscious glance. "Not in bed, no. Our relationship wasn't overwhelmingly physical. We never had time—*I* never had time," she corrected. "We didn't make love often, but when we did, it was good, and it still was, at least for me. I thought he enjoyed it." She squeezed her eyes shut. "I thought it was okay to have quality over quantity. I feel like a fool."

"You're no fool."

"Can you imagine him making love to me and thinking of her?"

"He may not have done that."

"*Eight years.* How could I have missed it?"

"If you didn't catch it in the beginning, it would have been nearly impossible to see later on. Over eight years' time, whatever he was doing would have become the norm. There wouldn't have been anything out of the ordinary for you to see."

Angie shot her a dry look. "*The New England Journal of Medicine* hasn't written this one up. I'm out of my element."

Paige smiled. "So how did you leave it with him?"

Taking a long, slightly uneven breath, Angie settled against the edge of the table, seeming, to Paige's relief, calmer. "I didn't kick him out, though I'm sure Mara would have told me to do that. 'Sue him,' she would have said. 'Take him for everything he's worth. If he likes Nora Eaton so much, let *her* wash his socks.' Mara adored Ben, but she hated infidelity."

Paige smiled again. Angie's analysis of Mara was right on the mark. For all the softness Mara may have had inside, she had her militant moments. "But that doesn't take into consideration the fact that you love him."

"I do," Angie breathed.

"Did he say what he wanted?" She couldn't quite get herself to use the word *separation*, much less *divorce*.

"He left the house after we argued. He came back later, but we didn't talk. He stayed in bed when I got up this morning." She pressed a shaky hand to her upper lip, then wrapped her arms tightly around her middle and looked at Paige beseechingly. "What should I do?" she whispered.

"Talk to him. Go home now and do it."

Angie shook her head. "There's too much to do here." She pushed away from the table and blotted her eyes in the reflection on the microwave door. "My patients are waiting."

"So are mine, but don't you think this takes precedence? This is your husband, Angie."

"I know. But I need time."

"Time is a luxury. We ran out with Mara. Ten times a day I wish I could turn back the clock and talk with her. Talk with Ben, Angie."

Angie paused with her hand on the doorknob and her back to Paige. "I don't know what to say. Do you know how disconcerting I find that? I'm rarely at a loss—but never in a million years did I expect something like this from Ben. I thought he loved me—I still do"—she shook her head—"I just don't understand. Maybe he's right. Maybe I haven't been giving him what he needs."

"Are you justifying it?"

"No, but I have to take part of the responsibility. You said it to Peter—it takes two to tango. If one of a pair isn't listening to the music, the other one may want a different partner."

"Angie, *nothing* condones infidelity."

"I *know.* But this is *Ben.* I need time to decide how to handle it."

Paige let her go and, soon after, started seeing her own patients, but Angie's dilemma was with her for the rest of the day. She felt it personally—the shaking of something that had been a rock. Angie's marriage had always been a paragon, a shining example of the way things should be. During those times when Paige wondered what it might be like to be married, she dreamed of a setup like Angie's that allowed both for work and family. At the hub of such a life was a husband, and though a different type of man from Ben turned her on, he was steadfast in the very same way.

Ben's infidelity crushed an ideal. It left an ache inside her, much as thinking of Mara still did, which was why she stopped home before going to Mount Court that afternoon. She told herself that she was checking up on Jill, but the fact was that seeing Sami eased the ache. It didn't matter that Sami wasn't biologically Mara's, that the two had never even met, but Sami seemed to be the little piece of herself that Mara had left to Paige.

Needing to feel the connection, she sent Jill off to see friends and took Sami with her to Mount Court. The team manager was happy enough to baby-sit while Paige ran with the team, then Paige held Sami while the girls did multiple sets of sprints. When practice was over, she strapped Sami into the stroller and, intent on taking advantage of a sunny September afternoon, started to walk.

She wound along the campus road, passing classroom buildings, the art building, and the library. She passed the administration building, walking at a leisurely pace, chatting with students, pausing to kneel by Sami's side and point out the sights. By the time she reached the dorms, a bulldozer could be heard. She followed the sound.

The girls had told her of the new Head's construction project, but telling was nothing like seeing. The setting was a wooded one beyond the last of the dorms and would have been beautiful had it not been for the widening hole the dozer was gouging in its midst.

Students of both sexes, wearing jeans and shiny hard hats, were standing around watching with the same kind of helplessness Paige felt. Just beyond, looking not helpless at all—indeed, intent on the work if the set of his jaw and the focus of his mirrored sunglasses went for anything—was Noah Perrine.

He wore jeans and a hard hat, too, though his hat was less new. He also wore a faded T-shirt. The way it seemed perfectly at home on his body surprised Paige. Likewise the way he was gesturing to the operator of the bulldozer. He seemed to know what he was doing, seemed at ease in the role of construction foreman. He looked taller and more rugged than he had the Friday before and less than ever like Head of the School.

Sami started to whimper. Paige lifted her out of the stroller and held her close. "It's okay, sweetie. Don't let the noise bother you. They're building a house. A new house. It's an incredible thing to do with the kids, I have to admit. For a prig, he's hit on something smart."

She watched Noah. He alternately gestured and stood with his hands on his hips. At one point, when the dozer stopped, he turned to the students and began to talk. In lieu of hearing, which the idle of the machine precluded, Paige tried to make out his expression, but the mirrored glasses stood in the way.

At his sign, the bulldozer started up again and kept at it for another little while until the driver cut the engine and climbed from the cab. Noah said more to the group, but even with the machine silent, Paige was too far away to catch his words. Then the students dispersed. Several stopped to talk with her—grumblings, which she passed off with an indulgent smile—but they were soon gone.

She should have returned Sami to the stroller and headed back to the car, but something kept her rooted to the spot as Noah approached. He stopped directly before her.

"Were you waiting for me?" he asked. The voice was as quietly steely as before, the sunglasses vaguely intimidating.

"Not on your life," she answered, willing her heartbeat to slow. "But it's an interesting project."

He took off the hard hat and the glasses, wiped his forehead with his arm, put the glasses back in place. "I thought it was. To hear it from these kids, it's an embarrassment. They think it's beneath them."

That was the gist of the grumbling Paige had heard. "They're spoiled."

"Among other things." He glanced toward the dorms. "We caught a couple in the woods last night."

"Doing what?"

"Don't ask."

"Drugs, alcohol, or sex—which was it?"

"Does it matter?"

"Sure does. Drugs and alcohol are illegal. Sex is simply unwise—at their age, at least." Her heartbeat sped when Noah shot her a look. Defensively she added, "Assuming the sex is by mutual consent, and I'm referring to the punishment. If I was the one deciding, I'd be harder on drugs and alcohol than on sex."

"You must like sex," he said.

She wished she could see his eyes. "That's not the point."

"You do, don't you."

She could have sworn she saw the start of a smirk. "That's neither here nor there," she insisted. "Your kids are the ones at issue. But, hey"—she held up a hand, then promptly took it back down and used it to put Sami in the stroller—"what you decide to do with them is your business. You're the Man." She secured the strap and started off. She needed to be moving. Noah Perrine made her uncomfortable.

"For the record," he said, falling into step beside her, "the two we caught were draining a fifth of vodka. They'll be suspended for three days and put on probation when they get back." He made a dry sound. "At the rate we're going, half the student body will be on probation by Halloween, which isn't any sweat off my back—hell, I'm only acting Head until they find someone permanent—but they'll have a tough time getting anyone to come with so much disciplinary action outstanding."

"You could always look the other way when rules are broken."

Sunglasses or no sunglasses, she felt his accusatory stare. "I should have known that a woman who keeps a baby strapped to her chest while she drives a car would say something like that."

"For the record," Paige informed him, tossing his own words right back, "now that I've learned how to use the car seat, she's in it. That was desperation you saw in action the other day. I don't make a habit of breaking rules."

"Neither do I," he said without raising his voice, "which is why I can't look the other way and let these kids do what they want. I may only be here for a year, but during that time it's my name that goes on the bottom line. It's my reputation that's at stake. It's my caring for the lives of these kids that makes me rigid."

"Whew," she said with a light touch, which was the only way she could think of to top off such a heavy speech.

"So don't tell me that I don't care for kids," he added, "because I do."

So he remembered their last conversation. "That was bothering you, huh?"

"Damn right. I'm doing my best in a sticky situation, and I'm doing it because I care. I didn't have to be here. I had a perfectly good job that I could have kept for as long as I wanted."

"Then why did you take this one?"

He had no fast retort. Finally, resignedly, he said, "It seemed like a good thing to do for a year. How's your team doing?"

With the shift away from himself, she dared a glance up at his face. The mirrored aviators added nothing of a personal nature. She wished she had a pair of her own, or a hat with a low visor—anything to make her feel less exposed. "The first race is Saturday. I'll let you know then."

"Have the girls calmed down?"

"There haven't been any more frantic phone calls, if that's what you're asking."

"Did they show up to talk on Saturday?"

"Most of them."

"The sophomores, too?"

"For a little while."

"Were they talking?"

"Listening, more. As you pointed out, Sara had never met my partner."

"And you pointed out that being new, she doesn't have a support group here yet. So how does she seem to you?"

"Okay. She's quiet, serious. She's my strongest runner. I'm guessing she'll place well on Saturday."

They walked on. Paige wondered where he was headed. She wished he would get to wherever it was. His presence disturbed the air around her.

"I identify with her," he said, and it was a minute before Paige realized he was still talking about Sara. "Being new and all. Do you think she's making friends?"

"She fits in fine with the team, but I have no idea how she is otherwise. What does her dorm parent say?"

"To me? Not a hell of a lot. I'm not much more popular with her than I am with the students. I'm the one making rules that she has to enforce."

"But she's your staff. Your staff is answerable to you."

"There are answers and there are answers. The ones they give are sometimes as begrudging as the ones the kids give. The last thing they want is to declare themselves my allies."

Paige reached the path that would take her to her car. Feeling imminent relief, she raised her hand in a quick wave and said, "Me neither. See ya."

Angie's palms were damp. She waited for Dougie to run ahead into the house, praying that he would go to his room so that she could have a minute alone with Ben. If the boy had heard any of the previous night's discussion, he hadn't let on. Aside from one comment, a vehement, "I'm starved," when he climbed into the car at school, they had talked during the drive home as though the disagreement the day before had never taken place.

She had no idea how Ben would be. One part of her would have been very happy if, like Dougie, he acted as though nothing were wrong. The other part—the hurt, angry, realistic part—knew that Nora Eaton existed. She would have to be dealt with. The question was when.

Angie preferred later. For now she would be satisfied to find the same old Ben watching the evening news. She could make dinner—she had taken chicken from the freezer that morning—and start a load of laundry. She could find strength in small, everyday accomplishments.

She came into the kitchen and called out a hello, trying to make it as cheerful as always. Ben didn't answer, but that was nothing new. Sometimes he didn't hear or was preoccupied listening to a news report; then, when he heard her puttering around, he would come in to say hello.

He didn't this night. She assumed that he was having doubts of his own as to how he would be received. After all, he was the one who had cheated.

When dinner was ready, she called out from the kitchen door. Dougie's footsteps on the stairs preceded his appearance. He slid onto his seat. "Where's Dad?"

"Coming," Angie said, hoping it was true. She started dishing out food; still he didn't show. "He may not have heard," she said, stopped what she was doing, and went to the den. Ben was just where she thought he would be. "Dinner's ready," she said.

He looked at her—unsurely, she thought. The look she returned was one of confidence. *Come to dinner, now. We'll work this all out later.* When she saw him start to rise, she returned to the kitchen. She had his food at his place and was fixing a plate for herself when he slid onto his seat.

"Hey, Doug," he said, holding out a hand for a high five. "How was school?"

Angie listened to a repeat of the stories she had heard in the car. When Ben asked a question that got Dougie going off in another direction, she tried to concentrate, but her thoughts were on the "later" she had been thinking of in the den. She managed to put in an appropriate word, enough to ward off suspicion that something was wrong. She even managed to eat a good half of her dinner, but all the while she was plotting. "Later" came just after she placed large pieces of chocolate cake before Dougie and Ben.

"I've been thinking," she said in what she thought was a reasonably conciliatory voice. "I know that neither of you is happy with the added hours I've been working since Mara's death. My new schedule isn't going over terribly well. So"—she cleared her throat— "I've decided to make some adjustments."

Both faces were wary.

"Dougie, you object to having to get up earlier in the morning."

"That's not it, Mom, but you drop me at school too early. It's embarrassing. Nothing's happening. The dorm kids aren't even *awake* then."

"They should be," Angie said, "if they want breakfast before school begins—but that's their problem, not ours. Now that Paige has a live-in to help with Sami, she can take her turn with the early emergency drop-ins so that I only have to do it twice a week. On those days, your father can drive you to school at the usual times. Same thing with picking up at the end of the day. On the three days that I have to stay late, your father will pick you up and bring you home. You can have a snack here, so that you won't be starved if you have to wait for dinner until seven."

Neither of them spoke. She looked from one face to the other. "Well? Does that sound better?"

Dougie looked at Ben, who had his lips pursed and was looking at his plate.

"What?" she prodded.

Dougie looked back at her. "You're missing the point, Mom. The point is that I want to be a boarder."

"We agreed last night that that wasn't feasible."

"You agreed. I didn't."

She tucked her napkin beside her plate, feeling genuinely confused. "Doug, why is this coming up now? Why not last spring? That would have been the appropriate time to decide whether you were going to board. Why now?"

"Because the kids are great this year, and I'm a year older, and if I don't board, you'll be on my back all year about using the telephone at night. Besides, if I board, I can eat dinner when the rest of the kids do."

"I just said that your father would pick you up earlier so that you could get a snack here."

"I don't want to come home earlier. I want to stay *later.*" He pushed away from the table.

"What about your cake?" Angie asked.

"You didn't bake it. It came out of a box."

"I can't do *everything.*"

"The cook at school makes it homemade," he said as he went out the door.

Angie was bewildered all over again, wondering what had gotten into Dougie. When she looked to Ben for help, he met her gaze.

"You don't listen, do you?" he said quietly. "He's telling you that he needs more freedom, but you don't hear."

"I accommodated him," she protested. "I told him that he could sleep later again, and that he wouldn't have to hang around school until six-thirty at night because you would pick him up earlier. I'm doing the best I can to make things the same as they were before Mara died."

"But that isn't what he wants. He's telling you that he wants to board."

Angie caught her breath. "Do *you* want him to board?"

"No, but that's not the point. The point is that you're still orchestrating things, which is what he's rebelling against. He needs freedom from that. So do I."

"A household can't function without organization."

"Organization is one thing, manipulation another. You've just informed Doug that I'll be driving him to school twice a week and picking him up three times a week, but you never even asked me if that was all right."

She was speechless, feeling overwhelmingly wronged. Finally she pointed a shaky finger at the floor. "Right here, last night, you told me that I emasculated you, that I never let you do things for our son because I was afraid you wouldn't do them right. Now I'm giving you a chance. I don't understand why you're upset."

"Because it's *your plan*. You came up with it all on your own. You didn't ask me what I thought, or if I had any better suggestions."

"Do you?"

"That's not the *point*." He ran a hand through his hair, made a guttural sound, and rose from the table. "It's a losing battle. I can't get through." He headed for the door.

"Where are you going?" A picture of Nora Eaton flashed through her mind.

"Out."

"Ben—" But the screen door slammed shut, and he was off toward his car.

Angie sank down on her chair and looked blankly at the uneaten servings of cake. When the numbness of his abrupt departure began to wear off, her insides were trembling.

She had been so sure she was doing all the right things. She had certainly *wanted* to do them. She didn't understand where she had gone wrong.

But there was no denying how deep the resentment ran against her. She might have attributed last night's flare-up to moodiness, had tonight's not followed it. Not only did the resentment run deep, but it struck her that it must have been building for years. And all the while she had been oblivious of it.

She wondered where had she been all that time, what she had been thinking. "You don't listen, do you?" Ben had asked, echoing all he had said last night. To one who took pride in having a firm grip on her life, his words came as a blow—and that, on top of the cutting fact of his infidelity. They hadn't even *touched* on that tonight. But perhaps rightly so. It was a symptom. Just as her schedules, and revised schedules, were placebos.

The problem was that for all her knowledge, for all her training and skill and competence, she didn't have the faintest idea where to turn.

Eight

Noah Perrine came from a family of academics. His father, his mother, and two older sisters were all teachers. It was understood that he would do the same. And he wanted that. Having grown up on the campus of the small southwestern college of which his father was a dean, he liked the sense of community that campus living offered. The seeming insularity of it didn't bother him at all. He believed that electronic communication made the world a smaller place, such that he could be cosmopolitan and provincial at the same time.

For the sake of tasting the cosmopolitan, he completed a doctoral program in New York, then took a position as the head of the Science Department at a prep school outside Tucson, but it soon became clear that his talents were wasted if limited to teaching. He had a way with adults. He had organizational skills and a feel for business that few others at the school had. Almost by default, he became involved in upper management and, in time, was named director of development. It was a position that allowed him to combine teaching with alumni relations and fund-raising, both of which were critical to the institution's survival. The fund-raising involved travel, and although he wasn't wild about that, he was paying his dues. His goal was to be named Head, if not of that school, then of another.

Unfortunately there was no appropriate headship available at the time when he had a sudden, dire need to leave Tucson. So he moved to northern Virginia to head the nonprofit Foundation for Environmental Awareness. There he was able to combine his knowledge of ecological issues and his teaching skill with his flair for fund-raising, and over the course of twelve years, he thrived. If there were times when he missed the warmth of small-campus life, he consoled himself with the knowledge that he had a meaningful job working for a cause in which he believed.

When he turned forty, though, he began to feel detached. He was as apt to wake up in Minneapolis, Boulder, or Boise as in Alexandria. People moved in and out of his life. He craved the centeredness of the life he knew as a boy.

A return to academia was inevitable, etched in his marrow like a spare gene, but he took his time, wanting just the right school, just the right setting.

Mount Court Academy wasn't it. Nearly insolvent, it had a dismal reputation punctuated by impotent leadership and a student body out of control. Academics had declined; disciplinary problems abounded. The school was a disaster that had already happened, waiting only for aftershocks, before imploding.

But the timing was right. Noah needed the change. The fact that the appointment was for a year gave him a built-in escape clause. And there was something to be said for the challenge.

He started in June and spent the summer cleaning up the administrative mess that his predecessor had left. By September he had worked out scheduling snafus with the registrar, weeded through a maze of alumni records with the development office, and, with the academic dean, critically examined every course being offered. While the basic curriculum was upgraded, electives were sorted through, tossed out, or restructured with an eye toward demanding a meaty academic load from every student.

More than a grumble came from a less than enthusiastic faculty that suddenly had to rewrite lesson plans, but those sounds were nothing compared to the reaction of the students when they returned after Labor Day.

Now, less than two weeks into the school year, Noah wondered if he was up to the job. To say that he wasn't a popular man on campus was putting it mildly. He didn't have a friend. The faculty treated him like an outsider; the students treated him like the enemy. The strength of his convictions didn't waver—he knew that he was doing right by the school—but that fact did nothing to make his work easier. He was lonely.

That was why, he supposed, Paige Pfeiffer caught his eye. She was a doctor, an intelligent woman who would support the changes he was trying to make, or so he had assumed—and it wasn't that he had assumed wrong, just that she was coming at things from a woman's point of view. She saw the emotional side of the issue, while it was his job to see the structural side. He was the rule maker, the disciplinarian, while she could be softer and more permissive, which was all fine and good. *She* wasn't the one who had to answer to an army of demanding parents and an even tougher brigade of trustees.

Still, he watched for her. She intrigued him somehow. He decided that it was her long, lean runner's legs. They were sexy as hell.

The inappropriateness of the thought brought home to him the sad state he was in. He needed a friend in

Tucker. More than that, he needed encouragement, a sign that what he was trying to do just might work.

Determinedly he showered, put on a clean pair of slacks and a fresh shirt, and went to the dining hall, but rather than taking his customary place in the faculty alcove and sitting through another meal with another teacher who would get in little digs about the extra class he had to teach that term, he plunked himself down in the middle of a group of freshman boys.

Those who weren't eyeing him warily exchanged nervous glances with each other.

"How're you guys doing?" he asked in a friendly way.

One brave soul found the courage to say, "Okay."

"Classes going well?"

Several shrugged. Others found sudden interest in their food.

"What do you think of the building project?" he asked to get them going.

They looked at each other.

One said, "It's okay."

Another said, "We're not old enough to do it."

A third said, "It may not look so good when it's done. Homemade stuff stinks."

"There's nothing 'homemade' about the house we're building," Noah chided. "The plans were drawn up by a legitimate architect, and the construction is being supervised by a legitimate builder."

Another boy said, "My brother's helping. It'll be a disaster."

"Uh-uh," Noah argued. "I can't afford a disaster. Everyone who's helping will learn to do it right."

"Yeah," said another with smug looks at his friends on either side, "so they'll be able to graduate and build houses."

"There's nothing wrong with that," Noah said.

"My dad isn't paying big money for me to learn to build houses."

"No, but that would be a great little side benefit to the formal education you're getting. Let me tell you, there's satisfaction to be had in building a house."

"You've done it?"

"More than once."

"Your *own* house?"

"No. They've always been houses for other people who wouldn't be able to afford it without a little help from their friends."

One of the boys groaned. "Here comes the pitch."

"What pitch?" Noah asked him.

"You're going to tell us that the community service requirement is the best thing to hit campus since the salad bar, but I hate salad."

"That doesn't mean you have to hate community service."

"In Tucker? Are you kidding? The town is the pits. There's nothing here."

"There's a grocery store, a library, and a post office. There's a hardware store, a lumberyard, and a book-store. There's a crafts collaborative. There's the Tavern. And the inn. There's an ice-cream shop, and there's Reels. And the hospital."

"Tucker General," someone snickered.

"From what I hear," Noah said, "Tucker General's saved many a Mount Court kid from disaster, so don't knock it."

There were several more snickers with no words attached. Then someone mumbled, "I wouldn't want to have a heart attack there," and the others laughed.

"Why not?" Noah asked. "The doctors at Tucker trained at the same hospitals that you know and trust. They just choose to live in Vermont. If I were a betting man, I'd wager that Tucker offers more personal care than the big city hospitals do."

"That's because the nurses are hicks. They don't know any better."

Noah was disappointed by the boy's cynicism, but not surprised. Spoiled was never far from arrogant and arrogant never far from jaded. These fifteen-year-olds were all three. "John, is it?" he asked the boy who had spoken last and found satisfaction in his surprise. "I tell you what. You do your thirty hours at the hospital and then tell me you still believe that, and I'll treat you and three of your buddies to sundaes at Scoops."

"Thirty hours?" John asked, looking appalled.

"That's the requirement."

"Where are we supposed to find that kind of time?"

"Saturday mornings, six weeks' worth, five hours each," Noah said. "Or Saturday afternoons, or Sunday afternoons, if you can't get out of bed early enough. The hospital is always in need of help on weekends. Or if you don't want to work at the hospital, you can tutor math at the elementary school, or read to the elderly at the nursing home, or work at the recycling booth at the town dump. The point is," he concluded, "that you all are a privileged lot. You have advantages that others don't have. You owe it to society to give something back."

"We pay taxes."

"Your parents pay taxes," Noah corrected. "You're the ones taking so much without giving back."

"We're too young to give back."

"You're never too young." He rose from his seat. Much more and he'd have indigestion, and he hadn't yet started to eat. "Who knows?" he added, tray in hand. "The concept of charitable giving might just sink in. You might find that you like it. You might leave Mount Court a nicer person." On the verge of saying something sharper, he took his leave. He ended up back in the faculty alcove and ate his dinner feeling somehow defeated. So, when he was done and back out in the early evening air, he tried again.

This time it was Paige Pfeiffer's group—Julie Engel, Alicia Donnelly, and Tia Faraday, plus Annie Miller and several juniors, plus two sophomores, Meredith Hill and Sara. They were sitting on the lawn, finishing assorted concoctions of the frozen yogurt that had been served for dessert. He slid his hands into his pockets and sauntered up.

"How's the yogurt?"

The girls eyed him with varying degrees of caution. Julie shrugged. Annie tipped her head. Tia said, "It's okay." They continued to eat, some licking cones, some spooning yogurt from dishes.

"An improvement over last year's food?" he asked.

They consulted each other with glances. Finally Alicia said, "This is."

The implication was clear. Noah waited for someone to elaborate on it. When no one did, he elaborated himself. "But you didn't like the tofu we had for lunch, is that it?"

Annie made a face. Tia grunted. Julie said, "It was vile."

"Tofu takes on the flavor of the foods it's cooked with," Noah explained. "Our cook hasn't gotten the idea yet. But he will. I thought his pizza was great." It had been covered with extra cheese and an assortment of vegetables and, more important, had been prepared without the extra dollop of oil that school cooks mistakenly assumed added flavor.

No one commented.

Noah pushed on. "He's doing okay with the salad bar. And the sandwich bar." They had been Noah's ideas, too, the theory being that there would be less waste if food was prepared simply and presented in such a way that students could take what they wanted and leave the rest. They much preferred bagels for breakfast than burned corn muffins that the cook had spent an hour preparing. Noah had had the dubious honor of tasting the latter during his visit to the school the spring before.

Alicia stretched out her legs. Tia whispered something to Julie. The juniors took extra crunchies from a dish and sprinkled them on their cones. Meredith and Sara reached for napkins from a wad that sat on the grass.

"How's your dad feeling, Lindsey?"

The girl, one of the juniors, looked up in surprise. "How did you know he was sick?"

"I talked with him on the day he and your mom dropped you here. He said he was having surgery."

"He did. He's better."

Noah nodded his satisfaction. He looked up in time to catch a wayward Frisbee that had sailed out of control from the game in progress farther down the lawn. Good catch, Noah, he told himself when none of the girls said a word. He sent the Frisbee off again.

"This time last year," he told the silent group, "I was in the hills of northern Virginia. I thought fall was beautiful there, but it's even more so here. Another few weeks and the color will be spectacular."

The girls looked at each other. Julie said, "That makes it even harder to concentrate on classwork."

"And on official school business," Noah said, "but it has to be done. Besides," he added on a note of humor, "concentrating when it's the hardest is what builds character."

No one laughed. No one even smiled. Noah felt a tangible resentment directed his way.

Alicia pushed herself up from the grass. "I'm taking this back to the dining hall." She was immediately handed other dishes and spoons, which she stacked, and left.

Julie rose, said pointedly, "I have to get ready for study hall," and started off. She was quickly joined by her friends.

The sophomores were the last to leave. Noah would have liked to talk with them, but when his eye caught Sara's, the abject fear he saw there kept him still.

He worried about her. She had come from San Francisco and a mother who was unable to cope with a teenage daughter, which had to be one blow for the child. Another had to be leaving all her friends behind, and a third, starting over in the middle of high school.

She was a sweet girl. Beneath the stoicism that kept her feelings hidden, she was sensitive. He was sure of it, and because of that, he had doubts that this was the right school for her. He liked Meredith, and others of the sophomores seemed nice enough, but he wasn't wild about the seniors in the cross-country gang. Paige Pfeiffer seemed fond enough of them—she could afford to be fond of them, since her time with them was limited—but they struck him as tough. He didn't know whether he could get through to them in a year. The underclassmen were something else. He had a chance with people like Sara, assuming they weren't turned off by the seniors. He vowed to do everything he could to prevent that, but it wouldn't be easy.

Nothing was, it seemed, where Mount Court was concerned.

Feeling sad, tired, and alone, he crossed the campus and followed the path through the trees, behind the library and the art center, to the headmaster's house. It was a beauty, a small brick Tudor covered with ivy, and had been one of the lures of the Mount Court job. That was before he had taken a closer look.

One could call the place dignified, elegant, even stately, but the most appropriate word was old, and although Noah had nothing against old houses that had been cared for, this one hadn't been. He had already personally replaced nonfunctional doorknobs, front and back, put weather stripping around the windows, and reshingled large sections of the roof when the storms of late August had sent rain dripping inside. He had had a plumber in to replace the hot-water heater, all the while wondering if the Head before him had enjoyed cold showers, and when the refrigerator had proved nonfunctional, he had purchased a new one himself.

It was a small house, as fitted the image of the Head whose children were grown and living on their own. Noah wasn't of that ilk, but he liked the intimacy. The first floor held the living room, dining room, kitchen, and den that were used from time to time for official entertaining. The kitchen and den jutted out from the back of the house as offshoots of an original, smaller kitchen. With their pre-dominance of windows looking out onto the woods, this was Noah's favorite part of the house.

The second floor had two bedrooms, each with its own bath. He had found the wallpaper so depressing that he had stripped it off within days of his arrival. Now, replacement rolls sat in boxes. He fully intended to do the repapering himself when he had the time.

One part of him thought he was crazy. It wasn't *his* responsibility, during a temporary stint as Head, to make improvements in the physical facilities, at his own expense, no less. The other part knew that doing things like papering the walls would be therapeutic. At the rate he was going in the popularity sphere, come the cold weather, when he would be spending more evenings and weekends at home, he would be desperate for things to do.

There was satisfaction in working with one's hands. Lord knew he needed satisfaction from some quarter.

He took *The Washington Post* from the pile of daily mail and felt an instant comfort. The *Post* was a relic of his life before Mount Court. It represented a world that valued Noah and awaited his return. Whether he chose to return to it was another matter, but the choice was his, and in the meantime the knowledge that he was appreciated somewhere was a solace.

He headed for the kitchen, intent on reading the paper at the round table in the glassed-in breakfast nook. The sun had fallen behind the trees. Dusk was approaching. He flipped the switch to illuminate the lamp that hung over the table. When nothing happened, he jiggled the switch, and when nothing happened still, he swore.

He dropped the paper on the table, unscrewed the bulb from the lamp, tossed it into the wastebasket, and took a new one from the storage closet in the back hall. The lamp remained dark when he flipped the switch, so he removed the bulb and tried another.

This time when he tried the light, fireworks flew from the switch on the wall with such force that he jerked back. He swore again and louder, then stood with his hands on his hips, his heart banging an unhappy message against his ribs, and his head bowed in defeat. He knew enough about electrical systems to know that this particular light switch would have to be rewired. He wondered how many others were in like state.

He didn't understand how a house that was so beautiful on the outside could be so broken-down inside— and, in his frustration, he wondered if there might be a broader message in that. He had come to Mount Court with the best of intentions. If they, too, blew up in his face, he didn't know what he would do.

Hating decrepit things, detesting snotty little rich kids, and, mostly, despising the thought of failure, he grabbed his car keys and made for the garage. Soon after, he was in his Explorer, winding over the Mount Court roads, curving around the main drive toward the wrought-iron archway. He kept his eyes straight ahead and his foot on the gas, and didn't let up for a minute until the image of Mount Court, as seen through a rear window dotted with decals from another life, was a memory.

"She's been dead more'n a week now. So how's it going?"

The question came from Charlie Grace. As one or another of Peter's three older brothers often did, he had slid into Peter's booth at the Tavern uninvited. Normally Peter didn't mind. His brothers had made so much less of their lives than Peter had that letting them sit with him was an act of charity. But Peter was tired. He had just ended another long day filled with questions about Mara from parents of her patients.

"It's going fine," he told Charlie, but he didn't gesture the waitress—Beth was on that night—for a beer for Charlie, as he usually, benevolently, did. He was in no mood to encourage his brother to stay. He needed time alone before Lacey arrived.

"She was a strange one," Charlie mused. "She could be a class-A bitch—Jamie Cox is the first one to say that—but her patients loved her. My kids think she's the greatest." He gestured Beth for a beer.

Peter wished he hadn't. More than that, he wished Charlie wouldn't put him down. "They think Mara's the greatest simply because I precluded myself from being their doctor. If I hadn't, they'd think *I* was the greatest."

"They still think you're the greatest," Charlie said with a sincerity that made Peter feel like a heel, "but she was a woman, and a woman has something else going for her. She was like a second mother to the kids. She had half the men in town in love with her, too."

"If you're going to tell me about Spud Harvey, save your breath. That's old news."

"Spud? Him, too? I was thinking about Jackie Kagen, and Moose LeMieux, and Butchie Lombard. She dated them all."

"Once or twice, each one, that's all," Peter specified. "You make her sound loose, but she wasn't. She was decent when it came to men. She never led one on. She never promised more than she was willing to give."

"Hey," Charlie said, raising a pacifying hand, "I'm not accusing her of anything. Besides, Norman agrees. She didn't have any enemies. He told me so at the doughnut shop this morning. He checked it out." He grinned an over-the-hill football hero's grin at Beth. "Thanks, doll."

Peter felt an uncertain alarm, though he was careful not to let it show. "What do you mean, Norman checked it out?" he asked with commendable nonchalance.

"Checked out her love life. Talked to the guys she dated. Talked to the guys she didn't date but who wanted to date her. He didn't talk to you?"

"I'm her partner. I didn't date her."

"Come on, Pete," Charlie chided in a lowered voice, "I saw you two out on the old covered bridge at dawn more than once."

"We're both camera nuts. We used to photograph it."

"At dawn?" he asked skeptically.

"Pictures are always more interesting when the lighting is oblique. Dawn and sunset are the best. Trust me. Mara and I didn't date. So Norman had no cause to talk with me. He must have annoyed the others but good."

"Nah. They had nothing to hide. They knew Norman was just doin' his job. Poor guy. I half hoped for him that he'd come up with something exciting."

"Like what?" Peter asked against the rim of his beer.

"Like Mara had something kinky going on with someone in town. Like that person knocked her out and left her in the car with the engine running."

Peter choked. He coughed, cleared his throat, then shook his head. "Coroner ruled that out. There wasn't a single bruise on her body."

"I know that, Pete, but where's your imagination?"

"I'm a doctor. I'm not into imagining ugly manners of death."

Charlie sighed. "All I'm saying is that Norman could have used the excitement. Hell, we *all* could have used it. This town is pretty quiet." He looked up. "Hey, Donny. Go on back. I'll be along."

Donny swatted Peter's shoulder as he passed. Peter raised a hand in greeting.

Charlie leaned forward. "So, tell me the truth. I swear I won't tell anyone. Was she good?"

"Who?"

"It's me. Charlie. I'm your big brother."

"Was who good?"

Charlie sat back. "Okay. I can play the game. But I have to warn you that when old Henry Mills gets a couple under his belt, which is nearly every night right over on that barstool, he starts to talk. He says he used to drink with her and that when she was half-crocked she'd be talking about you. He says if there was any man in this town she loved, it was you."

"That's flattering," Peter said with a smile.

"Was it true?"

"She never said so to me."

"Not even in the heat of passion?"

Peter didn't answer. He figured that silence, coupled with a bored stare, was his best denial.

Charlie offered a defeated, "I gotcha." Beer in hand, he slid from his booth. "You're one dull guy. I swear, if you weren't my brother, I wouldn't love you at all."

He gave Peter a fond nudge and walked toward his booth in back, leaving Peter in worse spirits than ever. Once, just once, he wanted a legitimate reason to hate his brothers. He waited for them to say something disparaging about his profession. He waited for them to call him a nerd, or blame him for misdiagnosing one of their friends' kids, or criticize him because he wasn't married. But they never did. They were good guys, all three of them, stagnant in their lives, but good guys. And he, with his academic accolades and his advanced degrees and the reverence of the townsfolk who loved putting one of their own on a pedestal—he was still bringing up the rear when it came to character.

"Hi," Lacey breathed, sliding into the booth. "Sorry I'm late. The most incredible thing happened to me when I left the estate. Jamie Cox was waiting by the gate, wanting to talk."

Peter relaxed. Jamie Cox was harmless, more an annoyance than anything else. He might own half the town, but he didn't own Peter. "What did he want to talk about?"

"Mara O'Neill."

Peter should have known. He couldn't escape her.

"And you," Lacey went on. "He wanted to know whether you were going to pick up the fight against him where Mara left off. He said he got that impression when he saw you here, and I can see why he did. I remember what you said. I told Jamie that your points were valid. He argued that they weren't and that they'd only get you into trouble."

"Was that a threat?" Peter asked.

"I asked him that, and he denied it. Still, it sounded that way to me. I told him that as a doctor here, it was your responsibility to speak up when you felt that the well-being of the people was being compromised."

"What did he say then?"

She smiled. "He asked me to repeat what I'd said. He hadn't understood it. So I repeated myself. I'm not sure whether he understood it the second time, either, but he started to defend everything he was doing around town. He paints himself as the good guy and everyone else as the bad guy. You're going to fight him, aren't you?"

Peter hadn't really thought about it. Up until the week before, he hadn't had to. Mara had appointed herself his opponent. "I don't know."

"You have to," Lacey said in alarm.

"Why do I have to?"

"Because someone has to, and you're in a better position than anyone else to do it. You knew Mara. You knew what she stood for. You know that she was right."

He didn't like Lacey's tone. He didn't like her suggestion that she knew what he knew. He didn't like her telling him what to do. "That doesn't mean I have to take on her fights."

"But it's the right thing to do," Lacey pressed.

"It may also be futile. Jamie Cox has a perfect legal right to do what he wants with his property. Sure, lower Tucker looks scummy, but that's a matter of aesthetics. There's nothing illegal—or unhealthy— about that."

"What about the old movie house? You said it was a fire trap."

"Jamie has a permit to keep it open, issued by none other than Tucker's building commissioner."

She sat back, looking disappointed. "You said that there was a conflict of interest, since the commissioner lives in one of Jamie's buildings."

It struck him that her disappointment was aimed at *him*. Angry, he leaned forward. "Look, Lacey, if you want to throw down the gauntlet, be my guest. You can fight Jamie Cox. You can take him to court, but it'll cost money. Why do you think Mara didn't do it?"

"She died before she could."

He shook his head. "She didn't want to spend the money."

"She didn't have to. She had an ongoing working relationship with the public defenders in town. They would have gone to court for her. They'll do it for you."

"Christ, that takes time and more energy than I have. I'm up to my ears in patients because Mara O'Neill decided to off herself, and you want me to take over her causes, too? Dream on."

Lacey didn't respond. She frowned at a gouge in the table. Finally, in a quiet voice, she repeated, "It's the right thing to do."

Peter swore. He knew that it was, but, damn it, he had enough on his mind without taking on Jamie Cox. He couldn't believe that Mara had saddled him with that one, too. So now he looked somehow less of a man because he refused to fight her cockamamy wars.

Struggling to contain his annoyance, he said, "I see patients from eight in the morning until five-thirty or six, and in between I squeeze in phone calls to parents, pharmacists, labs, radiologists, schoolteachers even, sometimes"—he glanced at his watch—"and in thirty minutes I have to address the Rotary Club two towns over. I think I do pretty well, with or without Mara's noble causes. I'm more productive than most everyone else in this town. If that isn't enough for you, what is?"

"Peter, I wasn't saying—"

"You were." He pushed himself out of the booth. "You were saying I'm not good enough. Well, fine. Go find someone who is. Better still, go back to the city. You want big-time philanthropists? You want die-hard do-gooders? You sure as hell won't find them in Tucker."

Disgusted, he stalked out of the Tavern. He didn't care if Lacey *did* have to pay for his beer. If she thought so poorly of him already, a little more was of no account at all.

Nine

Paige stood on Mara's front porch only until the Realtor had backed her car from the driveway. Then she reentered the house and went to work. She wasn't up for it, but she didn't have much of a choice. When one had a house to sell—when one hadn't even put it on the market before a Realtor approached saying that the new family in town was asking about it—one didn't waffle. One tidied up the house, moved the furniture around a little, set the fireplace with the new birch logs the Realtor suggested, and packed up anything and everything that was lying around loose.

The fact that Paige wasn't emotionally ready was secondary to practical considerations. Besides, she wasn't sure that emotionally she would ever be ready. Like Sami, Mara's house was a little bit of Mara. Paige had known wonderful times within its walls. Selling it was final, another nail in the coffin, further proof that Mara was dead.

One of the problems was that Mara, in death, had become a mystery as she hadn't been in life. She was unfinished business. Paige couldn't stop thinking about her.

So maybe it was just as well that the Realtor had forced the issue of selling the house. On her own, Paige might have postponed it forever.

She had promised the Realtor that the house would be sparkling clean and ready to show by nine o'clock the next morning, which gave her little time to waste and even less to change her mind. She was wearing a T-shirt and the cut-offs that she had changed into when she had come back from Mount Court. Now she called Jill and explained that she would be late, left Mara's number, and told her to forward calls.

Armed with a dustcloth, a can of furniture polish, a roll of paper toweling, a bottle of glass cleaner, and the vacuum that she had herself given Mara as a house-warming gift six years before, she set to work in the low orange glow of the evening sun, polishing the table in the front foyer, wiping down the mirror above it, polishing the swirling mahogany bannister, vacuuming the stair runner. She cleaned the front parlor in a similar manner, doing her best with furniture that Mara had collected much the way she had collected people. Just as she had always been drawn to the wounded, so the long leather sofa was an irregular with one discolored cushion, the woven carpet had a pattern that ran off the edge, and the coffee table was gouged in a way that only Mara's magnanimous eye thought artistic.

The back parlor was another story. The furnishings there were simple—a Shaker bench, two Windsor chairs, bookshelf upon bookshelf of planks stretched over bricks. Three things saved the room from being stark. The first was Mara's cushion collection—a wild assortment of pillows bought in a wild assortment of places and clustered in masses to rival the softest, deepest sofa. Paige smiled at the memory of Mara's wards running and jumping, tossing and turning, laughing hysterically right along with Mara.

The second was her work bench, an old barn door with legs attached. It held books and magazines, mail— some opened, some not—and road maps, a basket of fabric scraps, a half-finished pillow, and an instruction book from the quilting class she had been taking.

The third were the photographs that graced every free wall. They were ones Mara had taken and developed under Peter's watchful eye, and whereas one would have expected the pictures to be of children, they weren't. They were pictures of nature—trees, bridges, meadows, animals—each capturing a feeling that was every bit as intense as the emotion on a child's face might have been.

Given her druthers, Paige would have sealed off this room. The memory of Mara was nearly overpowering here, engulfing her with the same disbelief that she had felt so strongly during the first few days after Mara's death. Then came sadness, because the mind knew what the heart still could not accept.

Taking a breath and delving in, Paige cleared the desktop, spritzed it, wiped it down. After fanning several of the magazines on the table, she put the rest, along with the mail and the maps, in the trunk of her car. She arranged the quilting materials as artfully as she could, feeling all the while as though she were fashioning a tribute to Mara. She took even greater pains with the pillows, arranging them one way, then another, then a third when she felt that neither of the previous arrangements properly caught the spirit of Mara.

And that was important. Paige had promised Mara on the day of the funeral that she would find a family that would love the house as she had, and she was determined to do it. If the Realtor's family disliked this room, they couldn't have the house.

Dusk arrived. She switched on lights, moved into the dining room, and began polishing its contents. Mara had bought the long table and chairs at an estate sale. The pomposity of them had amused her—or so she had always claimed. Now, rubbing a cloth over the cherrywood, Paige wondered if there hadn't been a deeper attraction. She had seen a set like this before. She could have sworn it had been at the O'Neills' house in Eugene.

The sadness hit her in waves, occasionally so strong that she sank onto a chair until inertia proved worse. So she set a feverish pace in the kitchen. When she began to sweat, she tied up her hair with a piece of yarn from Mara's basket, pulled her T-shirt free of her shorts, opened the window, and pushed on. When her muscles complained, she ignored them. She was willing to do most anything to blot out the sense of emptiness that seemed to have settled over her life.

It didn't make sense, that emptiness. Mara had been a vibrant part of her life for twenty years; that her death should leave a gap was understandable, but that the gap should be so large—and *spreading*—was unfair.

She was cleaning the oven, scrubbing angrily, when the doorbell rang. It was just after ten. She wasn't in the mood for guests, couldn't begin to imagine who was there other than a neighbor curious about the lights. Traipsing through the hall to the front door, she switched on the outside light. A large form lurked beyond the wavy glass panel. Definitely a neighbor, she thought, picturing Duncan Fallen. He was the gatekeeper type and would be wanting to know who was in Mara's house. Strange he hadn't recognized her car.

But it wasn't Duncan. It was Noah Perrine. One look at him, and she groaned.

"Bad time?" he asked in that soft voice of his.

"Yeah." Her heart was pounding—a delayed reaction to the surprise of the doorbell, she told herself. "I'm tired and dirty. I'm not up for sparring. Maybe another time?" Then she frowned. "How did you know I was here?"

"Your baby-sitter."

"Did you stop by at the house?"

He shook his head. "Called."

"Ah." She nodded. It was a minute before it occurred to her to wonder why he had come, and then her eyes went wide. "Oh, God. Something happened—"

"No," he broke in. "Everything's fine."

She pressed a hand to her chest. "I had a horrible image of—of—just a horrible image." Pills, a car—her own imagination couldn't match that of a teenager intent on self-destruction.

But he repeated, "Everything's fine."

"Thank God." The doorknob steadied her. "So, were you just out driving around?" It was a nice enough night. He should have kept on driving.

"Campus was oppressive. I had to get away."

"Oppressive? Mount Court?"

"You aren't the Head there." He took a deep breath, something of a sigh that didn't know where to go. "I get tired sometimes. That's all. So I thought I'd drive around town, but the loneliness of that was as bad as it was at the school. It might have been nice to stop off and visit someone, but the locals I've met since I came here aren't wild about Mount Court. I didn't think they'd appreciate my dropping by."

"To tell you the truth," she hinted, but he was looking beyond her into the house.

"Glad to hear you have a baby-sitter. It wouldn't be good for the little girl to be here this time of night. This was your friend's home?"

"Uh-huh."

"Nice place."

Paige sighed. "The Realtor thinks she has a buyer. She's showing it in the morning. I'm getting it ready." She glanced disparagingly at her shirt and shorts, which were smudged and spotted. Self-conscious, she looked back up.

"You wear it well," he said with a crooked grin. "Can you take a break?"

She shook her head. "Not if I want to finish in time to get a little sleep before work tomorrow."

"Just down the street for a hamburger?"

Paige never ate hamburgers. Between the red meat and the fat, she figured most anything else would be better.

But a hamburger sounded mighty good just then.

Still, she shook her head. "I have a ways to go in the kitchen, and I haven't even hit the second floor." Besides, she was a mess. She couldn't go anywhere without a shower, much less anywhere with Noah Perrine. He made her nervous. He looked too good.

"Let me help, then."

"Oh, no, that's uncalled for."

"Four hands can do a hell of a lot more, faster than two."

"But—" She took a step back when he came inside.

"Where should I start?"

"But you look so nice," she protested, feeling slightly overwhelmed. Noah Perrine was an academician, she told herself, but when she tried to picture him pushing papers around his desk, the image of the construction worker came instead. "You'll ruin your clothes."

"We're not talking feeding the pigs in a mud storm, here. I've cleaned house before. My clothes won't be ruined."

"Really, Noah. I appreciate your offer, but—"

"You have the guilt to work off," he said, looking her in the eye.

Her protest fizzled. His directness was sobering. "Yes," she said quietly and with some surprise. She hadn't pegged him for the insightful type. "How did you know?"

"I lost a close friend once, too. It's been six years, now."

"Was it suicide?"

"In a way. Gin was his thing. He swore he never had more than one or two with dinner and explained away the occasional late night drunk driving citation as an aberration. I took him at his word until the night he drove into the back of an eighteen-wheeler at a toll booth, and then it was too late."

Paige couldn't deny the analogy to her situation with Mara. "I should have done more for her while she was alive. I should have been more aware of her state of mind. I should have been able to help. But I wasn't, and I didn't." Flexing her back, she braced her hands on the tired muscles above her waist and ran her eye up the winding staircase. "This is all that's left. And I feel guilty about that, too. I promised I'd have the place painted and get a new screen for the door and replace one of the shutters upstairs. But if the family that's coming tomorrow loves the place and buys it, I won't have time."

"Use my kids."

She had no idea what he was talking about and said so with a look.

"Community service. It's my thing. They may kick and scream, but they'll have the place painted in a week."

She shook her head. "If they're going to paint any house, it should be one in lower Tucker. The people there could use the help. Me, I can afford to pay. And I may have time. Who knows, the people tomorrow may not be the right ones. The house may be on the market for months."

"I hope not, for your sake. You need closure."

It was another direct eye-to-eye statement, a succinct summation of the problem. "Closure," she said with a sigh. "Painful, but it needs doing. Like the oven." She gestured toward the kitchen. "I have to get back."

"So what can I do?"

"Nothing. Really."

"Please," he insisted, "I have to do something. It's either help you here, or drive around for another few hours. I can't go back. Not yet."

Paige wondered why but didn't ask. She didn't feel strong enough to take on his woes. She had work to do, and the longer she lingered, the later it would be before she finished.

"Upstairs," she finally said with a wave toward the cleaning goods. "There are four bedrooms. Two are empty. You can start with those—dust, vacuum, do anything that might make them look more inviting. The Realtor suggested putting a small piece of furniture in each, but I can do that later. I'll be up to do the other bedrooms myself when I finish with the kitchen."

"Can't I help with that?"

She shook her head and set off down the hall feeling sadder than ever. There was something about Noah's unexpected kindness that was touching. It wrenched her at a time when she didn't want to be wrenched. She wanted to do the job she'd set out to do and go home.

So she finished the oven, scrubbed the stove top and the counters, then wiped out the refrigerator, which looked as forlorn as she felt with its single carton of milk, half loaf of bread, quarter stick of margarine, and gouged wedge of cheese. At first she left them there and mopped the floor. Then she returned, sniffed the milk, and, in a burst of furious action, dumped it into the sink, stuffed the bread, margarine, and cheese into the disposal, and ground it all up. They smelled of things gone bad. She was devastated.

Desperate for fresh air, she went through the bowed screen door to the back porch. She kneed the swing and watched it creak back and forth, but the knowledge of Mara's fondness for it brought her no solace. An empty swing was a desolate sight.

With a sound of despair, she left the porch and, by the frail light that filtered from the house, wandered into the yard. The birds were still for the night, leaving a hollowness in the air that the chirp of the crickets and the rustle of dying leaves in the breeze barely touched. It was a warm night, but she was chilled. Rubbing her arms, she walked farther into the dark.

At the spot where grass gave way to the woods, she sank to the ground. The black of night matched the dark thoughts she held, enlarging them until they encompassed the whole of her future. The years lay before her, a continuation of the ones that had gone past, yet different. More quiet and, like Mara, alone. Increasingly empty. Profoundly sad.

She heard his footsteps but didn't look up.

"What are you doing?" he asked.

"I needed air."

She heard him settle in the grass and wanted to protest. Noah Perrine, with his rules and regulations, wasn't the kind of person she was normally drawn to. But he was human and alive. His presence made the night less ominous.

His voice came from that softer place. "Was she a childhood friend?"

"We met in college. Something clicked."

"Were you very much alike?"

"In looks more than personality. She was more feisty than me. More intense. And selfless. Of all the things I remember about Mara, that's the best. She put most anyone else's welfare before her own. If the tables were turned and I was the one who had died, she'd probably be out there trying to memorialize my life. She wouldn't be sitting here brooding about her own future."

He pulled up a blade of grass and tossed it aside. "Reflection is inevitable, when a friend dies."

"Is self-pity?"

"Sometimes, when the reflection shows us things we don't like."

"But I like my life. It's a fine one. I'm doing worthwhile things."

He pulled up another blade of grass.

She heard herself say, "But there's an emptiness that's been there since Mara died. I'm busier than ever, especially now with Mara's little girl. Still, there are times when I feel I'm drowning in it, *drowning* in it, and I keep wondering whether this was what Mara was feeling when she drove into the garage that night."

She took a breath. When it came short and hard, she took another.

He touched her neck.

"I'm okay," she said, but she wasn't sure. Alongside the emptiness was a yearning, nearly as puzzling as the other in its depth. "I'm okay," she whispered, this time against the hand that was by her cheek, and then there was a greater warmth along the side of her body.

She leaned into it with an awareness of intense relief.

The night didn't protest. The sough of the wind in the trees grew rhythmic, hypnotic, lulling. She breathed in Noah's warmth, the faint smell of his skin, and when he drew her closer, she went. The emptiness seemed suddenly less sharp, and if the yearning was more so, it wasn't unpleasant.

That was why, when he kissed her, she kissed him back. His mouth was firm, demanding in quiet ways that reminded her of his voice. But he didn't say a word, simply kissed her again, for a longer time now and more deeply.

Later, she would wonder what had come over her, but just then, sitting behind Mara's house in the dark of night, there seemed no better way to keep emptiness at bay than this. Her body came alive, responding to his with a need that rose as quickly as instincts long suppressed.

She tasted the inside of his mouth and touched his arms, leaning into him, finding comfort in his strength. The chill she had felt moments before waned, replaced by a heat that started at the points he touched and stole inward. She gave herself up to it. It was the first relief she had had in days. Wanting more, needing more, she opened her mouth, and when the kiss was done, she was breathless.

She wasn't alone. His breathing was ragged. Given pause by its sound, she put her fingertips on his mouth, then his cheekbone, then the curve of his glasses.

He was a stranger. Nothing about his features was familiar in the way of an old friend or lover, yet she inched closer. His mouth welcomed her again, more hungrily this time. And the hunger was contagious. It swelled, creating a barrier against reason such that she could think of nothing but feeding it.

He tossed his glasses aside and buried his face in her neck, breathing faster and harder, and all the while his hands were at her back, holding her closer, moving her against his chest.

The heat spread. She made a sound of relief when he touched her breasts, then another, moments later, when he slipped the T-shirt over her head, released the catch of her bra, and took her bare flesh in his hands.

He might have been a stickler for rules and regulations at school, but there was nothing prescribed about what he did on the grass. He was a masterful lover, blessed with an intuitive sensitivity, even in the heat of his own passion, that told him what Paige needed and when. In due time his shirt joined hers, then his pants, and just when she thought she would die if she didn't have more of his body than even his nakedness allowed, he pressed her back and entered her.

Reality had no chance then. Between the dark of night, the friction of his thrusts, and the greed of her body, she was lost. He drove her higher and higher, intuitive still and hot, so hot, until, with a small cry and the suspension of every muscle in her body, she broke into a shattering climax. She was still in its throes when he found his own release.

Sanity returned in wisps, fighting its way through a foggy pleasure, surfacing and sinking back as she fought it. Inevitably it prevailed. With the steadying of her breath, the cooling of her heat, and the clearing of her head, she found herself lying naked on the grass beside an equally naked man whom she barely knew. Worse, he had come inside her, and she was unprotected.

"Oh, God," she moaned, pushing up. She wrapped her arms around her knees and held them close. "I can't believe I did that."

"Shhhh" was all he said.

She looked back, but the night hid his expression. So she buried her face against her knees.

He touched her back. She wanted to move away, but, incredibly, the comfort was there again, so she let it stay.

"I won't give you a disease, Paige," he finally said, "but I may have made you pregnant. Is that a problem?"

In a higher than normal voice, she cried, "Yes."

He moved his hand lightly. *We'll deal with it if it happens,* Paige felt him say, then laughed, vaguely hysterically, at the absurdity of her imagination.

"What?" he asked.

She shook her head.

"Tell me," he coaxed.

The hand was a connector, she realized. It kept something going between them, a relationship that was innocent in ways that their coupling hadn't been, but that made it somehow less wrong. "It's ironic," she said. "I make my living in part teaching adolescents the facts of life. I encourage abstinence, and when that doesn't work, I drum safe sex into their minds. Smart, huh? So what do I do?" She made a disparaging sound and groped for her clothes. His hand stayed with her until she moved out of reach. Then she felt a chill and dressed hurriedly.

He didn't move. She was on her feet before he said, "Why the rush?"

"I have work to do." She ran on into the house and went directly to Mara's bedroom. "That didn't happen," she muttered as she looked around. Seconds later, she was dusting the collection of tiny bottles on the dresser and polishing the oak beneath. She did the same with the oak pieces at the head and foot of the bed, with the night tables, with the rocker that sat in the corner. She puffed up the comforter, straightened the cushion on the rocker, vacuumed every inch of the bare floor and the wildly colored rag rug.

Then, breathless from the exertion, she paused. When she reached back to massage the muscles above her waist, she realized that they weren't the only muscles that were strained. Her thighs were shaky.

But she wouldn't think about that. She couldn't. So she crossed the room, sank onto the rocker, and hugged her knees. She relaxed only when her eye fell on the large, covered wicker basket that stood beside the rocker. It was Mara's knitting basket, filled from the bottom up with remnants of projects.

Swallowing, she lifted the lid. She might have guessed that the ongoing project would be pink, but although she would have put her money on a sweater, the piece proved to be an afghan, a delicate expanse of crocheted shells, just about the size of a crib.

She held the wool on her lap and rocked. After a while she looked again into the basket and found the sweater. Knitted into a yellow field were the same distorted blue stars with which Mara had decorated Sami's room.

Vowing to finish both pieces, Paige dug deeper. Though there were no other projects in progress, the yarn balls of varying sizes were like the rings of a tree, marking Mara's history from the most recent to the past. Paige found a ball of the nubby green yarn of which Mara had made a cardigan sweater for Tanya last spring, the variegated worsted she had used last Christmas to make hats and mittens for the poorest of her patient families, the fluffy chenille from which she had made a voluminous sweater for herself the fall before that. There was a handsome maroon of hand-loomed wool that Paige didn't recognize, but she recognized the brilliant orange of a sweater for another of Mara's foster children and the purple and pink from a scarf. There was the white wool, left over from the shawl Mara had crocheted for Nonny years ago, with which Mara had taught Paige the rudiments of the craft, and

interspersed throughout were knitting needles and crochet hooks of every size and length.

Hooked on the activity as she might have been on
sifting through a picture album, Paige dug deeper. She
had pulled out remnants of two other projects when her
hand hit a pack of papers. Assuming they were knitting
instructions, she pulled them up.

They were letters, written on cream-colored stationery, bound together neatly by a piece of green yarn. The
top one, the only one immediately visible, was addressed
to a Lizzie Parks in Eugene, Oregon, and Mara's own
address was where the return address should be, but the
letter had neither been stamped nor, obviously, sent.

Lizzie Parks. Paige didn't recognize the name. A
childhood friend? A letter written before Paige had
come to know Mara? But the return address was for
this house, which Mara had owned for six short years.

She held the bundle of letters in her hand, feeling
its weight for a time, until curiosity got the best of her.
Then she untied the yarn and thumbed through the
pack. There were half a dozen letters in all, each addressed to the same Lizzie Parks.

She repeated the name, yet still it didn't ring a bell.
Her first thought was to stamp the envelopes and mail
them. Her second thought was that if Mara had wanted
them mailed, she would have done it herself, rather than

keeping them in a neat collection, tied with a ribbon. Clearly she hadn't wanted them sent, and while Paige might still have decided that Lizzie Parks had a right to the letters, she wasn't that noble. Mara had been her friend. Now Mara was dead. Paige wanted to know what was in the letters.

She turned over the top envelope and found that it hadn't been sealed. After withdrawing the letter, she unfolded it. Her heart started to thud when she saw that it had been written less than a week before Mara's death.

"Dear Lizzie," she read:

Exciting news! As I write, the little girl I'm adopting is about to leave India. I can't describe my relief. It's like I've been thrown a lifeline.

If I had an extra picture of her, I'd send you one. She's a beautiful child, has brown hair and brown eyes, like me. I still can't believe that she'll be mine once she's here. I'll have to file adoption papers with the state of Vermont, but the adoption agency assures me that it's a formality. The tough part was getting the approval of the Indian authorities.

My parents don't put much stock in adoption. When I told them about Sameera, they said that it wasn't the same and that I could call them when I was married and pregnant. But that's easier said than done. When I didn't get pregnant with Dan-

ny's child, I thought it had to do with his problem, but then I didn't get pregnant after Danny either, and I tried. I tried so hard. Maybe too hard. They say that happens.

Paige wondered whom she had tried with. She couldn't think of anyone Mara had dated seriously. Unless there were men she hadn't known about. Wounded, she read on.

I think something's wrong with my body. Sometimes I think something's wrong with my mind, too. I can do so much right, but then the things that I want the most fall through. Like having a baby. So I'm adopting Sameera, and I don't care if my parents never recognize her as their granddaughter, she'll be mine.

Since Tanya ran off, things have been hard. Everyone tells me that it wasn't my fault, but if it wasn't mine, whose was it? I thought I was helping her. She was starting to sleep through the night. She wasn't wetting the bed as much. She was talking more than she ever had. I still don't know what went wrong, some bizarre thing must have snapped in her head. Either that, or I unwittingly said something that set her back.

So I need Sameera. I need to prove to myself that

I can do it right. It's like there's a little window of time open right now, and if I don't take this opportunity, it will close for good.

I can't afford another failure. There have been too many.

Paige let her hand fall to her lap. *Another failure.* "You weren't a failure," she insisted. "If you had seen the people at your funeral, you would know that. You were as successful as any one of us."

But these letters hadn't been written by the professional Mara. They had been written by the private Mara.

"Not a failure," Paige whispered, and opened the second letter in the pile. It had been written shortly after Tanya had fled.

"Dear Lizzie," she read:

The Lorenzos were in the office today. They have six children under the age of ten, and every ailment imaginable. One of the children is diabetic, another has a hearing deficiency, and the rest are continually in the throes of one infection or another. I kept thinking that nights in their house must be a circus of coughing, crying, and vomiting, and to hear the parents' complaints you can believe it. Still, I was envious. Nights in my house are silent—

dead—barren. I do what I can to fill the void, but inevitably I end up lying in bed listening to the nothingness that is my life.

Sure, I have a satisfying career. But that doesn't count. What counts is what happens at night. That's when the trappings of a life fall aside and the truth comes out. That's when I'm all alone. It's a sad statement about what I've accomplished in life. I've tried to change it, but nothing seems to work, and now I'm tired of trying. I'm feeling defeated. The nights are empty, long and lonely, and unless this adoption comes through, the future will be more of the same. I'm not sure I can bear that.

Feeling chilled, Paige refolded the letter, put it back in the pile, and tied the bunch with the yarn. "You should have told me," she said, studying the packet. "I might have helped."

But the truth was that she didn't know what she might have done. Granted, she wasn't feeling defeated as Mara had, but neither were her nights filled with the things Mara wanted. Moreover, the sense of emptiness Mara described was eerily like what Paige had been feeling of late.

It was as though Paige had inherited it along with the other threads of Mara's life.

Not caring for that idea at all, she replaced the wool and the letters, neatly and in as close to the way she had found them as possible, in the wicker basket, set the lid firmly on top, and turned to the one other bedroom that hadn't been cleaned. It was to have been the baby's room and was empty now, its contents in Paige's house. She started to vacuum but halfway through had a sudden, dire urge to be with the living. Within minutes she had the cleaning equipment put away and the lights turned off and was driving through the center of Tucker toward her own house.

For just a minute, leaving Mara's, she wondered when Noah had left, then she pushed the thought from her mind and drove on. She was greeted at the door by kitty, who wound in and around her legs with such excitement that Paige didn't have the heart to say, as she usually did when she lifted the small animal, ruffled its fur, and gave it a hug, "Only until I find you a home."

Jill was asleep on the sofa. She woke her gently and sent her to bed. After changing into a nightgown, she followed, climbing the stairs first to check on Sami.

The little girl was asleep on her back. Paige would have turned her onto her stomach had she not learned that this was the custom in India, and, besides, she wanted to see Sami's face. Forearms braced on the crib rail, she leaned down. The small night light cast the child's tiny features into relief. Paige touched her cheek; it felt soft and pleasantly warm.

The child stirred. Her eyes opened, focusing on nothing for a minute until they found Paige's in the dark. Against every instruction she had given parents for training their children to sleep through the night, Paige picked her up.

"Hi, Sami," she said with singsong softness. "How are you?" She kissed her forehead. "Did you have a nice time with Jill? I can see that she washed you and changed you. You feel nice and dry, and you smell wonderful. Did you have something good to eat before you went to bed? Milk? Apple juice?"

Sami scrunched up her eyes and scrubbed her nose with a fist.

"Ahhh, you're such a sleepy baby. And I'm keeping you awake. Come over here. We'll rock awhile."

Paige settled down with Sami curled comfortably against her and began a slow rocking. She hummed a song that had no words, something Nonny might have hummed, and could tell by the sag of Sami's body that she was asleep within minutes.

Still Paige held her. There was something peaceful about the rocking, about the warmth of the child nestled against her, even about the soft purr of kitty, who had settled on her thigh. She hummed another wordless song, one that came from a nameless place in the past, and rocked until each of the thoughts that might have kept her awake were gone from her mind. Then she tucked the little girl under a light blanket in the crib, went downstairs to her own bedroom, and, with kitty conforming to the curve of her body, fell quickly asleep.

It wasn't until her alarm went off the next morning, when she rolled over and came slowly awake, that the scent of Noah's body on her own reminded her of what she had done.

Ten

If Paige had been able to avoid going to Mount Court, she would have, but with a race on Saturday, daily practices were a must. So she poured herself into each one, running with the girls, recording their sprint times on a chart, coaxing, sometimes goading them on, giving them her undivided attention. She didn't look up when people passed. She didn't once glance in the direction of the administration building to see if anyone stood watching from the steps. Her sole purpose at the school was to coach the team. As far as she was concerned, Noah Perrine didn't exist.

Under normal circumstances, she would have looked forward to Saturday. On game weekends the campus was alive with activity, abuzz with visiting teams and parents, feeling like family to Paige. This weekend, Angie's Doug was playing soccer, which added to the lure. Paige would have enjoyed putting Sami in the stroller and watching that game once her own race was done—and she still planned to watch, but the enjoyment part was in question. Not only was there the issue of the Head of School wandering about, but Ben would be there. Paige hadn't seen him since learning of his infidelity. Given how hurt she was on Angie's behalf, and how angry, she wasn't sure what she would say.

As it happened, Saturday dawned rainy enough to preclude Paige's taking Sami to Mount Court. The games would go on, but with people huddled in their rain gear trying to stay warm, dry, and upbeat, there would be less pleasure in the watching.

Along with the rain came a chill in the air that told Paige the girls wouldn't run their best. True, the two teams against whom they were racing faced the same handicap, but that was small solace. She had been hoping that some of her runners would record personal bests. Morale at the school was low, and they needed a boost. She doubted they would get it this day.

Still, she kept her spirits up, dressing—as she always did on the day of a meet—nicely, in gabardine slacks and a sweater. On this day she also wore a long raincoat and carried an oversize umbrella. The raincoat would keep her camouflaged, the umbrella would keep her hidden. If either kept her dry, so much the better.

The girls stretched beforehand in a corner of the gym, wearing identical warm-up suits and glum looks. They weren't thrilled to have to run. "It's a mess out there," Julie whined. "This meet should have been canceled."

"Nonsense," Paige said lightly. "The course is largely through the woods. You'll be in the shelter of the trees, far drier than us."

"But it's cold," Alicia complained.

"Cool, not cold, either of which is preferable to hot," Paige reasoned.

Tia said, "My muscles are rigid."

"Then stretch," Paige urged. "And do an extra set of warm-up runs. You'll do fine. All of you. Just remember everything I've taught you. Pace yourselves. Don't let an opponent who jumps out in front get you running so hard at the start that you die on the home stretch. Stay focused."

"We can't beat Wickham Hall," Annie said. "They're incredible."

"So are we," Paige replied.

"They were undefeated last year."

"That was then, this is now. Come on, girls. If you don't think positive, you'll be defeated before you begin. Every one of you has bettered her times in practice this week and by significant amounts."

"When you start at rock bottom," Julie groused.

"You," Paige said, pointing a finger only half-playfully at Julie, "keep still." She turned to the others. "So much of any battle is believing in yourself. The course is three miles even. If you want to break twenty-one minutes—if you tell yourself that you can and keep repeating it—you will. I don't care if we win. What I *would* like to see is for each of you to run a race you feel proud of. I believe you can do it. The rest is up to you."

She followed them out of the gym and talked with the visiting coaches while the girls did warm-up sprints. Then, under cover of the umbrella, she moved aside and waited for the race to begin.

"That you, Paige?"

Her heart gave a little pit-pat but settled when she realized the voice was wrong. She peered out at Peter, who was covered with a hooded slicker. The friendly face warmed her into a smile. "What are you doing here?"

He shrugged. "Had nothing better to do." He patted a bulge in the center of his chest. "Thought I'd snap a few."

"In this rain?"

"Sure. The lousier the weather, the greater the drama. Mud shots are fun."

Paige recalled Mara saying something similar. Actually, it wasn't mud. It was snow. Mara had loved taking pictures in the middle of snowstorms, when the snow formed a veil through which the rest of the world was muted. Now, in hindsight, Paige wondered if that muting was a softening of things Mara had found too harsh.

On a lighter note she asked, "How did it go in the office this morning? Any interesting visits?"

"You'd have to ask Angie," Peter said. "She took my hours. Said she wanted to get ahead a few, just in case Doug had a sick day, but by my figuring, she's ahead a whole lot. She's been working like a fiend lately."

Paige could understand it. There was nothing like pouring oneself into one's work to obliterate other, more painful thoughts.

But she figured that Angie hadn't told Peter about Ben, and she wasn't about to do it herself. So she stated the obvious. "Doug is growing up. He's at school longer hours, and when he's home he should be spending more time with his dad."

"Hey, Dr. Grace!" several of Paige's runners called on their way past. They had wide grins for Peter, something Paige rarely saw. It struck her that Julie, for one, was quite striking.

Peter grinned back and flashed them a thumbs-up. "Cute girls," he told Paige.

She watched them go. "Yup. They're growing up, too. Those three will be graduating in June. Hard to believe." Time flew. She remembered when they had first come to Mount Court, more innocent and less cynical, albeit spoiled even then. In the short time she had with them each day, she had tried to teach them the concept of mental discipline. Whether it had taken hold remained to be seen.

The runners took up position. Peter removed his camera from his slicker and snapped a few shots. Paige moved closer to the starting line, thinking, *Confidence, confidence, confidence,* in the hope that a brain wave would carry the message to her runners. The gun went off. The bystanders cheered, each for his own team. Paige shouted her encouragement. Peter trotted along the sidelines with his camera to his eye, until the runners veered off into the woods.

"Lousy day," Paige heard from just beyond the tip of her umbrella.

The little pit-pat started and didn't stop this time, and it was accompanied by a rise in temperature in the air around her. It was always that way when he came near. There was an energy about him that stirred things up.

She kept her eyes on the woods, into which the last of the runners was disappearing. "Could be better."

"How are their spirits?" he asked.

She hummed out a high, "Could be better."

"And yours?"

"Just fine," she said in what she thought was a convincing way.

"Dr. Pfeiffer?" It was the race official. "I don't have the placement sticks." As each girl finished, she was given a Popsicle stick with the number of her place on it. When everyone had completed the course, the sticks were turned in, the score tallied, and the winning team named.

Paige spotted her manager talking with friends. "Sheila!" she called, and pointed to the official. The girl dug into her pocket and ran the sticks to the official, who moved off.

Paige should have moved, too, but that didn't occur to her until it was too late and Noah was ducking under the edge of her umbrella.

"I'm not sorry," he said in a voice that was at the same time soft but steely and defiant.

Paige scanned the handful of parents who had made the trip to Mount Court for the race, but she recognized none.

"I'm only sorry that I didn't have anything with me," he went on more quietly. "The last thing either of us needs is for you to be pregnant right now."

Paige didn't want to think about that possibility. She didn't want to think about *anything* to do with what had happened in Mara's backyard. She cleared her throat, then said, "Can we talk about this another time?"

"What's wrong with now?"

"I'm in the middle of a race."

"And you have nothing to do for the next fifteen minutes, when, if we're lucky, someone will come out of the woods." He straightened, lifting the tip of the umbrella so that he could see her. "Frankly, this course sucks. Bystanders can't see a thing. How can we expect to attract alumni and parents if everything takes place in the woods? And that's not to mention the safety factor. What if something were to happen in there?"

"The girls rarely run alone. If one gets hurt, another can run out for help. It happens to be a beautiful course. And on a day like this, they're better off in the woods than out here."

She scanned the road for Peter, intent on excusing herself to speak with him. But he was nowhere in sight.

"So," Noah said. "How will our girls place?"

Safer ground. Official business. That was all right. "My guess? For our team, Merry third, Annie second, and Sara first."

"Sara's that good?"

"That good."

"It's remarkable, really," he said, sounding almost buoyant. "This is only the second year she's run. She started last year in high school. Reluctantly."

"Why reluctantly?" Paige asked, daring him a glance. He was wearing a slicker not unlike Peter's. Its hood had a visor that protected his glasses, though not very well. The lenses were spotted with rain.

"Reluctantly was the way she did most everything," he said. "She was having trouble getting along with her mother, and it tinged every aspect of her life. Her grades fell. She withdrew, even from friends. There were several instances of shoplifting."

"*Sara?*"

"Sara."

Paige couldn't imagine it, but Noah seemed to know what he was talking about.

"It was never much of anything," he went on, "a lipstick here, a hair ribbon there. She was clearly trying to punish her mother. But it was the old story—she wasn't hurting her mother so much as she was hurting herself. Rather than prosecuting, the local police put her on probation. One of the stipulations was that she be involved in afternoon sports at school. So she started running. Took her anger at the world out on the pavement."

Paige knew well the stern look Sara often wore when she was running. "That explains it, then. She's still doing it. But you'd think the anger would be dissipated some by now. Out of sight, out of mind kind of thing."

He grunted. "It's never that easy."

"Will she talk about it?"

"Not to me, that's for sure," he said in a way that gave Paige pause. There were obvious reasons why Sara wouldn't talk to Noah—his position of authority, his unpopularity with the students. Still, she caught a sudden glimpse of familiarity—an expression, a gesture, a look.

"Why's that?" she asked, though suddenly, absurdly, she knew. At least, she thought she did. There was the different last name—but the same long legs, the same sand-streaked hair, and the interest Noah took in Sara, an interest that he passed off as the empathy of one newcomer to Mount Court for another but that was suspiciously intent. It seemed suddenly too convenient that they were both new to the school, both alone, both runners.

Noah looked uncomfortable.

"Why didn't you tell me?" she asked, feeling hurt. They had been as physically intimate as two people could be, yet he had withheld this very basic fact from her. But then, perhaps "withheld" was the wrong word.

They didn't know much about each other, period. Physical intimacy had been totally premature. Unpremeditated. Impulsive. Wrong.

He took off his glasses, shook them, put them back on. "We agreed that it would be easier for her to assimilate if she didn't have the onus of being the Head's daughter. It was a wise move, given my dubious popularity."

Paige knew that the "dubious popularity" was mutual. Noah wasn't wild about Mount Court, either. "Did you take this job solely because of her?"

"Not solely. Being Head of School has been a long-time goal of mine. But we had to do something with Sara. She needed to be away from her mother. I had been on the lookout for positions, and while Mount Court wouldn't have been my first choice, it was the only opening at the time."

So he was a father. It was a new thought, a strange thought that of necessity altered her image of him. "What about her name? Is Dickinson part of the ploy?"

"No. It's her legal name."

"Your wife's?"

"Ex-wife's, and no. It's the name of Liv's second husband. Sara's been using it for years."

He didn't like that. Paige could tell by the steel in his voice. "How old was she when you were divorced?"

"Three."

"Wow. So young."

"Too young to feel the sting of the breakup."

"Not too young to miss her father. Did your wife have custody right from the start?"

"It made the most sense," he argued defensively.

She wondered about the nature of the man, that he could leave a three-year-old child. Granted, she didn't know the details of the breakup of his marriage—and didn't care to, thank you—still, it smacked of the insensitivity that she had accused him of the very first time they'd met.

He put his hands in his pockets. "We can't always dictate the timing of highly emotional things." He shot her a look that had nothing to do with Sara.

She shook her head. "Not now, Noah. Please."

"Then when? Tonight?"

"No."

"Tomorrow?"

"No."

"Do you regret it that much?" he asked, and there was something in his voice, not steel now but hurt, that started a vibrating inside her. He leaned in. "Was it that awful?"

"No," she cried. "It wasn't awful at all. It was just plain dumb. And inappropriate. And ill timed. I was thinking about Mara and feeling empty, and suddenly there you were."

"It was my fault, then?"

She wished it had been, but no amount of denial on her part could support that premise. "I was doing my part," she admitted, staring straight ahead.

"Actively," he said with what she could have sworn was a grin and a smug one at that, but when she shot him a look, his lean lips were carefully controlled.

Intent first and foremost on flight, she started off down the drive in the direction of the woods, wanting to be there when the first of the girls appeared. But there was Noah, beside her in no time at all.

"That's a very rude habit," he informed her from the edge of the umbrella.

"What is?" she said without breaking stride.

"Turning and walking away. You do it a lot."

"You'll get poked if you stay there." The umbrella was bobbing with each step, its spiked tips perilously close to Noah's face.

"Raise the umbrella."

"I'll get wet."

"Okay, then stop walking and tell me why you can't stand still."

His saying she couldn't do it was reason enough for her to prove him wrong. She stopped walking and stood still in the rain. "I walk away because I have places to go and things to do. My life has become complicated in the past two weeks. I'm feeling stressed. Besides, I don't know how to deal with you. You're intimidating."

"Me?"

She stared at him.

"Okay," he conceded, "so I'm authoritative."

"And large and imposing and persistent."

"Those are qualities that get things done."

She thought of their night on the grass. He had been large and imposing and persistent then, but in incredibly appealing ways. Given her frame of mind, she hadn't had a chance.

She started walking again. He was beside her in an instant. She tried to steady the umbrella.

"I know what you're thinking," he said.

She humored him. "What am I thinking?"

"You're thinking that you were vulnerable that night and that I used those same qualities to accomplish the seduction that I'd had in mind right from the start, but you're wrong. If I'd had sex on my mind when I was driving over there, I'd have brought a rubber."

Paige glanced around nervously. "Can't we talk about this another time?"

"I'd like to, but you keep shooting me down. Tell me when, and we'll talk."

But Paige changed her mind. She didn't want to talk. She wanted to forget that anything had happened that night, and God willing, once she got her period she could do that. "Look," she said with a sigh, stopping again well short of the crowd waiting at the edge of the woods, "there really isn't any point in talking. What happened the other night was an aberration. It was a weak moment for me. I promise it won't happen again."

"Why shouldn't it?"

"Because," she said deliberately, "there's no future to it. My life is chock full. I have more than enough to keep me busy without juggling a relationship with you, and besides, you're here for a year, then you'll be gone, so what's the point?" She started walking, quickening her pace when a runner emerged from the woods.

It wasn't one of Mount Court's. Nor was the second runner. Or the third. Sara, who was indeed the first of the Mount Court girls to cross the finish line, was the seventh overall to do it. Annie placed second for Mount Court, eleventh overall, Merry third, fourteenth overall.

It was a dismal showing for Paige's team.

She didn't say as much to the girls. Nor did Noah, who commended each—with enthusiasm—on a fine run as she crossed the finish line.

Unable to forget what he had told her—fascinated, actually, the more she thought about it—Paige watched him with Sara. He asked her how the course had been, asked her where she had felt strongest and weakest, and told her no less than three times how well she had run. She answered him in a bare minimum of words, and when he put a hand on her shoulder, she turned away.

Paige felt for him. She didn't want to, but she did. It seemed to her one of the great tragedies of life that families couldn't get along.

"Dear Lizzie," she read later that afternoon, as she sat on the floor, rocking Sami in the portable swing:

I'm not sure when it started, I think way back when I was little and couldn't seem to do things right. My mom wanted me to be her little helper, but I had too much energy to be cooped up in the house. I wanted to be with my brothers. They were out running around all the time, going back and forth from town. I wanted to be meeting people and seeing how the rest of the world lived, not stuck at the house.

You were lucky. Your parents were different. You could do what you wanted.

Paige put down the letter. She was the intruder, the eavesdropper, the Peeping Tom on Mara's thoughts.

She knew it was wrong to read another person's mail, had deliberately left the packet of letters at Mara's the night before so that she wouldn't be tempted, but it hadn't worked.

On her way home from Mount Court she had detoured to the house, which the family moving to town had adored. Preliminary papers had been drawn up. They were hoping to move in within the month, which left Paige the unenviable task now, on top of all else, of disposing of its contents. On this day, her sole conscious intent had been to take home the best of Mara's photographs, but with little more than a fast glance at the photos she had gone to the wicker basket and dug through the balls of yarn until her fingers had hit the packet of letters. When she drew it out, she found that it was a different packet from the other, these letters written on blue stationery, tied with red yarn. On impulse she had upended the wicker basket and found four packets in all, each containing anywhere from six to ten letters. Taking a single photograph to ease her conscience, she had brought the letters home.

She would send them on, perhaps, one day when she could bear to part with them. For now they seemed the only source of clues to the mystery of Mara.

"Do you remember the time," Mara wrote on:

when I turned eight and wanted to have a birthday party at the rodeo that came to town? My parents said no. They said a rodeo party wasn't right for a girl, and the more I argued, the angrier they grew, but I wasn't giving in. I spent my eighth birthday alone in my room, and they let me sit there. I kept thinking that if they loved me, they'd come get me, but they didn't, and then when I finally came out they told me how much I had disappointed them.

I did that a lot, I guess. I still do. Next week is Dad's seventy-fifth birthday—

which dated the letter to three years earlier, Paige realized, and read on:

They're giving him a party. I wouldn't have known about it if Chip's wife, Bonnie, hadn't called and said that the boys talked with my mother and they all agreed that I ought to be there. When I mentioned a gift, Bonnie said that the best one I could bring my dad was a son-in-law. She said it with a laugh, but I knew she wasn't kidding. They all keep hoping that I'll turn up with a husband and a pack of kids, and buy a house right down the street just like Johnny and Chip did, but I won't. I can't.

What's wrong with being a doctor? Most people think it's a noble profession, but every time I think of it, really stop and think of it in the overall scheme of life, I feel guilty. Okay, so my dad had an ear infection that was misdiagnosed long enough for him to lose hearing in that ear. So my mom would have had another girl after me if the doctor had gotten to the hospital in time to unwind the umbilical cord from her neck. Does that mean all doctors are bad?

I wonder what another girl in the family would have been like. Probably just like they wanted me to be. Maybe they'd have stopped harping on me if they'd had her. Then again, maybe not. I could never be the invisible type, though for the longest time, I tried. I steered clear of them all and just went about my own business, but I annoyed them doing that, too.

Your life is so different from mine. I always envied you that. You make people happy, and that makes you happy. You may not have a fancy degree, but you feel satisfied with your life. Me, I can't seem to keep things together, not the things that matter most. I do so much, and still I fail.

Pained, Paige set the letter aside. She didn't understand how Mara could consider herself a failure, but the thought had been in the first letter, too.

"How are you doing, sweetie?" she asked Sami, who was a small lump in the formless seat of the swing. Carefully she lifted her out, and in a voice so light that it belied the gist of the words, said, "She wasn't a failure, but she was coming from a different place from her parents. Like me, I suppose. Only I have Nonny." She folded her legs and propped Sami in the middle, then squiggled a finger toward the little girl's tummy, tickled for a minute, withdrew, and squiggled forward again. "I think you're putting on weight. There's more here than there was this time last week." She tickled. "Come on, Sami. I want a smile. Just a little one to let me know I'm doing things right." She was in the middle of another squiggle when the phone rang. She answered it with Sami propped on her hip.

"Hello?"

"You asked what the point was," Noah said without preamble, "and I say that the point is pure fun. You have too much going on in your life to be involved, and I'll be outta here at the end of the year, but in the meantime it might be nice to have some fun."

She took a steadying breath. Even his *voice* upped the temperature a notch. "Fun is watching a movie or playing Boggle or discussing a book. What we did wasn't fun. It was sex."

"Sex is fun."

"It was an escape. It wasn't rational. I'm not sure I was aware of what was happening."

"And you're a totally rational creature," he said on a note of exasperation that didn't bother her one bit. Let him be exasperated. In the long run, it was better that way.

She thought of Sara, amazed all over again at the relationship between the two. She wondered how often Noah had seen her over the years, wondered how close they were. If there was caring, Sara had never let on—neither when the other girls had been denigrating Noah nor when he had reached out to her after the race. And then there was Noah's own declaration that Sara wouldn't confide in him. Clearly their relationship had problems.

Paige wondered if he ever felt like a failure where Sara was concerned.

"Well," he went on, all business now, Head of School to cross-country coach, "for a totally rational creature, you're missing something when it comes to your team. They ran terribly."

When Sami reached hesitantly for the phone cord, Paige nudged it into her hand. "The conditions weren't ideal."

"They were the same for the other squads, and they ran better than we did. You're too lax, Paige. That's the problem. I've watched practices where you and the girls sit talking."

"When something important comes up, we talk. I believe in doing that, and I don't care if we lose every race we run, if my talk can help these kids through the nightmare of adolescence. Actually, though," she thought aloud, "we haven't done much talking lately. Lately we've worked hard."

"So why such a lousy showing?"

Paige sighed. "No great mystery. Our girls don't see themselves as runners, and they sure don't see themselves as winners. But that's what we need, a win. One win. That's all. It'll turn the tide."

"How do you get the win without changing the self-image first?"

"That's what I have to figure out. Any suggestions?"

Noah had one, but he wasn't sharing it with Paige. He was annoyed with her because not only had he thoroughly enjoyed making love to her, but he couldn't stop thinking about it. She might have been unaware of what was going on, but he sure hadn't been. He remembered every detail, from the way her hands had stolen over his body, to the way her nipples had hardened under his tongue, to the tiny sounds that had come from her throat at the moment of climax.

Her desire to dismiss the whole thing annoyed the hell out of him. So he didn't say a word about his plan—it was none of her goddamn business—and at that moment he wasn't sure it would work, anyway. There were permissions to secure and equipment to buy, steal, or borrow, and even then he was taking a chance. Granted, history was in his favor, but he was still going out on a limb for a project that could fail. Given the Mount Court community's questionable opinion of him, on top of Sara's decidedly negative one, failure was the last thing he needed.

Eleven

Angie came home from work early. She had shifted appointments to free up a few extra hours, not quite sure what she would do with them, knowing only that she had to do something. She had been working longer and longer hours, hoping that the demands of her job would blot out painful thoughts, but the thoughts remained. If pushed aside, they crowded back at the first chance. She couldn't escape them. Her life had become a nightmare of going through the motions of the ordinary, while nothing about it was ordinary at all.

Dougie, who had always before been free with words and affection, was suddenly miserly with both. During drives to and from school, he sat silently in the car, giving the briefest answers to her questions, volunteering little. It wasn't much better at home, where

he spent the bulk of his time in his room, either studying or on the phone. Clearly he had issues that weighed
heavily on his mind, not the least of which, now, was
the tension between his parents.

Ben barely looked at her, rarely spoke to her, certainly never touched her. He was living at home without being there—although even the latter was in doubt
now. She had thought he would be working when she
got home, but the house was deserted. His studio was
dark, pens capped and papers neatened. The television
was off. His car was gone.

She sat down at the kitchen table, not waiting so
much as trying to decide what to do next. If Ben had
been home, they might have talked. She supposed that
had been at the back of her mind when she had left
work early. But the house was as silent and empty as her
mind. She felt helpless. The paralysis of not knowing
what to do was nearly as bad as the not knowing itself.

The irony of it was that she knew plenty, just not the
right things. She knew how the human body worked,
had taken course after course on its intricacies, and had
become a skilled mechanic. She could take what was
there, clean it, patch it, and get it working again, but
she couldn't create. She couldn't produce something
where nothing was before. She couldn't take emptiness
and fill it with meaning.

With neither her husband nor her son talking to her, she felt as though something vital had been removed, as though her body were continuing to function on the force of momentum alone. But it couldn't continue for long. The hollow inside was large and growing. Like a black hole, it would swallow her up in time.

She wondered where Ben was. Wondered if he had gone to the post office. Or the Tavern. Or the library.

She laced her fingers together on the table, them unlaced them and laid them flat on the inlaid tiles. Her hands were slender, straight, and efficient hands, their fingernails neatly filed and unpainted. After years of being washed umpteen times a day, moisturizing was little more than a placebo. She had a worker's hands. They showed their forty-two years in every crease, every tiny scar, every vein that hadn't been as prominent the year before.

She sighed and looked at the window. Her reflection looked back, midnight black hair that was cut on an angle toward her chin to give a look of practical chic. Her face was pale and slim. She was a petite woman whose knowledge level had always added inches to her height.

Her knowledge level was zip now, making her feel small, forlorn, and powerless. She laced her fingers together again, unlaced them seconds later, then tucked them in her lap. She thought about the past and how efficiently she had run her life, thought about the trauma of the present, worried about the future. Once Dougie was off to college, it would be just Ben and her in ways that it had never, in the entire course of their marriage, ever been.

She heard Ben's car turn into the driveway and, shot through with sudden jitters, rose from the chair. There were things to do, always things to do. Idleness accomplished nothing and only left more to be done down the road. She could start dinner, or put in a load of laundry, or water the plants, or call the bank about the new bankcard that was overdue.

But she didn't do any of those things. It was as though the paralysis that was in command of her mind now spread to her knees. She sank limply down on the chair.

He parked the car. She heard the door slam shut, heard his footsteps on the walk, then the steps. He opened the kitchen door, came in, and stopped short.

"Angie. I didn't know you were home."

"I parked in the garage," she said, wondering what would have happened if she hadn't, whether he would have driven on past. He wasn't pleased to see her; she could hear it in his voice. Uneasy, she rubbed her fingers together, steepling the thumbs.

"Is something wrong?" he asked warily.

She nearly laughed. Was something wrong? The most basic thing in their lives was wrong. She gaped at him.

"I meant," he specified, "are you sick?"

She shook her head.

"Dougie isn't due home for two hours," he pointed out.

"I know."

He regarded her cautiously, waiting, poised at the door as though he could go either way, in or out, with a word.

"Why is it I feel like the guilty one?" she asked when she couldn't stand him staring at her, silent, guarded, subtly accusatory. "You're the one having the affair, but I'm guilty. It doesn't make sense."

His look said it made sense indeed. She was the one who had deprived him during their marriage and driven him to seek comfort in another woman. If he had been wrong in taking a mistress, she had been wrong long before that.

She felt a heaviness in her legs, her middle, her arms, and for the first time wondered if there was a positive side to paralysis. It freed its victim from action, from response and responsibility.

But if she didn't act, no one would. Ben had always taken his lead from her, and she had never minded before. Right now, she did. She wished that for once he would be the initiator.

But she had trained him well. He waited.

Finally, with a sigh, she said, "I think we have to talk."

"We?" Ben asked. "Or you?"

"You," she shot back, pouring into that single word every bit of the negative feeling she had. Ben had hurt her beyond belief. Nothing she had done to him merited that. "I need you to tell me what's happening here. We go through the bare motions of life as usual, but it's a farce. Our family is falling apart. We walk around each other. We avoid looking each other in the eye. There's zero communication."

He didn't move a muscle.

"Ben?"

He shrugged. "What can I add? You just said it all."

She took a shaky breath. Old habits died hard; he wasn't helping in the least.

Quietly, wearily, humbly, she said, "Please, Ben. Tell me what you're thinking. What you're *honestly* thinking. I'm not telling you anything, I'm asking. I don't know what's going on in your mind. I don't know what you want. I don't know what I'm supposed to do."

"That's a change," he said.

She looked at her hands. "Okay. I deserved that." She looked away. "But it's been a way of life, knowing what to do. I've always taken pride in it, and no one—including you—ever discouraged me from being that way. But I never thought I was putting you down. You may have felt that, but I didn't intend it. I was just being me."

"Little Miss Perfect."

She studied her hands. The force of his resentment continued to stun her with sharp, grazing blows. Gathering the tatters of her self-esteem, she said, "Obviously not, or I wouldn't be sitting here right now. Talk to me, Ben. Tell me where we go next. Tell me what you want to happen. You say that I never hear you. I'm trying to do that now, but I can't hear unless you speak."

He stuck his hands in the waist of his cords and stood thinking for a while before finally saying, "Okay. We have to do something about Doug. He's annoyed with both of us right now. I doubt he says any more to me than he does to you. I got a call from his Spanish teacher this morning asking if there was a problem at home."

"How did *she* know?" Angie asked in sudden horror. She suddenly imagined the whole *world* knew, and she was appalled.

"He failed a test yesterday. He's never done that before."

"Not by a long shot," Angie said, feeling an awful defeat. It wasn't the grade. No one made it through school without an F or two. He could make up the test or average it in with his others. That wasn't the point. The point was that he wouldn't have failed a test if he wasn't deeply upset.

"So," Ben said, "we have to talk with him."

Several weeks before, Angie would have done that on her own. But Ben had accused her of being controlling and manipulative. So she asked, "What should we say?"

He shifted one shoulder. "I don't know."

She studied her fingers. If he didn't know, and if she wasn't supposed to tell him, where did that leave them? Holding her tongue, she looked up and waited.

After what seemed an eternity, he said, "There are two issues. One has to do with what's going on between us. The other has to do with him and the space he needs."

"They're connected," she said, and regretted it the instant she heard his drawl.

"Obviously, but one is more easily solved than the other." The drawl gave way to something more serious. "I think we should let him board at school."

She shook her head fast. Everything inside her rebelled at the idea, but she didn't say a word until Ben asked, "Why not?"

She calmed herself. "Because he's too young."

"He's in eighth grade. Mount Court kids start boarding in seventh."

"But if he's failing Spanish, he may need more supervision." She had a cursory knowledge of the language and tested him regularly on vocabulary.

"He isn't failing Spanish," Ben corrected. "He failed one test. And he might get better supervision at school, what with mandatory study halls every night."

"He'll be overwhelmed, being with kids constantly."

"Maybe. He'll probably say that that's better than being here every night. You smother, and I work. And he's a lonely only. It would be different if he had a sibling."

"We agreed that one would keep us busy enough."

"You agreed. Another Angie dictum."

"Well, damn it, you didn't argue, so you're every bit as much at fault!" She thought back to when Dougie was little. She couldn't even remember their discussing having another child. They had planned everything just so to allow for Angie's return to work.

They had planned? Or *she* had planned? She had the awful thought that it was the latter.

"Well," she said with a discouraged sigh, "it's a little late to be talking about this now. Just like it's a little late to be talking about Dougie boarding. The semester's already begun. I doubt they'd take him."

Ben guffawed. "Mount Court? For the price of room and board, they'd take a baboon."

Angie felt as though she were in a game of tug-of-war, with Dougie in the middle and Ben on the other side. "Do you have no qualms at all?" she asked, bewildered.

"Of course I have qualms. I love the kid, too. I like having him around. But he wants this, Angie."

"He also wants a car for his sixteenth birthday, but that doesn't mean we have to give him one."

"Not the same at all," Ben said. "A car is a luxury. Granted, boarding is, too, but at least it's an experience with some merit to it."

"You're right. Boarders learn great things."

"You don't think he'll learn those things anyway? You don't think he knows that some cigarettes don't have tobacco in them? You don't think he knows what the term *druggie* means? Come on, Angie, get real. He's a bright kid. He's a *normal* kid. He'll be discussing girls' breasts with his friends whether he boards or not, and if he wants a condom, he'll get one without asking you to buy it."

"He's only fourteen!" she protested.

"It doesn't mean he's going to *use* one, but guys talk about it for years before they do it." He put a hand on the back of his head and held on tight. Angie hadn't seen that gesture since the day they had moved to Vermont, when the moving company had dropped his computer. "Jesus, Angie, think about it, will you? You raised the boy. For fourteen years you've been teaching him to be honest and considerate and hardworking. Those values are part of him now. It's not like all of a sudden he's going to forget them—unless you put him in a little cage and make him break his way out by whatever means he can find. Give him air, Angie. Trust him a little."

"Like I trusted you?" she blurted out.

The words hung in the air. For the very first time, she saw guilt on his face.

"I did, you know," she said more quietly. "I assumed you believed in fidelity. It never occurred to me that you would have an affair. Never *occurred* to me."

His hand was on the back of his neck now. He let out a breath. "It wasn't intentional. It just happened."

"For eight years?" she cried. "Ben, *you* get real. If it had happened just once, I might have been able to buy the fact that it wasn't intentional. But to continue it for that long? You're a bright guy. You know what's happening in the world. You can sit over dinner and tell me about the latest scandal that's breaking in the government. Sometimes it has to do with money, sometimes perks, sometimes sex. I can't count the number of times you've talked about some man who was cheating on his wife. Didn't you see that you were doing it yourself?"

He looked away. "Of course I did."

"Do you know how much it hurts?"

He looked back at her, and though she hadn't planned it, tears came to her eyes. She brushed them away, lest he accuse her of being manipulative, but they came back. Ignoring them, she asked, "How did you get together with her?"

"It's not important."

"It is to me."

"Well, maybe I don't want to talk about it."

"Because it's special? Because it's yours and not mine? Because you're afraid I'll try to control it somehow?"

"Because, damn it, I shouldn't have said anything. I knew you didn't expect it. I knew it would hurt you. I may have blurted it out in anger, but that isn't how the thing itself has been all this time. I didn't do it out of defiance. I did it because I had a real need that wasn't being met."

A need Angie hadn't filled. She felt grossly inadequate for the hundredth time in a week, such that it wasn't quite as shocking as it had been at first. She couldn't do everything, be everything. She was coming to accept that.

Ben leaned against the wall with his arms folded and his ankles crossed, studying his deck shoes. In a weary voice he said, "I always go to the library to read the periodicals. She was there. We became friends."

"When did it become more?"

"I don't know."

Angie waited.

Finally he said, "We probably knew each other a year before it happened."

"Where do you go? Her house?"

"Angie, this isn't—"

"It is," she said, but quietly, sadly. "This is a small town. I know most of the people in it. I see many of them professionally. It matters to me how many of them know."

"Your image."

"It's more than that. My self-confidence has been shot to threads around here. You tell me I've been wrong. Dougie tells me I've been wrong. I want to know if I can leave here and pretend that I can still do something right."

"You do plenty right. Let's not get overdramatic."

She shot up from her chair. "Overdramatic? I'm the *last* person to get overdramatic. I've been walking around for days like nothing's wrong." She sank back down and, quietly again, added, "I'm feeling my way through this. It's new to me. I'm doing my best, but if I ask something that you think is inappropriate, bear with me. You're not seeing things from my perspective." She sighed. "All I want to know is if everyone else in town knew about this before I did."

"No one knows. We've been careful."

"Are you still? Now that I know?" It was an oblique way of asking that other, more frightening question.

"I haven't been with her since you found out. Not that way, at least."

"But you've talked."

"She's my best friend."

"I always thought I was that."

"You used to be. Then you got so that you didn't have time for me. I was like a piece of furniture. Once I was put in place, all I needed was a little dusting once in a while, a little fluffing up, a shifting one way or another to suit my surroundings. The original buy was the only critical part. After that"—he made a disparaging sound—"habit set in."

"Is this a midlife crisis?" she asked, half hoping it was. Midlife crises passed.

He shook his head. "It's more fundamental than that."

She pressed her lips together and nodded. "Are we breaking up?"

He was a long time in answering, a time of staring at the floor and frowning. Finally, in a quiet voice and with a wary look, he said, "I don't know. Is that what you want?"

At least it hadn't been an outright "no." She had been worried about that. Belatedly she started to tremble. "I don't want it, no. I like our marriage—"

"Like you like our goose-down comforter?"

There it was, the bitterness again. Given its depth, it amazed her that he had been able to hide it for so long. Unless he hadn't hidden it at all, and she had just been oblivious, which was his contention. She couldn't believe she had failed to see or hear something so strong. "You're very angry."

"Yes, I am. I'm angry that you weren't more attentive. I'm angry that your work is so important to you. I'm angry that you put Dougie before me. I'm angry that I was put in the position of needing something so badly that I had to betray you to get it."

"I am not the bad guy," she insisted softly. "I didn't intend to do any of that. If you had spoken up sooner—really spoken up, like you are now, instead of just dropping vague suggestions—we might have avoided all this. Eight years is a long time for you to be feeling bad about something without saying a word."

He lifted a shoulder. "It's done. Water over the dam."

"So what do we do now?" They were back where they started.

He realized it, too. She could see it in the slump of his shoulders. She remembered when she used to massage those shoulders, when as a couple they were younger, more dependent on each other, and yes, best of friends. At the earliest months of their marriage, she had loved touching him. Then time had become scarce, and she had lost the knack.

She wondered if she could get it back, wondered if she wanted to. But before she could give the problem the thought it deserved, she was diverted.

"We start," Ben was saying in delayed response to the question she had asked, "by letting Dougie board. It can be for a trial semester, with the understanding that if at any point it doesn't work out, he'll come back home."

Angie was fighting a losing battle. She was on the short end, two against one. "I'm very uncomfortable with this."

"Then let him be a five-day boarder. He can come home on weekends."

That didn't sound quite so bad—still bad, just less so. "Will he agree to it?"

"If that's the only option we give him."

But there were drawbacks to that, too. She could think of them all and would have blurted them out, if she didn't have a sudden attack of unsureness. Once, she had known almost everything there was to know, and where knowledge left off, intuition picked up. Lately— first with Mara, now with Ben and even Dougie—she was way off the mark.

"What?" Ben prodded impatiently.

She shook her head.

"I'd rather you say what's on your mind now," he said, "than hit me with an 'I told you so' later."

She was half-tempted to do just that. He wanted to let Dougie board; she could go along with it and then let him take the blame if things went wrong.

The only problem was that this was Dougie's life they were talking about. She didn't want things to go wrong for him, not ever, which was one of the very rea- sons she was hesitant to let him board at Mount Court. Okay, so she could hear Ben's arguments in favor of it; she could even give them some credence. Still, there was this other.

"It has to do with timing," she began hesitantly. "If we send him off to live at school now, he's apt to think it's because we want him out of the house so that we can either fight or get a divorce. He's apt to worry more there than he will here."

Ben thought about that in silence. In the past Angie might have filled that silence with more of her thoughts. Now she remained still.

Finally Ben said, "He'll do fine, if we handle it right."

Angie waited for him to go on. She was anxious to hear what he was going to say, because it went to the heart of the matter.

Incredibly, he looked to her for help, but she kept her mouth shut.

Finally he said, "We can tell him that we're letting him do this because he wants it so badly."

Which didn't address the issue at all. Angie remained silent, but her expression must have said something—either that or Ben's conscience had— because, snappishly, he said, "We can tell him that we'll both be here waiting for him to come home each weekend."

"Will we?"

"I will," Ben said. "I wouldn't let him down by not being here."

Which said nothing about what he wanted to do with, for, or about their marriage.

"What about you?" he asked when she didn't respond.

"This is my home. I have nowhere to go. But we're avoiding the issue, I think."

He drew himself up and glanced at his watch. "I'll go pick him up. It's time. I won't mention this until dinner. We can discuss it with him then."

Swinging back out the door, he left her alone and more troubled than ever.

Peter was similarly alone and troubled when he left the Tavern. He hadn't stayed long, just for a beer. With no one to talk to, all he could think about were the pictures drying in his darkroom.

He had spent hours on them the night before. He had found just the right negative this time—or so he had thought—and had made every sort of print imaginable. Then he had gone through a day of seeing patients, of talking to parents and suggesting solutions to ailments, all the while feeling extra good about himself because he had been so sure that he had it. Back home, in the light of day, he had seen that none was right. None captured the feeling he wanted. None did her justice.

The beer hadn't eased his disappointment at all. It had only made him aware that he was alone while everyone else was paired up, and that he would have been with Lacey if Lacey hadn't gone holier-than-thou on him.

Taking his camera with him, he walked to the end of the block and turned onto Main Street. The sun was lowering in the sky, creating shadows to give depth to the stores there. He took a head-on shot of the bookstore, extended his zoom lens for a shot of the church at the end of the street, retracted the zoom, and took a shot of the whole of the three blocks that made up the center of town. The amber stone looked more golden in the sunset, the signs more authentically antique, the window displays more quaint.

He parked himself against a trash receptacle, opposite the block that held the drugstore, the card store, the package store, and Reels, and extended the zoom for shots of the latter. Mount Court kids were in town; he could see them through the store window. They were gathered in groups, some actually searching through the videos for one to rent, some simply talking to each other, some sitting on stools at the back of the store where the soda fountain stood.

He caught sight of Julie Engel. Her head was bent over a videocassette. She read it, replaced it, and picked up another. He crossed the street, stopping where the cars were parked diagonally, and snapped several shots of her through the glass. If striking when she had her hair pulled back and her skin bare, she was even more striking now. Her long hair was shiny and gently waved; her makeup was light but put focus on her eyes; her clothing was demure in ways that suggested the opposite.

As he watched, she separated herself from the group and wandered idly toward the front of the store. Then she saw him. She smiled and waved. After turning to say something to her friends, she came outside.

"Hi, Dr. Grace."

"How're you doing, Julie?"

"Not bad."

"Did you find something to rent?"

"Nah. I've seen everything good three times. It gets boring after a while." She gestured toward his camera. "Are you taking pictures of anything special?"

He tossed his head back toward the street. "Just the town. The light's right."

"Take some of me?"

"Of you."

"My stepmom's birthday is next month. I'd love to send her something good. She thinks the worst of me most of the time. Wouldn't it be nice if she could have something angelic?" She glanced toward the church, beside which was a small park. "We could go there," she said, taking his arm and leading him off.

Peter felt a tiny qualm. Julie Engel was as wily as she was beautiful, if the stories he had heard were to be believed. He wasn't sure her stepmother's birthday was in October. He wasn't sure she had a stepmother at all. And he could hear Mara's voice, warning him against wily young women.

Then again, the park was beside the church, which was certainly safe ground.

"What about your friends?" he asked.

"It'll be ages before they pick something and have a soda and maybe even an ice cream across the street. We don't get ice cream at school anymore. Mr. Perrine thinks frozen yogurt is healthier." She slipped her elbow through his. "He's an incredible bore, don't you think?"

Peter eased her arm from his. Tucker was a small place. People saw things; what they didn't see, they imagined; and what they didn't imagine their neighbor imagined for them. He didn't want anyone getting the wrong idea. He didn't fool around with kids, never had, never would.

"To tell you the truth," he said now, "the man seems fine to me. I like his rules."

"That's because you don't have to live under them. You don't have to be in a dormitory at ten on week nights and eleven on weekends—and that's for the *seniors*. Let me tell you"—she scooped her hair back from her face—"it's a bummer. I shouldn't be restricted this way. I'm eighteen."

Peter didn't believe it for a minute. Seventeen, maybe. Maybe seventeen and a half. But not eighteen.

She ran ahead, stopping against the side of a tree on the edge of the park. The sun caught her hair and gave it life; Peter raised his camera and captured the image as he approached, then did it again from different angles close up. He was in the act of refocusing when she trotted deeper into the park, stopping this time on a long wooden bench. She sat there innocently, looking into the camera's eye for one frame and away for the next.

"Lift your chin. . . . That's it. Great. When did you say your stepmom's birthday was?"

"November. There's plenty of time to get a really good shot. I'll pay you, of course. You'd be my official photographer." She jumped off the bench. "How about there?" She pointed to a stand of birches. The sun's final rays were snagged on bits of protruding bark, creating the hint of a conflagration in the works.

Peter, who had no intention of charging Julie for one print for her stepmother, whose birthday was in either October or November as the girl's whim went, held her off while he photographed the trees. He had the camera to his eye when she moved in but lowered it when he saw what she had done.

"Julie," he warned.

"Just a few," she whispered, slipping off her shirt as she approached. "The light is great."

"Put it back on."

But she had tossed the shirt aside, and if she'd been wearing a bra, it too was gone.

Her breasts were high and full, fresh in the way of a young woman approaching the height of her physical appeal. She might have been eighteen, twenty-one, or twenty-five. But she was a patient, a student at the school of which he was the doctor of record, and trouble.

Peter deliberately threaded the camera over his shoulder. "I won't take pictures of you nude."

"I'm not nude," she said, coming closer still. "I'm wearing pants."

"Get dressed, Julie. Let me walk you back to your friends."

She shook her head. With the confidence of one who knew her power, she held his eyes. "Touch me," she whispered from inches away.

"Un-uh," Peter said with a slow shake of his head.

"Don't you find me attractive?"

"Very, but you're my patient, for one thing, and for another, you're a child."

"I'm not a child. I'm eighteen. And I'm Dr. Pfeiffer's patient, now that Dr. O'Neill is dead."

Now that Dr. O'Neill is dead. Mara would be *shrieking* if she could see him then. Focusing on that thought, he moved aside and reached for Julie's shirt, but she moved with him.

"You are," she said, "the most attractive man in this town."

He stretched the shirt over her shoulders, only to find that the sleeves were inside out. He took it back off and set about righting them.

"Half the girls at school are in love with you." She put her lips to his jaw.

He tugged harder at the sleeves of the shirt, fixing one and attacking the other.

"I'm not a virgin, if that's what's bothering you. I've done this before."

"Spare me, Julie," he warned as he pulled the second sleeve through. He hurried the shirt to her shoulders, only to find that he had hemmed her to him. Her hands went to his belt. One slipped lower.

"You do want me," she said with a victorious grin.

"No," he shouted, and stepped back. "No," he said more quietly, holding up his hands in token surrender. "I'm flattered. You're a beautiful girl. But anything between you and me is impossible."

"I felt it," she taunted.

"What you felt," he said with a sigh, "was the difference between a boy's body and a man's. And what you did," he added with gravity, "was an invasion of my privacy." He put his hands on his hips. "Now, I can easily walk you back through town with your shirt off, so that everyone can see the goods, but if that isn't what you had in mind, I'd suggest you button your shirt."

She buttoned the shirt, but her eyes said that she didn't believe he hadn't been aroused. The occasional smirk she shot him as they walked back to Reels said the same thing. He was relieved when she ran off to join her friends. She had begun to make him feel like a eunuch, but he wasn't that by a long shot. He had a normal, healthy appetite for attractive women—an appetite that would have been well satisfied even then, had it not been for Lacey's trying to tell him how to run his life. He could tell her a thing or two right back. It struck him that he ought to.

He crossed the street, walked back the way he had originally come, turned the corner to the Tavern parking lot, and slid into his car. Minutes later he was on his way to the Weeble estate.

He pulled up in front of the garage, climbed the narrow stairs to the apartment above, and knocked on the door. He could hear the sound of Tucker's own rock band, Henderson Wheel, which had hit it big to the tune of three successive platinum albums. He knocked again, louder.

"Yes?" Lacey called over the music.

"It's me. Peter," he tacked on, because he wasn't sure what his reception would be. He hadn't talked with her since the night he had walked out of the Tavern and left her behind.

She was a long time in opening the door, and then she wore a long robe and a sober expression. "You should have called first. I'm very tired."

"I won't stay long," he said, and went past her into the apartment. He waited to hear the door close. When it didn't, he turned to find her standing with her back to him and her hand on the knob. Her blond hair spilled down her back to the point where the robe cinched in her waist, just above the gentle flare of her hips. He felt a sharp tightening at his groin.

He returned to her and buried his face in her hair, pushing the door closed as he pressed into her.

"Peter, don't," she protested, and tried to move away, but his arms hemmed her in.

"I know I'm a bastard," he said before she could, "but we have unfinished business, you and me." He began to knead her breasts.

She squirmed. "Don't do that."

He let her turn herself around before he pinned her to the door, and while he moved against her, he held her face with one hand and lowered the other. "You like it. I know you do."

"Peter—"

"I know just what places feel the best"—his hand found its mark—"especially when you aren't wearing underwear. Did you do this for me?"

"How could I have?" she cried, exerting a steady pressure against his chest. "I didn't know you were coming. Peter, I don't want—"

He stoppered further words with his mouth and devoured her lips while he stroked her, but even as he felt her body begin to move to his rhythm, she tore her mouth away.

"You have *no right* to walk in here like this," she panted, pushing against him weakly, "and expect me to put out."

"But you love it," he said, opening her robe, then his pants. He felt powerful and male, hard as a rock, ready to explode.

"Damn it, I don't want—"

"You do, yes, you do," he said, holding her less gently. He ground his mouth against hers at the same time that he drove into her. He didn't know whether her cry was of pain or pleasure and didn't care, because the need inside him was too great, too male, too total.

The door behind her rattled under the force of his thrusts, but it, like the band of her legs around him, was something far removed from the tension building, building, building inside him. He ground his teeth together, bit out a guttural cry, and reached a climax that seemed to go on and on. In its midst he was aware of nothing but the extraordinary pleasure that had taken him over.

Very, very slowly, he regained an awareness of where he was, of the boneless slump of his body against Lacey and the raggedness of his breath against her neck. It was another minute before he felt her rigidity.

Drawing back, he met eyes that were cold as ice. After slipping from beneath him, she tied her robe as she crossed the floor, closed her hand around a stone obelisk that stood on the coffee table, and faced him again. "I think you'd better leave. Now."

The way she was holding the obelisk kept him where he was at the door. He rezipped his pants. "What are you upset about?"

"I don't want you here. I didn't want you here in the first place, but you barged your way in. You're a rude man, Peter."

"Ahhh. You're pissed at me because I left you with the bill the other night."

"The bill was nothing. I could afford to pay it. But you walked out when I dared to criticize you. I hadn't realized how insecure you are."

"There you go, psychoanalyzing again."

She was shaking her head even before he stopped speaking. "Not psychoanalyzing. Stating the obvious. You can't take the least bit of criticism, and you can't take rejection. That spells insecurity to me, and it's the last thing I'm looking for in a man. Contrary to what you choose to believe, I *don't* need you, Peter. I'll be heading back to Boston in a month. It's been nice, but it's over."

He wasn't sure he believed her. After all, he was the best Tucker had to offer, even for one last month. "Are you annoyed because you didn't come?"

She shot a sound of exasperation at the ceiling. "*Listen* to me. It's *over.* We've had some fun, but the fun is done. Don't even *think* of coming here again. If you do, I'll prosecute."

"Prosecute?" he asked. "Prosecute *what?*" He wasn't getting tripped up in that one. "What happened just now wasn't rape."

"Maybe not in the end, because, you're right, you know the buttons to push. But another time you won't be getting *near* the buttons. I'll call the cops first." She shifted her hands on the obelisk. "Now, leave."

Peter gave her a last, long look. She was attractive, but far from the best lover he'd had. He didn't need her, not by a long shot. Let her finish her work and go back to Boston. He could function just fine without her.

With a shrug, he opened the door. "It's your loss," he called over his shoulder as he trotted down the steps. With the slam of the door above him, another small chapter in the book of his loves ended, which didn't bother him in the least. Another would begin. He was a big man in town, an important man, a respected man. Women loved that. He wouldn't be alone for long.

Twelve

Noah was amazed at how well his plan gelled. He wasn't sure whether the credit could be laid to the plan itself or to the fact that he had any plan at all. Mount Court had been stagnant for so long. The prospect of someone doing something new and untried created instant enthusiasm.

Permissions arrived by fax from each of the parents involved, along with more than one encouraging phone call. The equipment was donated by a graduate who had gone into the business of orienteering and was curious, given the reputation of the current Mount Court student body, to see how it would be used. Noah called on old contacts to provide two professional climbers, a young married couple who would offer him badly needed backup in exchange for a welcome, albeit small stipend.

He picked his group with care, selecting the thirty students and four faculty members he felt most needed the challenge. The male-female split was even, as was the division among sophomores, juniors, and seniors. He included Sara in the group for the same reasons that applied to the others, plus several more. The mountain climb was, first and foremost, an exercise in group cooperation and trust. If all went as planned, there would be a bonding among the participants. He wanted her to experience that. He also wanted her to see that her father wasn't the bad guy everyone thought, but that he was experienced, knowledgeable, and adventurous.

The night before the trip, he called the faculty members to his house and told them his plan. They were resistant, but he had been expecting that. The four had the same kinds of attitude problems as the kids, which was precisely why he had included them.

"Katahdin?" one asked. "That's ambitious, for a group that's never climbed a mountain before."

Another shook his head warily. "If the new emphasis here is on discipline and academics, missing classes is a big mistake."

"Taking those kids is the mistake," a third warned. "Your list includes some of the worst troublemakers in the school. They're apt to go on a sit-down strike halfway up."

"They won't," Noah said. "They'll be too scared of being left behind. We'll leave tomorrow afternoon, immediately after class. It's a four-hour drive to Baxter State Park, which means that we'll reach the base camp in time for dinner."

"Are there decent restaurants nearby?"

Noah slowly shook his head. "We cook."

"*Us?*"

"You four, plus two guides, plus thirty kids, plus me. Everyone helps, everyone eats. We'll spend the night at the base camp and set off from there before dawn."

"Before dawn."

He ignored the echo. "All we'll have to carry are small day packs. The vans will meet us at the other side of the mountain tomorrow night to drive us back here, so we'll only miss a day of classes."

"Why go during the week and miss any classes at all?"

"Because I don't want this mistaken for any old weekend hike. It's serious stuff. An impromptu part of the curriculum. It's as important as any class they have."

"But if it's a four-hour drive from here to Baxter State, we could be getting back in the middle of the night. How can you ask the kids to go to classes on no sleep?"

The question came from Tony Phillips, a math teacher, football coach, and ex-player who was the laziest one of the bunch. Noah wasn't surprised that he would be worrying about sleep—and not about the kids' sleep, either. He was thinking of himself, no doubt about it.

"Kids can push themselves when they want," Noah said with a confident smile. "They'll sleep like logs Friday night."

"But we have practices Friday afternoon and games Saturday."

Noah nodded. "Right, and the kids will be grumbling about that, which is why I need you all to be upbeat and encouraging. They can do it all, climb Katahdin and still make practice and their games, and they'll be feeling on top of the world. The point of this is to give them a sense of achievement."

Abby Cooke, who taught history, made a dubious sound.

"What?" Noah asked.

"Nothing," she said.

"It didn't sound like nothing. Do you have reservations about the plan?"

She hesitated, then said, "Actually, yes. I do. These students have no appreciation for mountain climbing. They couldn't care less. There won't be any sense of achievement."

"Maybe not," Noah admitted. "Then again, they just might. I'm not looking to kindle an interest in were the worst of the complainers, protesting the food, the bugs, and the lack of bathroom facilities and talking wistfully about being back at school as though Mount Court were paradise. The boys weren't into complaining as much as swaggering around as though they knew just what had to be done when and were bored with the entire show.

Noah had assigned Sara to a group of what he considered to be the least troubled of the students, but he spent no more time with that group than he did with the others. He didn't dare approach her, though he was dying to know what she was thinking and feeling. Favoritism would backfire for sure.

When everyone had finished, he made a second round of the groups to make sure the clean-up was done properly and explain what would be happening the next day. Then he passed out tarps and demonstrated how to stretch them between trees to form a shelter for the night. He made a final round to make sure that the tarps were secure.

The rain began at midnight and continued for several hours. Noah wasn't sleeping so soundly that he didn't hear the group that stole into one of the vans to sleep, but he didn't force them back out. The others would be feeling that much more pleased with themselves come dawn, and, indeed, that was what happened. There was

mountain climbing, just give them a taste of success. I've been with groups like this before. Even the most reluctant are usually touched in some way."

There was silence, then, "What's the weather forecast?"

Noah shrugged. "Whatever."

There was another silence, then, "When will the kids be told?"

"They'll get notes at the end of their last class asking them to report to the auditorium. You four and I will be there to explain what's happening and give them a list of the things to put in their day packs. They'll have half an hour to get ready, then we leave. I already have the okays of their parents. Any other questions?"

"Just one," said Gordon McClennan, who taught Latin. "Can we opt out?"

Noah shook his head slowly.

Gordon looked around. "But why us?"

Because you four are lazy and bored, he thought. Because I'd put money on the fact that none of you has ever tried anything like this before, because you've all been thorns in my side since I took this thankless job, and because you could use the exercise.

Diplomatically he said, "Because you have better rapport with the students we're taking than some of the others. You're right; this is a difficult group. These kids aren't used to roughing it. They aren't used to exploring the great outdoors, or functioning as a group, and they sure aren't skilled in survival techniques, which is why I have two hired hands to help teach. Not that we'll be in any danger, assuming everyone pays attention and follows either their lead or mine, but Katahdin is no snap. The operative word is 'challenge.' That's what this is about."

Noah said as much to the students who gathered in the auditorium the following afternoon. They looked horrified and shot one excuse after another his way until, finally, losing patience, he said, "This trip is not optional." He looked at his watch. "You have thirty minutes to get ready and meet at the bus."

"What if we don't?" one of the boys asked. Noah knew him well. He had already broken enough rules to put him in extra study halls for a month.

Now Noah smiled. "Funny you should ask that, Brian," he said. "Your parents thought you would. They said that if you don't go, you can spend next weekend with them," which was the last thing Brian would want, given the friction between his parents and him. Noah's gaze spread. "I have similar promises from others of your parents." He rubbed his hands together. "Any other questions?"

Thirty minutes later they were off. Noah sat alone behind the bus driver. The other front seats were empty, as were the four immediately behind. Beyond that, all the way to the back of the bus, were successive pairs of grim faces.

They reached the base camp on schedule. There they met up with the hired hands, Jane and Steve, and not a moment too soon, as far as Noah was concerned. Not only were the faculty members as unwilling participants as the students, but not a one of them knew the first thing about cooking on a small camp stove, much less digging a latrine, much less raising a tarp.

Working from a prepared list that separated friends and troublemakers, he divided the thirty students into groups of five plus one adult, then went from group to group detailing what had to be done. Jane and Steve backed him up, taking over with their own and adjacent groups while Noah circulated. Grunts, moans, and muffled oaths notwithstanding, the students cooperated. They seemed to understand that no one would eat until the cooking was done and that the more everyone chipped in, the sooner that would be.

Dinner consisted of beef stew from a can, rolls from the Mount Court kitchen, and hot apple cider. Through it, Noah moved from one small circle to another, answering questions and fielding complaints. The girls

razzing galore of the van sleepers. He might have taken pleasure in the satisfaction of those who had remained outside if those hadn't quickly joined the others in grumbling about the ungodliness of the hour.

At least the rain had stopped. The air was damp and chilly, though the chill eased with the coming of light. Breakfast consisted of apples, oatmeal, and hot chocolate and was eaten to the tune of intermittent squabbles, which Noah deliberately ignored. When everything had been cleaned up, the vans took them another forty-five minutes to their starting point. After Noah described the trails they would be taking to the top of the mountain, the pace they should keep, the difficulties they might expect to find, and the rules they were to follow, they set off.

Those who had been wearing sweatshirts and sweatpants soon peeled them off and either wrapped them around their waists or stuffed them into backpacks as the air warmed. They walked in a long line that snaked through the trees, six clusters of five students and one adult each. Noah led; one of the experienced climbers and his group took the midpoint; the other and her group brought up the rear.

Noah listened both to the mountain sounds and to those of the climbers immediately behind him. He could hear their hiking boots on the dirt path enough to know that they were keeping up with him. He wanted to think that they were getting into the spirit of the thing, though he suspected that their silence was defiance.

Two hours of easy hiking up the mountain, they reached Chimney Pond, where fresh water and a ranger awaited. The air had begun to cool; sweatshirts and sweatpants went back on. They snacked on gorp and water and, after refilling their bottles, moved on.

They followed Cathedral Trail until the trees thinned and grew stunted. Noah put on a wool sweater and waited while the others did the same.

"This was where Thoreau turned back," he called down in an attempt to goad the kids on. "He was tired. Thought he'd never make it to the top."

There were grunts and mutterings. He caught the words *wimp, smart,* and *nuts,* a mixed review that left him in the dark as to the success of his ploy.

They passed the treeline. Earth gave way to open expanses of rock. The clouds thickened. "What if it rains?" one of the girls behind him asked, less complaining than apprehensive.

"We have rain gear," he answered gently. "It'll keep us dry."

"Won't the rocks be slippery?" another asked.

"Not terribly."

"The more slippery the better," one of the boys called. "We could use some excitement. This is pretty boring."

"You call that boring?" Noah said. He turned to study the view, which was spectacular even in spite of the clouds. Growing up in the Southwest, he had adored climbing the desert hills and imagining himself two hundred years back in history. The hills were higher here, greener, and the sense of history every bit as rich.

"When will we be able to see the top of the mountain?" a girl asked from close by his side.

He waited for a small group to gather around him. "It's right there." He pointed. "Wait. The clouds are moving. . . . There. See?"

"That's so far!"

"It must be *freezing* up there."

"We can't make it."

"Sure we can," he said. "It looks farther than it is." He slid off his backpack and took out a windbreaker.

"But it's in the clouds. We can't go there."

"Sure we can," he repeated. By this time the lower climbers had caught up. He saw Sara in their midst and called, "Add another layer," in her general direction. "It'll get colder before it gets warmer."

"This is nothing compared to what we ski in," one of the boys said. He was the captain of the soccer team and one of the few who hadn't yet put anything on over his shorts.

The others were busy pulling sweaters from their packs and hurrying into them. Noah, who had taken a wool hat from his pack, gestured the boy aside. In a voice that wouldn't carry beyond them, he said, "I'm sure you've seen worse, Ryan, but the fact is that it could be damn cold up a little farther. Once you get chilled, you'll have a hard time warming up."

"I'm fine," Ryan said, and returned to his friends.

Noah pulled on the hat along with a pair of wool mittens. He looked down the line, relieved to see that many of the others had done the same, including Sara. When the backpacks were in place again, he led them on.

They scrambled over the rocks for an hour before stopping for peanut-butter crackers and more clothes. When an argument broke out in one of the groups, he started toward it, then stopped. Ryan was saying that it wasn't cold; his group was telling him that it was, and that he'd slow down the others if he got cold later on, and that that wasn't fair. In the end he put on a sweatshirt and sweatpants. Noah was pleased, in part because he didn't want the kid to freeze for the sake of his pride, in part because group dynamics were finally kicking in.

This time when they moved on, those at the front stuck closer to Noah than before. They were frightened, which was fine, as far as he was concerned. Without fear there would be no sense of achievement, which was what he wanted most for them.

The rain started slowly, in random drops that came and went and caused more apprehension than damage. Though wearing rain suits now, they were exposed and vulnerable, a ragged cord of climbers moving six by six through the lowering mist toward a point they couldn't see.

Noah felt the anticipation building, both in himself and in those around him. "Tired?" he asked, and was gratified to receive head shakes instead of complaints. Yes, there was fear, but they had come too far to turn back. Stubbornness had set in, and determination. The troop huffed and puffed but climbed on.

When the skies opened and the rain came in earnest, there were some complaints and open epithets from the faculty members, but the voices were quickly drowned out. Leaning into the deluge and the shifting fog, the group closed in and climbed more slowly, moving higher and higher until finally, on what looked like little more than another of the plateaus they had reached so many times before, Noah stopped.

"Here we are," he said. "Knife Edge."

There was utter silence behind him. He dared a glance back to find those who had been closest to him staring in horror at the path ahead. As lower climbers joined them, all, save the young couple who had done the climb many times before, looked similarly horrified.

Knife Edge was a span of rock barely ten feet wide that undulated along the top of the mountain. They would be following it single file for a mile until they reached their trail of descent.

Noah could feel their terror, even shared some of it, and in that instance wondered if he had made a mistake. Even with two experienced climbers along, as the Head of Mount Court Academy, he was the one ultimately responsible for the group. Knife Edge had thrown better climbers than he into a tailspin.

"We can't go on that," came one cry.

Then another: "There's nothing on either side but clouds."

And another: "There's nothing to keep us from falling off."

"No one's falling off," Noah said. "I've been here in the snow, and no one fell off then. Jane, Steve," he called to his backup, "are you planning on losing anyone here?"

"Nope!"

"No way!"

"The path is perfectly safe," Noah told the group. "We'll just take it slow."

"I'm not crossing that."

"Me neither."

"Let's go back the way we came."

Noah had wanted a challenge, and a challenge he had. He shook the rain from his glasses. "We can't go back the way we came. The vans will be waiting for us here." He put the glasses back on. "Look," he said calmly, but loud enough to be heard above the rain, "the path is safe. We'll go single file and stay close. Anyone who is uncomfortable walking alone can hold on. Okay?"

Knowing that the longer they stayed there, the more frightened they would be, he called Abby Cooke to the front. His voice brooked no dissent. "You lead the way with your group. Steve and his group will be right behind you."

Abby stared doubtfully at the path, which at that moment looked like the thinnest ribbon of rock in a swirling cauldron of fog. Noah was acutely aware that more than one climber had died falling off its edge in a panic. He put a hand on her shoulder. "The rock looks wider when you're actually on it. It just rolls across the top of the mountain. Go slowly, but keep it steady. The day is wearing on."

He hated to pressure her, but the fact was that if they didn't traverse Knife Edge and start down, they would be engulfed in darkness long before they reached the bottom. That would be a challenge in and of itself.

Pale and quiet, Abby started off. Noah sent each member of her group off after her with the squeeze of an arm and quiet words of encouragement. "Just keep to the center of the path and relax. One after the other. . . . That's right. Good. . . . That's it. Hold on to the jacket of the person in front of you if you're frightened."

This was Sara's group. He figured it would be more able to handle Knife Edge than some of the others and would set a good example. If someone freaked out, he preferred that it happen in Jane's group or Steve's, better still at the back of the pack, where few would see and catch on.

Steve set off with his five, then, cautiously, Gordon and his.

"In the center, Sherri," Noah coaxed. "That's it. Good, Morgan. Hold on. That's fine."

By the time the third group was making its faltering way along the rocks, Abby's group was lost in the clouds ahead. The rain came steadily. The fog rose on either side of the path.

The fourth group set off, a reluctant caterpillar making its slow and uneven way behind Jane. The fifth group gathered around Noah. Annie Miller was in tears.

Noah put an arm around her and spoke by her temple. "You can do this, Annie. You're as physically coordinated as they come."

"But I can't see the path."

"Sure you can. It's wider than you think, much wider than you. Remember that, and take it one step at a time." He reached out for Ryan and brought him close. "Annie's following you, Ryan. She'll hold on to the back of your jacket. Just take it slow and steady. Got that?"

Ryan nodded, though he looked none too steady himself.

Noah gave Annie a squeeze. "We'll be right behind you. You'll do fine."

She started off gingerly, gripping Ryan's jacket, hunching into herself, but moving.

"Stay together," Noah urged the others as one by one he sent them off, leaving only Tony Phillips and the final five students. He turned to find one of the latter sitting on the ground and knelt beside her. "Julie?"

She shook her head. She wasn't budging.

"Can't stay here forever," he coaxed, acutely aware of the passage of time, the rain, the chill.

She nodded vigorously.

The others in the group knelt around her, dripping wet and shivering. "We have to go, Julie."

"It's too cold to stay here."

"You can do it."

"I never asked to go mountain climbing," Julie cried.

"Neither did we, but we're here."

"We've come too far to turn back."

"We made it up the mountain. Now's the easy part."

"That isn't easy!" Julie screamed in a tone that suggested she was on the edge.

Noah, who knew that things wouldn't get better until she saw for herself that the path wasn't made of thin ice, put an arm around her and pulled her to her feet. The others crowded in.

"You can hang on to me, Julie," said Mac, the only senior boy in her group. He had been heavily disciplined for using sexually derogatory language to a female faculty member, but his chauvinism was welcome now. "I'll go right in front of you."

"I can't," Julie wailed.

"I'm scared, too," one of the other girls cried, "but no one ahead of us has fallen off."

Julie backed up, right into Noah, who didn't move an inch.

"Come on, Jules," Mac said, taking her hand. Between his gentle pull and Noah's small nudge, they moved her to the start of the path. Tony Phillips set off, followed by Brian, then Hope, then Mac, then Julie, and Marney, who squeezed in between Julie and Noah and put her hands on Julie's waist.

"I won't let you fall off," she called over Julie's wet shoulder, then shot a terrified glance over her own shoulder at Noah. "Don't let me, either."

"I won't," Noah said. He stayed close behind her, talking to her so that she would know he was there. He called encouragement to Julie and those in front of her and peered through the clouds ahead for sight of the others, but the visibility was too poor to see much of anything.

He pushed the thought of tragedy from mind, but it kept coming back, along with every sort of remorse imaginable. He cursed himself for thinking that he could successfully lead so large, untried, and reluctant a group, even with two experienced climbers along. He cursed the mountain, cursed the weather, cursed the Mount Court Board of Trustees for hiring him in the first place.

Knife Edge should have been crossable in half an hour, but they spent three at it. The weather slowed them to an agonizing pace that was further delayed by panic stops. When the group worked together, the panic passed. That was some solace, what with the self-reproach Noah was feeling.

The sky darkened. Dusk was fast approaching and so was foreboding. "Can we pick it up any?" Noah called, then quickly muttered, "Forget that. You're doing just fine."

They stumbled along in the rain, crossing one stretch of rock to the next. "Center of the path," Noah yelled from time to time when someone strayed perilously close to the edge. He was in a cold sweat by the time they finally reached the spot where Knife Edge ended and the rock flared out into a wider, safer plane.

They were greeted by the wild applause and cheers of the waiting groups, then by hugs and laughter—even *he* hugged and was hugged—and in that short period, before the reality of the descent could loom before them, Noah knew that the trip had been worthwhile. The climbers were cold, wet, and tired, but spirited and enthusiastic enough to include him in their glee. They had tasted a kind of victory that not one of them had ever tasted before.

It kept them bolstered, even when night fell and the descent grew labored. What with rest stops and snack stops and stops when someone stumbled in the dark and fell, it was midnight before they reached the vans and four in the morning before those vans finally turned in under the wrought-iron arch and pulled around the campus drive to the dorms.

"Sleep in today," Noah told them as he sent them off to bed, and for once no one argued.

Exhausted, he headed for his own house, but exuberance kept him awake. He stood for a time at the back window with a cup of hot cocoa, thinking how much he wanted to tell someone what had happened, if only to keep it real. But he didn't have anyone, and the sadness of that seemed all wrong, given the victory he had scored. So, when the first hint of dawn cast its slim line of light on the horizon, he put on his running shorts and set off for town.

Paige awoke at six to tiny sounds coming from the monitor that linked her room to the baby's. She crept upstairs to change Sami's diaper, then brought her down, warmed a bottle, and settled back into bed. Kitty joined them, curling in a ball at Paige's feet.

"There," Paige whispered to Sami. "How's that?" She gave the pillows another nudge. "Better?" Comfortable and lazy with the pleasure of staying warm in bed on a cool October morning, especially when she knew she'd have to get up before long, she watched

Sami drink. Tiny hands framed the bottle, overlapping Paige's. Sami's eyes held hers.

"Taste good?" Paige whispered with a satisfied smile. "I'll bet it does, warm milk going down just the right way." As she said it, she ran her thumb down Sami's tummy. Sami drew up her legs and made a gurgling sound that Paige chose to think was a laugh. She gave the little girl a kiss on the tip of her nose.

Settling back onto the pillow, she was struck by the loveliness of the moment. It had become a miniroutine, this early morning time with Sami, stolen moments before the day began. The house was quiet, save for the soft sound of sucking and the gentle beat of rain on the leaves of the trees in the yard. Between those lulling sounds and the warmth of the bed, of Sami, and even of kitty, she felt an unexpected peace. She knew it couldn't last. Sami and kitty both were temporary fixtures in her life, and it was surely the novelty of their presence that gave the illusion of peace. Still, it was nice for now.

A tap came at the window. Paige guessed it was a branch from the nearby maple and ignored it, until it came again, more insistently. She looked at the window and gasped. After setting Sami down, she climbed from bed and raised the sash.

"What are you doing here at this hour?" she asked in an urgent whisper. The last thing she wanted was for Jill to wake up, look down, and see Noah.

"Running." He was out of breath. "Had an incredible experience. Had to tell you about it."

The incredible experience was seeing him there with what precious little he was wearing clinging to his body. "It's six-thirty in the morning!" she managed to say.

"Can I come in?"

"No!" She tried to pull her nightgown more tightly around her, but it was a poor substitute for a robe, and then Sami began to whimper, so she hurried back to the bed. "Shhhh, sweetie, it's just Noah." She sank down, returned the bottle to the child's waiting hands, and looked up just as he climbed through the window.

Her protest came too late. He was already in the room, shutting the window behind him. "Noah, this is *my* morning, *my* house." And he was disturbing her peace.

He looked around, spotted the bathroom, and disappeared, only to emerge seconds later wiping first his glasses, then his face and neck with a towel. His shoulders were leanly muscled and gleaming.

"Still raining," he said unnecessarily. His sneakers, running shorts, and singlet were all drenched. "But it was incredible. We were up there at the top of the mountain." He peeled the singlet over his head, tossed it aside, and rubbed himself down with the towel. "I thought for sure I'd made one hell of a mistake. I mean, the rain was coming down. The path was obscured by the clouds. The kids were terrified"—he shimmied out of his shorts between swipes with the towel—"and I mean *terrified*. I thought we were in for a major disaster"—he kicked off one sneaker and bent to dry his leg—"someone falling over the edge, someone pushing someone *else* over the edge." He kicked off the other sneaker. "And then they came together. I mean, it worked the way it was supposed to, but I didn't think it would. So help me, I didn't."

Tossing the towel aside, he came to the bed and then slipped under the covers. "God, am I freezing," he said, sliding closer to her. "And tired. Haven't slept in twenty-four hours." He tugged off his glasses and closed his eyes. "Just wanted to tell you. The good news."

Paige wanted to say something. She tried to think of what it was. But the sight of Noah Perrine naked had swept every other thought from mind, and then it was too late. While she stared in astonishment, his features slackened, his breathing slowed, and he fell into a deep sleep.

For a minute she didn't know what to do. He couldn't stay long; having a naked man in her bed was the worst kind of example to set for Jill, and she wasn't sure whether Sami should be seeing him, either, though the little girl seemed no worse for the experience. She was drinking her milk happily, making the same sweet sucking sounds, now mixed with the slow sough of Noah's breathing.

Kitty rose from her ball, stretched herself shoulders to rump, and hopped over the lumps in the bed until she reached Noah's face. She explored it with her nose. He didn't move. She caught sight of a corner of the sheet extending beyond his shoulder and bounded toward it. He didn't move then or when she began to play.

It struck Paige that for someone who had spent years enjoying a wide expanse of bed in solitude, she had quite a crowd in it now. Assuring herself that it was a temporary condition, she felt an odd pang low in her stomach. But the pang wasn't unfamiliar. She let Sami finish her bottle and burped her, then sat her in the playpen and retreated into the bathroom.

A short time later, she emerged freshly showered. Noah hadn't moved an inch. His damp hair looked darker than usual, all the more so against the white of her pillow, and his limbs seemed to stretch forever under the covers. He had the solid build of a casual runner, not skinny as a fanatic would be, but well toned. Even as she told herself that he had no business being in her bed, she couldn't deny that he did wonderful things to the shape of her sheets.

Sami was still sitting—the skill had come quickly, as Paige had known it would—and was gravely studying a small stuffed dog while kitty struggled to climb the mesh walls of the playpen and join her. The tiny animal made it halfway up before losing her footing and tumbling back down, but on the next try she crested the top and scrambled inside. Sami looked at her, made a soft sound of greeting, and reached out.

Something was agreeing with her here, Paige thought with more than a little pride. Granted, someone else would be taking over her care before long, but Mara would be pleased with what Paige had done. Not that it had been hard. Sami was an incredibly easy baby. She ate and she slept. She took her shots with barely a peep and put up with the exercises Paige did morning and night. The amoeba infection she had come with had cleared itself up, and if there had been emotional problems, they were responding to love.

Wrapped in a large towel, Paige bent over the playpen. She reached in and stroked Sami's head. "That's kitty. Can you say it? Kit-ty. Look at her play. . . . Oooops, she has your ball. Let's get it." Paige reached for the knobbed toy. She squeezed it into a squeak, then held it out for Sami to grab.

Sami stared at Paige.

"Here," Paige said. She rubbed the ball against Sami's hand. Sami looked down, studied the ball, cautiously put her hands on either side of it. "That's right," Paige encouraged. "That's my girl."

She straightened and looked at Noah, who remained dead to the world. So she dressed and dried her hair, then scooped Sami from the playpen. The silence from the second floor told her that Jill was still asleep, which was nothing new. She was a typical teenager. Paige didn't have the heart to wake her until it was absolutely necessary.

Holding Sami on her hip, a shield against temptation, she came down on a knee on the bed and called a soft, "Noah? Wake up, Noah."

He breathed deeply in, deeply out.

"You can't sleep here," she sang. "I have impressionable children in this house."

Actually, Sami didn't seem impressed at all. She was studying Noah the same way she had her stuffed dog, curiously but unattached.

"Noah?" Paige called more loudly, then gave a staccato, "Noah."

He drew in a breath and turned over.

She sighed, straightened, and said in a full voice, "Okay. Just until Sami and I have breakfast. Then you have to leave."

She shut the door tight with kitty inside and told Sami, "Let her pounce on him for a while. He'll wake up."

But he didn't. Twenty minutes later he was sleeping as soundly as before. This time Paige shook his shoulder. "Noah?" She shook it again. "Wake up, Noah."

He made a disgruntled sound.

"Noah."

One eye came open. Paige saw no sign of recognition in it.

"You have to get up, Noah. You can't sleep here. Jill will be waking up soon, and a representative from the adoption agency is coming by. The last thing I need is for either of them to see you."

He stared at her for another minute. "Paige?"

She rolled her eyes.

He looked around in confusion, until understanding slowly came. Then he made a tired sound.

"Look," she said, and one part of her wasn't lying, "I'd like to let you sleep here, but this is a really bad time. The rain has let up. You can run on back to Mount Court."

He had both eyes open now, focused on her in a muzzy way. "How long have you been up?" he asked.

"A while now."

"You look great."

She didn't want his compliments. They were too potent at a time when she had other things on her mind. "You have to leave, Noah."

"Did I tell you about the trip?" he asked without raising his head from the pillow.

She nodded. "I'm glad it worked out well, given that half of my team missed practice yesterday. So now who's the stickler for discipline?"

"I was taking your advice and being flexible." He shifted under the covers. "Your bed feels great."

"You shouldn't be here."

"Did you get your period?"

She nodded.

"Thanks for telling me."

"It happened just this morning."

"Ahhh. Are you relieved?"

"Very. Aren't you?"

"You bet. Kids should be planned. I bought a box of condoms the other day. Of course I didn't think to bring any along when I ran over here."

"That's fine, because nothing's happening," she said, though there was a stirring inside that belied the words. Something was happening all right. He hadn't touched her, and he was turning her on, particularly incredible given the ache her period caused. She stood up and begged, "Please leave, Noah. I have to get on with my day, and I can't do it while you're in my bed."

One long arm came from beneath the covers. It lay on the comforter for a minute, before the rest of him emerged.

Paige stepped back. She told herself to leave the room—then told herself to stay and make sure *he* left—and all the while she watched him dress. When he was done, he put on his glasses and finger-combed his hair. Then he looked at her and kept on looking.

"What?" she asked, none too steady.

He said nothing, simply came forward, took her face in both hands, and kissed her on the mouth.

It wasn't until she heard the front door closing that she realized he was supposed to have gone back out the window and snuck off through the trees.

An hour later Paige was sitting in the living room, holding Sami on her lap, while the adoption agency's Joan Felix looked through the papers Paige had just passed her.

"Financial report, personal report, medical report, professional record, birth certificate—everything seems to be here," she said and smiled up at Paige. "There was never any question about a temporary placement, of course. You're eminently qualified for that. I don't have to study these papers to know that you're every bit as qualified for a long-term placement. I take it you're willing to do that?"

Paige turned one bright plastic key after another around a plastic key ring, while Sami watched in fascination. "From the start I said I'd keep Sami until an adoptive family is found. The last thing she needs is to be passed from foster home to foster home."

"Will you have a problem attending the preadoptive sessions we run?"

Mara had told Paige about those. Held biweekly in Rutland, they were group meetings of the agency's foster and adoptive parents of foreign-born children. Their purpose was both educational and supportive.

"I have no problem with those," Paige said.

"It may take a while to find the right family."

"I understand that."

"Do you?" Joan asked kindly but bluntly. "Given Sameera's background, placing her won't be as easy as placing some babies, not in as homogenous a state as Vermont. Of those families currently in our files, none are appropriate. New families are always coming forward, and we do coordinate with agencies in other states, but I think you ought to know what we're up against."

Looking at Sami, adorable in a green-and-white-striped playsuit with a white ribbon in her hair, Paige couldn't understand why any parent-to-be wouldn't snap her up in a minute. She was healthy, even-tempered, and bright. Paige also could swear that she saw the germs of affection, if the way the little girl was clinging to her arm was any indication.

"What if it takes a year or two?" Joan asked.

A year or two. Paige felt a twinge for Sami's sake. "Won't placing her get harder the older she gets?"

"Yes and no. The older she gets, the more personality she has, and the more appealing she may become. Parents are often scared off by statistics. Knowing that this little one was nearly killed at birth because she was born female, knowing that she was stashed away for the first two months of her life before being passed from orphanage to orphanage, is pretty gruesome. The older she gets, the more that fades away. The older she gets, the more Americanized she becomes. Vermonters like that."

Paige grunted.

"The problem," Joan cautioned, "is that the older she gets, the more attached she'll be to you and vice versa. It's a problem all foster parents face. When the time comes, will you be able to give her up?"

"I think so," Paige said. She didn't look at Sami this time. "There's so much else going on in my life."

"Do those other things make taking care of her difficult?"

"Oh, no." She held Sami closer, loving her warmth and her sweet baby smell. "Not at all. It's working out fine. She's doing well."

"That's obvious," Joan said. She sat back, looking from Paige to Sami and back. "Would you consider adopting her yourself?"

"Me? Oh, I couldn't. I never planned on having a child."

"That doesn't mean you wouldn't make a wonderful mother."

But Paige had her doubts. Her own mother had been lousy at it; she had needed her freedom, and though Paige was much more of a homebody than Chloe, everything was relative. Being a homebody to Paige didn't mean staying home with a baby. It meant being daily on the go within the confines of a small town and returning home quite happily each night. Now she had Jill to baby-sit, but Jill would have her own baby before long, and Paige would have to hire another sitter, which wasn't fair to Sami. She deserved a full-time mother.

"Well . . ." Joan sighed and slipped the papers into her briefcase. "Do think about it. I'll file these and be back next week to talk more. In the meantime, we'll be on the lookout for an adoptive family, if you're sure that's what you want."

"It's the best thing for Sami," Paige said, and believed that it was, all the more so when Peter cornered her the next morning.

Thirteen

W hat's up?" Paige asked, settling in at her desk with a cup of coffee and a curious look at Peter.

"We have to talk," he said from the door. He slid a look at Angie, then folded his arms over his chest. "What's going on around here is absurd. I'm tired, Angie's tired, you're tired. Things were supposed to level off once the trauma of Mara's death passed, but it hasn't happened. We need help. We need a fourth doctor."

Angie groaned, expressing Paige's sentiment exactly.

"I know it's hard for you both"—he looked from one to the other—"you're still feeling an allegiance to Mara, but, damn it, she's dead. She's up on that hillside, cold as stone. She doesn't know we're working our butts off, so what's the point?"

Paige couldn't put the point into words.

"Okay," he tried, "so you don't want to see someone else walking in and out of her office, but you sold her house, didn't you?"

"I had to," Paige said, defending the action, reluctant though it had been. "The monthly mortgage was going to waste. And besides, the Realtor had a buyer." Paige liked the family. Husband and wife were stockbrokers, fed up with city life, determined to work by computer out of their home. They had two children and believed in feeding the birds. "But it wasn't easy for me. It doesn't seem right that Mara isn't there."

"She's *dead*," Peter snapped. "Why can't people accept that? It's bad enough here in the office; not a day goes by without someone asking about her, like she has a cold and will be back at the end of the week, and it's worse in town."

"She was loved," Angie said with envy and no small amount of sadness.

So are you, Paige thought, and tried desperately to catch Angie's eye to convey the message, but Angie was looking at Peter, who was scowling.

So she reached into her pocket and unfolded the letter she had been reading that morning before work. "Mara didn't think she was loved."

"Are you kidding?" Peter asked sharply. "People thronged to her. She *adored* that."

"Listen," Paige said, and read, " 'Life is so busy here sometimes that I fool myself into thinking that there's a deeper meaning in it, but the fact is that everyone has his own life and it's separate from mine. They see me, they talk to me, they even tell me how wonderful I am, then they go home to their own lives and don't think of me at all. I'm incidental in the overall scheme of things. I come and go in people's lives, just as people come and go in mine. Relationships go only so far, then stop, always short of the deep connect. I wonder what's wrong.' "

Angie was stunned. "Mara wrote that?"

"When?" Peter asked.

"I couldn't find an exact date," Paige answered. "It's one of a whole bunch of letters. None of them were ever mailed, but they're all addressed to a Lizzie Parks. Do either of you know that name?"

"Not me," said Angie.

"A *bunch* of letters?" Peter asked. "Have you read them all?"

"Not all. They're pretty heavy. I can only take them in small doses. She truly saw herself as a failure."

"What did the other letters say?" he asked.

"Most of the ones I've read have to do with her family. She would have had us believe that she didn't care about them, but the opposite was true. Calling it an obsession might be taking it too far, but she thought about them a lot."

Peter left the door, took the letter from her, and stared at it front and back. "Why didn't you tell us about these before?"

"Because I felt guilty reading them, they seemed so private, and now I'm betraying her by reading them aloud."

"Then why did you?"

It had been unpremeditated, an impulsive thing, but Paige didn't regret it. "We're all pretty uptight. I thought maybe sharing them would help. It's easy to feel sorry for ourselves, picking up the remains of Mara's life like we are, but the fact is that compared to Mara, we're in good shape. The deep connect—what a phrase. She felt so *alone*, it boggles the mind."

Peter tossed the letter onto the desk. "She was unbalanced. I've been saying that for weeks." He glanced at Angie, then back at Paige. "So, can we interview for a replacement, or should we sit around agonizing over Mara a little longer?"

Put that way, Paige felt foolish. "You're right, I guess. It's silly to wait. We'll need someone else eventually. Eventually might as well be sooner."

When she thought Peter would savor the victory, he was checking his watch. "I'm off for an allergy meeting in Montpelier. You're both covering, right?"

Angie sat straighter. "Not right. I had the afternoon off. What allergy meeting?"

"My usual."

"But that's on Mondays."

"This is a supplemental one."

"Ginny didn't have it on the schedule."

"Then Ginny messed up." He went to the door. "This is why we need a fourth. We're stretched too thin. Can you help Paige, or should I skip the meeting?"

"I can help," Angie said, and he left.

Paige turned to Angie, who was sitting at the side of the room looking peaked, and not only from lack of sleep, Paige knew. Dougie was boarding now, which left her home alone with Ben or, more aptly, waiting for Ben, who wasn't doing much more than making brief appearances there. They were tiptoeing around each other, and though Paige had urged Angie to talk to him, argue with him, even beg him to see a counselor, she refused. She had been burned for years of taking charge, so she was lying low, waiting for him to take the initiative. It was a painful wait. She was dying a little more each day.

Paige, in turn, felt the agony of seeing a friend suffer and wanting to help but not knowing how. "Is working now a problem, Angie?"

Angie let out a breath. "No problem. I didn't have specific plans. I never do lately, it seems. I feel like I need time to think, only when I sit down to do it, I can't."

"Did you talk with Dougie last night?"

"Sure did. He's having a ball, and that's a quote. Don't ask me what it means. He may be doing very little of what he should and a whole lot of what he shouldn't, but one thing's for sure, he's pleased to be free of me."

"Don't you think that's taking it too personally?"

"Maybe." She picked her cuticle. "At any rate, Ben isn't upset. He believes that whatever Dougie does at Mount Court is important for his development."

"You must agree on some level," Paige pointed out, "or you wouldn't have gone along with the decision to let him board."

"I do agree. I guess." She tucked her hand in her lap. "I don't know, Paige. I'm terrified when I think of the harm that could be done to my son's mind, body, ego, if this doesn't work out. But then, some of Ben's arguments have merit. I have been protective. Maybe overly so. I can see that now. I just wish that we could have found an in-between measure. Boarding is so *total*." She rubbed her palm against her skirt. "Then again, he's home on weekends, and on those times he's his old affectionate self, so maybe Ben's right. Maybe the problem was me, after all."

Paige could hear it coming. She left the desk. "Angie—"

"I've failed as a mother."

"No way." Paige perched on the edge of the chair by Angie's. "No way *at all,* and you have an incredible kid to prove it. Think about it, Angie. We've seen hundreds of kids over the years. Some of them have been troubled in ways that stem directly from their parents. Think of the Welkes, the Foggs, the Legeres—*they* are failures as parents, but you aren't in any way, shape, or form related, even with a gross stretch of the imagination, to any one of them. Dougie isn't troubled. He isn't suicidal. He doesn't skip school to play body games with girls behind the maintenance building. He doesn't drink on the steps of the war memorial. He doesn't steal hubcaps from tourists passing through town. He's a well-adjusted kid who has reached the very normal stage of needing to share more of his life with his peers. It's possible that if Mount Court had been three hours away, he would never have wanted to board, but it was an incredible temptation to him—to board and still have his parents close by. The kid has the best of both worlds. He's a smart little guy."

"Not so little," Angie mused. "I have to keep reminding myself of that—and of the fact that he's rooming with one of the top students in his grade, and that his dorm parent is new and very good, and that the Head of School has enough confidence in the system to let his own daughter live in a dorm. Did you know he had a daughter at Mount Court?"

Did she ever; but Paige had thought it a secret. "Who told you?"

"Marian Fowler," one of the few Tucker natives on the Board of Trustees. "I called her right before Dougie moved into the dorm. I knew she'd give me a positive picture of the school, but that was what I wanted. She said that if the new Head trusted the school with his child, I should, too." She paused, cautious now. "I heard something else about the new Head."

Paige arched a brow, understating her curiosity.

"I heard," Angie said, "that he was seen leaving your house early one morning. Do you run with him?"

The front door, rather than the window. Paige had known that would come back to haunt her. "Uh, not really. But we are friends. He was out running one morning and stopped by to say hello."

"Good friends?"

Paige shrugged as casually as she could. She didn't know what to call the kind of friend Noah was. She wasn't even sure she should be calling him a friend, but the alternatives were either boss or lover, neither of which would do.

"He's a handsome man," Angie invited.

Had Paige denied it, Angie would have been instantly suspicious. So she didn't try. "That was the first thing that struck me. I would have thought the girls at Mount Court would have crushes on him right and left." She shook her head. "They can't stand his rules. Neither can I. He can be rigid."

"Reassuringly so, from a parent's standpoint," Angie commented. "It was only after I talked with him that I felt at all at ease about Dougie boarding."

Paige imagined Noah at his desk talking with Angie. No doubt he would be reassuring. He was articulate, smooth, clearly dedicated to his cause. Given that his was only a year's appointment, he might have easily maintained the status quo. Instead he had gone out on a limb, taking unpopular stands. Paige might not agree with some of those stands, but she had to respect his courage.

She hadn't seen him since the morning he had left her bed. Not in real life, at least. In her mind, a dozen times, and each time in the buff.

"Paige?"

"Hmmm?"

"What's that look?"

"No look," she said, embarrassed. "Just irrelevant thoughts."

"Then add these. The last school Noah Perrine worked at was a private school on the outskirts of Tucson. He had worked his way up from science teacher to director of development and was on a direct track to the headship when he suddenly resigned his position. It seems that his work required a fair amount of travel. His wife, who was a native New Yorker and wasn't wild about being in the desert to begin with, was even less pleased when he was gone. She felt he was abandoning her to raise their daughter alone. So she took up with another teacher at the school. By the time Noah returned from his last trip, the whole school knew what was going on."

Paige's heart went out to Noah. "How awful."

"It was a small school. Word spread quickly. He knew right away that he couldn't ever be Head there, so he left."

"He must have been humiliated," Paige argued. She didn't believe he had left solely because he would never be Head. He didn't strike her as that ardently ambitious. "In such a close environment, it would have been an untenable situation."

Angie went on, seeming steadier now that she was imparting information. "The wife and her boyfriend left soon after he did. They moved to San Francisco and married, and for years they were part of what they thought to be the academic elite. Last year they split."

Ahhhh. That might explain problems between Sara, whom Paige had always seen as more wounded than malicious, and her mother. If the tension of a failing marriage was rocking the home, if Sara blamed her mother for it, if she was losing the father whose name she had taken years before and turning to Noah as a source of stability, the move made sense.

Of course, that said nothing about the dubious involvement Noah had had with Sara over the years and the fact that their relationship was far from strong.

Angie was looking crushed. "It seems to happen more and more, parents splitting, kids suffering. That's what worries me most."

Paige forced herself back. "Dougie?"

"What he's thinking about Ben and me."

"What are *you* thinking about Ben and you?" Paige asked just as the phone buzzed. She pressed the intercom. "Yes, Ginny."

"The examining rooms are filled."

"Be right there." She hung up, looking at Angie expectantly.

"I'm not thinking much," Angie said in dismay, and rose. "I'm trying to get through one day at a time."

"But if you talk with Ben—"

"If I talk with him," she went to the door, "I may hear things I don't want to hear."

Paige was right beside her, holding the door shut. "Like what?"

"Like without Dougie there's nothing. Like we've grown in different directions. Like he wants a divorce. Like he loves *her*."

All painful things. Paige wanted to deny each, but she wasn't an expert on Ben or on any other man, where matters of the heart were concerned. The only thing she knew was that she didn't want the demise of Angie's marriage to haunt her the way Mara's death did.

"So you're not saying anything, hoping the problem will go away. But it won't, Angie. It may recede for a time, but if it's there, it's there. You can only ignore it for so long. Talk with him. You have to."

"I know," Angie wailed softly. "I know." She drew herself up, the professional once again. "Have to go to work."

"Will you talk to him?"

"I'll think about it."

"Please, Angie? Talk soon?"

With a look that said, "Enough," Angie opened the door and left the office.

Paige and Angie saw all of the scheduled patients and then some between that midmorning point and the lunch break that was built into the appointment book.

As happened often, Paige lingered with her last patient, leaving herself ten minutes to eat a tuna sandwich and call home to check on Sami, before starting on the afternoon cases. She had until three, when she would pick up Sami and head for Mount Court. Jill had asked for the afternoon and evening off to help the mother of one of her friends prepare a surprise birthday party for the girl, and Paige wasn't about to refuse. Jill needed to be with her friends. And Paige liked taking Sami along.

Shortly after two, though, Jill called, out of breath and upset. "I took Sami for a long walk, like I told you I would, and when we got home, the back door was open. Someone's been in there, Dr. Pfeiffer. Someone's gone through your things."

Paige's stomach lurched. "Someone *broke* in?"

"Well, I didn't lock the door. But I'm sure I shut it. I wouldn't leave it open. Not with kitty running around. I called to her, but she didn't come."

"Is Sami all right?"

"She's fine."

"Where are you now?"

"Next door at the Corkells'. I don't know what to do."

Paige put her fingertips to her forehead and tried to think. Her heart was pounding. "Don't do anything, Jill. Just stay where you are. Whatever you do, don't go near the house until I get there. I'll call Norman Fitch. He'll meet me there."

Fortunately Peter had returned and could see the last of her patients. She paused only to call Mount Court and cancel the afternoon's practice, and within minutes was driving across town, trying not to let her imagination run wild. Nothing like this had ever happened to her before, not during her growing-up years in the kind of wealthy suburb thieves loved, nor during her school years in the city. The last place she would have thought it could happen was in Tucker—small, friendly, law-abiding Tucker.

But it had. Someone had entered her house uninvited. Drawers had been rifled, books removed from bookshelves and set aside, papers and magazines fanned. Pieces of clothing lay on the closet floor, seeming less thrown there than inadvertently dropped, but that made the violation no easier to swallow. A neat intruder was an intruder nonetheless. Only the medicine chests showed no sign of trespass, suggesting that the search hadn't been for drugs.

Nothing appeared to have been taken except kitty, who was nowhere in sight. While Norman and his deputy dusted for fingerprints, Paige ran to the Corkells'. She took Sami in her arms and held her tightly, then carried her back to the house and went from room to room.

"Kitty? Kitty? Where are you, kitty?"

She made a second round of the rooms, this time shaking a box of kitty treats, usually a surefire way of drawing kitty from hiding. But there was no small fur-ball scampering out, and Paige grew frightened.

She returned to the front hall to find Norman talking with none other than Noah Perrine.

"I heard you'd canceled practice," Noah said by way of explaining his presence, but Paige's mind was on a single track.

"I can't find my kitten. She must have run out of the house while the door was open." She slipped past, out the door to the front porch, calling, "Kitty? Come here, kitty!" She ran down the steps and began a search of the perimeter of the house, looking behind bushes, into trees, down the window wells of the basement. "Where *are* you, kitty? Here, kittykittykitty!"

Noah met her at the garage. "I don't see her."

Paige was close to tears. "She's just a baby. She isn't used to being outdoors. She can't possibly protect herself against other animals, and if she wanders too far, she'll never find her way back." Still holding Sami, she set off for the neighbor's yard and searched it the way she had her own. Jill was searching, too, and Betty Corkell, and before long the search had spread down the street. Paige's shoulders were aching by the time she returned home. She sank down on the front stairs, propped Sami on the lower step between her legs, and buried her face in her hands.

She didn't have to see to know that it was Noah who settled beside her. The solidness of him was a tangible thing, and that was before he began to rub her shoulders. His hands were masterful. They knew just where she ached.

"She'll show up, Paige. She can't have gone far."

"But she doesn't have a collar. I was just keeping her for a little while, only until I found a permanent home for her, and since she was staying inside all the time, I didn't bother with a tag, but now no one will know where she belongs."

"Maybe someone will find her and keep her. Isn't that what you want?"

"No!" She shot him a glance. "I want to find a home for her myself. A good home. Not just some place she wanders into. Do you know what people do to cats they take on the spur of the moment and then tire of?"

"Don't assume the worst."

"She was abandoned once. Now she's probably wandering around, thinking it's happened again. She was so *sad* then. She may be bigger now, but she's just as helpless."

"Cats aren't helpless. They can fend for themselves."

"This one doesn't know how."

"It's instinct."

"But she's just a baby," Paige said, and put her chin in her palm. On one level she knew she was being foolish. On another she was feeling devastated. "I'll put signs up. Someone must have seen her." Assuming whoever had broken into the house hadn't taken kitty in a car and dumped her far away. Noah's fingers continued their work. After several minutes, leaving one hand on her arm, he slid to the step below. "Hey," he said softly, studying Sami. To Paige he said, "She's getting bigger. Looks none the worse for the excitement around here."

Paige shifted Sami to her lap. The little girl didn't belong to her any more than kitty did, but the worry was there. "Thank God she and Jill weren't home." Her throat grew tight with emotion. She forced words past it. "If anything had happened to either of them, I don't know what I'd have done."

"Do you have any idea who might have broken in or why?" Noah asked.

She shook her head.

"Nothing's missing?"

"Nothing obvious. Television, stereo, CD player— they're all there. Same with my parents' silver, which would have brought in a bundle on the black market."

"Do you keep any patient records, confidential reports here, that someone might have wanted?"

"None."

"Then robbery wasn't the motive, at least not robbery in the traditional sense. Stealing your peace of mind is something else. Do you have any enemies who may be out to give you a scare?"

"Enemies? In Tucker?"

"A difficult case that may have upset a parent? Maybe an *unstable* parent?"

"I have several, but I can't imagine they'd do this. Small-town doctors have a kind of protection. You might disagree with something they say, but you can't tell them to go to hell, or next time you get sick, you're out in the cold." She stood suddenly and went down the stairs. "Kitty?" She looked back up at Noah. "I thought I heard something." She moved aside a rhododendron branch. "Kitty?" But there was neither movement nor noise.

Discouraged, she returned to the stairs. She leaned heavily against the wood railing and looked up at the house. Inside, Norman was making notes on a pad. She had a sudden sick feeling in the pit of her stomach.

"Are you okay?" Noah asked.

"I guess. It's just the thought of a stranger going through my things. The intrusion. The violation." Her imagination took her further, to an image of kitty mutilated and left to die, meowing piteously but with fading strength.

Noah left the stairs and started thrashing through the rhododrendron.

"She's not there," Paige said. "I'll have to go through the neighborhood putting up signs."

But he moved to the next bush and worked his way toward its base. He straightened with a wide smile on his face and kitty in his hand. "You heard something all right."

Instantly relieved and grinning, Paige took kitty in her free hand and hugged her against Sami. She buried her face against the animal's neck, which was soft, warm, and blessedly intact. "I was so worried." At that moment she couldn't imagine sleeping without kitty on her bed.

"Paige?" Norman called from the door. "Can't find any sign of forcible entry, but since the doors weren't locked, that's understandable. Mickey's staying here to dust more while I go asking around the neighborhood. It's possible that whoever it was went in and out the back way through the trees so no one would see, but it's worth a try. Do me a favor and don't move anything until Mickey's done?"

Paige nodded. She looked toward the house and swallowed hard. Her skin crawled when she thought of touching her own private things after a stranger had touched them.

"I'm calling the girls on your team," Noah said. "They'll help neaten up when it's time."

"No, no," Paige said, though she was touched by the offer, "don't do that."

"Why not?"

"Because it'll upset them. They're too young."

"Not too young to help someone who has helped them out many a time. It's a good lesson. Besides, they like you, and they'll like being off campus."

But Paige hated the idea of the girls giving up their evening to clean up her house.

"I'll let them out of study hall for it," Noah coaxed.

At that, she couldn't resist a crooked smile.

Pushing off from the step, he said, "I'll be back." A handful of long strides took him across the lawn to his car.

The van was packed with Paige's team and pizza. By the time it pulled into her driveway, Mickey had left and the local locksmith was at work installing the dead bolts that Paige would never have bought if she were the only one involved. But there was Sami now, and

Jill; Paige wouldn't be able to go to work with a free mind, knowing that they might be prey to a thief on the loose.

Then again, this thief may have deliberately waited until they left the house, may have sat in the bushes and watched. While it was reassuring to think that they hadn't been in danger, the thought that someone had been so calculatingly determined was terrifying.

She tried to think of who it might be and what he might have been after. She still couldn't find anything missing. While the girls neatened the living room and kitchen, she tackled the bedroom.

"This is the worst," Noah observed from the doorway.

Nearly every drawer had been opened and searched, leaving mounds of femininity stuffed haphazardly back in. The closet shelves had been rearranged none too neatly. Mara's knitting basket had been overturned, scattering skeins of yarn hither and yon.

Paige tossed underthings into a laundry basket. She didn't care how many washes she had to run, she would run them *all night* if that was what it would take to restore a sense of purity to her life. "I can't imagine why anyone would do this."

"The world is full of perverts."

Angrily, disgustedly, she tossed a nightgown into the pile. "I always thought Tucker was different."

"No place is different. Not that this had to be the work of a dangerous criminal. It could have been someone with a weird sense of humor. Are you sure nothing's missing?"

She had checked her jewelry box, but nothing was gone. She had checked the closet file that held the official paper on her mortgage, her insurance, her IRA. Nothing was even out of place, as it might have been if the papers had been photographed.

With a sudden pang, she thought of Mara's letters. Pushing aside dresses, blouses, and slacks, she pulled from the closet the apron that Mara had made for her several birthdays before. It had been a joke; Paige had never been much of a cook, despite Mara's attempts to humiliate her into it. The last of those attempts had been this apron. It had no less than a dozen pockets on the front. Mara had claimed that they were deep enough to hold every ingredient Paige would need to bake a chocolate cake in an organized fashion.

Paige didn't know about that, since she still hadn't tried to make a chocolate cake, but the pockets were more than deep enough to hold packets of letters. They were intact, all four, each with its own bow neatly tied.

"Nothing's missing," she said, and wondered why she had thought of the letters with such a pang. Probably because they held great personal meaning. But for that same reason, a thief would be disinterested. Which apparently he had been, since the letters hadn't been touched. Unless he hadn't realized they were there.

But why would anyone want Mara's letters?

"What is it?" Noah asked.

She shook her head. "Nothing special."

"You sure went pale looking for those."

"They're personal."

"Letters from a lover?"

She shot him a droll look. "No, not letters from a lover. I've never had a lover who was that sentimental."

"Would you want one?" he asked, leaning against the bureau, "or would you consider sentimentality a sign of weakness?"

She began tossing T-shirts into a second laundry basket. "Sentimentality isn't a sign of weakness. Nor, though, is it enough to make a lover top-rate."

"What else does it take?"

"Strength, individuality, conviction—traditional values in a man, but macho when they stand alone. Mixed in with a little sensitivity"—she sucked in her breath—"potent."

"You've never found a man like that?"

"No."

"Is that why you've never married?"

"I never married," she said, attacking the drawer with slips and stockings, "because marriage as an institution never held much of a lure. I didn't need it."

"Didn't need the commitment?"

"Didn't need the burden."

"What burden?"

"The *burden.* Obligations. Expectations that can't be met."

"You mean, you don't want to be tied down to one man?"

She made a face to show the absurdity of that.

"Then what expectations can't you meet?" he asked.

"I work, for one thing, and not nine to five. I'm on call many evenings and weekends, and I *like* my work. If someone were waiting for me at home, he'd be in for a long wait."

"Maybe he'd have things to do himself. Maybe he wouldn't mind."

"Maybe not, but it's a moot point, seeing as I haven't fallen madly in love with anyone from Tucker."

"What about me?"

"A, I'm not madly in love with you, and B, you'll be gone in a year. You don't count," she finished with what she thought was a confident flourish, then caught a movement at the door. She looked that way to find Sara by the jamb and quickly crossed the room. "Hey, Sara. How's it going out there?"

"The baby's crying. Can I get her? I have a little brother at home. I know what to do."

Paige took a quick breath. "Sure." She watched Sara leave, then turned back to Noah, who was picking up a scattering of clothes from the closet floor. "I didn't realize there was a child from the second marriage." That complicated things even more.

"Are you washing these?" Noah asked darkly.

She shook her head. "Dry-cleaning. Put them on the bed."

"But you have to sleep there."

"Then the love seat."

"I'll put them in the car," he said, and went to do it.

Facing two filled laundry baskets, Paige piled one on top of the other and carried them to the laundry room. She started the first load of wash, then went up the stairs.

Sara was leaning against the bars of Sami's crib, not touching, just looking. Paige crept to her side and whispered, "She fell back to sleep?"

"I guess." She dropped a hand into the crib and touched kitty, who was curled in a ball. "Did he send you after me?"

"No. He's outside putting things in my car."

"You know, don't you."

Paige didn't pretend ignorance. "That he's your father? Uh-huh." She didn't believe in playing games with adolescent girls who were often smarter than she was. In Sara's case, honesty was a must.

"Did he tell you not to trust me?"

"No. Why would he do that?"

"Because he doesn't trust me himself. He knows I lie."

"Well," Paige said, unable to say one way or another what Noah knew, "I've never seen you lie."

"You have." She looked at Paige with quiet defiance. "There's no baby back home. My mom had enough to handle with me. She wasn't about to have a second."

The hurt rang familiar to Paige. "Did she tell you that?"

Sara fingered kitty's paw. "No, but I could tell. Everything was fine as long as I was invisible, but after a while that was harder to be."

"I know."

"No, you don't," Sara scoffed.

"I do. My parents had me when they were nineteen. I was one major chain around their necks. They wanted to be flying all over the world, not staying home to raise a child."

"But did they?"

"Stay home? For three reluctant years. Then they were gone."

"So who took care of you?"

"My grandmother."

"Was she happy about it?"

"Very. It gave her another shot at parenting. She felt she could do everything right the second time around."

"Don't say that's what my dad's feeling, because he didn't do *anything* the first time around."

"Maybe he sees that was a mistake. Maybe he's trying to correct it."

She didn't answer. After a minute of fiddling with kitty's ear, she nudged the animal closer to Sami. "Do you like him?"

"Your dad? Sure. He's a nice guy."

"I mean, *like* him," she drawled.

Paige drawled back, "I don't *know* him enough to say."

"He looked right at home in your bedroom."

"He was helping pick up. Giving moral support. It's scary, this kind of thing," she said, and looked around. "Whoever was here even went through the baby's things. Why would he have done that?"

"I don't know. Breaking and entering isn't my thing. I just steal from stores."

Paige sighed. She put an arm around Sara's shoulders and said softly, "I'm glad you told me that. If you only steal from stores, then my parents' silver is safe, and

my grandmother's Waterford, and the diamond earrings my father gave me when I turned sixteen." She
tugged Sara toward the door. "Let's go down. You can
help with my room. More appropriate you than your
dad. It's women's stuff."

Late that night, after a semblance of order had been
restored to the women's stuff and everyone had left,
after Sami had taken the evening bottle that she was
on the verge of giving up, and Jill was asleep, and
the new bolts on the doors had been thrown, Paige
crawled into bed. While she absently tossed a tiny
paper ball for kitty to retrieve, she opened another
packet of Mara's letters.

"I love him, I think," she wrote. Paige looked for a
date but could find none. It was pretty old, if Mara was
referring to Daniel in the present tense. Daniel had
been dead for fourteen years.

*It seems I've known him so long, and half the
time we're arguing, but there's a side of him that
few people see. He comes across as a guy who's totally confident, when the opposite is true. He was
the youngest in his family and the least able to do
things the others did. I identify with him in that,
which is maybe why I can understand so much of*

what he's feeling. When I tried telling him that once, he got angry. He doesn't think he's insecure. So I don't tell him anymore, but I can see it in everything he does, especially when he's with me and needs the upper hand.

Poor guy. He tells himself that he's the kingpin of the practice, when everyone knows that he isn't. He brought his local contacts to the group, but he has no business sense. He had his office on the opposite side of Tucker—

Tucker?

—when we arrived. Paige was the one who booked space right next to the hospital, which is where he should have been all along. Paige was the one who put the group together. She was the one who decorated the offices and designed the letterhead and hired Ginny and Dottie.

Paige set down the letter in astonishment. Mara was talking of *Peter.* She snatched it back up and read on.

She did it purposely, of course. She let him take the credit. Maybe she was being polite, or diplomatic. Or maybe she knew how insecure he was, too. What she didn't know then, and doesn't know now, is how hard he fought against that insecurity. He studied his way through school and went into medicine, and he came back to Tucker to hold his head high. I admire him for that—and because he's a good doctor. He may be arrogant sometimes, but there are other times when he's that little boy sitting alone in a corner of the schoolyard, steeling himself against the taunts he is sure will come. Those are the times when I melt. Paige tells me I have a thing for the wounded. She should only know the extent of it.

Paige skimmed the remaining lines of the letter, set it aside, and opened another. Halfway down, she read:

He comes in the middle of the night and never stays long. He says that it wouldn't be good for the group if the others knew we were involved, and maybe he's right. Paige and Angie wouldn't understand the attraction. He can be a pain in the butt sometimes. But they don't know how good it is with him. In the middle of the night, he's a clinger. He holds me like he's afraid someone will come along and snatch me away, and even if he's doing it in his sleep, I don't care. It makes me feel good.

Mara and Peter. So it was true. And Paige hadn't known a thing.

She skimmed that letter, then several more, moving quickly over passages that were blatantly physical. At the next to last letter in the bundle, she slowed.

I shouldn't be surprised, really. I never could sustain a relationship for any length of time. Something always goes wrong.

But it wasn't my fault this time. We were cleaning up after working in his darkroom when I found the pictures buried under a pile. At first I thought they were cut from a book, they were so striking, and then I recognized the model. She graduated from Mount Court two years ago. Peter claims she was of age at the time he took the pictures, and she might have told him that, but he was fooling himself. He could have checked the medical records and found out. She was barely seventeen, posing in the nude in ways that would put him behind bars for years.

He says it's art. I say it's trouble. He says I'm a fine one to talk after giving my husband the pills that killed him, but that wasn't what happened at all. The problem is that if he tells, I can kiss my career goodbye. So it's a draw—I don't tell on him and he doesn't tell on me.

Paige folded the letter with unsteady hands. She didn't want to read more, not that night, at least. She was feeling sick.

That morning Peter had learned about the existence of Mara's letters. He had suddenly had an allergy meeting that hadn't been on the books, and while he had been out of the office, someone had searched Paige's house.

It was too coincidental for comfort.

Fourteen

Paige phoned Peter early the next morning and arranged to meet him at the coffee shop around the corner from the hospital. His house would have offered them more privacy, but she wasn't feeling sure enough of him for that. If the worst-case scenario were true and he was guilty of everything she'd imagined in the course of the long night just past, he was a far different person from the one she had thought she knew.

Oh, she knew he was insecure. During their weekly group meetings, he jumped to his own defense more often than the others. Moreover, she had always suspected that his feelings for Mara ran deeper than he let on. Angie had called it a love-hate relationship; Paige agreed.

But the rest—it was hard to accept.

"Hey, Paige," he called in greeting, looking dapper as always in a tweed blazer and slacks. He winked at the cashier as he strolled past to the table Paige had taken. "What's up?" He pulled out the chair and sat down.

"Coffee?"

"Sure." He turned the mug at his place right side up.

Paige poured from the pot the waitress had brought but left her own mug facedown. She was jittery enough without the caffeine.

He added cream and two sugars and took a drink. Satisfied, he took another, then set the mug down. "Problems?"

"I don't know." She was trying to gauge his mood, without luck. He was the same nonchalant Vermonter he had been the very first time they had met. Whether the nonchalance was natural or deliberate was the question. "You're the only one who can tell me that."

He put his elbows on the table. "Shoot."

"Mara's letters? The ones I told you about yesterday?"

"Mmmm?" He took another drink of coffee.

"I was reading more of them last night. There were a bunch that talked about you."

He set down the mug with a thud. "Does that surprise you? I told you she was hung up on me."

"These were very specific," Paige said in a lower voice. "They talked about a love affair. They talked about accusations each of you made against the other, and a stand-off whereby neither of you would tell if the other didn't."

He was visibly shaken. "Mara was nuts."

"She didn't sound it in the letters," Paige argued. "They made perfect sense. They implicated you as much as they did her."

"Implicated me in what? A love-starved woman's dreams?"

Paige felt suddenly less sympathetic. Mara might indeed have been love-starved, but Peter, in his way, was no less so. "Don't put her down so quickly," she cautioned. "She wrote some upsetting things. I can't just put the letters away and forget about them."

Peter looked disgusted. "You're talking about the pictures. She made a goddamned big deal about those. They freaked her out—mostly because they were artistically superior to anything she could produce herself. They were beautiful pictures."

"She said that."

"They weren't pornographic."

Paige leaned forward. "But she said that your model was underage, and if that's true, we have a problem."

"She was eighteen."

"At the time the pictures were taken?"

"She told me she was eighteen."

Paige pressed her fingertips to her temple. "The problem," she said, trying to remain perfectly calm when she wanted to shriek at Peter for being a fool, "is that she might have lied. I haven't seen these pictures, so I don't know how they'd be regarded by a jury—"

"A jury! Christ, Paige, this isn't a legal case. It never was. It's over and done."

She raised a hand. "Hear me out. I don't know where the line lies between art and pornography, but I do know that you're a pediatrician. You earn your living working with children. You're in a group practice that devotes itself to them. Do you have any idea what would happen—to you, to *us*—if someone, anyone, were to see those pictures?"

"You're assuming they're obscene," he accused, and started to get up. "Thanks for the vote of confidence."

She grabbed his arm. "Please, Peter. This involves all of us. I don't want to assume anything. That's why I'm talking with you now. I haven't said a word to Angie. This is between you and me. *Sit.*"

He gave her a disdainful look but did as she asked.

"Thank you," she breathed in relief. "This is very difficult for me. It's one more hit in a whole string of them. All I'm doing is trying to hold things together."

He cracked his knuckles. "At my expense."

"No. You're part of what I want to hold together. I like you, Peter. I always have, and I respect your medical ability. If not, I never would have hung my shingle beside yours in Tucker, much less dragged two of my friends up here." The responsibility was hers, and an awesome one at that. "Maybe it would have been better for Mara if I hadn't."

Peter's features tightened. "I wasn't responsible for her death."

"I didn't say you were, but apparently she needed something that none of us could give her. The feeling of despair, of total and utter *failure*, that permeates her letters is heartrending. When her father came for the funeral, he said that this wouldn't've happened if she'd stayed home in Eugene."

"But then she wouldn't have been a doctor. That was her greatest source of reward."

"I told him that. Still, there are times when I wonder—" She broke off and chided herself, "Pointless. It's over and done." To Peter she said, "But we aren't. We're still here, and I want it to stay that way. I like what we have, which is why this is all so upsetting for me."

Peter pushed his mug around. "There's no cause for upset. The pictures don't exist anymore. I destroyed them, negatives and all."

"But why, if you thought they were art?"

"Because I'm not dumb, Paige. You're right. We don't know how a jury would judge them. If they had fallen into the wrong hands, I could have been in deep shit. They weren't worth it." He paused. "Aren't you happy? The condemning evidence is gone. The practice is saved. No one can ever accuse one of the pediatricians of diddling with his patients."

She studied her hands, not quite sure how to say what needed to be said. Peter could be volatile when threatened, and he was definitely threatened. Gently she said, "The evidence may be gone, but if there's a problem, it still exists." She clutched his arm before he could rise. "Don't blow up. Just answer me. Is this a problem? Was Mara more upset about the photographs or about the fact that you made them? I have to know, Peter. We deal with children. I can't risk the chance of one of them being hurt."

"This is an insult," he said very quietly.

She squeezed his arm. "I'm simply asking."

"If you knew me, or trusted me, you wouldn't have to ask."

"This has nothing to do with trust. It has to do with what turns people on, and that can't always be controlled."

Peter drew his arm free. He gripped his mug with both hands, looked her in the eye, and in a low, angry voice said, "I'll say this once, and once only.

I love children because they're innocent and trusting and inherently good human beings, but I don't desire them sexually. I desire women. It's a healthy drive, shared by any healthy males, and while I'm on the subject, let me say one other thing. Legally, I have every right to screw a willing eighteen-year-old female."

"I know you do, but that's a technical matter. I can guarantee you—*guarantee* you—that if it came out that you were having an affair with an eighteen-year-old, you'd lose half your practice."

"You're right. That's why I'd never do it."

"How about breaking into my home," Paige threw in, thinking that being a thief was more reputable than being a child pornographer and that since he'd defended himself against the last without going bonkers, he could handle the first. "If you thought Mara's letters would be incriminating, would you try to steal them?"

When he rose from the table, this time she didn't reach out. "You really don't trust me, do you?" he asked.

"I want to. But I've been racking my brain about who else might have done it, and I can't think of anyone with motive but you."

He turned and, slipping a hand in the pocket of his slacks, left the coffee shop without another word.

———————

He didn't talk with her that day or the next. On the instances when their paths crossed, he was either studying a file or otherwise preoccupied. When Angie commented on his distance, Paige shrugged it off, but she felt like a hypocrite. *Communicate,* she told Angie. *Communicate,* she told the girls at Mount Court. *Communicate,* she told her patient families every day of the week.

So she tried. After several days of silence, she cornered Peter in his office. "I know you're furious, but if we don't talk, we can't resolve anything."

"There's nothing to talk about," he said, regarding her coldly. "You made it clear what you thought. I don't need a repeat."

"I didn't say that you did it. I simply asked."

"That was enough."

"But I *had* to ask," she argued in her own defense. "Look at it from my point of view. Circumstantially speaking, you had opportunity and motive. If it wasn't you, I need to know who it was. *Someone broke into my house.* It's not only my safety that's at stake, it's Sami's and Jill's, too."

"Sorry. I can't help you out." He jotted some notes on the report he'd been writing.

"Peter." She sighed. "We can't practice together if we can't talk."

"Oh, we can talk." He tossed his pen aside and sat back. "We can talk about any patient you want. Go ahead. Ask away."

"Did you love Mara?"

"Mara wasn't a patient."

"Did you tell her that she killed Daniel?"

"Daniel," he said, growing angry again, "was a drug addict. She fell in love with him because he was needy, and married him because she thought that the strength of her love alone would haul him out of the pit he was in. When that didn't work, she tried pharmaceutical treatment. I can't say if she killed him. I wasn't there. But by her own admission, she did give him drugs."

"She was trying to wean him off them gradually."

"The guy died of an overdose. That's a fact. Whether Mara was the one who supplied the pills that did it, or whether the local pusher did is something that a medical board would spend months trying to determine."

"Did you actually threaten that?" Paige asked. She didn't believe for a minute that Mara had been responsible for Daniel's death, but if the suggestion was made, if it came before the medical board, if Mara was found at fault such that she lost her license to practice, it would have killed her as surely as the fumes from her car. Her career meant everything to her.

But Peter wasn't thinking that way. "You bet I threatened it. She was on her high horse telling me what a medical board would do with *my* prints, so I turned it right around. Mara could be one hell of a bitch." He pushed a hand through his hair. "Still can. We can't get rid of her. She keeps hanging on."

Did she ever, Paige thought. Nothing had been the same since Mara had died. She wondered if things would ever be the same again.

Discouraged, she leaned more heavily against the door. "So. Where do we go from here?"

"I don't know."

"We can't continue this way. The tension is awful."

"Then we'll split. You take your patients; Angie will take hers; I'll take mine."

"But I don't want that," Paige cried. Splitting up was her solution of last resort. "I like your patients as much as I like mine, and I like working in a group. I want things to be like they were before. It was such a *comfortable* life."

Peter didn't respond. Nor did he look at her. When he picked up his pen and returned to work, she resignedly let herself out of the office, and when the last of her patients had been seen, she set off for Mount Court.

Practice went well. Paige ran from the demons of the day, pushing herself and the girls farther, faster, than usual. She was therefore more tired than usual when she returned to the car and drove home. She was also more distracted, which was why, in hindsight, she didn't sense anything amiss until she pulled into her driveway, climbed from the car, and reached across to the passenger's seat to get the clothes she had worn to work. She cried out in alarm when a face rose from the backseat.

"Sara!"

Sara eyed her somberly.

With a hand to her chest, Paige calmed her breathing. "You scared me half to death. I had no idea you were there. Why didn't you speak up?"

"If I'd spoken up, you'd have turned around and taken me back."

"I can still do that," Paige threatened, but Sara climbed out of the car, crossed the front lawn, and planted herself on the steps.

Paige came to sit beside her. As anxious as she was to see Sami, instinct told her Sara was in greater need at that moment. The girl needed a friend. Paige liked the idea of being one. "Just visiting?"

Sara nodded.

"Does anyone know you're here?"

"I signed out."

"For how long?"

"Until ten."

"Ahhhh." The evening. Once a sacred time for Paige, now a time for visiting with Sami. And Jill and Sara. Family time, in a make-believe way that was rather nice, as novelties went. "Then you'll stay for dinner?"

Sara shrugged. "If you want me to."

"Sure I do. But I have to warn you, I'm on call. If the phone rings, I'm off to the hospital. Did you bring any work to do?"

Sara shook her head.

"No homework?"

"I finished it before practice."

"Ah. That's good. I took chicken from the freezer this morning. Sound okay?"

Sara shrugged.

Paige gave her shoulder a squeeze as she went on into the house. She reached out for Sami, who was playing with Jill on the living room rug. "Hello, sweetie. How's my girl?"

"Gaaaaaaaaaa."

"What a nice greeting! You'll be talking up a storm in no time. Jill, this is Sara. She's from Mount Court." To Sara she said, "Jill is living in to help me with Sami. She was with friends the other night when you all came."

Sara looked suddenly uneasy. "I thought it was just you and Sami."

"One more's no trouble." She put Sami in Sara's arms before Sara could say that she had never held a small child before. "Want a break, Jill?"

Jill ran upstairs to phone her friends. Paige lifted kitty. "Hello to you, too. How's my second girl?"

Kitty meowed.

Sara, who was awkwardly trying to shift her arms around Sami, murmured, "I don't think I'm doing this right. Maybe you'd better take her."

"Let her straddle your hip. . . . That's right. There you go."

Sara and Sami were exchanging wary stares.

"Are you adopting her?" Sara asked.

"No. I'm just keeping her until a permanent placement is found."

"Do you think she knows that?"

Still cradling kitty, Paige came close. "I think she's too young to understand. She knows if she's clean and dry, and if her stomach's filled, and if her world is peaceful. She certainly knows if there's noise and upset, and she knows if she's with people who care. Yes, she's aware if those people change. She knows new people from old, but does she understand that she's come thousands of miles and has more to go before she finally settles? I doubt it."

Sara continued to stare at the child. "It's awful to be bounced around."

"Were you?" Paige asked in response to the suggestiveness of the statement. She wanted Sara to know that she could discuss anything with her.

"Not really. A little, maybe. My father would come to town and take me for the day. I hated it."

"Why?"

"He was strange."

"Strange?"

"A stranger. I didn't know him. I didn't know why he was coming."

"He wanted to see you. He loved you."

"No. It was in his mind. I was his daughter, therefore he loved me. It wasn't an emotional thing."

"You underestimate him."

"If it was real, why didn't he visit more?"

"Maybe he felt awkward, what with your mom and her husband."

"But he was my father."

"He may have thought you wanted to forget that. You didn't have his name."

"That was my mom's idea, and he didn't fight it."

Paige wished she knew more of Noah's side of the story. "Did you ever ask why he didn't?"

Sara scrunched up her nose and shook her head.

"Maybe you should."

"We don't talk about things like that."

"Maybe you should. If it's bothering you—"

"I didn't say that it was," Sara said quickly. "I don't care why he did what he did. He lives his life, and I live mine."

"Seems to me the two are overlapping now."

"Not much. I don't see him often. He avoids me."

Paige let kitty down and gestured Sara toward the kitchen. "I was under the impression that he avoided you because the two of you agreed to keep your relationship a secret." She took a package of chicken from the refrigerator and unwrapped it.

"That was the idea, but it's not working. People are finding out anyway."

"Is *he* telling?" Paige couldn't imagine it. Her impression was that Noah felt a definite loyalty toward Sara. He hadn't told Paige that Sara had lied about having a younger brother, when he might easily have done so.

"Kids find out. They ask questions. They want to know where you come from and who you live with and what you're doing on Thanksgiving vacation."

"Ahhh. So *you* told them."

"Just a few," Sara said defensively. "My closest friends. I had to." Her expression soured. "The rest will find out soon enough. Fall weekend's coming up.

Most everyone's leaving, but I'm not. They'll want to know why."

"You could always tell them California is too far to go for a weekend," Paige suggested. "Then again, you might want them to know the truth. They know you now. Their opinion of you will have already been formed. And maybe their opinion of your father is softening."

Sara looked noncommittal.

"Is it? Is there as much grumbling as there was at first?"

Sara shrugged.

"Didn't the mountain climb help?"

"A little, I guess."

"Well, that's something, then." She took two bottles from the refrigerator. "I have to warn you, I'm not the most imaginative cook in the world. I always do my chicken on the grill out back, but I can do it either with honey-mustard sauce or teriyaki sauce. Which would you like?"

"Honey-mustard," Sara said, then, "Did you mean what you said the other night about not being in love with him?"

Paige took the cap off the honey-mustard sauce. "I don't know him very well. How could I be in love with him?" She coated the chicken with sauce.

"Do you think he's handsome?"

"Very."

"Do you think he's smart?"

"Very. But those things are low on my list of priorities. When I fall in love with someone, it'll be because of the person inside." She grabbed a match. "Hold that thought. I'll be right in." She went out back, lit the grill, and returned to find that Sara had held the thought all right, only it was a slightly different thought from Paige's.

"Would you like to be in love with him?" she asked.

"Actually," Paige said, taking salad makings and a loaf of French bread from the fridge, "I'm not sure I'd like to be in love with anyone right now. My life is a mite busy."

Sara nodded. She shifted Sami in her arms.

"Too heavy?" Paige asked.

"No."

Jill returned, looking excited but unsure. In response to Paige's questioning look, she said, "My friend Kathy has tickets to the Henderson Wheel concert. She says I can have one if you don't need me that night. It's a week from Saturday at the movie house."

Paige didn't like the thought of *anything* at the movie house, but she knew that the concert would go on with or without her approval. She also knew that Jill needed a pickup.

"I don't need you. It's perfect, actually. I work in the morning, but then I was thinking of staying over at my grandmother's. She adores Sami."

"So I can go?" Jill said with an enthusiasm Paige didn't see often enough on her face.

"Call Kathy and say yes before she gives the ticket to someone else." Jill ran off.

It struck Paige that the concert was on the same fall weekend that Sara would be one of the few at Mount Court. "Are you a Henderson Wheel fan?"

Sara made a dubious sound.

"Is that a yes or a no?"

"It's a so-so."

"I could try to get a few tickets if you like"—Forgive me, Mara, but it's for a good cause—"for whoever is left at Mount Court with you."

Sara shook her head. "It'll be a local crowd. They don't like us much."

"Who told you that?"

"Everyone knows. They think we're spoiled little rich kids. They like our money, but that's all."

Paige wished she could have denied it, but years of misbehavior on the streets of Tucker had formed a definite image in the minds of the locals. "Maybe that will change under your dad. So far this year, there haven't been any embarrassing incidents. His rules must be paying off."

She left the kitchen long enough to put the chicken on the grill, then was back to make a salad. By the time she was done, Jill had returned. Paige reached for Sami.

"This little one needs to be changed. Jill, you know where things are, why don't you set the table. Sara, the chicken should be done. You can bring it in."

Paige played with Sami all the way up the stairs and through a diaper change. She was seeing the beginnings of smiles and laughed every time she did. What she loved, though, was the way Sami's arms naturally went around her when she picked her up.

"That's my girl," Paige said, hugging her all the way down the stairs. She set her in the high chair in the kitchen, gave her mashed chicken from a baby food jar and a sliced banana, and sat down to eat with Sara and Jill. She had taken no more than two bites of chicken when the phone rang. She looked at Sara. "I warned you. I'm on call."

But it wasn't her answering service. It was Noah. "I'm a little frantic here, Paige. I need your help. We've searched the entire campus, but we can't find Sara. She hasn't been seen since practice."

"She's with me," Paige said quickly.

"With you? Really?"

"She left campus with me. We're just having dinner."

"Thank God," he breathed. "I've been imagining horrible things."

"You shouldn't have. She signed out."

"No, she didn't."

Paige caught the guilty look on Sara's face. "Aaach. I guess she didn't." To Sara, chidingly, she said, "He was in a panic. They've been looking all over for you."

If Sara was touched, she didn't let on. Paige wanted to shake her.

On the other end of the line, Noah sounded dismayed. "The girls kept talking about the Devil Brothers, saying that it was only a matter of time before they abducted one of the female students. Who in the hell are the Devil Brothers?"

"Not Devil. DeVille. They're two sweet, simpleminded lugs of guys who are Tucker's perennial scapegoats. They're harmless."

"Ahhhhh. The girls were working themselves into a frenzy, taking me right along with them. I'm afraid our secret's out, Sara's and mine. So she's there. Thank God." In the next breath he said, "God help her, the little minx. If she thinks I can give her dispensation from disciplinary action, she's wrong. Particularly now that people know we're related, I'll have to go out of my way to be impartial. She went AWOL. That's worth a detention times ten."

"What's he saying?" Sara whispered.

"You don't want to know," Paige whispered back, then said into the phone, "Can she finish dinner, at least?"

"I'll be there in half an hour."

"Make it an hour."

"Half." He took a shaky breath. "Thank God. I was thinking that I'd taken her away from her mother only to subject her to unspeakable horrors." He took another breath, a steadier one this time. "So, anyway, what are you eating?"

"Chicken, but there's none left for you. Come in an hour and you can have some brownies." She hung up the phone before he could argue.

"Brownies?" Jill said. "We don't have any brownies."

Paige looked from one girl to the other. "Then we'd better get a mix down from the shelf and whip up a batch real quick, don't you think?"

Noah loved the brownies. He didn't love the awkwardness that accompanied Sara and him in the car back to Mount Court. Talking with teenagers was his forte, which was one of the reasons why the difficulty he had talking with Sara upset him. The other was that she needed a father as much as he needed a daughter.

But talking about feelings, perhaps criticizing and being criticized, was risky business for two people who didn't know each other very well. After several minutes of silence, all he could think to say was "I was worried."

"I'm sorry," she answered, though she didn't sound it at all.

"Why didn't you sign out?"

"I didn't think of it."

It's one of the most basic of the dorm rules, he wanted to say. When you leave campus, you sign out. If everyone came and went as the mood took them, we'd never know where they were. Parents entrust the care of their children to the school. We are responsible for our students.

"You know," he mused, "when I envisioned having my own daughter at the school where I taught, I thought I knew the drawbacks. After all, I was in a similar position as you once. So I was thinking how difficult it might be for you, but there's another side to it that I hadn't thought of. Me. Normally parents are miles away and don't know about the little problems at school until those problems are resolved. They don't go through the hell of the worry I did."

She was quiet for so long that he wondered if she'd heard. When he looked at her, she said, "You can always send me home. Then you won't have to know about the problems."

"I don't want to send you home. I want to have you here."

"Maybe I don't want to be here."

"Don't you?"

She didn't answer.

"Sara?"

"I don't know," she mumbled.

"Are you missing California that much?"

"Maybe."

"Looking forward to going back for Thanksgiving?" When she didn't answer, he shot her a glance. "You talk with your mom every week, don't you?"

"Uh-huh."

"Is she doing okay?"

"Sure."

The fact was that Noah had received an irate call from the woman several days before saying that she could never get through on the dormitory phone and asking why Sara hadn't called her. According to Liv, the two hadn't talked in three weeks.

Given Sara's history, Noah tended to believe Liv. But he couldn't say that to Sara. He was doing his best to trust her, in the hope that she would earn that trust in time.

Unfortunately it was taking longer than he had thought, and his patience was growing thin.

For that reason he set great store in the upcoming fall break. It was only five days, Thursday through Monday, but it would be the first time that Sara had stayed at the house with him. It would also be the longest period of time they had ever spent together alone. The annual week with his parents didn't count. This was major parenting.

The prospect of it might have unnerved him if he hadn't been so excited. He wanted her to come to like him and to that end planned a dinner out and a shopping trip to Boston. He would take her to a movie, if she would go. He would play Boggle with her. He was hoping to involve her in redecorating the house, if only to make her feel that it was hers.

He was also hoping to take her canoeing on the river north of Tucker. Canoeing was relaxing and peaceful. It was a tandem activity involving coordination and cooperation and created the kind of atmosphere in which the beginnings of a relationship might be forged, or so he hoped. He knew he would meet resistance along the way, but he was determined to persist. If the weekend proved a bust, it wouldn't be for lack of trying on his part.

Fifteen

Angie, too, was looking forward to fall break. Well in advance, she told Paige and Peter that they wouldn't see her in the office on those days. She wanted lazy time with Dougie—sleeping late, having a leisurely breakfast, knocking around the house, lighting a fire. She wanted him to feel the pleasure of being home.

Had she been the only one involved, she might have pulled it off without a hitch. But there was Ben to consider. For two days, a normal weekend, they could pretend that things were fine, but five days would be harder.

They had canceled the New York trip. Ben hadn't wanted to go in the first place and was happy enough to let his agent do the honors. Once upon a time, Angie would have insisted that they be there, but her days of insisting were done. She didn't feel qualified to insist on much where Ben was concerned. Where once she had spoken for him, she was silent now. She didn't know what he was thinking, didn't know what he was feeling. He wasn't saying much to her but came and went, leaving her imagination to account for his time. She had taken to stopping at his house during the day, but he was rarely home. He did his work, then was gone.

She didn't know where he went and didn't have the courage to ask, mainly because she wasn't sure she wanted to know. She did know that the thought of his being with another woman continued to cut to the quick.

Telling herself that something had to be resolved before Dougie came home for a long and potentially awkward weekend, she drove to the house the afternoon before he was due home, saw Ben's car gone, and kept on driving. She went to the post office in the center of Tucker, but the blue Honda wasn't there, so she continued on down Main Street, past the row of cars parked diagonally in front of the grocery store, the hardware store, the bookstore. She turned the corner and tried the parking lot of the Tavern, then the parking lot of the Tucker Inn. She returned along Main Street, past Reels and the ice-cream shop, thinking she might have missed the Honda the first time around.

Then she went to the library. It was a small gray building with crisp white trim, a relic of Colonial days that was nearly as revered by Tuckerites as the church. When Dougie had been little, Angie had taken him to story hours there; when he had entered school, she had helped him research reports there. When judged by the number of volumes it held, the Tucker Free Library fell short. When judged by the charm of the place and the warmth inside, nothing could beat it.

The blue Honda was parked under a tree. Angie pulled in beside it and sat with her head bowed. From time to time she looked up, but the view was discouraging. Leaves that were a brilliant crimson and gold the week before were starting to fade. With their edges curled, they looked smaller, sadder, more self-contained. Every few minutes, given a fatal nudge by the breeze, one fell from its branch to the ground.

Therein lay the good news. Ben's car didn't have enough leaves on it to suggest that it had been parked for long. The bad news was that it was there at all.

As she had so often in the past weeks, Angie recalled the first time she had set eyes on Ben. She had been drawn first by the air of quiet certainty about him, second by the dryness of his wit, third by the way his smile curled her stomach. He could coax her into taking time off from studying to go to a midnight movie, spend an evening laughing with friends, or climb into the car and drive for hours with the radio blaring their favorite songs.

His lightheartedness had complemented her seriousness. They brought out the best in each other.

She wasn't sure when that had changed. The years between that first day and the present seemed crowded together, twenty-one years of doing everything that had been productive and profitable. Somewhere along the line whimsy had been lost. Their lives had become programmed.

To suit her. He was right. Okay, so she was at fault there, but that didn't justify his taking up with Nora Eaton.

She heard a light tap on the window and looked up as Ben settled against her car mere inches from where she sat. He was wearing the leather jacket she had given him several years before, open to a plaid shirt. His hands were tucked in the pockets of his jeans. He looked healthy, even roguish with the smattering of gray in his hair, but there was neither quiet certainty about him nor a smile. He looked at the Honda, then at the ground, and in that instant, if she had been able to, she would have started the car, backed around, and sped off down the street. But Ben would have been injured, for starters. And then there was the matter of her tears. They came from nowhere and started pouring down her face. It took both hands to hide herself from him.

The passenger door opened and shut. He reached for her and held her with surprising ease over the gearshift. "Come on, Angie. It's not that bad."

"It's terrible!" she cried. The closeness of him, the familiarity of his touch, and the rightness of his scent drove home her dilemma. "My life is coming apart at the seams!"

"It's just us having some troubles."

"But that is *my* life. *Us* is the key to the rest. It's what holds everything together."

He didn't say anything to that, and she herself was wondering where it had come from. She hadn't planned to say it. But the words had popped out, and she couldn't take them back. They were more right than, career woman that she was, she wanted to believe.

It was a minute before she regained a semblance of control, and then she drew back, groped in her jacket pocket for a tissue, and blew her nose.

"I'm sorry. I didn't mean to break down. It was a buildup of things, I guess." When he didn't say anything, she took a deep breath. It shuddered on its way out. "I never thought life could be so fine one day and so terrible the next. Since Mara died—" Her throat grew tight again.

"What's happening to us has nothing to do with Mara."

"I know." She wanted to say that Mara's death had set off a string of events, because that was truly the way it seemed, but he was right. The problems with their marriage had nothing to do with Mara.

"Why aren't you at work?" he asked.

She looked anywhere but at him. "I, uh, take time off in the middle of the day sometimes thinking that maybe we can have lunch together, but when I go home, you're never there. Usually I don't want to know where you are. Today was different."

"How so?"

She would have mentioned Dougie's fall break, had she not realized that it was as irrelevant as Mara's death. So was Dougie if they were talking about the future. For the first time, she could accept that.

Holding the tissue tightly in her hand, she said in a broken voice, "I can't keep on this way. I'm not focusing in on much of anything I do, because my mind keeps wandering back to us. I need to resolve things." She felt an overwhelming defeat. "I had to know if you were with her."

"Today's her day off. Lately I only come here when she's off."

Angie looked up to find him staring at her. "Is that true?"

He nodded.

"She must have a lot of days off. Your car's never at home."

"I drive around," he said in such a begrudging way that it had to be true. "I can't bear the quiet, so I get in the car and drive. There are some days when I start as early as ten in the morning."

Angie might have found solace in the fact that he was upset, had she known something about the nature of that upset. In the past she might have presumed to know that something, but she'd learned better.

"What do you think about while you're driving around?" she asked.

He snorted. "Us. What else?"

He was looking out the window now. Angie didn't feel as much on the hot line herself. "What about us?" she asked.

"I think about the things we used to do that I liked."

Like what things, she wanted to prod, but she held her tongue. She had to stop directing conversations. Ben was a big boy. If he wanted to elaborate, he would.

Sure enough, after a minute he said, "I liked it when we used to do spontaneous things, like cook on that little hibachi out on the rickety balcony of that first apartment we had, or play backgammon until three in the morning. I liked it when we used to be snowed in, when we slept late and went for a walk. Things like that."

"Then I got too busy to be snowbound."

"And I let you," he admitted. "I let it happen. So I'm at fault, too."

Yes, thank you, she thought. If the hours he had spent driving around in his car had produced this realization, she forgave him the driving. The infidelity was something else.

"Are you suing for divorce?" he asked, looking at her now.

She shook her head. "I'm not ready to give it up, but I need to know what's happening with her."

"Nothing. It's off between us."

He looked earnest, but she had to know more. "Why?"

"She was a substitute. A way to fill the time."

"She's been that for eight years. What's changed now?"

"You know now. And I feel like shit."

The angry part of her was glad to hear it, the demoralized part felt a redemption of sorts. She had always thought Ben a man of conscience. Indeed, politically, his cartoons threw a punch for those who couldn't fight for themselves. Mara had loved that. And Angie had been proud.

Despite a lapse, conscience had prevailed. It was gratifying to know that she hadn't been totally wrong.

"What about us?" she asked quietly. "Can we put something meaningful back together?"

He straightened his leg and rubbed its thigh. "I don't know. I'm still angry sometimes."

"When I'm at work?"

"Mostly."

"Do you want me to quit?"

He eyed her cautiously. "Would you?"

She had asked for that one. But there was no weaseling out. "Would isn't the issue," she tried to explain. "It's could. Could I?" She took a shaky breath. "I don't know. Being a doctor is part of who I am. I don't know if I could give it up completely, any more than you could give up drawing."

"I've been drawing since I was two."

"I've been wanting to be a doctor nearly as long."

"Art is part of the psyche."

"So is the need to heal."

A silence settled between them, heavily on Angie's heart. In the back of her mind were Paige's desperate urgings—*Talk to him, Angie, tell him how you feel*—and then Mara's writings—*I come and go in people's lives, just as people come and go in mine.*

At that moment, Angie identified with Mara. But it was the last thing she wanted.

"There has to be a compromise," she burst out. Meekness wouldn't do when one had reached a crossroads in life. "It can't end like this. We have too much in common, too many things we both like. We have a history together—"

"And a child who's coming home for vacation tomorrow," Ben broke in with an echo of the sarcasm that had been so prevalent of late. "Is that what this is about?"

A dead leaf fell on the hood of the car, dull and drab, discouraging enough to spur Angie on. She shook her head. "No, Ben. I've come to see things I couldn't see before. You were right about Dougie. I'm not saying that I'm thrilled he's boarding—I don't think I'll *ever* be thrilled about it, but it's like the times when he was little and used to climb across the top of the swing set, and I'd close my eyes and let him do it because I knew that he'd never learn unless he did. He's doing okay as a boarder. It's what he wants. It may even be what he needs." She took a breath. "No. This is about us."

Which brought them full circle.

"So," Ben said to the dashboard of the car. "Where do we go from here?"

Angie wasn't touching the question. "You'll have to tell me that. I'm feeling gunshy where giving direction is concerned."

"I can't do this alone."

"But I don't know what to say. I know what I want. I want us to stay together and try to make things work, but I don't know if that's what you want at all."

He was still. After a long minute, quietly, he said, "It is."

"Then there have to be solutions. Maybe we should think about them for a while, then talk again." It sounded a little like carrying on long-distance negotiations, but Angie didn't know what more to say. If there was hope, she could wait.

"And Nora?" he asked. When she looked at him in alarm, he added, "Can you forget about her?"

"Can you?" seemed the more appropriate question to Angie. She waited anxiously for an answer.

"She's been a good friend. I'm not sure that if I hadn't had her, I wouldn't have run away."

Angie felt a sarcasm of her own. "I'd thank her for that, except I hope I never see the woman again. She slept with my husband. I don't know if I can forgive her for that. Besides, maybe if you had run away, I would have learned about the problem sooner. I didn't know, Ben." She was bewildered all over again. "Honestly I didn't."

He looked at her for the longest time. Then, with a tenderness worlds away from sarcasm, he said a quiet, "I know," and let himself out of the car.

Students started leaving campus at the end of Wednesday classes. Vans headed for the airport in shifts through the afternoon. Parents arrived in cars, loaded up kids and suitcases, and left.

Knowing that Sara had cross-country practice, then a study hall that was part of her punishment for leaving Mount Court without signing out, Noah didn't expect her at the house until dinnertime. Rather than cooking in, he had made a reservation at Bernie's Béarnaise, thinking that would be a special way to start the break.

Five-thirty came and went. He gave her more time, figuring that she would be packing up a few things, but when she hadn't shown by six, then six-thirty, he set off for the dorm. In the course of the two minutes that it took him to walk there, he imagined that she'd run off, or been abducted, or taken refuge at Paige's again.

He wouldn't have minded the last. He liked having an excuse to see Paige. They had no future, yet still she fascinated him, and not only sexually, though there was that, too. She gave him a run for his money when it came to repartee. If she was down, put off balance by something he said or did, she was never down for long. She could look him in the eye, tell him he was all wrong, and turn him on like there was no tomorrow.

Besides, she was a good role model for Sara.

MacKenzie Lounge was deserted. He strode through, swung up the stairs to the third floor, and went down the hall to her room. The door was closed, but there were sounds inside. He knocked, called, "Sara?"

"Yes?"

He jiggled the handle, but the door was locked. "Open up."

It was a minute before she did. She was wearing jeans and a sweatshirt, socks but no shoes. A small television provided background chatter.

"Where ya been?" he asked, trying to keep it light. She couldn't have forgotten that it was fall break. All her friends had left. The dorm was empty. The dining hall was closed.

She shrugged. "I was just sitting around."

"But I've been waiting for you."

"Why?"

"Because you're staying with me over break."

"I didn't know that," she said.

He sighed. "Sara, how could you not have known it? I left a note in your mailbox. I said we'd go to Bernie's Béarnaise. I said we'd go canoeing."

"You didn't say anything about staying with you."

He took an impatient breath. "Well, where else would you be staying?"

"Here. There are other kids around."

"Not many, and not in MacKenzie. They're over in Logan. That's the only supervised dorm this weekend." He tried to be level-headed, but he was frustrated and hurt. It was the same hurt he had felt time and again when he had come to visit Sara and been greeted coolly. He felt rejected by the one person he most wanted.

"Okay," he said, looking around the room, "just put together a few things and let's go. We can stop by for more tomorrow."

"I'd rather stay here."

He flipped off the television. "The backpack will do fine. You don't need to take much."

"I have tons of homework to do."

"You'll need a skirt or dress for tonight. Remember that purple outfit you wore to the play last weekend? You looked gorgeous. Wear that."

She turned away. After a minute she crossed to the desk. Keeping her back to him, she said, "You don't have to do this. I'll be fine with the other kids."

He exploded. "Well, I won't, damn it. You're my daughter, and this is my fall break, too. I've been good. I've left you alone to get acclimated to the school like any other student, but this weekend is for regenerating, and

I need it. It's been a whole lot of long, lonely months. I need my daughter. I need my family, if that's what you and I can be called."

"We aren't a family," she argued, but more meekly.

"We sure as hell are. I'm the father, and you're the daughter."

"We barely know each other."

"That's why I've been looking forward to this weekend. It's about time we *got* to know each other, don't you think?"

She shrugged. "Things weren't so awful before."

"They were *terrible.* I respected the fact that your mother had her own life, a new life with a new husband, and I tried to give her room to raise you without getting in the way. So what happened? I saw you for a day here and there, and a week once a year with my folks. If I were to do it again, I'd do it differently. I'd fight to see you more. You'd have *my* name. I wouldn't be so damned deferential to Liv."

He caught himself before he said more on that score. He had sworn not to bad-mouth Liv, though he held her at fault for the breakup of their marriage. Tempering his voice, he said, "Those years are done, Sara. I can't force you to like me, but I'm sure as hell gonna try."

Her shoulders hunched. It was a minute before he realized she was crying. He crossed the floor and took her in his arms. "Ahhhh, baby. Don't cry. We'll work things out. I promise."

She cried quietly. While she didn't wrap her arms around him, she didn't pull away, and suddenly the years disappeared. She was a toddler again, crying over a fall, and he was comforting the little girl he adored. "I know it's hard. Your life's been turned upside down in the past few months. It's natural that you're feeling unsettled. That's why it's so important for us to try with each other."

"I didn't think you wanted me around," she hiccoughed.

"This weekend?"

"All those years."

"Are you *kidding?*" he asked. "You saw the pictures I kept on the mantel. I couldn't pry many out of your mother, but whenever we were together I snapped away. You hated it when I did that—you always tried to turn away, remember?—but I *lived* through those pictures at times."

"You never came."

"I thought I was doing you a favor, minimizing the confusion about who your father was, but there's another side to that, Sara. You never *asked* me to come. When I'd be leaving you off at Liv's, you never asked when you'd see me again. I was never told about things like dance recitals, even though your mother had pictures of those all over *her* mantel, and when you started running—which was my thing, you knew that because you'd seen me running when we stayed with my folks— you never said a word."

"I didn't think you'd want to know."

"Well, I did. I thought about you all the time. I never let a birthday go by without a visit or a call, certainly never without a present. There were cards for every other kind of holiday, and I didn't just sign them 'Love, Dad,' I always wrote something that I thought would be meaningful, either about what the card meant or what I was doing with my life or what I thought you might be doing with yours." He smoothed aside a swath of long hair that was just the color as his. "I cared, Sara. I cared all those years, and I care now."

"But you *hate* it here. You only took the job because you needed somewhere to put me. At the end of the year, you'll be gone, and I'll be stuck here alone for two more years."

"If you stay, I stay."

She grew still. After a minute's quiet she asked, "You're not leaving?"

"I don't know, but if I leave, you come with me."

She was quiet for another minute. "That's because I get a free ride at whatever school you're at."

"Cutie, I'd pay tens of thousands if you desperately wanted to be at another school that didn't happen to be mine. It's not the money. I want you with me. That's all."

She started crying again.

"This was always the best and the worst about being a parent," he mumbled against the top of her head. "It was the worst, because crying meant you were unhappy, and the best, because I got to be the one who made it better. I wish I could do that now, the way I could when you were a year old, but the issues are more complex." He held her until the sobbing slowed, then he said, "I do love you, Sara. I know you don't believe me, but it's true. Give me half a chance and I'll prove it to you."

She sniffled. Turning away from him, she pulled a tissue from the box. "I don't know why you'd love me. I'm not a very lovable person."

"Whoever told you that?" he asked, suspecting that Liv had said as much more than once. He held up a hand. "No matter. I don't want to know. Whoever it was was wrong. Everyone in this world is lovable in some way, shape, or form. It's sometimes just a question of getting around—getting around—" What the hell: "Getting around the shit to the lovable part."

She was standing by the dresser with her back to him.

"So, let's start getting around the shit," he said more gently. "How about it?"

When she remained silent, he knew it wouldn't be easy, but then he had never thought it would be. One didn't wipe out years of misperception in a single conversation, no matter how ardent the speaker was. Whether because of Liv, Liv's husband, Jeff, or something in Sara herself, she had grown up thinking the worst of him. Changing that would take time.

"I really did love that purple outfit," he coaxed. "Come on. Stick a few things in the backpack, give me some clothes on their hangers, and we'll go over to the house. I have something to show you."

The something was a bedroom set for Sara's room. Noah had shopped around for days, not only for the bed, nightstand, and dresser, but for a thick quilt that matched soft floral sheets, which matched a pale green wall-to-wall carpet. Sara didn't say anything when she saw it, but he could tell that she was pleased. She stood at the door for a long time, just looking with wide eyes and what might have been, with an optimistic stretch of the imagination, the tiniest ghost of a smile.

Pleased, he hung her clothes in the closet and left her alone to change. Fifteen minutes later, lightheaded with his stunning daughter next to him in the car, he directed the Explorer toward Bernie's Béarnaise.

Passing Tucker General and the medical building beside it, he could have sworn he saw Paige's car turn in.

Had he been alone, he would have stopped and shared his little victory with her. He thought about her often, usually in the middle of the night when he awoke in a bed that seemed too large, too cold, and too sterile—which was incredible, since he'd been sleeping in the very same bed for years and had never felt quite those things. Paige was a tickle at the base of his spine that, if left to its own devices, spread to his front and lower. She was unfinished business.

For a minute, even with Sara, he thought of stopping. Then he decided against it. This was a time for Sara and him. It was important that nothing at all intrude.

Paige parked and trotted into the building and up the stairs. When she entered the office, Ginny was standing by the phone clutching a brown paper bag.

Worriedly she whispered, "I bought a quart of milk during lunch and left it here by mistake. When I stopped back to get it, I saw him."

Paige patted her arm. "I'm glad you did. Thanks, Ginny. I'll go see him."

Peter was in his office, sitting at the desk, but barely. He looked as though the weakest nudge would send him crashing to the floor.

"Hey." Paige smiled as she approached the desk. "What're you doin'?"

Peter moved his forearms over something that had been crushed and unfolded. "Jus' neaten' up." His fingertips glanced clumsily across two bottles of Scotch. The nearly empty one fell over. He grabbed for it and missed. Paige set it straight. While he swore under his breath about the waste of good brew, she mopped up what little had spilled.

"You're usually over at the Tavern by now. Have you had any dinner?"

"Don' wanna eat. No point."

"Sure there is. You have to keep up your strength. You have patients who depend on you." None of whom, she prayed, would be calling with an emergency this night. Then again, she could cover any emergencies, but if he went staggering down the street, the whole town would know by morning that its favorite son had been drunk.

Paige had never known him to be drunk before. She wondered what was behind it.

He moved his forearms again, as though trying to hide what was beneath them.

"Whatcha got there?" she asked.

"Not a thing," he answered, enunciating each word.

It was a photograph. She could see that much, though no more, and felt a wrenching depression deep inside. "Oh, Peter. You told me you destroyed them."

"Tried," he said. "Right in the basket. But I pulled 'em back out. Therrrrre all I have of 'er now."

"But it's not right," she pleaded. "You know it's not. Those pictures are inappropriate, whether she was eighteen or not."

He barked out a laugh. "Hah! She wazzzzn't eighteen! Maybe wished she was, but she had these teeny-weeny lines on 'er hands"—he gestured—"and on her neck, and these teeny-weeny veins on 'er thighs, she din't like *those*, lemme tell you."

Paige took the opportunity of his gesturing to lift the photograph from the desk, but even before she turned it right side up she had an odd sense of what she'd find. It was a picture of Mara, fully dressed, grinning for the camera with a silliness that few people ever saw in her.

The great depression widened inside her. Not pedophilia, but what? Fascination? Obsession? *Love?*

"It's beautiful," she whispered. "I didn't know you'd taken pictures of her."

He reached for the photograph, put it back on the desk, and scrubbed its surface with his palms in an attempt to erase the creases. "Hunerds," he said, then, "More'n hunerds."

Paige pulled up a chair and sat close beside him. "She must have liked that. She must have felt wanted."

He frowned. "She wazzz . . . wazzz . . . wanted."

"Loved, too?"

"Loved. Mmmm." He frowned again. "She said I ruined things."

"Ruined what?"

"Us. That I always found ways to wreck things." He looked up at her and added, "With women," in a knowing way before returning brooding eyes to the photo. "Said I din't think I was worthy of anything good. Zzzz'at stupid?" he asked, looking up again, but before Paige had to answer, he reached for the Scotch.

She held the bottle. "Don't you think you've had enough?"

"Never enough when you're 'lone."

"You're not alone. You have friends all over town."

"But she's gone," he said, and suddenly his face crumpled. To Paige's horror, he began to cry.

She touched his shoulder. "Oh, Peter. I'm sorry. I'm so sorry." Love. Tragically so.

"She'zzz th'best," he said between sobs.

"I know."

"An' I never told 'er. She killed herssssself 'cause she din't think anyone cared."

"That wasn't why. It was a combination of things—"

"I did it I did it."

Paige gripped his arm. "No, Peter. It wasn't you, any more than it was me or Angie or Mara's family. We all thought she was tougher than she was, so we made mistakes with her, but it wasn't any one of those that sent her over the edge. It was lots of things, some of which we had absolutely no control over."

Peter was shaking his head.

More softly, Paige said, "We don't know that it was suicide."

"I did it, me."

"It might have been pure exhaustion. Mara was always pushing herself. This time she might have pushed too far."

When he reached for the Scotch this time, she moved both bottles to the credenza behind the desk.

"I need it," he whined, then added, "I don' feel so good," just as he turned an ominous shade of green.

Paige got him to the bathroom just in time. After he had lost the contents of his stomach, she helped him clean up. Then she walked him to the kitchen, sat him on a chair, and made a pot of coffee, caffeinated and strong, which she proceeded to force into him until he was marginally sobered.

"Better?" she asked finally.

He had his head in his palms. His hair was sticking out every which way. "Hardly," he grumbled. "I can think now." He was silent for another little while, then, "Did I say much?"

"Nah."

"No damning confessions?"

She smiled and shook her head. There seemed no point in kicking the man when he was down. "Just that you did like Mara, and that you miss her, which makes me feel a little more normal. I think about her so much."

"That's your own fault," he grunted. "You're stalling on hiring another doctor."

"No, I put an ad in the journals, but they don't come out for another week. We'll get someone."

"And you wake up and see her little girl every day."

"But I like that."

"She reminds you of Mara."

"She helps me over the hump. By the time they find an adoptive family for her, I'll be better." She was in the process of pouring him a final cup of coffee when she thought of the bottles of Scotch that should, under no conditions, be found.

"Drink up. I'll be right back."

She returned to his office and was taking the bottles by the neck when something on the credenza caught her eye. It was a letter, handwritten on fine pink vellum that had a familiar scent to it. When she tried to place it, she conjured up a picture of Mount Court.

Uneasy, she raised the letter. Center top was an embossed monogram so swirly it was indecipherable. The handwriting was not, though. It was neat and pretty, the kind of script that lacked the character of maturity.

"Dear Dr. Grace," she read:

> *I just wanted you to know that I'm sorry if I put you in an uncomfortable position at the park. I only wanted to be with you. It seemed like I'd been waiting forever for you to see me like that. I'm not the little girl I was when I first came to Tucker. I'm grown up. You know that now. I'm sure that the pictures you took will be awesome.*

Paige didn't read further. Furious, she stalked back to the kitchen and tossed the letter onto the table before Peter.

"What's this?" she demanded.

He frowned, studied the paper, mumbled, "A letter from Julie Engel."

"Obviously. But what does it mean?"

He held his head. "Don't shout."

"You said you didn't have a problem," she shouted. He winced. "I don't."

"Then why is Julie Engel sending you scented letters?"

"Because she has a warped imagination. She came on to me, not the other way around. I walked away from her. The letter is an apology."

"And a thanks for the pictures you took. What pictures, Peter?"

"Pictures of her. For her stepmother's birthday."

"Oh, please," Paige said, rolling her eyes. After listening to Peter's drunken sobbing, after cleaning him when he was sick and sobering him up, she felt betrayed.

"They were," he muttered. "At least, that was what she told me. And the pictures I took were innocent. The minute she unbuttoned her blouse, I walked away. When I got home, I exposed the film." He braced the coffee cup between both hands, but it still shook on its way to his mouth.

Paige sighed. "I hope so, Peter, because, while I'm at it, it will be just as easy to fill two MD spots as one. I'm asking you a final time. Do you have a problem?"

"Ask Julie," he grumbled.

"I'm asking you. I need your word. For the sake of all the children we see in the course of a year, I want to know whether there is any reason, any reason at all, why you shouldn't be practicing here."

He pushed himself to his feet, looking tired but steady. "There's no reason." He tossed his chin at the half-empty coffee cup, murmured, "Thanks for nothing," and left.

She watched him walk a straight line down the hall before turning back to clean up the kitchen.

Sixteen

Saturday night, shortly after ten, Peter turned onto the cemetery road and gave the car enough gas to make the top of the hill. He parked and climbed out, then reached back in for a small bouquet of flowers and crossed the grass to Mara's grave.

A crescent moon hung low in the sky, too slim to cast a shadow, but the darkness didn't frighten him. Nor did the field of headstones marking this the land of the dead. He had been living with a ghost for weeks. Nothing he found here could be worse.

He was stone-cold sober. Nothing stronger than V-8 juice had passed his lips since the night he had made a fool of himself in front of Paige. The details of that night blurred, leaving only frayed bits of conversation, but they were enough to confirm his worst suspicions.

It had been all he could do to look Paige in the eye the next morning and assure her that he was more than capable of seeing his patients.

Mara's headstone was a solid slab of local granite, left raw and natural for all but the polished square on which had been carved her name, the dates of her life, and the epithet "Dear friend and healer, once loved, never forgotten."

He brushed several leaves from the top of the stone, then from the ground at its base. After tossing aside the bouquet he had left the week before, he set down the fresh one. The flowers were yellow and red, vibrant, as Mara would have liked, and though he knew that they wouldn't last long, he felt good bringing her something.

Better late than never, he thought, and sat down on the mound of leaves that he'd made. "Just visiting," he told her. "Life is lonely."

He hadn't seen Lacey and wasn't about to. Their relationship had run its course and died a death that was, ironically, more permanent than this one. That relationship had been less substantial than this one. He had admitted it to Paige, could certainly admit it to Mara.

"There aren't many women around like you." He missed her in a visceral way. "So I don't know what I'll do now."

You could date someone local, he heard her say.

"I've never done that in my life, and you know it."

You could start.

"Why should I? They didn't want me when I was growing up, so I don't need them now. Besides," he added, "they know too much. They know my brothers."

And they'd make comparisons? That's bullshit, Peter. No one compares you to your brothers anymore. It's all in your mind.

"Maybe, but it's just as real. And don't tell me I'm insecure. Did you write about that in your letters?"

I didn't have to. Anyone who knows you can see it.

"Gee, thanks. You always had a way of making me feel great. Would it have been so awful to say glowing things for once?"

I did.

"You did? About what?"

What do you think?

"About that? Really?" The thought of it pleased him. "Wonder if Paige was impressed. I could use a little boost in her eyes. Right now she's thinking I have a thing for little girls. I told her that I only like adult women, but she doesn't believe me. She doesn't think I should be practicing medicine at all."

Bear with her, Peter. She's under a strain.

"Well, damn it, so am I. She's dragging her tail about hiring someone new, even though you'd be the first one to tell her to do it."

So if she's dragging her tail, you do it.

"Me? Nah. That's Paige's job. She'll interview people, then present them to me for approval. That way I don't have to waste time on the dregs."

There's a flip side to that line of reasoning.

"Yeah?"

Yeah. You don't get half as much a say as to whom you hire. Paige may rule someone out—like a gorgeous young female—with whom you'd enjoy working.

She had a point.

"I suppose. Paige makes too many decisions herself. She has too much power. It gets to making her feel too important, like she could take unfounded allegations against me to the medical board and have my licensed revoked. If she ever tries to do that, she's in for a fight. My license to practice means as much to me as it does to you." Quietly he corrected, "Did to you. I'd be dead without it."

A siren wailed in the distance. "Uh-oh. Car crash. Wonder where it is this time." He pulled up the collar of his coat against the chill of the night. "Probably one of the good ole boys driving his pickup into a tree."

You're awful.

"Nah. Factual." He shivered and shot a look at trees that were growing skeletal. "Winter's coming. We'll have snow within the month." He wondered if she'd be warm enough six feet under. Then he caught himself. If factual was what he was, then he had to accept that she wouldn't be feeling anything at all, not this winter or the winter after, or one ten years down the road, or a hundred. She was dead. D-e-a-d.

He hoisted himself to his feet before the finality of it all got him down. "Gotta run. I can hear another siren coming our way. Somethin's goin' on. Could be they'll need a doc."

He started to leave, then did an about-face and returned. Kneeling at the very base of the stone, he moved the flowers closer, touched his fingertips to the letters of her name, and whispered, "I'll be back."

Feeling a huge throbbing in his chest where his feelings for Mara had been, he crossed the grass, climbed in his car, and cruised back down the hill in search of diversion.

With the canoe strapped to the top of the Explorer, their camping gear piled in the back, and Tucker less than half an hour away, Noah felt the kind of exhausted satisfaction that came from physical exertion and emotional reward.

Sara was asleep on the seat beside him, leaning against the door, pushing the limits of her shoulder harness. He checked—for the tenth time—to make sure the lock was down and even then would have given anything to shift her so that she was leaning toward him. Body language spoke volumes. But he could be patient.

They had come a ways together in the past few days, not talking as much as he would like but cooperating nicely. Sara hadn't complained, not about portaging the canoe, or setting up camp the night before, or waking up to a brief and unexpected snow squall that morning. Sure, he would have loved it if she had showed enthusiasm. He would have loved it if she'd said "Wow, Dad, this is *great!*" or "You're so *good* at this!" or "I'll bet none of my friends are doing anything this cool on *their* fall breaks!"

The flashing lights of an ambulance appeared in his rearview mirror, followed soon after by the rise of its siren. He pulled as far to the right as he could without ramming the guardrail that bordered the two-lane road. He didn't care to know what was beyond the rail; the topography of the area suggested a thirty-foot drop past trees and boulders to a stream; he checked Sara's door for the eleventh time.

The ambulance flew by. He pulled back onto the road and returned to speed. It was ten-fifteen. They had been awake since dawn, warming up, having breakfast, breaking camp before putting into the water. By mid-morning the sun had brought a warmth that made the snow squall seem a joke.

He was glad they had come canoeing now. Another few weeks and a snow squall would escalate into something more. He loved the thought of that—nature was beautiful cloaked in white, reduced to the basics of size and shape and therein more bold—but he wasn't sure Sara was up to it. Maybe in a few years. They might go farther north. Make three or four days of it. Even shoot the rapids.

A crescent moon poked through the bare arms of the trees. A month before, it would have been kept out by the leaves. A shame. With the ghost of its entirety holding it there in the sky, it was a testament to the stalwart source of its light.

His rearview mirror flashed with the approach of another ambulance, and again he squeezed right. It wasn't one this time, but three in succession, whipping past with a speed he would have judged unsafe had he not known that everything was relative. Three ambulances meant serious trouble. He wondered where.

Sara stirred. She raised her head as the last of the flashing lights disappeared around a curve in the road. "What happened?"

"I don't know, but something must have. They're bringing them in from all over."

She righted herself on the seat. "Maybe it's a car crash."

"That's a lot of ambulances for a car crash."

"Or a bus crash. Or a madman opening fire in the Tucker Tavern."

He shot her a humorous look. "Good God, sweetie, you have a vivid imagination."

She shrugged. "It happened back home. At a fast food place, with families and kids all around."

"That was urban violence. Chances of something like that happening in quiet little Tucker are more remote." But he saw another ambulance coming up behind them. There were two in this group. When they had passed, he said, "Maybe you're right."

"Can we follow?"

"No. We'd only be in the way." And he had no intention of letting Sara see blood and gore. "We'll go home. If it's something big, we'll hear about it pretty fast."

"At Mount Court?" she asked. The dashboard illuminated her "get-real" expression. "We're as far as you can get from Tucker and still be within the town limits."

"That," he said with a sigh, "is an astute observation. It's true on more levels than you'd want to count."

"They hate us."

"No. They don't know us. They have a preconceived notion of who we are, what we stand for, and how we behave, and unfortunately the blatant misbehavior of a small group of students in recent years has fed into it. We're off to a better start this year."

Another ambulance approached, passed, and whizzed off. By Noah's count, that made seven. He was beginning to think that Sara's vivid imagination might not be far off the mark when she asked, "Do you think Dr. Pfeiffer's involved?"

Paige hurt? "God, I hope not!"

"But if there are enough injuries to fill all these ambulances, wouldn't they need her help?"

He corraled his runaway heart. "As a doctor. You're right. They would."

"Only she's away this weekend. She went to her grandmother's. I heard her telling the baby-sitter that, the night I had dinner at her house."

Noah was relieved that she was out of harm's way. "Well, if they need her, I'm sure someone knows where to reach her."

"That must be awful."

"What?"

"Being on call all the time. You can be having a nice dinner, even at a restaurant, and you get a call and have to stop eating and leave whoever you're with and race to the hospital."

"That's part of being a doctor."

"Well, I'm sure glad she's not *my* mom," Sara said so pointedly that Noah would have had to be totally ignorant of the workings of children's minds not to get the message.

Angie was feeling better about herself and her life than she had felt in weeks. She and Ben had taken Dougie to Montpelier, had spent several hours wandering through town before having an early dinner. Then they had returned to Tucker, rented two movies at Reels, and were now done with one and starting on the other.

The best part was that she hadn't arranged a thing. The day had been Ben's doing from start to finish— except for the popcorn, which she had just air-popped and over which, as a splurge, she was in the process of dribbling melted butter.

She didn't splurge often. Dribblng melted butter on popcorn defeated the purpose of the air popping, but she wanted to do things differently. She was determined to pull herself out of the rut she had settled into in recent years, and if that meant dribbling melted butter on popcorn, or overlooking the fact that the late show had been Ben's choice and was R-rated, or ignoring the sound of the sirens that had been wailing in the distance, on and off, for the last ten minutes, she would do it.

"Wonder what's going on," Ben remarked when she returned to the den with the popcorn.

"Beats me," she said with determined nonchalance. "Peter's on call tonight. He'll handle whatever comes up." She didn't look at Ben to see whether he was pleased. He had to be. Her statement said that her family came first, which was at least part of what he wanted. "Sit here, Mom." Dougie moved over to make a place for her between Ben and himself. "The movie's starting. This is a good one."

"How do you know?"

"Because I've seen it before."

Angie dared a glance at Ben. "When?"

"At school. Some of the kids have rented it."

"But it's R-rated."

"They're old enough."

"Ahhhh," she said.

"There isn't much difference if he sees it with them or with us," Ben pointed out, though gently. He was trying. Angie could tell. That made it easier.

"Better with us," she said lightly. "That way we can answer any questions he might have. Or give a blow-by-blow commentary on what's happening," she teased, "or cover his eyes at the explicit spots."

"The R isn't for sexually explicit," Dougie informed her. "It's for violent."

"Violent. Lovely." Another siren wailed in the distance. "What with the sound effects out there, and the violence you say is in here, I may be the one who'll have nightmares," she quipped, but the truth was that she didn't care. Sitting between her husband and her son, with a warm bowl of buttered popcorn floating back and forth along with an atmosphere of goodwill, she couldn't have cared if she had nightmares for days. The moment was worth it.

Ben reached back and hit the light switch, plunging them into a darkness broken only by the flicker of the television. Just as the opening credits of the movie filled the screen, the phone rang.

Reflex brought Angie forward, but second thoughts had her elbowing Dougie. "It's been for you most of the weekend. Go on. We'll pause the movie." She thought it was a brainstorm. After all, Ben said she smothered the boy. What better way to ease her grip than by letting him answer his own calls. It wasn't asking much, just a short walk cross the room.

From across the room a minute later, he called, "It's for you, Mom."

"Oh." She got up. "Sorry." She took the receiver from him. "Yes?" She knew it would be business. No one would be calling for fun this late on a Saturday night.

"Angie," she heard Peter's voice say, "we have a problem."

If he was saying that he was in bed with a woman and wanted her to cover for him, the answer was going to be no.

"The movie house?" he went on. "The Henderson Wheel concert that's been sold out for days? The one Jamie Cox was so damned proud to be packin' 'em in for?"

"Yes?" she asked with a sense of foreboding.

"The friggin' balcony collapsed. A hundred people on top of another hundred twelve feet below, with rotted wood and plaster and chairs between them." He made a sound of disbelief. "No one knows how many people are hurt, or worse. They're just pulling them out best's they can. The ER at Tucker is a zoo. Ambulances are coming in every two minutes, making drops and going back for more. The criticals are being flown out, but we'll have the rest. They need us, Angie. Do you know where Paige is?"

Angie's mind focused on the horror of it, so real, and in that far worse than any R-rated movie. Hugging herself against a chill, she looked at Ben. He had risen from the sofa and was approaching.

"*Where's Paige?*" Peter repeated.

"Uh, at her grandmother's. I have the number. I'll call."

"And get here as fast as you can. We're talking wholesale carnage." He hung up the phone.

"My *God*," she whispered.

"What happened?" Ben asked.

"The balcony at the movie house collapsed in the middle of the Henderson Wheel concert. Hundreds of people have been hurt. They're pouring into the ER."

"The concert?" Dougie echoed, his face pale. "Half the *town* was going."

Angie put a comforting hand on his shoulder while she looked at Ben beseechingly. "Mara saw it coming. She knew the place was unsafe."

"But she couldn't have stopped this concert," he said. "Cox has been planning it too long. He'd never have let her stand in his way."

"Do you think he had her killed?" Dougie asked.

"No," Angie and Ben said in unison.

Angie softened her voice. "No. But people will be thinking a lot about her in the days to come." She looked at Ben again, questioningly this time.

Almost imperceptibly, he tossed his head toward the door. "Go," he said. "They need you."

"I wanted to be here."

"I know, but this is an emergency. You're not choosing them over us. They just need you more than we do right now."

Something stole around her heart, warming the fringes of the chill that had come with Peter's words. She nodded, gave Dougie a hug, then, on impulse, gave one to Ben. Without looking up, she opened the desk drawer, flipped through her address book for Nonny's number, and punched it out.

Paige was asleep on the red shag carpet in front of the fire when the phone rang. The noise was so out of place that she jumped up, but Nonny, who had been reading on her white wicker chair, simply extended an arm and picked it up.

"Hello?" she said with the same sweetness that was there night or day. She listened, looked at Paige, and said, "No, of course, you didn't wake me, Angie. Paige, here, was sleeping, and my little pumpkin's been sound asleep in her Portacrib for hours, but it'll be another hour or two before I turn in. Is something wrong? You sound breathless."

Paige came to her knees, ready to take the phone.

"Oh, dear," Nonny said, then, "Uh-huh. Yes. . . . No, dear, it's really no bother at all. She woke up when the phone rang. Here she is."

"Angie?" Paige asked, squinting at the clock.

"Something awful's happened, Paige. The balcony at the movie house collapsed during tonight's Henderson Wheel concert."

"What?"

"Scores of people have been hurt. Peter just called. I'm on my way to Tucker General now. They'll need every able hand. It must be a madhouse there. I hate to ask you to drive back from Nonny's, but there's a good chance some of our kids were at that concert."

Paige pressed a hand to her chest. "More than a good chance. Jill was there with her friend. They're ours. It *collapsed*?"

"That's what Peter said. Will you come?"

"I'm on my way. Angie, are there any—" She broke off, but Angie understood.

"I don't know. We'll find out soon enough."

Paige hung up the phone and told Nonny what had happened. "Tucker isn't prepared to handle anything like this." Her thoughts swirled. "Mara always predicted a fire, so instead of burns we have crushed bodies. I have to go."

"Of course you do."

"But I can't take Sami." *Especially* not if Jill had been hurt.

"She'll stay here with me."

It seemed the simplest thing, since Sami was already there. "I hate to ask."

"You didn't. I told you. She'll stay with me."

"But I'll be back first thing in the morning to pick her up."

"Not if you've worked all night and need sleep. She's fine with me, Paige. Really. You brought a diaper bag filled with enough supplies to keep her a week."

"Just until tomorrow. Okay, maybe the afternoon, if I'm dead tired and stop home to sleep for an hour. Can I call you?"

"Please do. But if I don't answer, don't be concerned. I may take her out. Just leave me that little stroller we used this afternoon. I liked that one. My friend Elisabeth took her grandchildren out walking in the fanciest something I've ever seen. She said it was state of the art, but I tell you there were so many layers of padding and shock absorbers and sunshades, and that was before she put in little blankets—well, you could barely see the child. So leave your little stroller. I want to *see* my Sami."

She isn't your Sami, any more than she's mine, Paige wanted to say, because it had been such fun taking Sami to visit Nonny that it could easily be habit forming. Regular reminders of the facts of life were in order.

But the facts of life at the moment, given the tragedy in Tucker, were brutal enough without an addition. So Paige simply gave her a hug. "You're a lifesaver."

"That's what keeps me going. Now drive carefully, do you hear?"

Paige took the roundabout way into Tucker so that she wouldn't have to pass the movie house. The street would be a logjam of ambulances and other emergency vehicles, and the helicopters—she saw two rise and head in separate directions—would cause delays of their own. The last thing she wanted was to be hung up in traffic.

The access to Tucker General wasn't much better, so she pulled into the parking lot of her own building next door, parked, and ran across the yard and several driveways to the emergency entrance of the hospital.

Havoc reigned within. The sound hit Paige first, the discordancy of whimpering that cried of pain and fear, then the smell, antiseptic from preliminary treatment overshadowed by the mustiness that anyone who had ever been in the old movie house would know.

The waiting room was packed with victims strewn in varying postures. Some were sitting, some were lying down, some were propped fragilely against pieces of furniture or the wall, cradling one body part or another. Clothes and skin alike were torn, bloodied, and filthy.

Paige's medical training had included discussion of the mass casualty incident, but she had never experienced it personally before, much less in a town she knew well. She would have suffered a rush of cold dread even if the crowd had been wholly adult, but too many of the faces she saw were those of adolescents. Too many were familiar, though she didn't see Jill, or the friend she had been with, among them. Some of the injured were being comforted by parents and siblings who had rushed to the scene. Others clung to those who were similarly hurt.

The triage nurse stood by the door, clutching an overflowing clipboard and looking bewildered.

"Has everyone been tagged?" Paige asked. She could see a flash of green here and there.

The nurse nodded. "I think. But there's so many. The criticals were flown to the trauma center in Burlington. A couple of them were brought here until they were hemodynamically stable, but they've been taken out now. You missed the worst."

"Fatalities?" Paige whispered.

"Three at the scene," the nurse whispered back.

Paige closed her eyes for a second, but that was all she allowed herself. Better than an hour had passed since the collapse. Those of the red priority one cases that hadn't been airlifted would be upstairs in the operating room or beyond. The stable but serious yellow-tagged victims would be doubled up in ER bays. She was needed.

She tried to make a beeline there, but there was no speeding through the maze of broken humanity. The injured ranged from their midteens through their thirties and were grouped with their friends. She saw patients and former patients and tried to touch or give each an encouraging word. When she missed one, she was called.

"Dr. Pfeiffer! Here, over here!"

She worked her way toward a sixteen-year-old girl whose family had her propped on a windowsill.

"They say Leila only has a broken arm and has to wait," Joseph complained, "but she's hurting awful. Can't someone look at her, at least?"

Paige carefully lifted the packing that covered Leila's arm and examined the spot where the bone had broken through the skin. Gently she said, "It's a compound fracture. It'll need to be set surgically, but if the OR is backed up, that might take a while. I just got here and have no idea what's going on inside." To Leila she whispered, "You're going to be fine. Think you can hang in there just a little longer?"

Leila nodded as another voice cried out, "Dr. Pfeiffer?" Paige looked around. "Butch is hurt bad, Dr. Pfeiffer."

Butch was slumped against a wall beside his sister Catherine. Former patients of Paige's, Catherine was now twenty-one and Butch nineteen. He was trying to press a wad of gauze to his forehead and hold his ribs at the same time.

Paige lifted the gauze and surveyed the gash. "A little stitching will take care of this," she said, and lifted his arm enough to gently prod his middle, "and some wrapping here," assuming the rib hadn't punctured anything. "I know you're uncomfortable"—she broadened her gaze to include Catherine—"but there's nothing to be frightened of. Were you there, too, Catherine?"

Catherine nodded. "I was up front. The music was so wild and loud and *strong* that when we heard this *cracking* we thought it was part of the show, y'know, a special effect or something. Then the cracking got louder and we heard screaming and looked around and right there in back of us the balcony just crumbled down on top of all the people underneath. Butch was in the balcony. The people underneath were, like, *crushed.*"

"Did either of you see Jill Stickley?" *Three fatalities. Three fatalities.*

"They were two rows down from me," Butch said, which told Paige nothing. He added weakly, "This hurts real bad when I talk."

"Then be real quiet," Paige coaxed softly, "and remember, the pain is only temporary. You've broken some ribs"—she hoped it was nothing more, though that wouldn't be known for sure until he made it to an examining room—"but they'll heal. Now, I'm going on in to help. The sooner we can move people out of those bays, the sooner we can get you in."

She worked her way through the crowd, thinking all the while about Jill being on the balcony rather than under it, which was small solace since she might have been down front with Catherine and not injured at all. If she was among the least hurt of the green tags, the walking wounded, she might have been taken by bus to a more distant hospital, which was standard procedure during a mass casualty incident. In that case, news might be slow in coming.

Paige prayed she was in that group.

The hall off the waiting room was lined with loaded stretchers and wheelchairs. Relatives of their occupants huddled around each.

"When will Trisha be taken, Dr. Pfeiffer?" asked one distraught mother.

Paige bent down—"Hey, Trish"—and gave the mother a reassuring touch in passing. "As soon as we possibly, possibly can."

"Dr. Pfeiffer, Patrick can't move," cried another.

The boy was on an immobilizer. Paige put a hand to his brow. "That's deliberate. We don't want him to move until we can determine the extent of his injury. The hard collar, the blocks by his ears, the straps holding him to the longboard—they're there to make sure he stays as still as possible."

She gave them a bolstering smile and slipped into Room A, where the chief of the ER staff, Ron Mazzie, was bent over one of the two patients there. He was being assisted by a nurse and a technician. When he looked up, she asked, "Where do you want me?"

"Room F. Maybe G. Whichever's without. There are patients waiting in both. Thanks for coming, Paige. We need you."

"Glad to help. You haven't treated Jill Stickley, have you?"

"No. Maybe one of the others has."

Nodding, she let herself out. She would have stopped at each of the rooms to ask about Jill, if it hadn't been for the patients waiting for her down the hall. She didn't waste time looking for a lab coat, nor did she scrub up, other than to wash her hands in Room G, which was the one without the physician. A nurse was already there. Both patients were yellow-tagged. While she wiped her hands on a paper towel, the nurse showed her the vital statistics on the more serious of the two.

His name was John Collie. He and his siblings had all been patients of Peter's. John was now twenty-two and no longer coming to the office, but he recognized Paige. She talked softly, reassuringly, to him as she worked.

He had a gash on his chin and another, longer one on his arm. But it was the pain on the left side of his upper abdomen, just below his ribs, that concerned Paige. She felt a distinct rigidity there. If a rib had broken and pierced his spleen, if blood filled that spleen to the point of rupturing, he would be in bad shape.

"I want a CAT scan done," she told the nurse, and wrote out the order. "Let's find out if his spleen is bleeding. The ribs need to be X-rayed, but that's not the first priority. Is there someone who can take him to the scanner?"

The nurse stuck her head out the door, hollered, *"Bartholomew!"* and returned.

"Bartholomew?" Paige echoed with a wink for John. She took a closer look at his lacerations. The one on his chin looked worse than it was. She cleaned the movie house dust from it, then examined his arm. "This one should be stitched, but it'll wait until after the CAT scan." She rechecked his vital signs and made notations on his chart, then looked up when the door opened.

Bartholomew was an orderly who was large, white-haired and bearded, and nearly seventy. His greatest problem getting John's gurney out the door were John's mother and two of his sisters, who had been waiting in the hall and now crowded in. In a voice aimed to calm, Paige explained what she had found and where John was headed. After sending them to follow, she turned to the patient in the second bed.

Her name was Mary O'Reilly. She was twenty-four years old, married, and the mother of two young children who were patients of Paige's. Mary's husband, Jimmy, had been red-coded and taken to one of the other hospitals, and Mary was in such a panic about him that she was paying little heed to herself, which was just as well. Her thigh was a mess. It had been impaled by a shard of wood that had crashed from above. The shard had been removed at the scene and the gash temporarily bandaged, but it was deep enough to expose the bone. Paige called on every bit of her medical skill to repair layers of muscle, tendon, and skin. When she was done, she smoothed Mary's hair back from her damp and ashen face. "You'll have to stay off this, Mary."

"But I got my kids to take care of. And I gotta find Jimmy."

"Who's with the kids now?"

"My landlady." Her voice rose to a hysterical pitch. "She was doing us a favor. We don't go out much since the kids were born."

"Do your parents live nearby?"

"There's just my father, but he's up in St. Johnsbury and he won't talk with me since I married Jimmy."

"What about Jimmy's parents?"

"They're here in Tucker." She looked horrified. "Someone has to tell them about Jimmy."

And about Mary, Paige thought. She couldn't be kept at the hospital long, what with the crowd, but she certainly couldn't go home alone. She was going to need help with the children for some time to come.

"I'll have someone call them," Paige assured her.

"Maybe they heard. Maybe they're looking for him already."

"Then your landlady will stay with the kids until they get back, and in the meantime we'll try to get you some news on Jimmy."

"What if he's dead?" she cried.

"Don't even think it," Paige scolded gently, and stood back when an orderly wheeled her from the bay. She followed only long enough to stop at the desk, which was being manned by a harried charge nurse and a handful of eager volunteers, and see to contacting both Mary's in-laws and her landlady. She returned to Room G in time to be accosted by an unhappy parent.

"That's my boy in there. Name's Alex Johnson. When's a doctor gonna see him?"

"I'm a doctor, Mr. Johnson. I'll see him now. If you wait here, I'll be out as soon as I can to tell you what I find." She backed into the room and let the door close.

Alex had multiple lacerations and a fractured femur. Paige corraled the portable X-ray unit into the bay and had pictures made of the fracture. When it proved to be a simple one, she casted it and stitched his cuts.

To the father she said, "Ideally, I'd keep him here overnight, but given the situation, I just can't. He has crutches. We'll wheel him out to the car and help you get him in. He'll have to stay off that leg."

"You tell him. He don't listen to me."

"It's important, Alex. You can't put any weight on it." To both of them she said, "Keep it elevated to minimize the swelling. Take aspirin for the pain. If it gets terribly uncomfortable, if the cast starts feeling too tight or too loose, let us know. Okay?"

She turned to the patient whose stretcher had replaced Mary O'Reilly's on the other side of the bay. Tim Hightower, age twenty and strapped to an immobilizer, had been a patient of Mara's. He had bruises and cuts and was mildly concussed, but the possibility of a cervical spine injury was the real cause for fear. Paige examined him with care, using her fingertips on the base of his skull and his neck to detect swelling or tenderness. She worked her way down his back, questioning him all the while. To her relief, he had neither paralysis nor inhibition of movement. His reflexes were as they should be, as were the sound and feel of his stomach, liver, and kidneys. But his back hurt, which was what had prompted the paramedics to immobilize him.

"I'll clean up your cuts and send you to the X-ray unit upstairs, but unless something shows up on the pictures, we can assume that a lower back muscle strain is the source of your pain."

She sent him along and turned to the next, a twenty-eight-year-old woman with enough broken facial bones for Paige to defer to a plastic surgeon. Next was another heartrendingly familiar face, a seventeen-year-old with fractures of the collarbone and the humerus, then a thirty-three-year-old with a broken rib and a question-able punctured lung, then a twenty-nine-year-old with abdominal injuries that would require surgery.

And so it went. Over the next few hours a steady rota-tion of patients kept her at work without a break. When one patient left, she turned to another; when that one left, she turned to the next. Every few patients was one of her own, a teenager who had been having the time of his or her life and now lay bruised, broken, and in pain. But alive. She kept telling herself that. Some recoveries would be slow. There would be problems with school, with after-school jobs, with playing sports in a town that revered its varsity teams. But at least these children were alive.

Adrenaline pumped through her system, masking fatigue, while she set bones, stitched lacerations, cleaned abrasions, and forwarded to the surgeons more compound fractures, internal hemorrhaging, and edemas than she had seen during her three-month ER rotation in medical school.

There was no sign of either Jill, her parents, or her friend. During one brief coffee break, Paige found Angie, but Angie hadn't seen Jill, either.

Three fatalities, Paige kept hearing. *Three fatalities.*

The night waned before the last of the yellow tags were seen. With the dawn came the green tags, injuries that were less serious but no less in need of attention. Paige gulped down more coffee and a candy bar from the machine in the staff lounge and delved back into the suturing, casting, and splinting.

At midmorning, when she took a short break, she called the Stickleys' house. There was no answer. On the chance that Jill had escaped injury entirely, she tried her own house. Nonny answered.

"What are *you* doing there?" she cried in surprise.

"We got up early and walked all around my neighborhood, then we decided to help you out and drive back here ourselves," Nonny said, sounding chipper and no worse the wear for the trip with a child. "Are you all right?"

"I am," Paige said wearily, "but so many aren't. What a nightmare."

"Have you gotten any sleep?"

"Not yet. Soon. You haven't heard from Jill, have you?"

"No. Should I have?"

"Ideally, yes. I can't seem to locate her. If she calls, will you call the ER and leave me a message?"

Nonny agreed, and Paige returned to work. It wasn't until noon, when she sank down wearily in the physician's lounge to await the return of enough energy to get her home, that Peter approached with the information she wanted.

"Jill's upstairs. She was one of the first to be seen. She has a pelvic fracture."

Paige groaned in distress. "The baby?"

He waved a hand. "It's touch and go. She's had some bleeding, but the baby's still in there. For how long, no one knows. She and her friend were in the middle of the crush that came down from the balcony, but Jill got the worst of it. The other girl was bussed to Hanover."

Weary and heartsick, Paige closed her eyes. No matter that Jill hadn't planned to be pregnant—no matter that she was going to give the baby up for adoption—to lose it would be a tragedy.

"I have to go see her," she said, and pushed herself up from the sofa, but she hadn't taken more than two steps when an alarmed face appeared at the door.

"We need help. They've pulled seven more from the rubble."

It seemed to go on and on and on.

Paige shot Peter a horrified glance and set off on the run beside him.

Seventeen

Peter hung his head over the sink in Room D and tossed water into his face. He was dead tired, yet he felt a sense of satisfaction that he hadn't felt in a long, long time. He had helped. No doubt about it. He had done his share, had worked right along with the others, had held up his end even with those last difficult cases.

If he were to go to the Tavern—which he wouldn't, since it was two in the afternoon and he planned to go home and sleep for the next seventeen hours—he would be hailed as a hero. He had treated more than a few of his brothers' friends' kids. They'd be buying his beer for years.

A fine thought. Once he got some sleep.

He wiped his face, tossed away the paper towel, left the room, and headed for his car. When he rounded the corner, he nearly fell over a single gurney that stood there. On it, strapped to a longboard and looking as white as the sheet that covered her, was Kate Ann Murther.

"Please help me," she pleaded in a shadow of a voice. She was on oxygen and an IV. "Please help me please help me."

Her head, like the rest of her, was immobilized, so that she couldn't see him, and either no one at the nearby nurses' station had heard her or no one cared to respond. Kate Ann might well have been invisible, which was pretty much what she'd been all her life. She was an introvert to the extreme, a quiet creature who lacked the courage to reach out for niceties such as friendship, physical comfort, and respect.

Peter didn't owe her anything, certainly not compassion for having suffered through childhood as he had. The last thing in the world he wanted was to be associated with a nobody like Kate Ann Murther.

She was seven years younger than him. She had never married. To his knowledge she had never even dated. She lived alone in a tiny house on the edge of town that always had one problem or another—frozen pipes, a leaky roof, racoons in the cellar. Same with her car, which had a way of breaking down at the most inopportune of spots. She supported herself by doing simple bookkeeping work for several of the smallest businesses in town, though none of those broadcast the fact. They dropped their books at her house and picked them up when she was done, all after dark so no one would see, and if there was snickering in the Tavern about what else happened at the time those books were exchanged, no one believed it. Kate Ann was so shy as to be pathetic, so pathetic as to be sexless. She wasn't someone anyone in town wanted to take credit for knowing.

What stunned Peter was that she'd been at the concert at all.

"Please help me please help me."

More words than he had ever heard her say at one time.

"Someone pleeeeeease."

So soft and sad and *terrified* that he couldn't have turned around and taken the back way out of the hospital unless he'd been made of stone.

He came to the side of the gurney where she could see him. "What's the problem, Kate Ann?" he asked kindly. The generosity of the night was still in effect. He was giving of himself to the less fortunate. Mara would be pleased.

Kate Ann looked up at him through tear-filled eyes. "I can't move," she said so quietly that he might have missed the words if he hadn't heard them once too often in the hours just past.

He took the chart from the foot of the gurney, read it, and, against his better judgment, felt a twinge of sympathy. He wondered what her doctor—according to the chart, it was Dick Bruno, though he wasn't a neurosurgeon—had told her.

"You can't move," he said gently, "because we're trying to keep you perfectly still. There may have been some damage to your spinal chord. The CAT scan says there's some swelling. One of these IV bottles contains Solu-Medrol to fight it. The immobilization is to prevent further damage from being done and hopefully let things start to heal."

"But I can't *feel* anything," she whispered with eyes large as a child's.

Caught by them, Peter was suddenly back in med school, starting his rotation in pediatrics, facing his first patient. The hurt, the fear, the dependence, then the absolute adoration when the hurt eased, had sold Peter on being a pediatrician.

Kate Ann Murther wasn't a child. She wasn't his patient. She wasn't any of his business. But, doctor to patient, he felt bad for her, so he said, "The trauma of the injury will have numbed things up," which was the truth, though not the whole truth.

She didn't say anything immediately but continued to hold him with those large, child's eyes. He had the sudden impression that he had told her more than anyone else had that night.

"Have they mentioned getting you into a room?" he asked.

"No one answers when I ask."

"I'll ask for you," he said, and forgetting his exhaustion, he marched to the nurses' station. "What's the story on Kate Ann?" he asked of the charge nurse, who looked up blankly.

"Kate Ann?"

"Murther. Kate Ann Murther." He tossed his head toward the gurney.

The nurse peered around him in surprise, as though she hadn't known anyone was there, which bothered the hell out of Peter. Okay, so Kate Ann was the forgettable type, and in times of turmoil the forgettable types were forgotten. But the turmoil had tapered off. And Kate Ann had spinal damage and possible permanent paralysis. She had a right to be terrified. It wasn't fair that she should be ignored.

In a low but firm voice, he said, "I'd like to get her to a room *stat*."

The nurse waved a hand at the papers on her desk. "Where should I put her? We're bulging at the seams."

"I want Three-B. That's where spinal injuries are usually kept."

"It's filled."

"Tell you what," Peter said. "I'll wheel her up there myself while you call and have them look around, they'll find a place. I don't care if they have to empty out a stockroom, but the woman is seriously injured. She needs to be monitored." He glanced at the clock. "You have five minutes. That's how long it'll take me to get there."

He returned to Kate Ann, whose eyes begged for help.

"I'm wheeling you upstairs. Are you warm enough?" He touched her arm. It felt like ice. "Christ, Kate Ann, you have to speak up." He wheeled her down the hall to a supply closet, ducked inside, and emerged with the last three blankets there. He tucked two right up to her chin, left the third on her feet, and wheeled her on.

The head nurse on 3-B was looking harried when he arrived. "We haven't any more room. Our doubles are tripled."

"All we need's a corner," he said, then, so tired that he was punchy, added, "Hold on, Kate Ann. I'm about to get you the best view in town."

That was just what he did. He found a small window spot in a quad that already had a fifth and might just as well have a sixth. She couldn't look out, but she would be able to feel the warmth of the sun on her face.

Once she was set up there, with her chart firmly in place at the nurses' station and a warning, barely veiled as a promise to the head nurse, that he would be back to see how Kate Ann was doing early the next morning, he took the elevator back down. He stopped at the front desk only long enough to write a note to Tucker's chief of neurosurgery asking him to give Kate Ann some time. Then, with exhaustion suddenly back in a gust, he went straight to his car and drove home.

It wasn't until much later that he realized he should never have signed the note. If word got out that he was championing Kate Ann Murther, he'd be done for, for sure.

Paige was later leaving the hospital than Peter. Her last case had been perhaps the worst of all, a young man who not only worked for the highway department, a physical job in itself, but was also the star of the intertown basketball league. He had been caught under an extraordinary weight of rubble that had fallen from above. To free him, emergency workers had had to amputate his leg.

In the commotion of bringing him in, Paige had been swept into the operating room to assist the two surgeons there, and when the other doctors had left she remained with the patient's family. They talked of recuperation from the surgery, of physical therapy and a prosthesis. They mentioned the possibility of his return to work. No one mentioned basketball.

Paige stayed with them until she simply couldn't a minute longer. Then she trotted up the stairs to the second floor, trotted all the way down the hall, and breathlessly singled Jill out from the four in the room at the very end.

She went straight to the bed, took Jill's hand, and leaned low. "How're you doing, hon?"

Jill struggled to open her eyes. Paige knew that it would be a while before the grogginess wore off. Beneath the sheets, a cast ran from her waist to her knees. At the head of the bed, a fetal monitor beeped steadily. On a nearby chair, looking drained, sat her mother.

"I feel weird," Jill mumbled.

"You will for a while. But you're doing fine."

"My baby . . . they don't know."

"That's why they have you on a monitor, to tell them if the baby has any trouble."

Jane rose. She didn't speak, but stood there looking uncomfortable enough to tell Paige that she wanted to.

"Let me go calm your mom," Paige told Jill. "I'll be back." Once in the hall and out of earshot, Jane said,

"They were thinking of cutting it out, but they thought it might be too little. They say they'll do it if there's any trouble. I hope they do. The sooner it's gone, the easier things will be, especially now. She can't have a baby now. Not with the cast and all."

"She can. They'll simply wait until the baby is able to function on its own, then take it by cesarean section."

"But don't you see, it's no good. She can't stay with you anymore. She needs someone to take care of her, but he won't have her in the house. He pretends he doesn't have a daughter. He's been uglier than ever." She didn't have to elaborate.

Paige wanted to scream. "You don't have to suffer through that, Jane. I've told you before. You could speak with someone."

But Jane was shaking her head. "That'll make it worse. He'll beat me something awful if I tell anyone."

"We can get a restraining order."

"But I don't want one. I don't want to kick him out. He's my husband."

Paige had long ago learned that she could express all the fury in the world, but it wouldn't change the fact that many women who were mistreated would choose that mistreatment over being alone. She neither understood it nor agreed with it, but then she had never been married. She had never loved any man, much less one with problems.

Mara had. Mara would be *so much* better talking to women like Jane Stickley than Paige was.

But Mara wasn't there, and Jill was lying alone in the other room. Paige gave Jane's arm a little rub. "Think about it. I can help, if you want it. In the meantime, we have to support Jill. The baby's fate will be decided without any help from us."

With Jane in tow, she returned to the room and sat with Jill for a short time. When Jill fell asleep again, she left and, heavy-hearted, set off for home. She pulled into the driveway, parked behind Nonny's car, and let herself in the front door.

Nonny was in the living room playing pattycake with Sami while kitty looked on curiously. The three offered such a heartwarming picture, in contrast to the harrowing tableau at Tucker General, that Paige felt a sudden giddiness.

"Oooooooo," Sami said, and held up her arms.

Paige swept her up and gave her a hug. "How's Mommy's little girl?" She rocked her from side to side. "It's so good to see you. Both of you," she said to Nonny. "All of you," she said to kitty. "I feel like it's been a year and a day since I left." She sank down on the sofa and curled up in a corner with Sami still in her arms. Kitty jumped behind the crook of her knees.

"Is everyone taken care of?" Nonny asked.

"For now. We lost another one in Burlington. That makes four. More than a hundred hospitalized between Tucker and others. Half again as many treated and released." She closed her eyes. "The old movie house. Mara knew." She breathed in deeply. "Mmmmm, this little one smells so good. So clean and healthy, after all that." By contrast she felt filthy, but she was too tired to move. "Jill is in rough shape. She has a fractured pelvis. The baby is teetering."

"Oh, dear. I'm so sorry."

"Me too." The words were an effort. Sami was so warm against her that she snuggled closer. "I won't crush you," she whispered, but the next thing she knew, Nonny was shaking her shoulder.

"You should be in bed, sweetheart."

"In a bit," Paige said, and dozed off again. This time Sami's squeal brought her awake with a start. The child was standing against the side of the sofa with her face inches away.

"She squirmed out of your arms half an hour ago," Nonny explained, "but she refuses to go far. I think she missed you."

Paige smiled and touched Sami's mouth.

"Geeeeeee," Sami said, crinkled her nose, and smiled back.

Paige planted a kiss on her cheek. "Such a sweet baby. But Mommy's dead tired. I have to sleep." With an effort, she pushed herself up. "Just for a couple of hours. Can you stay, Nonny?"

"I intend to."

"Just for a couple of hours," Paige repeated, but the last few words were slowed by the realization that she no longer had a baby-sitter.

"For as long as you need me," Nonny assured her. She wrapped an arm around her waist and propelled her toward her bedroom. "You smell musty."

"Movie house dust. It was worse than the blood."

"If I run you a bath, will you fall asleep in it?"

"Definitely. Later." She stumbled into the bedroom, but without Sami's sweet baby smell, she couldn't bear herself. So she stood under the shower, soaped, rinsed, toweled herself dry, then climbed into bed and was instantly asleep.

Noah and Sara learned about the movie house disaster when they went into town Sunday afternoon for brunch. They didn't have to ask any questions. No one in the coffee shop was talking about anything else. All they had to do was to sit in their booth and listen to the conversation around them.

"Horace's boy was there. He broke a leg. Porter's broke two arms."

"Half the town was there. Broken bones is the least of it."

"The balcony fell right down on the ones underneath. Horrible. Horrible."

"Shoulda known it would happen, place was so old."

"Too old to be having a concert with jumping and foot stomping and all."

"Jamie's in big trouble, lawyer says."

"Serves him right, th' old coot."

"They should make him add a new wing to Tucker General. I hear it's filled to brimming."

"But how many's patients and how many's family?"

"No matter. Everyone's trying to help. We don't have enough nurses. I hear they bussed some in from Hanover."

"And doctors from Abbotsville. Every one of ours has been working round the clock."

Sara leaned forward. "Do you think Dr. Pfeiffer is there?"

"Probably," Noah answered. "One of her partners would have called her."

"Her baby-sitter was going to that concert. I wonder if she was hurt."

He shrugged and shook his head. He had no way of knowing. But he kept thinking about it, and about

Paige, through the afternoon while he and Sara put up the new wallpaper in the bathroom. It was a hard pattern to match. He kept waiting for Sara to complain, but she wouldn't give him that satisfaction, so when he was feeling distinctly cross-eyed, he called for a break.

On the pretext of seeing if she was home and, if so, getting the scoop firsthand, they drove to Paige's.

"I think she has company," Sara said when they found two cars in the driveway.

"That's okay. We won't stay long. If she's here, she'll be tired."

"Dead asleep," her grandmother said, introducing herself only as Nonny and seeming to know just who they were. "But you're welcome to come in and visit with Sami and me. We like having guests."

Noah gave Sara an inquiring look. She shrugged and said, "I like Sami."

So they went inside. Sara was the one to ask about Jill and was upset when Nonny told what had happened. "Will she be in the hospital long?"

"For a little while, I'd guess."

"Is her family with her?"

"I'm sure."

"Who will baby-sit Sami while Dr. Pfeiffer's at work?"

Nonny tipped up her chin. "Me. Oh, she hasn't acknowledged it yet, but she will. I'm the best baby-sitter around."

"I can baby-sit," Sara offered. She was sitting on the floor opposite Sami, rolling her a ball.

Noah was thinking that she looked happier and sounded more affable than she had in a while. He could imagine that it was this house, which had a warmth to it. Or maybe the warmth came from Nonny, who was a seventy-something pixie wearing red leggings and an oversize red sweater. Or from Paige, who was sound asleep in the other room wearing God only knew what.

Of course, Sara couldn't possibly baby-sit Sami.

Nonny, bless her, said, "You can't possibly baby-sit, Sara. You have school. That's far more important for you. And besides, I *need* to baby-sit. The older I get, the more useless I feel. This will make me functional again."

Sara kept on playing ball with Sami. "Dr. Pfeiffer said that she lived with you while she was growing up. Is it true?"

Noah listened closely.

"Oh, yes. It's true," Nonny said. "My daughter—her mother—is a very charming woman, but she wasn't cut out to be a mother. Some women aren't. It's usually better if they realize it before they have children, but in this case it worked out all right. Of course, Paige didn't always agree. She missed having a mother and father. At times, she still does."

"Where are they now?" Noah asked.

Nonny screwed up her face and looked at the ceiling. "Uh, Capri? No. Siena. That's it. Siena."

"What do they do there?" Sara asked.

"Not—very—much," Nonny ennunciated with care and a certain helplessness. "My daughter married a man with too much money. They became playmates when they were eighteen, and they're still at it. They've never grown up. They've never had to accept any sort of responsibility."

"But they had a child," Noah pointed out. "That's a responsibility."

A sheepish Nonny said, "I'm afraid I made it easy for them to shirk it. From the start, Paige was my little girl. She was a cuddler in ways her mother never was, and I loved it. I was always quite happy to send my daughter and son-in-law back off to their villa or chalet or dacha, or wherever it was they were living at the time. I enjoyed having Paige to myself." She grinned. "And now I have Sami." Her grin widened, seeming to overtake her small face in a way that was so cheerful, Noah nearly laughed. "And now I have you both. It's so *lovely* to have guests." The grin vanished, replaced by wide little eyes and an earnest entreaty. "You'll stay for dinner, won't you?"

Put that way, Noah could no more have disappointed the woman than he could have dragged himself back to wallpapering a bathroom. "We really shouldn't impose."

"No imposition!" she exclaimed, just as he had suspected she would. Her eyes were bright. "I was only ordering in. So I'll order in more." Leaning close to Sara, she said, "Do you like Mexican?"

Sara nodded vigorously. "But my father doesn't. It upsets his stomach. Every time he came to visit me in California we had a problem. He'd ask me where I wanted to eat, and it would always be Mexican. The places *he* wanted to eat were boring."

"Ach, then we'll make him a cup of chicken soup. As for me"—she rubbed her hands together—"I'm in the mood for something hot. Say, some chili. Or nachos with jalapeño pepper cheese."

Sami grew red in the face. Nonny stroked her head. "No nachos for you, either? No chili?"

"Do they upset her stomach, too?" Sara asked.

"Actually," Nonny said, lifting Sami, "that isn't the problem." To Noah, with a charming delicateness, she said, "Would you excuse us while we go to the ladies' room to repair ourselves?"

Noah chuckled. "Of course."

Sara got right up and went with Nonny, leaving him alone in the living room. Not one to pass up a prime opportunity, he headed for Paige's bedroom.

He didn't see her at first. She was lost in the patchwork designs on her bed—comforter, a slew of pillows, sheets—all in warm shades of brown, gold, green, crimson. He saw what he thought was a patch of hair, but it turned out to be kitty, curled in a ball against one of the pillows.

Then he saw Paige. Her body was a faint diagonal line under the comforter and her hair was strewn over the patchwork, camouflaged, but it was her, no doubt this time. His body was telling him so as surely as his eyes, though precious little of her was exposed. The comforter crowded under her jawline. He couldn't begin to guess what she had on.

Drawn closer, he studied her face. It was pale, clean, vulnerable in sleep. Her hair looked as though it had been damp when she had fallen into bed. It was a riot of waves. He smoothed several back from her cheek, then, unable to resist, returned to touch the smooth skin. Then the straight line of her nose. Then her mouth. Her breathing was slow and far more even than his. Her eyelids were still.

He sat down on the bed. Still she didn't waken.

He thought of the time she had just spent at the hospital, hours that had to have been brutal, and felt a swell of respect. He also felt respect for Nonny, who had raised an irresponsible daughter's daughter to be eminently responsible.

He felt another swell, this time a physical one centered in his groin. The attraction was strong. It was chemical, had been so from the first, and the more he saw of her, the stronger it became. The time they had been together, way back in Mara's yard, seemed a dream now. Or maybe it was because he had dreamed it so many other times that the first was just blending in.

He kissed her temple and waited. When she didn't respond, he kissed her eye, then her cheek, lingering there to enjoy the fresh scent of her skin. Tendril by tendril, he trained her hair back over the pillow. He traced the sculpted line of her ear. He slid his fingers under the comforter and let them soak up the warmth of her neck.

She gave a soft hum of pleasure. He moved his fingers lightly.

Her eyes flickered open. They focused straight ahead, then shifted slowly to Noah. She seemed disoriented, asleep with her eyes open, but he didn't give a damn. Her mouth looked too soft, too sweet, to resist. He lowered his head and kissed it. He ran his tongue around it. He nibbled on her lower lip, sucked it, caressed it.

A soft sound came from her throat. She had closed her eyes, but her mouth was his for the taking, and he was too hungry to abstain. He took it in its entirety, devouring it wetly, using his tongue to explore what was inside.

She made the same soft sound, accompanied by the beginnings of response. Her breathing was no longer as steady. Her mouth clung to his.

He framed her chin with his hand, then slid it lower, under the comforter, then the sheet. The route was paved with bare flesh, silky and warm, rising and falling with the sough of her breath. He found her breast and caressed it, drew her nipple hard between his fingers, then pulled the comforter back only enough to put his mouth where his hand had been.

This time it was a cry, a soft but needy one, then the sound of his name on her breath. Her body was swelling, arching to his. She repeated the cry when he drew her nipple deeply into his mouth.

Rising up, he braced himself over her face. Her cheeks were flushed, her lips moist. Her eyes were open again, disoriented now in an eddy of pleasure. He slipped a hand under the sheet, lower over her abdomen, until he found what he sought.

She gasped.

"Shhhhh." He covered her mouth and ate at it in time with the motion of his hand. He swallowed her breath when it came faster, then her cries when they rose, when her body went tight and seconds later shook with a powerful release.

He was slow in retrieving his hand and then brought it up, fingers spread wide to feel everything he could before he withdrew. Her breasts were tight, her nipples hard. She pressed her hands over his to hold them there until, it seemed, reality hit. Then she made a sound that held more than a touch of embarrassment and rolled over, away from him and so far under the comforter that nothing showed but the top of her head.

Noah wanted to talk. He wanted to tell her not to be embarrassed, that her pleasure was his, that the release was good for her. He wanted to give her another one. Mostly he wanted to strip down, join her under the covers, and bury himself deep, deep inside her until nothing remained of the outside world but bits and fragments of memory.

But the outside world was still there. He could hear it moving over his head and guessed that he had Nonny to thank for keeping Sara occupied. Which was nice, but not overly responsible on his part.

Reluctantly he rose from the bed. He straightened and took several deep breaths, grateful just then that

Paige was buried under her comforter so that she wouldn't see the shape of his pants. In the bathroom, he tossed cold water on his face, but between the bra that lay with her discarded clothes, the damp towel on the rack, and the scented soap that was so thoroughly reminiscent of her skin, his body tightened again.

Back in the bedroom, he stood at the window and studied the backyard. With the loss of leaves from the birches and maples, the conifers captured the limelight in the late afternoon sun. Soon that sun would be lower and weaker. Soon snow would cover the firs. Soon the Board of Trustees would be picking a permanent Head of School and Noah's time at Tucker would be done.

It occurred to him that the place wasn't all that bad. But some things were written in the stars, and this was one. He was destined to head a *great* school. Not Mount Court.

A glance over his shoulder told him that Paige remained under the comforter, and just then the second-floor sounds picked up. Taking his cue, he left the room.

Paige dreamed of things so seductive and passionate and downright erotic that she awoke in a sweat. The room was dark. She was alone. It was a minute before her body stopped trembling, a minute before the reality of her exhaustion and its cause hit her, and then she brushed her hair back with a forearm and moaned.

The clock glowed a green ten twenty-two. She figured she had been sleeping for more than seven hours and had every intention of going for another seven, but in this short break she thought of Jill and her baby and all the others who'd been hurt. Life was fragile, taken for granted day to day, but such a tenuous thing. Paige's own parents had had that close call in an airplane, but how many close calls had there been in automobiles? Or walking along streets? Or sitting, oblivious of danger, in theaters whose structural stability was in doubt?

She thought of coming home that afternoon to Nonny and Sami, and then there were visions of Noah—had he been there or had she simply dreamed him? Months before she had thought her life rewarding—she still thought it so—but these new elements fit into it with frightening ease.

Fragile. Tenuous. Happiness that could get a firm grip, then tear your flesh away when it left. Was it truly better to have loved and lost than never to have loved at all? She didn't know. The pain of wanting things one couldn't have was devastating. It was sometimes better to push them from mind and pretend that they just didn't exist.

So much for dreams. Reality was harder to ignore.

Reality, just then, was tens of patients for whom Paige was no longer responsible but whom she wanted to visit. Reality was a thriving group practice meant for four, with only three left and working double time. Reality was Nonny, who was seventy-six going on fifty, and Sami, who was sixteen months going on twelve months. Reality was a cross-country team to coach every afternoon, and a baby-sitter to heal, and too few hours in the day.

The exhaustion of it put Paige back to sleep, but she awoke the next morning knowing that of the four doctors coming to Tucker to interview that week, one of them had better be good.

One was. Her name was Cynthia Wales. After completing her residency in pediatrics, she had spent four years on the staff at Children's Hospital in Boston, but she was an outdoorswoman. She wanted to be closer to mountains and rivers, and she wanted the less pressured practice that would grant her time to explore them. Best of all, she had come to interview at the start of a two-week vacation and was willing to postpone that vacation and start working right away.

Cynthia was an easy sell. Paige, who got glowing reports from colleagues who had worked with her and felt the sheer energy level of the woman, liked her from the start. Likewise Angie, who was looking to spend more time at home. Ironically, after pushing to hire someone, Peter was hesitant.

"What bothers you?" Paige asked him.

He was looking everywhere but at her. "I don't know."

"Her credentials are impressive," Paige coaxed. She didn't think it was a power play on Peter's part. He looked legitimately bewildered.

"There's something about her," he tried, sounding pained, then defeated. "No, maybe it has nothing to do with her."

"She isn't Mara."

"No." He cracked his knuckles. "She isn't."

Paige was grateful that he could finally admit it. She didn't know what he remembered of the night he'd been drunk, but he had been less critical of Mara ever since.

"She isn't Mara," Paige repeated, "but she may be wonderful with our families. Why don't we give her a try? You said it yourself, Peter. We have to move on."

He met her gaze then and sighed. "You're right. Let's do it."

The relief was immediate. Cynthia was a bundle of enthusiasm, received so well by the patient families she saw that by week's end the group sent out a letter explaining that she would be taking over Mara's practice.

Paige began to breathe more easily. With a fourth doctor to normalize things at the office, she could run back and forth to the hospital, where her services were snapped up. Every bed in the place was taken and then some. Doctors were in demand, hospital services stretched thin. Specialists had been brought in to treat many of the patients Paige had seen, but there was always something for her to do. And then there was Jill, who was lying in her cast listening to the fetal monitor, wondering if the baby would live and whether she wanted it to. With her father still ignoring her, her mother trying to hold her job and visit Jill on the sly without her father finding out, and her best friend still hospitalized in Hanover, she spent much of her time alone.

For that reason Paige was pleased to walk into her hospital room on the Saturday morning after the collapse and find Sara standing by her bedside. "What a nice surprise," she said, putting an arm around Sara, then as quickly drawing back. "Don't you *dare* tell me you thumbed in this time, Sara Dickinson."

"No. I came with my father."

"Ahhh. Better." She felt a flicker of heat at the thought of Noah nearby.

"You didn't tell me Jill was pregnant," Sara said.

"I felt it was Jill's decision to make as to whether she told or not."

"She asked what the monitor was for," Jill explained. "But I don't mind. Everyone knows."

Paige smiled her encouragement and asked softly, "Are you okay?" The floor nurse had caught her on her way past and told her that the baby had appeared distressed at one point during the night. For a short time, the doctors had considered doing a section. Then it had stabilized.

"I'm okay," Jill said. "Just hurting. They won't give me much for the pain."

"They're afraid it would affect the baby."

"I'd think the baby would like it," Sara said, and did something with her eyes to give the illusion of their spinning in opposite directions at once.

"How do you do that?" Paige asked, laughing, but Jill had laughed, too, so the answer was moot, and Sara was barreling on, looking slightly awed now.

"Jill said that the guys from Henderson Wheel were in to visit."

Paige looked at Jill. "Yes?"

"Last night. After you left. Robbie Howe—he's the drummer—is so cool. He sat with me for ten minutes. He said he'd have stayed longer but that they had to fly to New Jersey for a gig."

"What did you talk about?" Sara asked.

"Music. The concert. Where else they're playing. They never had anything happen to them like happened here last week, and this is their hometown. It's like, too much. They feel awful. They're going to keep coming back to see people. He said that if I needed anything— like if I had trouble with money for all this—I should let him know. They want to help."

"So does my dad," Sara said. "He's downstairs talking about it with someone now. He thinks it would be great if the kids at Mount Court could help some of the people who were hurt. I mean, we can't do medical things, but we can visit, or help with homework."

"How about baby-sit?" Paige asked, thinking of Mary O'Reilly. Her husband had suffered a broken back and would be hospitalized for months. Once he was transferred to Tucker, Mary would want to visit, but she had limited mobility herself. For now her in-laws were helping her out, but they both worked.

"We can baby-sit," Sara said with confidence.

Baby-sitting was only the first of the things Paige thought of. The list was endless once she got going, and it included helping both those injured in the movie house and those who had relied on the injured for help. She passed on her ideas to Noah, who was determined to take the opportunity to teach his students a lesson in community cooperation. The time it took for Tucker General's social services director to organize things allowed for fall sports to wind down.

Diligently, Paige prepared her team for the last few races of the season. Several were running better than ever—girls who had climbed Noah's mountain and found a measure of self-confidence at the top. Sara was one; her times continued to improve, along with her comfort level, if telling friends of her relationship to Noah was any measure of that. Then again, it struck Paige that Sara might have felt comfortable telling friends that he was her father because the tide had turned. He wasn't winning popularity contests yet, but he had earned a modicum of respect on campus.

As for Paige, when Noah stopped by to watch practice it was all she could do not to shake. She still thought him gorgeous. She had even come to like him. And then there were the dreams that she had all too often.

So she limited her interaction with him to discussion of the girls, which was, after all, the only business she had at Mount Court. And there was plenty to talk about, particularly where Julie Engel was concerned.

She was a problem. She skipped class and was put on detention; she left the dorm after hours and was put on detention; she smoked in her room and was put on detention. While the others had generally responded well to Noah's tactics, she had not. Rather than being buoyed by the experience of Knife Edge, she felt humiliated.

"I couldn't do it," she complained when Paige raised the issue in an attempt to get to the heart of the problem.

"You *did* it. You made it across."

"I was a total wimp."

"But you got there. That's what counts, Julie. You have to stop regarding the glass as half-empty. It's half-full—and you can fill it the rest of the way if you want, but you have to *want*."

Unfortunately the only thing Julie wanted related to the opposite sex. Of all the senior girls, she was the one most aware of herself as a woman, which, given the letter she had written to Peter, made Paige a mite uneasy.

Peter, fortunately, was aware of the problem and had started sending Cynthia to Mount Court when the infirmary called. What with the return of normalcy to the office, he, like Paige, was spending time each day at the hospital, helping with patients injured in the movie house collapse.

Given the negative thoughts she had had about him, Paige found his dedication to be redeeming. When she made a casual reference to it, though, he was far from casual. "It's the least I can do, don't you think? Okay, so it wasn't a fire, but Jamie Cox had no business packing people into the movie house. I knew it just as well as Mara did, but I was too cowardly to pick up the fight where she left off. If I had, the collapse might never have happened."

Paige felt duly chastised. "I'm as guilty as you. I did nothing either."

"Yeah, but look what else you're doing. You've taken Mara's child. That's a major obligation."

"No obligation," Paige replied. "An obligation is something negative. Sami isn't at all."

"She's work and responsibility."

"But not negative. And only temporary."

Paige kept reminding herself of that. Weekly visits from the adoption agency's Joan Felix helped, as did biweekly sessions with the agency's other parents. Those discussions focused on the ups and downs of adoption in general and interracial adoption in particular, and while those ups and downs didn't faze Paige in the least, the sessions were a touchstone to reality. Without them she might have pretended that Sami would be forever hers.

The little girl was a treasure, a blossoming little person to wake up to in the mornings, to stop home at noontime to see, and to have supper with at night. As a pediatrician, Paige had known about the miracle of a child's development, but seeing it in other people's children was one thing, seeing it in her own another. Each day Sami did something new, something that gave Paige a special pride. The child was thriving, putting on weight, catching up with her age with astonishing speed. Paige was sure that when she hit school she would be the smartest little girl in the class.

The problem of hiring a baby-sitter haunted her. She knew she should be looking but kept putting it off. As guilty as she felt imposing so deeply on Nonny's life, the fact was that she didn't trust anyone else with Sami as she trusted her grandmother—who had, for all practical purposes, moved in with her. She had taken over the second upstairs bedroom and had brought enough things from her house, including a red-and-white rag rug, a huge heart comforter, and a white wicker rocker, to make the room her own.

They were a family—Nonny, Sami, and Paige. They went out together driving, shopping, and visiting, and Paige loved every novel minute of it. Those times when she felt guilty having such fun, she simply reminded herself that it was temporary and the guilt eased. Likewise when Noah invited the three of them out to dinner.

He was passing through Tucker, like Sami and Nonny. The transiency made it safe.

So different was this makeshift life from the one Paige knew to be permanent, and so shielded did she feel from reality, that when the middle of November arrived, and with it her birthday, she decided to break with tradition. Normally she filled the day with every commitment she could find for the purpose of arriving home at night too tired to do anything but fall into bed—certainly too tired to think—and by the time she awoke the next morning the dreadful day was gone.

This year she felt braver.

Eighteen

Paige's birthday fell on a Thursday. She arranged to take the day off from work, and since the cross-country season had ended the weekend before, there was no practice to interrupt a lazy day. She planned to spend it at home with Nonny and Sami.

"I see it in patients sometimes," Mara had written in a letter that had spoken directly to Paige, "those few lucky families who know the pleasure of being together for no other reason than being together. It takes a meshing. It takes the acceptance of one person by another, differences and all. It takes the kind of love that doesn't demand, simply is."

Paige was regarding Nonny and Sami as her family in many of those same regards. In the wake of the movie house tragedy, she was grateful they were there.

She wanted to have a big breakfast at home, then read the paper. She wanted to bundle everyone up against the nippy air, take a walk into town, and put Sami in the kiddie swing in the park by the church. She wanted to go back home, listen to music and knit while Sami napped, then take her and Nonny across the state line to Hanover for a birthday dinner at the Inn.

As it happened, she had barely finished devouring the last of Nonny's Belgian waffles when the first of the year's snow started to fall. By the time she had read the newspaper cover to cover the flakes were coming more steadily. She took Sami from the playpen and joined Nonny at the picture window that looked out from the kitchen onto the backyard.

"Beautiful, isn't it?" Nonny asked.

"It is. Look, Sami. Snow." To Nonny she said, "It's her first one. A milestone."

Sami had her little hand flat on the window.

"Can you say snow?" Paige urged. When no sound was forthcoming, she said, "How about Nonny? Non-ny. Come on, give it a try. Non-ny. No? Then try Ma-ma. Mmma. Mmma."

Nonny arched a brow her way.

"It's generic," Paige assured her.

"It doesn't have to be. You could adopt her."

"Nah. She needs a full-time mother."

"Between you and me, she has one, and before you know it she'll be going off to school, and then you won't even need me. You could do what Angie has done all these years, work while the child is in school and be done in time to pick her up. What do you think Mara was planning?"

"Exactly that," Paige conceded, "but I'm not Mara. She had a *thing* for being a mother. She was obsessed with that kind of relationship." The deep connect, she had called it. "I don't have quite that need."

"You're more independent?"

"Self-reliant."

"Poppycock. You need family just like the rest of us."

"Yes, but not as *immediately* as Mara did. Not as intimately. I was perfectly satisfied with my life as it was before Mara died."

"But you love having Sami."

"Um-hmmm. It makes me feel good knowing that I can give her love while the agency searches for permanent parents."

"What if they don't find any?"

"They will. It's just a matter of time."

"And in the meanwhile you're becoming more attached to her. You can't fool me, Paige. I see you creeping up to her room every night long after she's asleep."

"I'm checking to make sure she's all right."

"You're standing over her crib for fifteen, twenty minutes sometimes. Face it, sweetheart, you're hooked."

Paige brought Sami's hand to her mouth. She kissed it, then shifted the small fingers to her chin. "Mara wrote about being a foster mother in some of her letters. She said that there was always a problem with separation, but that the satisfaction of helping a child made it worth the pain. I've helped Sami. I've given her a good start here. I feel the satisfaction of that."

"And the pain? Will you feel that, too?"

"When the time comes."

Nonny didn't say more, and Paige didn't invite it. This was her birthday, a difficult enough day on its own. She wanted to keep it as upbeat as possible.

So she played with Sami, then took her upstairs and bathed and dressed her, but when she would have gone out for a walk, the snow was falling harder than ever.

Nonny joined her at the front window. "It's mounting up."

"Mmm. What would you say, two inches?"

"Three. You're not wheeling a carriage far in that."

"No. I wish we had a sled. Maybe I can put her in the Snugli and cover her with my parka."

"She won't be able to see anything."

"I'll turn it around so that she looks out. Better still, why don't we get in the car and go to Hanover now. The driving can't be that bad."

The look Nonny gave her said that it certainly could be. Then the look turned sad. "I know what you're doing, Paige. It's the same thing you've been doing for years and years, modified, perhaps, but the basic strategy is the same. If you arrange to be out of the house, you won't be here when the phone doesn't ring." She looked pained. "They won't call, Paige. They might call in two weeks, or five weeks, but they aren't attuned to remembering your birthday. It's as simple as that."

Paige stared out at the snow. "I've never been able to understand it. If they had eight kids, okay. Dates can be confused. But I'm their only child. My mother gave birth once in her life, just once. Didn't that day mean anything to her?"

"It did. Just not the same thing it would have meant to me, or to you, if you'd been the one to give birth."

"I'd be anticipating the day for weeks. I'd be planning a party. I'd be thinking of all the things my child most wanted to do, and I'd have them planned without even having to ask her."

"That's because you're you. But Chloe isn't you, and she's not going to change."

Paige thought about that, then sent Nonny a small smile and a shrug.

"Still you hope?" Nonny said.

Paige's smile turned self-mocking. "Maybe one year, by some quirk of fate, it'll just hit them." She studied the snow. "But you're right. We shouldn't go out driving in this. How about I build a fire and we'll play Scrabble?" That demanded concentration. It would take her mind off the phone.

Nonny scowled. "You always win."

"I'll let you make a blank out of one letter per turn."

Nonny liked that idea. So did Sami, who had great fun poking at the letter tiles. Paige still won the game, but by that time Nonny was thinking about lunch and after lunch Sami went in for a nap and Nonny dozed off on the living room sofa.

Planting herself before the fire and out of sight of the phone, Paige picked up her knitting. She was finishing the afghan Mara had started for Sami. It seemed the perfect thing for Sami to bond with and then take with her to her next life. A gift from Mara. Via Paige.

Kitty wandered into the room. She had spent the morning as she always did, roaming the house, perching on one windowsill or another, clicking her teeth at anything that looked as if it might be a bird. Now she sat at Paige's feet and stared at the yarn as it came out of the skein. Every few minutes she pounced, took the yarn in her mouth, and shook it. When Paige gave a tug she released her hold, sat back, and stared at the new yarn coming out.

Paige set aside the knitting and scooped her up. She was getting bigger. Her fur was longer now and softer. Paige enjoyed the feel of her at the foot of her bed each night. There was something nice about reaching down to touch her and about the purr that started up when she did it.

"You going to get rid of her, too?" Nonny asked. Her eyes were open, though other than that she hadn't moved.

Paige felt the blunt edge of the question, particularly the "too." "It's not a question of 'getting rid' of her. It's a question of finding her a proper home."

"Are you still looking?"

"Theoretically. But I keep forgetting to ask. She demands so little."

"Are you willing to keep her?"

Paige rubbed kitty's neck. Kitty closed her eyes and raised her chin for more, which Paige promptly gave. "I may do that by default. She's here. It may be more of an effort to find her a home than to keep her." Hearing her own words, she looked at Nonny. "I know what you're thinking, but the same is *not* true about Sami. You don't keep children by default. Sami is a human being. She's a responsibility that gets bigger the bigger she gets."

Nonny didn't say anything. Nor did she look away.

"I'm a full-time pediatrician," Paige protested.

"Not full-time, now that you've hired a fourth."

"Then three-quarters time. Plus Jill. Plus helping organize the Mount Court kids to help around Tucker," which she felt was a wonderfully worthy cause. "Plus being on call once the mountain opens for skiing. Plus reading. Plus knitting. My life is still demanding, Nonny. Children aren't in my game plan. Not for a while, at least." When Nonny simply lay there staring at her, she set kitty down. "I know what you're thinking, but if the biological clock runs out, it runs out. I won't rush into something that I'm not ready to do."

Nonny neither moved nor spoke.

Paige sighed. "Look, I know I'm not giving you the answers you want, and I'm sorry to be imposing on you with Sami this way—"

"Don't use that word!" Nonny hollered, sitting up with a speed Paige wouldn't have expected from a woman her age.

"But it *is* an imposition."

"Damn it, Paige, that's the trouble with you! You're so smart when it comes to most things, but when it comes to parenthood you're way off the mark." She had pushed her small self from the sofa and begun to pace. "Not that it's your fault. Chloe and Paul made you feel like an unwanted limb. Growing up, you were good as gold for me, because you didn't want to be a burden, and you're still apologizing every time you ask me to do something. Still apologizing."

She stopped in front of Paige with her hands on her hips. "For God's *sake,* Paige, people who love people want to do things for them. Why haven't you *learned* that? Have I ever complained? Have I ever said I'd rather be playing bridge? My coming to baby-sit for Sami isn't a task. It's a privilege. It's a joy. Yes, it's work, but a labor of love. No obligation. No onerous task. No grotesque plague on my time. *I want to baby-sit.* And if you were truthful with yourself, you'd admit that you want to keep Sami. You adore her. She adores you. You have ample resources to raise her in comfort. But you're frightened of making the commitment, because you think of it as something that will smother. You mother everyone else's children, but that doesn't count, because you can leave them all behind at the end of the day. Well, let me tell you," she scolded as Nonny rarely did, "you leave behind the pleasure, too. No pain, no gain, as they say. You come home to an empty house, which, by the way, will seem twice as empty now that you're used to having Sami around."

She started to turn away but turned right back. "And I'll tell you something else. That empty house will seem *three* times as empty when you're fifty, and *four* times as empty when you're sixty, and by then it will be too late. I know." Turning on her heel, she left the room.

Paige waited for her to come back. After a bit, she went into the kitchen and made a pot of fresh mango tea, thinking that the smell of it steeping might lure Nonny down. When it didn't, she poured herself a cup.

The snow continued to fall. Paige watched it, sipping her tea, thinking that everything Nonny said made sense but that old habits died hard. It was one thing to tell herself not to feel that she was imposing, quite another not to feel it. She had always tried to be self-sufficient, precisely to avoid that dilemma.

As for Sami, Paige didn't know. She just didn't know. She supposed she had the time to be a mother. She supposed she had the intelligence and the resources to be one. And the love. Yes, she had that. She did love Sami. But it was such a responsibility. More than doctoring or foster parenting. Much more. She had always assumed she wasn't cut out for motherhood, which was one of the reasons why she had become a doctor.

Or had she become a doctor to give her an out when the weight of the responsibility loomed?

The phone hadn't rung. It would be nighttime in Siena. If it didn't ring very soon, it wouldn't ring at all.

She finished her tea, rinsed the cup, and set it on the drainer. Then she looked at the snow again and felt a sudden, dire need to be in it. After putting on her insulated running gear, a Gortex parka, a wool hat, and mittens, she left a note on the kitchen table for Nonny and set off.

The streets had been plowed but were deserted. She had them to herself, running at the side or the middle, as went her whim. It wasn't until she had reached the center of Tucker, rounded the hospital block, and started back down Main Street that she encountered a moving vehicle. It was Norman Fitch.

"Nasty day to be out," he called out his window.

"Actually," she breathed, "it feels great."

"Snow's not stopping for a while. We're expecting up to a foot. You'd best be heading home. Be dark before long."

But Paige wasn't heading home yet. She had hit her stride and was feeling too good to stop. If her parents chose to call so late, it would be their loss.

She made a tour of the streets behind the center, running up one and down another. The snow was mounting underfoot and her sneakers were getting wet, yet still she ran on. She headed north out of town, where the road was broad and beautiful, rolling through stands of trees whose arms held the snow in lieu of leaves.

In time she began to feel a chill, but her feet beat a rhythmic tattoo on the snow, and her will wasn't yielding to either cold, wetness, or encroaching dusk.

By the time she turned in under Mount Court's wrought-iron arch, she was starting to tremble. That was when she felt a qualm, but it was too late to turn back. She couldn't make it home. She didn't want to.

Since the drive had been first cleared, another several inches had mounted up. She plodded through them, tired now and laboring, but determined. She passed the academic buildings, the administration building, the library, and the first of the dorms. She turned onto the path between the second and third and, in the distance, saw the completed frame of the new alumni house, but she ran on to the Head's house and struggled up the low steps. Stopping at last, panting, she rang the bell.

Noah answered the door wearing a sweatshirt and sweatpants, with his round, wire-rimmed glasses perched on the bridge of his nose and a pencil between his teeth. He took one look at her, tossed the pencil aside, and hauled her in by the arm. "Brilliant," he declared, as he swung the door shut. "Absolutely brilliant." He pulled off her hat and mittens and set to picking at the zipper of her parka through the snow that had crusted there. "What in the world possessed you to run all the way out here?"

"Don't know," she said through chattering teeth. She was shifting from one foot to the other, too cold to stand still but unable to undress, which was fine, since Noah was doing it for her. "It wasn't conscious. I just ran. My feet took me here."

He had freed the tab of the zipper and was tugging it down. She turned from one side to the other to free her arms from the parka. Then she held his shoulder when he knelt to pull off her sneakers. "This'll all melt in your hall," she warned.

"Fine. I need an excuse to resand the wood. Do you know how much snow's out there?"

"They kept plowing. It wasn't so much."

"It's twenty-two degrees out. And you're wearing these skimpy running pants." After tossing aside the second sneaker, he took her hand and led her up the stairs and through the bedroom she assumed was his to the bathroom, where he turned on the shower. While he waited for it to heat, he pulled off her turtleneck jersey, then her running pants. He muttered a pithy oath when he saw her legs, which were bright red from the cold. When steam had begun to fog the door of the shower, he opened it and shoved her inside, underwear and all.

The warmth was heavenly. Paige's muscles ached. Her skin stung, then tingled. She held her face to the spray, turned, and let it pour over her head. Parts of her body that had been numb began slowly to revive. With the increased sensation, she pulled off her underwear, dropped it in a corner, and returned to the full force of the spray.

She was thinking that she might just stay in Noah's shower forever when the door opened and he joined her. His glasses were gone, and his clothes, but it seemed the best thing to happen to her that day. Without a second thought, she wrapped her arms around his neck.

If there was a birthday gift to be had, this was it. She had been wanting him forever, it seemed, and the waiting only enhanced the pleasure she felt. She was tingling now from the inside, all the more so when he circled her hips and lifted her so that their mouths could meet.

Their kiss was as wet as the shower. Paige lost herself in it and in the kisses that followed, each one sweeter, deeper, more consuming—and frustrating. For every kiss, every touch, she needed more. She strained closer, moving her hands through his hair and over his skin, craving the kind of possession for which her dreams had left her wanting.

Taking her weight on his thighs, he braced her against the shower wall, touched her breasts and swallowed her cries, and still it wasn't enough. She was feeling desperate, feeling that if she didn't have more, she might die. That was when she felt his entry.

The scraping glide, the fullness, the sense of every loose end of her life coming together, touched off a million tiny explosions inside her, and that was before he began to move. When he did, she could only catch her breath and hang on. Her body shook in a trail of orgasmic shocks, one dovetailing the next, never quite ending but going on and on and on.

She was gasping against his ear, trembling in the aftermath, when she realized that he was rock still and hard all over. She drew back, wiped the water from his face, and, with a hand on his cheek, met his eyes. They were as hard as his body, but hot and hungry.

"I can't finish," he ground out, "until I put something on."

"No need," she whispered. She slid off him and took him between her hands, and while she gave everything she could to his mouth, she stroked him below. It didn't take long. He was as primed as she had been—from dreams? she wondered, but didn't ask. That would have involved confessions and deeper discussions than those she was prepared to hold. Rather, when he came with a long, guttural cry, she held him until he could breathe again, then bathed him, then let him towel her off and lead her to his bed.

She was thinking how beautiful his body was, how well proportioned and manly, and that she wanted him again. But when he should have slid under the covers and taken her in his arms, he simply perched on the sheets, punched out a phone number, and looked at her while he waited for the other end to ring.

"Hey, Nonny, it's Noah. Paige is here." He listened. "She's fine. I'm just warming her up." He listened more, then asked, "Any problem if she spends the night?" He listened a final time. "Sounds good. We'll see you then."

Paige didn't move.

Looking at her all the while, he hung up the phone and said, "It's time we stop fooling ourselves. Something's going on between us, and I don't know as it's pure lust." His mouth curved. "But I'm willing to explore the pure lust theory for a while."

He reached for her as he slid under the covers, and if she had objected to anything he had said or done, she would have promptly forgotten. The coming together of their bodies was like nothing she had ever experienced. It was so strikingly new and special, so provocative, so incendiary, that to deny it would have been to deny her very existence.

The exploration was slower this time. It was a hand here, glancing over skin and through hair. It was a tongue there, tracing and taunting, dancing away when the arch of a body sought more. It was the visual study of a tactile response and the seductive effect of a word, a hum, a sigh, and the joint rise of breathing and need until only completion would do.

This time they climaxed together, then lay for a long time, reluctant to move. A sweet lethargy owned Paige's body. She felt warm and safe and incredibly at peace.

Noah stretched against her. He kissed her forehead and said in a crusty male voice, "When I applied for this job, the trustees asked me about my morals. They were concerned because I was single. Seeing how it's isolated up here. And the sweet young locals are always hungry for fresh meat. Wonder what the board would say if they could see me now."

Paige grinned against his chest. "I'm not a sweet young local. I'm a doctor. And this is the very first time I've come here."

"Why did you?"

She raised her eyes. "Nonny didn't tell you that?"

"Tell me what?"

She settled in again, running her thumb over the hair that trailed down the center of his chest. It was darker than that on his head, the color of warm maple against his skin. "It's my birthday. I figured I deserved a treat."

"Your birthday. No kidding?"

"No kidding."

"Did Nonny bake a cake?"

"No. Mara was always the one who did that. Last year she made a monstrosity of a cake, brought it into the office, and set it up in the waiting room where everyone who walked in could take a piece." She fell quiet, thinking of Mara, feeling lonely to be growing older without her.

Noah's arms tightened. The comfort was welcome, but it didn't divert Paige's thoughts. After a time she said, "She had a way of making everyone happy but herself. She was like the clown who was crying inside. So sad. Something I don't ever want to be. So when I started feeling sorry for myself this afternoon—because the snow had spoiled my plans, and Nonny was cross with me, and my parents hadn't called—I went out for a run. And ended up here."

He ran his hands through her hair. It was a lulling gesture. When she hummed her pleasure, he kept at it. Within minutes she was asleep.

Noah dozed, but not for long. He had no desire to sleep away as intense a pleasure as Paige Pfeiffer. For a time he just looked at her, studying her features as she slept, savoring the curl of her body against his, the swell of her breast, the sweep of her thigh. In time he kissed her, because to be near her this way and not do it was painful.

She came slowly awake, saw him, and smiled.

"You're tired," he whispered.

"Not that tired," she whispered back.

"Hungry?"

"Starved."

"Can I make you a birthday dinner?"

Paige found the thought of that eminently pleasing. "Sure. If you want."

"I want," he said, but he made no move to leave the bed. Instead he came over her and kissed her eyes, her nose, her mouth. Then he kissed the tip of her chin, then under it, then her throat, then the pulsing spot at her neck. The pulsing picked up as he worked his way down her body, over her breasts, her ribs, her belly, until she was a writhing mass of nerve ends waiting to connect, and when they did, when his tongue brought her to a release as no man ever had, she was too scattered to realize it.

But later, after he had indeed left the bed and prepared her the most simple, most kind, most delicious birthday dinner she could have wanted, she knew that something special had happened. She had tasted something, a nameless something that threatened to upset the order of her life as neither Mara's death, nor Sami's arrival, nor Nonny's moving in had yet.

One part of her wanted to run as fast and far as she could, but she didn't move. She stayed in Noah's bed, made love with him over and over through the night, and when he drove her home the next morning through the winter wonderland that Tucker had become, she let him kiss her a final time.

"This isn't over," he warned as though reading her mind.

She didn't answer. There were too many things she had to think about, not the least of which was sitting in a high chair with mashed banana all over her face when Paige walked in the door. When Sami gave her a mucky grin and said through the mess, "Ma-ma-ma-ma-ma," Paige wondered if there was a conspiracy afoot. They were trying to snag her by the strings of her heart and tie her down.

She was thinking that she was going to have to steel herself by immersing herself more deeply in those other things that made up her life, when the hospital called to say that Jill was in labor.

Peter called out to Paige as she ran down the hospital corridor, but she simply held up a hand and was gone.

So he continued on to the office. Angie was really the one he wanted to talk to anyway.

He caught her an hour later, between patients. "Got a minute?"

She tucked her stethoscope in the pocket of her lab coat and motioned him into her office. "What's up?"

"I need your opinion on a patient."

"Who is it?"

"Not one of ours, just someone I helped at the hospital after the accident. It's a thirty-four-year-old female in otherwise good health. She was in the balcony and fell clear of the worst of the debris, but she landed on her lower back. X-rays show a lapse in the spinal cord between T-twelve and L-one. She was a questionable red-code at the time. They considered flying her out, but since it appeared to be an isolated spinal injury and there were so many other patients with multiple injuries, they kept her here. She's had repeated CAT scans. The initial swelling responded to the drip they gave her, but she can't move."

"Not at all?" Angie asked.

"Not from the waist down. She doesn't have any sensation. No pain. No pressure. No tingling." Peter had done his own little tests when he'd seen her. "The neurosurgeon has been in and out. He says it's a done deal. Paralysis. I want to know if he's right."

"Was this Mike Caffrey?"

Peter nodded.

"He's good," Angie said.

But Peter hadn't liked his bedside manner. At a time when she had no one at all with her, he had bluntly told Kate Ann that she would never walk. Peter had come in hours later and found her in tears. He couldn't help but feel bad for her.

"What do you think about the case?" he asked Angie.

"I'm not a neurosurgeon."

"But you remember every detail of every rotation you did, and you know the neurosurgeon's bible by heart. Should I call in a consult, or is it a done deal?"

She thought for a minute. "The CAT scan says there's no swelling?" He shook his head. "But she has no feeling at all?" He shook his head again. Sympathetically she said, "Then it doesn't look good."

That was what he was afraid of. Too much time had passed with no physical response to suggest that movement might return on its own. "What about physical therapy?" he asked.

"Is that what they're suggesting?"

"They're not suggesting much. The poor woman is lying there all alone, day after day, not knowing what in the hell's going on."

"Does she have family?"

"Nope."

"Friends?"

"Nope."

"She was at that concert all alone?" Angie asked in surprise.

Peter sputtered out a facetious half laugh. "Yeah. That's the joke of it. She's the quietest, shiest woman in the world, but she happens to love Henderson Wheel. She'd never been to a rock concert in her life before this. It took every bit of her courage to buy the ticket, much less show up." Not that anyone had taunted her. Peter had asked. In the midst of the music and the lights and the beat, she had simply faded onto her paid seat in the balcony, which was largely the story of her life. Even now she lay in her hospital room, quiet, undemanding, and nearly invisible. Peter didn't know how anyone couldn't feel sorry for her.

"Physical therapy," he said, hauling his mind back on track. "Will it do much good?"

Angie shrugged. "It'll develop and strengthen the muscles in her upper body. It'll keep her lower body limber so that she can handle it better, and if there is a return of sensation, she can capitalize on it. Will it fix what's been broken? No."

Peter ran a hand up the back of his head. "That's what I thought." He swore softly. He had no idea what

Kate Ann was going to do. Neither did she—and she wasn't dumb, by a long shot. He was fast coming to understand that. She knew what she faced.

"The Spinal Cord Center in Rutland is a good one," Angie suggested. "Or the Rehab Center in Burlington. If she's willing to go to Springfield or Worcester or Boston, she'll have even more to choose from."

Peter knew all that. What he didn't know was how she was going to pay for the care that she needed. She didn't have medical insurance, hadn't been able to afford it.

"Who is she?" Angie asked curiously.

He took a deep breath, slipped his hands in the pockets of his slacks, and exhaled. "No one important." He took another breath and said more hesitantly, "There's something else. I'm thinking of suing Jamie Cox."

Angie looked startled.

Peter was instantly defensive. "You don't think I should?"

"I *think* you should. I'm surprised. That's all. He's one of yours."

"He's sleaze. Do you know what he's going around town saying? He's saying that the reason the balcony collapsed is that there were too many people up there. That there were more people than tickets he sold. That people snuck in and were sitting in the aisles and standing up in back and on the sides. He's saying that what happened was their own fault, and that no jury in the world would find him guilty. He's saying that no one can possibly prove that that balcony was structurally unsafe, and that anyone who tried would be a fool."

"A threat if ever there was one."

"And untrue. People can prove the balcony was unsafe. Any laborer in town who's done incidental work there has seen the weaknesses. The problem is, most of them won't come forward because Jamie owns the houses they live in. He's got 'em by the balls." Peter tucked his hands behind his suspenders. "But he doesn't have me that way. I own my own place. And he has money that can help those people who need care and can't pay for it themselves." Like Kate Ann. She was a perfect example. She had paid full price for a ticket and mustered up her courage to go to a concert for the very first time. Now she was a paraplegic. No one could give her back the use of her legs—it was too late for that—but someone could sure as hell make the life that she had left a little easier.

"The question," he went on, "is how to get that money. I was thinking I'd ask Ben if he knew of a lawyer, someone out of town, who's good and would be willing to take on the case. Maybe someone in Montpelier who knows how the state courts work. Think he'd give me a name?"

"Of course he'd give you a name. And in any case, I'm sure he'd like to see you. You don't stop over anymore."

Not since Mara had died. He used to like seeing her there. She had always been more laid-back in a family setting.

And then there was the matter of the trouble between Angie and Ben. That had started up soon after. Dropping by to see Ben would have been awkward.

"Why don't I mention it to him tonight," Angie offered.

"I'd appreciate it," Peter said, and started to leave.

She touched his arm. "Are you doing this for Mara?"

He considered that. "Maybe." And maybe a little for Lacey, though she had gone back to Boston, and he was just as glad. He didn't want her back. She had pricked his conscience, was all.

He shrugged. "Who knows. Maybe I'm doing it for me." He grinned. "Maybe I want to be a new kind of hero. With you ladies giving me a run for my money on the medical front, I need a new niche. Peter Grace, civic activist. Sounds impressive, don't you think?"

Nineteen

Angie saw the last of her patients shortly before three, left the office soon after that, and drove straight home. She was disappointed when Ben's car wasn't there, but not surprised. It was the third day this week that she'd come home early. He hadn't been there once.

Sometimes she drove around; sometimes she waited. This time she decided to make use of the time by going to the fish market in Abbotsville. Fresh fish was trucked there every morning from the coast of Maine, and the prices were high. But Ben loved lobster. As she saw it, the expenditure was an investment in her marriage.

Back home again, she waited. With the coming of darkness, she turned on the lights. She did a load of laundry, set the table, put the lobster pot on the stove, made a salad, spread garlic butter on bread that was ready for toasting. She read *Newsweek*. She called Dougie and left a message when he wasn't in the dorm.

It struck her that Ben might have gone to see him. The eighth-grade class was going to Acadia National Park that weekend, so Dougie wouldn't be home, but if he had called, needing something, Ben might have dropped over whatever it was. He might have taken him for ice cream. No, not ice cream. Hot chocolate.

He might have wanted to talk with Dougie about school. About Thanksgiving, which was approaching fast. About Angie.

She wondered what he would say about her.

Then again, maybe he was with Nora. He claimed it was over between them—the times she had driven around, she had driven by the library first and his car wasn't there—but if he wasn't with her, where was he?

Angie pulled the newspapers from the day's mail, one from Chicago, one from Seattle, one from New York, and opened to the editorial pages. Ben's cartoon was the same in each, a single-frame tongue-in-cheek drawing of three prominent members of the House of Representatives, each wearing a Boy Scout uniform, a halo, and a benevolent grin, each hiding a knife marked, in turn, THE POOR, THE ELDERLY, and THE CHRONICALLY ILL.

It was something he might have drawn twenty years before. His priorities hadn't changed. Not politically, at least. She trusted that he would always root for the underdog. But she wasn't sure what else she could trust.

She heard the Honda turn into the driveway and stayed where she was. Although he must have seen her car, he looked startled to find her sitting there when he opened the kitchen door.

"Hi. When'd you get home?" he asked.

"A while ago."

He glanced at the counter. "Wow. You've been working. What're you making? Hey, those are lobsters in the sink!"

"I bought them in Abbotsville. I thought they'd be fun."

"We haven't had lobster in ages."

"That's why I bought them."

He studied her. Innocently he asked, "Is something wrong?"

Was something wrong? *Was something wrong?* It was the wrong thing to ask her, in the wrong tone of voice. Something snapped inside, only this time there were no tears. "Is something wrong? You're *damn right* something's wrong. I came home early to see you. I've come home early three times this week, only you're never here. Where have you been?"

He pursed his lips, seeming defiant for a minute, before shrugging. "Here and there."

"Where's here and there?" She didn't care if she sounded shrewish. They had been walking politely around each other, pretending that everything was all right. Only it wasn't.

"You want a rundown?" he asked, defiant indeed.

"Yes. Yes, I do."

He leaned against the counter and started ticking off his stops in a robotic tone. "I started off at the post office. George Hicks was there. He suggested we go for coffee. I didn't have anything else to do. As far as I knew, you'd be at work. So we had coffee. Then I went to the hardware store and talked with Marty. While I was there, the Freemans came in. They said they were on their way to an estate sale in White River Junction, so I followed them there."

"An estate sale?" Angie asked. "Since when are you interested in antiques?"

"I'm not," he said in his own voice, looking her in the eye, "but the house the antiques were in was gorgeous. And there were other people looking around just like I was. That means human contact, which is a damn sight better than sitting here all by myself." He braced his hands on the counter behind him. "If you'd told me you were coming home early, I might have made a point to be here."

"You wanted spontaneity. I was trying to surprise you."

"Surprise me? Or check up on me? I told you before, Angie, I go out. I stop in town, I drive around, I do whatever I can to keep busy. And don't look at me that way. I wasn't with Nora. I told you *that* before, too."

"Okay." Angie held up a hand. "Fine. You weren't with Nora." Her hand fell. She felt overwhelmingly discouraged. "But this isn't right, Ben. Something's not working. I wasn't coming home to check up on you. I was coming home to spend time with you. I've been trying to change, really I have. I'm not telling you what to do or think. I'm not orchestrating our lives anymore. So what do we do? Nothing. We don't go places. We don't do things. And we don't talk. Not the way we used to. Not honestly. Not impulsively. Certainly not about hopes and dreams, the way we used to when we were younger."

He swore softly, let out a long, tired sigh, and looked away. "I don't know what those hopes and dreams are anymore. Seems like we should be living them out now, only we're not. And suddenly I'm forty-six. More than half of my life is behind me. What's ahead? I just don't know."

"What do you *want* to be ahead?" Angie asked with some urgency. Her future lay in the answer.

"I don't know. That's the problem. If I did, I could act on it. I just feel this goddamned . . . inertia. Like I wake up in the morning and see this guy in the mirror who has a successful career and makes lots of money that he's stashing away for a rainy day that may not ever come. I see the same road stretching before me, day after day after day. It's so fucking boring." He pushed a hand through his hair. "So maybe it wasn't you. Maybe the problem was me after all."

"Not completely. The things you said about me made sense. I didn't hear what you were saying. I was a doctor first, a mother second, and a wife third. I'm trying to change. But I need help from you. You were always the lighthearted one of us. You had the exciting ideas. I was the realist, the pragmatist, and that is boring if it dominates the other all the time." She paused, then asked in frustration, "So why did you let me do it?"

"Because it was easy," he shot back. "It seemed the thing to do. I knew my life would change once I left New York. I surrendered to the inevitable."

Angie felt a spark of anger. "Then what happened is your fault."

"That's what I'm *saying*," he answered, which took the wind from her sails and set them back to square one.

Rising from the table to stand at the window, she thought about what he wasn't saying. He wasn't saying that he wanted a divorce. He wasn't saying that he was bored with *her.* Taking courage from that, she went to where he stood and, shyly almost, slipped her arm through the crook of his. She had always found reassurance in his nearness; she still did; this was what she had missed most in recent weeks.

"So where do we go from here? You have to give me a clue."

"I wish I could."

"What do you want to do?"

"I don't *know.* That's what I'm saying."

"Now," she goaded. "Right now. If you had your choice of doing anything, anything at all, what would you want? What would give you a boost? What would be exciting enough to pull you out of this funk?"

She knew she was taking a chance. If he said that he wanted to see Nora Eaton, she was sunk.

He thought for a minute, then said, "Go somewhere."

"Me?"

"Us. I want us to go somewhere."

Relieved, she asked, "Where?"

He thought again. "Williamsburg, Virginia."

She grinned. "Yes?"

"When we were in New York, we used to talk about going, but you were always so busy and then we had Dougie, and somehow we never found the time."

"Okay." Her grin faded. "Let's do it now."

He looked surprised. "Right now?"

She nodded. "Right now."

"What about Dougie?"

"He's not here."

"What about work?"

She didn't have to think about it. She had put in more than enough hours to compensate, and now there was Cynthia to cover. Angie had a right to the time. This was a family emergency of sorts.

"They'll be able to function without me for a long weekend," Angie said. "How about you?"

"I'm always ahead a few days. I can swing it."

She left his side and went to the phone. But whereas in the past she would have been the one to make the arrangements, now she held out the receiver to him. He stared at it for a bemused minute. By the time he took it, his eyes held a hint of excitement and his lips a touch of the smile that never failed to curl her stomach.

He looked empowered—and Angie didn't care how much Mara would have denied it, an empowered man was a sexy man. With that thought and a smile of her own, she went upstairs to pack.

Paige didn't put on scrubs. She wasn't needed in the operating room. Jill was under general anesthesia and wouldn't know who was there and who wasn't. Her mother, on the other hand, was alone and frightened in the waiting room.

They sat together quietly, holding their breath each time the door opened, releasing it when the doctor who emerged wasn't Jill's. Paige thought of the parents she saw in prenatal sessions, the ones getting a head start on pediatric care, who came to her with questions shortly before their babies were to be born. Their excitement was always contagious.

There was no excitement now—just dread that the baby might be deformed, or too small to live, or ill in some way that demanded prolonged and expensive medical treatment, and fear that Jill, whose insides were already battered, would react adversely to surgery.

When the doctor finally came to see them, it was with a mixed bag of news. "Jill's fine," she said, "but we lost the baby. I'm sorry, Mrs. Stickley. The pelvic fracture caused other internal injuries. It's a miracle the baby stayed in so long."

Jane was holding a hand to her chest. "But Jill's all right."

"She will be. Once the baby was taken, we did some repair work. If all heals well, she'll be able to have other children."

"When can I see her?"

"If you go back to her room, she'll be along soon."

Paige had no intention of waiting. She sent Jane on, then made her way to the recovery room, where Jill was drifting in and out of sleep. As time passed, she was more out than in. Paige held her hand and waited quietly with her arms propped on the bars of the bed.

After a bit, Jill kept her eyes open long enough to focus on Paige.

Paige smiled. "Welcome back."

"What happened?" she whispered hoarsely.

"You're going to be just fine."

"And my baby?"

Paige's smile faded. She shook her head. "It was too little. It couldn't make it."

Jill swallowed and closed her eyes. "What was it?"

One part of Paige didn't want to tell her. Giving the baby a sex made it more real. But then, it had been real. To deny that would be to deny Jill the right to grieve as she needed to do.

Softly she repeated what the surgeon had told her. "It was a boy. Very tiny. There may have been some damage from the accident. It's for the best, Jill."

Jill nodded. She dozed off. Paige remained with her, holding her hand. A few minutes later Jill turned her head and opened her eyes again. She frowned, then remembered.

"A boy. Did he look like Joey?"

Paige smiled sadly. "I don't know. I didn't see him. My guess is he was too little to look like anyone at all."

"I kept wondering . . . kept thinking I'd be walking somewhere . . . see a little kid who looked like one of us." She made a face. "My stomach hurts."

"That's your incision. They took the baby by cesarean section. But you're going to be just fine."

"Only no baby."

"Not now. Another time. When it's right."

Jill nodded. Her eyes pooled. She closed them, but tears trickled from the corners.

Paige held her hand more tightly, letting her cry until the lingering effects of the anesthesia doped her again. When she woke up this time, Paige summoned an orderly and they wheeled her back to her room.

Jane was waiting there, along with Jill's father, who hadn't spoken with Jill since she had announced that she was pregnant. Apparently Jane had called to tell him that she no longer was.

As soon as Jill was shifted onto the proper bed and covered, he leaned over. "Jill? Jillie? It's me."

Jill opened her eyes. They took him in and filled with tears again.

"It's all right, honey," he said, taking her hand and patting it. "You'll be just fine now. Don't you worry about a thing."

Purposefully, Paige moved in close to him. Had he smelled of liquor, she would have summoned Norman Fitch to kick him right out of the hospital. That was how much she thought of Frank Stickley.

But he smelled clean.

So she touched Jill's shoulder and said softly, "I'm going home now, Jill. Your parents will sit with you for a while, but I'll be back first thing in the morning. If there's any problem, ring for the nurse and she'll call me, okay?"

Jill nodded.

Paige left the hospital thinking that Frank Stickley reminded her of Thomas O'Neill. Both men were stubborn; both considered their own values sacrosanct; both had the ability to cut off a child as though it were a fingernail rather than a piece of the heart.

Jill would never forget what her father had done. She might be able to set it aside for the present, but she wouldn't forget it. It was a piece of emotional baggage that she would likely carry for the rest of her life.

Rejection was like that. A borer, it drilled a tiny hole deep inside that never went away. In good times it might be filled with the overflow of happiness, but in bad times it got bigger and bigger, until finally it choked off the will to live. That was what had happened to Mara. Paige was convinced of it. Rejection had become synonymous with failure. Whether her death had been accidental or not was a moot point. She had lost the will to live.

Later, standing over Sami's crib watching her sleep, Paige wondered if children weren't the key, a perpetuation both of the species and of the self. For Mara certainly, they were a validation, a declaration to the world that "I am worthy, therefore I am worthy to raise a child." Jill, who was barely old enough to know what raising a child meant, had felt it on some level. And Paige? Her work had always been her validation.

Suddenly she wondered if it was enough.

Peter was the first to arrive at work the next morning and started seeing drop-ins as soon as they came. He was feeling better than he had in a long time, and that, *in spite* of Angie's call the night before. The fact of her taking Friday and Monday off would mean more work for him at a time when he had other things on his mind, but he could be generous. Angie had been through a rough period. If a long weekend together was what she and Ben needed, he could grant them that.

Fortunately, while the morning served up more than its share of seasonal colds, coughs, and earaches, the afternoon was acute free. He was out of the office by five, crossing through the parking lot to the hospital. What snow remained from the storm had become slushy and dirty, but that didn't discourage him. He was feeling energetic.

He had a regular roster of accident victims whom he saw daily, and daily the list shrank as patients were discharged. Only the more serious remained, which meant that those who needed the greatest care could finally, comfortably, get it.

He visited each in turn, saving Kate Ann for last. When he arrived, she was picking at her dinner. He stood at the door for a minute, watching.

There were only two patients left in the room, Kate Ann and another. The other seemed always to have visitors, while Kate Ann had none, which was one of the reasons Peter tried to save a little extra time for her each day. The other was that he felt bad for her. She faced an ominous future.

"Look who's here," came a familiar voice. A pair of arms circled him from behind, hands coming to rest on his chest with the same suggestiveness as the voice, which proceeded to croon against his back, "My favorite doctor."

He took the hands and lifted them off. As he turned, he saw a group of giggling girls slip into the stairwell down the hall. "Not appropriate behavior, Julie."

She gave him a crooked smile that said she disagreed. "You were looking pensive. Very sexy. Tell me you were thinking about me."

"Sorry, but I wasn't. What are you doing here?"

She pulled at her smock. "I work here."

Smock or not, he didn't believe it. He wouldn't have put it past her to filch the smock. "Uh-huh."

"I do. A bunch of us are helping out. After the collapse at the movie house and all. If it hadn't been fall break weekend, some of us might have been at that concert."

"There but for the grace of God?"

"You could say." She tossed her chin toward Kate Ann. "Has she eaten? I've been back twice looking for her tray. She is so-o slow."

"She has reason to be slow," Peter pointed out. "She has a slight problem with mobility. If you want to be helpful, you could see if anything needs to be cut. For that matter, if you want to be helpful, you could just go in and sit with her. She doesn't have any family. She lies there day in, day out, alone. She could use the company."

Julie looked at Kate Ann uneasily. "What in the world would I say to her? She and I don't have a thing in common."

"How do you know that?"

"Because she's much older than me."

"So am I."

"And she's a townie."

"So am I, but that's beside the point. Kate Ann is an avid reader. She's been through most everything on the bestseller lists. You could discuss one of those books with her. Unless you haven't read any." He took pleasure in Julie's flush, which for once had nothing to do with sex.

"I'm a full-time student," she argued. "I don't have time to read books."

"Then songs. She listens to the radio. You could discuss music with her. Or you could ask her how she's feeling. Ask her if she'd like her television set turned on. Ask her if she'd like the slant of the bed changed. She can't do much for herself. Any help will be appreciated. Come on. I'll show you how." Taking Julie's hand, he led her into the room. He dropped it when he neared the bed.

"Hi, Kate Ann," he said, pleased to see the brightening of her eyes when they caught his. "How're you doin'?"

"Okay."

"What'd you get for dinner?"

She looked dubiously at the tray, then dubiously at Julie. "Fish, I think. But I'm not very hungry. I'm sorry I've held you up. You can take it now."

"You haven't held her up," Peter said. "It's her job to wait as long as need be until you're done." He made the introductions. "Kate Ann, I want you to meet Julie. She's a senior at Mount Court Academy."

Kate Ann produced a rusty smile for Julie, but it was gone in a wink.

"If you ever need anything and she's around, she'll get it. Okay?" He gestured toward the tray. "Don't want anymore?"

"No," she murmured.

Peter gave Julie the tray. "All set," he told her by way of dismissal, and went to the foot of the bed to occupy himself with Kate Ann's chart. By the time he had read that there was no change in her condition, Julie was gone. He returned to the head of the bed.

"You look better, at least. I like the robe." He had picked it up at the mall. It hadn't cost much, but it made Kate Ann look as if someone cared.

"I like it, too," she whispered, fingering the collar. "But you shouldn't have bought it."

Maybe not, he thought to himself, but the teal green of it demanded attention. It refused to be invisible. If Kate Ann was to get the care she needed—which had become his cause—she had to emerge from the woodwork.

Besides, teal did interesting things for her skin, made it look less pale, more alabaster. He doubted she had ever worn anything as vivid. The Kate Ann his mind pictured was always dressed in dull browns and grays. If she did something with her hair, which was straight and long, parted in the middle, and pulled back into a braid, she might actually look attractive.

Then again, it was probably better to leave her hair as it was. Less work.

"And the book on tape," she added. "I listened to it this morning."

"I read it last night." It was a new legal thriller. "What did you think?"

"I thought that it wasn't as good as his first," she said.

Peter agreed. He tried to put his finger on what was wrong. "Too contrived?"

"Like the ingredients of the first mixed up and put back in a different order. Only it didn't work."

"Except for the ex-wife. She is well done."

Kate Ann's eyes sparkled. "She's the most sympathetic of the characters. I like her." The sparkle died. "I envy her."

"Envy?"

"She's resourceful. She finds ways to make things work. She fights for what she wants." Left unsaid was that Kate Ann couldn't do that.

"You could," Peter coaxed.

But she looked away. "I'm not good with people, not good at all. It hurts too much to try. And now, well, I can't—"

"Kate Ann, I've called another doctor. He's a neurosurgeon from Worcester. I'd like him to see you next week."

"I thought there was nothing left to do." She waved a shaky hand toward her legs and looked as though she might cry.

Peter took the hand in his to still it and said with quiet confidence, "There's always something left to do. If it's not surgery, then it's physical therapy." He refused to let her give up.

"But I can't afford another doctor."

"I told you not to worry about money."

"But I don't have any. I can't pay for any of this. And if I can't work soon, I'll lose all my accounts. Isn't there some way I can work? My mind works. And my hands. Can't I do work here?"

"You should be resting."

"I need to work," she whispered, the child again with the big eyes that held desperation and fear to the point of overflowing.

Those eyes did something to Peter. He touched her shoulder. "Be right back." He went to the nurses' station and returned with a piece of paper and a pencil. "Who are your major accounts?"

She was confused. "What—"

"I'll call them and see what I can do."

She gave him the information. "There aren't many," she said meekly, "but they do pay."

He folded the paper and put it in his pocket, feeling at the same time sorry for poor, pathetic Kate Ann Murther and pleased that he could help. It seemed to him that work, even on a small scale, was as valid therapy as the other.

"I'm really starved," he said, "but the stuff you had looked pretty grim. It'll be more of that in the cafeteria. What if I ran over to Harry's and brought back a veal sub. Would you have some?"

She looked startled, then shy. "A little, maybe."

He rubbed his hands together. "Good. I'll be right back."

He bought two subs, had Harry cut Kate Ann's into pickup-size pieces, and returned. She ate nearly half of the sub. He wrapped up the rest, put it on the table by the bed, and instructed the nurse to encourage her to eat more later. Kate Ann had always been thin; now she looked as though a good gust would blow her away. Peter wanted her to put on a few pounds. She needed strength for the long road ahead.

He was thinking about that long road an hour later while he nursed a beer at the Tavern. Familiar boot steps came from the back. His brother Charlie slid into the booth.

"Hey-ya, Pete. What's up?"

"Not much," Peter said.

"You look tired. Putting in extra hours at the hospital?"

"You could say that. The movie house thing is lingering. It'll be a long time before we're back to normal."

"Frenchy's boy got home yesterday, but it'll be a while before he's on his feet. Same with Duke's kid. The two of them toppled down with the rest of the crew in the balcony." He shook his head. "Shouldn't've happened. Frank Stickley's mad as hell. He was in here a little while ago saying someone ought to do something, and he isn't the only one. There's lots of grumblings this time. 'Course, they're just grumblings. No one that rents from Jamie Cox dares take him on." He leaned in and lowered his voice. "You gonna do it?"

"Me?" Peter asked, more curious than surprised.

"You're right for the job. You've seen firsthand the mess he made. And you don't owe a damn thing to Jamie."

"Neither do you."

Charlie made a sputtering sound and sat back. "Yeah, but I'm nothing. I don't know the first thing about taking someone on in a courtroom. On the street, maybe. In here, maybe. But not in a courtroom. And that's where it's gotta be. That's where it'll hurt him most."

"You've thought this out," Peter remarked.

"Hell, it doesn't take much thought," Charlie countered. "I'm not dumb. Neither are the other guys, though there are times you'd like to think it. We know what has to be done. We just don't know how to go about doing it."

Peter felt contrite. "You hire a lawyer. He'll do the rest."

"That's fine to say, but no local lawyer will take on Jamie, so where are we going to find someone good who can get the job done? You're the one with the outside contacts. You know city doctors. They know city lawyers."

Peter looked duly thoughtful. He didn't want to be a pushover. "The guys are really talking?"

Charlie nodded. "Mad as hell. They'd be grateful if you got the ball rolling, I can tell you that." He grew cautious. "Mara O'Neill woulda done it, if she were alive."

"Probably," Peter admitted. He was past the point of getting his hackles up the minute her name was raised. He and she had come to a meeting of minds.

"She was a fine person," Charlie said, then leaned forward again. "So what's this I hear about you and Kate Ann Murther?"

"Come again?"

"Kate Ann Murther. Don't ask me what she was doing up there in that balcony—don't ask me what she was doing at that concert at all—but word has it she's in bad shape. So. I hear you're taking a special interest in her."

"Where did you hear that?" Peter asked with what he thought was just the right amount of disbelief.

"Duke's sister-in-law works on Kate Ann's floor. She says you're there a lot."

"I've been following all the patients I treated in the ER after the accident."

Charlie winked. "But you didn't treat Kate Ann. Leastways, that's what Duke's sister-in-law says. You brought her upstairs after the accident and let it be known that she wasn't to be ignored."

"Damn right," Peter snapped. "The poor thing was lying there in the hall in absolute terror and no one was paying her the slightest heed. Just because she doesn't have family here who can make noise on her behalf doesn't mean she should be shunted aside. They just left her there. God knows when she would have gotten a room—*if* she would have gotten one—if I hadn't come along."

Charlie grinned. "Then it's true. You've become her savior."

"I wouldn't quite call it that," Peter hedged. "I'm making sure that she gets the care she needs. It's my job as a doctor."

But Charlie was still grinning. "Kate Ann Murther. She's the last person I thought you'd be drawn to. Lacey, I could understand. *Mara,* I could understand. But Kate Ann Murther?" He looked ready to choke with laughter, which irritated the hell out of Peter.

"What's so bad about Kate Ann?"

"She's from around here, for one thing. You always went for women from the outside. The natives knew you too well."

"What's *that* supposed to mean?"

"Aw, you know, Pete." He waved it off. "You were such a little runt of a kid. I can say that because you made good. You look good. You *do* good. You're smarter than any ten people in this town put together."

"Not Kate Ann. She's smarter than people think."

"She's a little mouse."

"She's shy. She's frightened of people. So she keeps to herself, and what happens? People think she's strange. They think she doesn't have a brain in her head. When she ventures out, she gets nervous and does things wrong, so what people think is reinforced. Then they laugh at her, which makes her *more* nervous, so she makes more mistakes. I'm telling you, beneath that mousy little front is an intelligent and sensitive woman. Not only that, but she's grateful for every little thing you do. I bought her a robe so that she wouldn't have to lie in the hospital all the time in those ugly wraps, and you'd have thought I'd bought her a diamond."

"You bought her a robe?" Charlie echoed.

Peter hadn't meant to say it, hadn't even realized he'd blurted it out until Charlie had caught him on it, but he wasn't backing down. "I sure did. It's about time someone in this town showed a little kindness to the woman. And respect. She does a job here. She keeps the books for a whole bunch of our businesses. You didn't know that, did you." It was a statement that Charlie's surprised look upheld. "Well, she does. And you didn't know it because no one wants to admit to it. How did you think she supports herself? She sure doesn't come from money."

Charlie sputtered out a laugh, but it was on the feeble side. And Peter wasn't stopping. He was on a roll.

"So maybe it's time we acknowledge that in her own quiet way Kate Ann Murther does a service for this town. We could start by showing a little sympathy for the state she's in. She's paralyzed. She'll never walk again. So here's this frightened woman, who's totally alone in the world—who isn't old at all but hasn't a snowball's chance in hell of finding a man, especially now—and she's facing a future in a wheelchair. How's she going to get into her house? How's she going to get around it, once she's inside? How's she going to get in and out of the shower? How's she going to get in town to buy food? Do you have *any idea* the panic she's feeling lying there in that bed all day asking herself these questions over and over again?"

"You sound like you're running for office," Charlie said, sounding mildly put off.

Peter threw up a hand. "Christ, it's common decency. The woman has lived a pathetic life to date, and now she faces one that's even worse. What would you do in her situation?"

"Probably go out back and put a gun to my head."

"Yeah," Peter breathed. The word hung in the air. "Well. One of my friends did something along that line, and she did it because the people around her—including me—didn't care enough to take her life's worries seriously." His voice was rising again. "I'm not letting that happen again."

Charlie patted the air. "Okay. Okay. I believe you."

"You'd better. Because as far as I'm concerned, sticking up for Kate Ann Murther isn't something a loser does. It shows character! And compassion! And you can tell Duke to tell his sister-in-law that if she wants to keep her job, she'd better make sure that Kate Ann Murther has the best possible care. I'll be watching!"

"*Okay.* Geez, Pete, calm down." He looked around uncomfortably. "So. Are you having Thanksgiving dinner with us, or are you flying the coop?"

"I'll be here." Peter had a brainstorm. "And I'm bringing Kate Ann. It'll be good for her to be out of the hospital and with people for a few hours."

Charlie gaped at him for a minute. Then, with a look in his eyes that said he feared for his brother's sanity but wasn't about to get him going again, he said, "Whatever you say, Pete. Whatever you say."

Angie slid onto the seat by the window and fastened her seat belt. Beside her, on the aisle, Ben did the same. She caught his eye. He caught her hand.

"Nice weekend," he said softly.

"Mmmm."

"Like old times?"

She thought about that. "A little. But better. I wish we had another day."

He nodded and studied their hands.

"You're not looking forward to going back, are you?" she asked. She had been aware of his reluctance for hours. It was flattering. And exciting. But unsettling.

He shrugged. "I have mixed feelings."

When he fell silent she said, "Go on. You have to tell me about them." That was the promise they had made to each other, and not in the heat of passion, though there had been plenty of that.

"This has been a special time," he said. "I'm worried that when we get back it'll all just . . . pffft, be gone and I'll be right back in the same old rut."

"If you know the rut's there, you should be able to do something to avoid it."

"I should. Only for the life of me, I don't know what to do. How do you fight boredom in a place where there isn't a whole lot to do?"

"I'll plan to be home more."

"So we'll both be bored." He looked at her then. "I don't mean that as an insult, Angie, but think about it. Tucker is Tucker. We can talk for hours, and make love, and have candlelight dinners, but after a while, Tucker is still Tucker. There's only so much we can do there."

"Then we'll go away more."

"Enough to fill the gap?"

"We could do it once a month," she urged. She wasn't letting him give up. Not after the weekend they'd had. Not after the progress they'd made. "We could plan ahead, plan to go somewhere we both wanted to go or do something we both wanted to do. The anticipation would be worth millions."

But he was shaking his head. "Maybe boredom is the wrong word. I need to be with people. Different kinds of people. Interesting kinds of people. Tucker just doesn't have those kinds." His tone sagged, as though what had been holding it up had simply dropped away, leaving the raw truth. "I miss New York."

"We'll be back there with our families for Thanksgiving."

"That's not what I mean. I mean for work."

Angie knew that. She had been feeling the undercurrent of it longer than she cared to think. Longer than she had been *willing* to think. She had chosen to ignore it because it wasn't what she wanted to hear.

"There's something about being where the action is," he tried to explain. "Fax machines are great, and E-mail, and conference calls, and Federal Express, but those don't put me where it's at."

A flight attendant passed, closing overhead bins and checking seat belts. Ben waited until she moved on, then said softly, "When you were in med school and doing your residency, we were in the city, so I had all that. Same when Dougie was born. Then we moved to Tucker, and I lost it."

Angie felt a thudding deep inside. "Are you saying you want to move back to the city?"

He looked up the aisle forlorny. "I'm saying I miss it. And if there were any way we could arrange it, yes, I'd move back." He shot her a quick glance before deflecting his gaze to her hand. He brushed her wedding band. "But there's your practice."

The thudding inside her picked up. After two months in which certain basic aspects of her life had been turned upside down, another loomed.

"Your career isn't portable like mine is," Ben reasoned, playing devil's advocate to his own thoughts. "You're established in Tucker. You know the people. You *like* the people."

"Don't you?" she asked in dismay.

"Yes. Definitely. They are really nice people. They're kind. They're friendly. Once they get to know you, they'd give you the shirt off their back."

He grew still when the flight attendant started talking about emergency measures.

Angie leaned closer. "It's more than just the people. It's the way of life. It's the ease. The slower pace. The peacefulness."

"If I could have those things *and* intellectual stimulation, I'd be in heaven."

"Maybe there's another solution. Montpelier's not far away. Could you tie up with a newspaper there?"

He shot her a telling look. "The *Gazette* isn't exactly the *Times.*"

"What about teaching? You could go to UVM, or Bennington, or Dartmouth. There'd be plenty of intellectual stimulation at any of those places."

"Maybe," he admitted, though skeptically. "If they'd want a cartoonist on their staff."

"Not any old cartoonist. A prize-winning political cartoonist. You're tops in your field. If they don't want an entire course devoted to it, what about a series of seminars? You could coordinate with an art department. Or better still, with political science."

"Maybe," he said again.

The flight attendant had taken her seat. The plane pushed back from the jetway.

"What if I were to commute to New York?" he asked.

Her mind buzzed. Three-hundred and thirty-some miles. Five hours without traffic, upward of seven hours with. "Uh . . ."

The plane moved forward.

"What if I spent three days a week there?"

She swallowed. Three days a week when she wouldn't see him at all? A bachelor pad in New York? Evenings doing God only knew what with God only knew who? "Sounds kind of like a separation," she said uneasily.

He looked her in the eye and spoke with the quiet assurance that she had always loved. "That's not what I mean at all. Especially after this weekend. All I'm doing is trying to think up ways to preserve your practice, my mental health, and our marriage at the same time. Three days a week might do it. Three days every *other* week might do it. Three days once a *month* might do it. I won't know until I try."

She wanted to say that it wouldn't work, that it would break up their marriage for sure. Except that many husbands traveled on business. Their wives got used to it. And it wasn't as if she'd be doing nothing the whole time he was away.

Besides, she knew he was restless. That was what Nora Eaton had been about—that, and a frustration that Angie had turned a deaf ear to. But she wanted to think she could learn from her mistakes. She wanted to think she could grow.

So, rational creature that she was, she said, "I could live with three days once a month."

The plane bounced over a seam in the tarmac and rolled on.

"Would you join me for a couple of days before and after?" Ben asked.

"I could." Rational creature that she was, she went a step beyond. "Or I could look for a job closer to the city."

Ben stared at her. "You'd consider doing that?"

"If it was the only way this would work."

"You'd leave Tucker?"

"You left New York for me once."

The pilot announced that they were second in line for takeoff.

"That was different, Angie. I can work anywhere. You—you have a successful practice in Tucker. You'd have to start over."

"Not completely. I'd have you. And my skills and my reputation. And Dougie, for as little or as long as he isn't at school." She smirked. "I'd also have my mother, and my brother and his wife and their five kids, and your mother, and your sister and her significant other, and your aunt Tillie."

"On second thought," Ben hedged, only half in jest.

"Why don't I look," Angie suggested. "I'll put out feelers to doctors I know in the New York area. If there's an opening in a small hospital in one of the suburbs, or with a group in the country north of the city, it might be interesting."

"You'd really do that?"

The plane turned onto the runway and waited.

Angie thought about it. "A pediatrician's practice is, by definition, transient. Children grow up and move on. New ones come along."

"But you love your families."

"Yes. And I'd love others just as well." She had the confidence to know that others would love her, too. "If I could find a comfortable setting and a group of doctors I respect, I could move."

"What about Paige? And Peter?"

"I'd miss them. Like you've missed the guys from the *Times*. But you've kept in touch. So I'd keep in touch with Paige and Peter. They could visit us. We could keep the house in Tucker and use it as a ski place. Or a weekend retreat."

"What about Doug?"

The plane started forward.

Angie's first impulse was to say that he would simply enroll in the school system wherever they were. Then she thought of all that had happened that fall. "He's doing well at Mount Court. If he wanted to stay, I'd let him."

"Even if we were a distance?"

"We didn't see him this weekend, and we've survived."

The plane picked up speed. She sat back in her seat.

"Do you *want* to move?" Ben asked.

She turned her head on the headrest. "No. But I do want you, and if moving is what it'll take to keep you, so be it."

The plane went faster. The front wheels left the ground, then the rear ones, and as it climbed steadily into the air, Angie wondered at her calmness.

She guessed it had something to do with the way Ben had laced his fingers through hers.

Twenty

Following the annual grief of her birthday, Paige always liked Thanksgiving. Over the years she had taken to spending the day with friends in Tucker, a group of twenty, give or take, all transplants like her. They were an eclectic surrogate family, diverse in age and background. Each brought unique talents to Tucker and a unique contribution to Thanksgiving dinner.

The festivities, which were held at a different house each year, began with hors d'oeuvres at one in the afternoon and ended with dessert at ten at night. In between, while a fire roared in the hearth, they came as close to capturing the feeling of going over the river and through the woods to grandmother's house as most families ever came.

Nonny was a bona fide member of the group, having attended enough of its Thanksgivings to know to bring along doubles of her pecan pie and leave her potato stuffing at home.

Sami, who was just starting to walk along furniture, was the center of attention this year. Paige had bought her a sweet denim jumper with a soft print blouse and matching tights. Between that, and the bow in her dark hair, and her sober face that lit brightly when she smiled, she was precious. The other children fought over who would play with her.

Paige had been half hoping Noah would join them, but he had gone to Santa Fe to see his folks while Sara visited her mother in San Francisco. And it was for the best, Paige knew. She had seen him nearly every day since her birthday. Either he caught up with her at the hospital after dropping the Mount Court group there to work or he came by at night. Several times he had slept with her—crept in after Nonny had gone upstairs and crept out at dawn—and as guilty as Paige felt, she couldn't turn him away. Being in his arms felt too good.

That was why this Thanksgiving breather was important. So much had changed in Paige's life that fall. She needed a reminder that some things, like Thanksgiving with the aliens of Tucker, as they called themselves, would be there long after Noah Perrine left.

Snow started to fall on Thanksgiving night and continued into the morning. Paige forged her way through it to get to the office. She and Peter were the only ones around, what with Angie and Ben in New York and Cynthia home in Boulder, and though the schools were out for the holiday, colds, allergies, and flus took no vacation at all.

She worked a long day, stopped at the hospital to visit with Jill, and went home feeling bushed. She decided that it had to do with the festivities the day before and the letdown the morning after.

She wondered if Noah had had a festive day, wondered if he had felt any of the same letdown. She doubted it. He hadn't called—not that he had said he would, but she had thought that if he was thinking of her at all, he would have picked up the phone. Clearly he was home with his family and in his element. No matter how much he claimed to be a man of all seasons, she knew him well enough to know that he adored New Mexico. The letdown for him would be returning to Tucker.

Sami was feeling something or other, too, because she pushed away far more of the supper that Paige put on her high chair tray than she ate. She even pushed her bottle away. She didn't want to bounce in the swing that hung from the ceiling in a corner of the kitchen. She didn't want to roll a ball to Paige. All she wanted to do was to be held, which Paige did gladly. When the phone rang at eight-thirty—not Noah, though Paige's pulse had been skipping—with an emergency call, she rushed to the hospital to treat a four-year-old whose leg had been spattered with boiling water, then rushed home.

Sami remained fretful. By the time Paige put her in her crib, her nose was starting to run. Paige wasn't surprised when she awoke in the middle of the night warm and sweaty. Children caught colds from other children. It was inevitable, and important in terms of building up immunities. It was also heartbreaking. Sami was small and helpless. She didn't understand why she felt lousy, and no amount of explaining on Paige's part made sense.

Paige bathed her and gave her baby Tylenol, then sat with her on the rocker humming the lullabies Nonny used to sing. Sami dozed and woke up crying. Paige wiped her face with a damp cloth. She gave her a bottle of apple juice, of which Sami drank barely half. She changed her sleeper and combed her hair. Then she sat with her in the rocker again, thinking that for all its wonders, modern medicine had yet to do much for the common cold.

It was a long night. For the first time, Paige understood the frustration her patient-parents had been talking of all these years when their children were sick and there was no way to help. "They'll sound worse than they are," Paige always told them, just as she told herself now. "Keep them as comfortable as you can. Encourage liquids. Definitely do not panic." And last, "Make sure that you get enough sleep yourself. A run-down parent is no good at all."

Paige barely slept. When Sami was awake, she rocked her to lull her to sleep, and once she was sleeping, she didn't want to risk waking her by transferring her to her crib. Shortly before dawn, exhausted, she carried Sami down to her own bed, but she had barely dropped off to sleep when Nonny ran in, alarmed when she hadn't found Sami in her crib.

"Paige Pfeiffer," she cried, taking Sami in her arms, "this child might easily have crawled to the edge of the bed and tumbled right off!"

"She wasn't moving far," Paige murmured groggily. "She doesn't feel well. Be an angel and give her more Tylenol. And wake me in an hour? Please? It's my Saturday in the office."

A shower revived her somewhat an hour later, but by the time she had finished up at the office and was heading home, she was beat. She napped with Sami in the afternoon, while Nonny took a walk in the snow, then went out for a run while Nonny stayed inside with Sami.

Inevitably she thought of her birthday and having run through the snow to Mount Court. There was no point in that now. There probably hadn't been a point in it then, except that she had needed a boost. Noah had certainly given her that.

Okay. So she could use a boost now—just a little one—the kind that came with a call from a friend to say that he was thinking of her. There was such a message when she got home, but it was from Daniel Miller. One of the newer aliens of Tucker, a computer whiz somewhere around her age, he wanted to say how much he had enjoyed Thanksgiving and that he would be going to an art exhibit at Bennington the following weekend and would like to take her, if she was free.

The fact that he had left the entire message with Nonny made a statement about the prospect of their ever being anything more than friends.

Paige spent the rest of the afternoon and evening as she had the one before, holding Sami. Fortunately, her temperature was down. The initial rawness of her cold had settled into a steady drip, and while Paige was relieved, and grateful when Sami fell into a sound sleep in her crib, she couldn't deny the special feeling that came when a child was sick and clung. A sick child was the ultimate in dependency. The parent with multiple children, all making demands on her, might dread that. Paige did not.

Neither had Mara. "I'm a way station in their lives," she had written about being a foster mother:

> which is perhaps what gives added meaning to those needy times they have. I can spend my day running from examining room to examining room, or from the hospital to the Town Hall to the court house, but when I come home and sit out on the back porch swing, holding a hand or talking out an upset, there's a completion that I feel. I'm not thinking beyond, to the future. I'm enjoying now for now's sake, and when now passes, I miss it.

Once Sami was asleep, Paige felt oddly lost. There was plenty to do that she didn't feel like doing. She played Scrabble with Nonny, but it didn't satisfy her the way holding Sami had, and it didn't keep her mind from wandering to the phone.

She turned in early and fell asleep quickly, though not deeply. Each sound Sami made—a cough, a tiny cry—came through the monitor and brought her awake. She checked upstairs from time to time, but the child was cool and sleeping.

She had just returned to her room after one such check when she heard a rapping on her bedroom window. Her eyes flew there and found Noah's face.

Not bothering with a light, she opened the window and helped him climb inside.

"What are you doing here?" she cried, delighted in spite the start he had given her. "You're not supposed to be back until tomorrow night!"

He tossed aside his coat, taking her in his arms, said against her hair, "I wanted to hold you," which he did, tightly, for a long minute before easing her back. In the darkness he studied her face, feature by feature, as though searching for a change that the few days apart might have brought. "How was your Thanksgiving?"

Paige had to struggle to think back that far. No man had ever cut short his vacation to be with her. No man had ever taken to stealing in her bedroom window. No man had ever held her with arms that trembled or touched her face with eyes whose hunger lanced the dark. No man had ever made her feel so full.

"It was okay," she managed to say, though her thoughts clung to all these things that made Noah unique. "Yours?"

"Nice. For a day. Then I got restless." He kissed her, then smiled down apologetically, then kissed her again. This time when he smiled there was a question in his eyes.

Paige answered it by pulling up the hem of his sweater. While he pulled it over his head, she started unbuttoning his shirt, and while he pulled it off, she kissed his chest. By the time she was ready to move on, his trousers were open. She slipped her hands inside and held him while she sought his mouth.

"I missed you," she whispered, and felt his response in her hands. He drew away from her only long enough to toss aside the rest of his clothes and her nightgown, then tumbled her back to the bed.

He didn't say anything. He didn't have to. His mouth was eloquent without a word, with his hands and body echoing all it said, and when he drew her up off the bed and settled her onto a magnificent erection, she felt beautifully and thoroughly complete.

He held her, one arm around her hips, one arm around her back, perfectly still. In her ear, in a faintly ragged breath, he whispered, "I was dreaming of this all the way home. Had a five-hour hard-on. Hope the flight attendant didn't notice."

Paige laughed. She ran her fingers through the hair on his chest, over the wall of muscle that was so comfortably broad. "You are a corrupter," she whispered. "I wasn't thinking about this at all."

"Not at all?"

"Not at all." It wasn't sex she'd been thinking of, but the completion. When she was with Noah, she felt content.

"There goes my ego."

But nothing else. He was huge inside her. She closed her eyes to more intently savor the pleasure.

He pulled her close again and drew in a long, shaky breath against her brow. "I love it when you do that."

"Do what?"

"Tell me that you feel good that way."

She coiled her arms around his neck and held on tightly.

"I love you," he whispered.

Her heart caught. "Me too."

"Yeah?"

"Yeah."

His body tensed. "Christ," she heard him murmur seconds before he pushed her back, and while her hips rose to meet him, he drove into her again and again.

It was a while later, after they had dozed in each other's arms and woken softly, that he said, "Did you mean it?"

She didn't pretend ignorance. She had never before told a man that she loved him. She hadn't even thought it about Noah until he'd said the words himself, and then the meaning of everything she'd been feeling seemed to congeal. "Yes. Did you?"

"Yes." He paused. "It's kinda nice."

"And kinda scary."

"*Lots* scary." He settled her more comfortably against him and drew up the quilt. In a quiet voice he said, "Something exciting happened while I was home. An old friend of mine is president of the Board of Trustees of a prep school there, my alma mater. He said that the Head has just announced that he's leaving."

Which meant that Noah would be applying for the job. And he'd get it. Which meant he would be moving to Santa Fe. Just when she'd fallen in love. It wasn't fair.

"The job isn't automatically mine," he cautioned. "There'll be a formal search, but everyone involved knows me and my family, and the fact that I'm an alumnus of the school is a plus."

"Is it a good school?" she asked against his chest.

"Not good. Great. Great reputation, great student body, great alumni support, great endowment."

"Everything Mount Court doesn't have."

"You could say. It'd be a feather in my cap."

She nodded against him.

"You could come with me," he suggested.

"Me? Oh, no. My life is here."

"You could move it there."

To *New Mexico?* "But I like it here."

"You say you love me," he said in the simplistic way men had of doing, as though love conquered all, as though love *forgave* all, as though love condoned the creation of havoc.

She was suddenly miffed. "Love is only one part of my life. The entire rest of it is here in Vermont."

"What if we were to get married?"

She took in a breath the wrong way and began to cough. When she had recovered, she pushed herself up so that she could see his face. It was a futile move. Between half-lidded eyes and the dark, she couldn't see much, which was nearly as unfair as his request. "Marriage has never been in my game plan."

"That doesn't mean it's bad."

"It was for you before."

"That was then, this is now. You and Liv are worlds apart." He took her chin in his hand. "Either you're very cynical, or very frightened. Which is it?"

"Neither," she said, then, "Both," then, "Hell," and sank down on his chest. Seconds later, when the baby monitor emitted a distinct cry, she bobbed back up. "Sami's been sick." She found her nightgown and, pulling it over her head, left the room.

Sami was only half-awake. She was congested, whimpering as she stood against the bars of the crib scrubbing at her nose and eyes with her fist. Paige lifted her out and held her close. "Shhhh, shhhh, Mommy's here," she crooned. "Is my little girl not feeling great?"

"What's wrong?" Noah asked from behind. He had pulled on slacks, but they weren't fastened. His chest was bare.

"It's just a cold, but enough to make her miserable. She doesn't understand what's wrong or what to do to fix it. Not that there is much," she murmured, and headed for the bathroom, where she wet a cloth and wiped the child's face.

"Will she take something to drink?" Noah asked when she returned to Sami's room.

"Maybe. I'll go down for a bottle after I change her."

"I'll get the bottle. What should I put in it?"

Nothing, Paige wanted to say. I don't need your help. I'm perfectly able to take care of myself. I've been doing it a lot longer than I've known you. Which, from a sensible, level-headed woman, was absurd. "Apple juice. She likes that."

"Is everything all right?" Nonny asked from the door. She was a petite wraith in a white nightgown and shawl, who suddenly saw Noah. "Oh, my. I didn't know we had guests."

Paige sighed. "Not guests, Nonny. Just Noah."

"And not exactly dressed for the weather, I see. I hope she isn't going to kick you out at dawn this time, Noah. Since it's Sunday. And since I already know you're here."

To Noah, Paige complained, "This was how it was when I was growing up. I'd tiptoe around her about something, then find that she knew about it all along."

Nonny had shuffled to the changing table in her tiny white mules and was feeling Sami's forehead. "Is my pumpkin hot again?"

"No. She must have been frightened when she woke up all stuffy. Noah's going down for a bottle. You go back to bed."

"And miss the fun?"

"Nonny."

"I'm going, I'm going." She shuffled out of the room.

Noah went down for the bottle. By the time he returned, Sami was cleaned up. Paige sat on the rocker and let her drink, while Noah leaned against the crib and watched.

"You did this just right," she said softly. "I'd have thought you'd be rusty."

"I always loved feeding Sara."

"Did you do it much?"

"Whenever I could."

Paige continued to rock. Sami, who was helping hold the bottle, took it out of her mouth and rubbed tiny teeth against her lips. "No more?" Paige asked. "Not even a little? For Mommy?" The mouth opened and the nipple went back inside. "That's my girl."

Sami drank most of the juice before taking the nipple out of her mouth for good. Paige set aside the bottle and rocked her a bit longer. Then she put her on her side in the crib, drew up a blanket, and rubbed her back.

"You enjoy her, don't you?" Noah asked. He was standing close beside her.

"She's a sweetie." But it wasn't Sami of whom she was most aware just then. It was Noah. The warmth of him was a physical thing, a lure when she didn't want to be lured.

"Have you thought any more about adopting her?"

"No."

"Not in your game plan, either?"

Paige didn't answer. As she rubbed Sami's back, she tried to remember what life had been like before Mara had died. Two and a half months. It hardly seemed possible.

Mara would have said that Paige would be insane not to accept Noah's proposal, because the deep connect was everything.

Maybe it was. But it scared the living daylights out of Paige.

Noah touched her arm. "I think she's asleep."

Paige nodded. She let him drape an arm on her shoulder and guide her down the stairs, because it was so *lovely* to be guided rather than to guide all the time; but when they were in her bedroom and he turned her to him and took a breath to speak, she put a hand to his mouth.

"Don't say anything. I can't think about the future now, Noah. Not yet. What's happened between us is new for me. Can't we just enjoy it, just enjoy the here and now?"

It was easier said than done, because the words had been spoken and couldn't be taken back. The following afternoon, leaving Nonny and Noah with Sami, Paige slipped into her room and curled up on the love seat with Mara's thoughts on men.

"We had such problems, Daniel and I, right from the start," she wrote.

> *But even when things were at their worst, there would be those few precious moments when everything clicked. They were like a dream. They made the hell worthwhile. I wasn't taking care of Daniel, any more than he was taking care of me. We were doing it together, really together, two people of like minds, in harmony.*
>
> *After he died, I thought I'd never experience that again, but I did. I had it with Nowell Brock—*

Paige was stunned, she had never imagined Mara with Nowell.

—for the short time that he lived in Tucker, but there was no future in it, because he was married. I sometimes felt that was why we clicked. It was a safe relationship. Nothing could ever come of it.

And Peter. I had it with Peter. We could be out in the woods at dawn, lying still as the dead on the ground with our cameras glued to our eyes waiting for the deer to feed on shrubs by the brook, and we'd be whispering back and forth, one finishing the sentence the other began. He knew what I was thinking, and vice versa. We were totally in sync. But we always lost it when we stood up. Had it in bed, lost it when we got out. That's the story of my life.

Paige lowered the letter.

"Who's it from?" Noah asked from the door.

Once before she had put him off. She didn't see any reason to do it now. "Mara. After she died, I found bundles of letters in her house. They're kind of like a diary. She wrote them over a period of years."

"What's in them?"

"Different things. Some are personal. Others are more philosophical. I've learned things about her that I never knew. It's sad. She was such a close friend." She frowned, haunted still by all she hadn't known about this close friend. "It makes you wonder whether any of us know, really *know*, the people we're with all the time."

"Of course we do," Noah said kindly. "But there are always those people who, for whatever their reasons, shield part of themselves. It's not that they're dishonest, just that they don't always tell the whole truth."

"If I'd known the whole truth, I might have been able to help."

"If Mara was one to tell the whole truth, your help might not have been needed. She would have been healthier and stronger."

Paige knew he was right. She gave the letter a nudge. "I keep thinking of the isolation she must have felt when she was writing these."

"It's too bad she didn't just give them to you at the time she wrote them."

"Oh, they're not written to me. They're written to someone else." Saying it, she felt a new wave of guilt.

"To a friend?"

"I guess." And Paige was a voyeur on the thoughts Mara shared. "Someone back in Eugene. Mara never mentioned her to me." She shot Noah a contrite look. "I know. I should package them up and send them on, and I will. I just want to read them a while longer. They make me feel closer to Mara. They help me to understand her death."

"Did this friend come to her funeral?"

Paige shook her head. "Only Mara's parents and three of her brothers came from Eugene."

"Do you think she knows that Mara is dead?"

"Good Lord, I hope she does. I assume she found out." But the guilt swelled again. "There haven't been any telephone messages from an old friend since Mara died. I mean, it's been two and a half months. If the two of them kept in touch, she would have tried to call. Wouldn't she have?"

"If they kept in touch, she would have," Noah reasoned. "But maybe they didn't. That would explain why Mara never mailed the letters."

"Then why did she write them?" Paige asked.

"She needed the outlet."

"But why to *this* person?" And why not to Paige? There was some hurt in that, Paige realized. Perhaps even envy. Surely, though, she hadn't kept the letters to deliberately deprive Lizzie Parks of something she wanted for herself.

Or had she?

Stricken, she took her address book from the nightstand and punched out the number of Mara's parents in Eugene. Mary O'Neill answered the phone. Paige had spoken with her several times in the course of disposing of Mara's things. Now, after a cordial greeting, she said, "I have some papers here, Mrs. O'Neill. They're actually letters written by Mara to a Lizzie Parks." She gave the address. "I'd like to send them on. Do you think Lizzie's still at this address?"

There was a silence at the other end of the phone. Paige imagined that Mary O'Neill was trying to decide if the address was indeed correct or, alternately, that she was flipping through a phone book to check.

As it happened, Mary O'Neill was doing neither of those things. In an awkward voice she said, "No. There's no Lizzie at that address. There's no Lizzie at all."

With horror, Paige imagined that Lizzie Parks, too, had died. "What do you mean?"

"There never was a Lizzie. Not in real life. When Mara was little she used to pretend she had a cousin just her age who lived here in Eugene. But there never was any cousin. Lizzie Parks was Mara's imaginary friend."

Paige's hand shook. She bowed her head and pressed her free fingers to her forehead. "Oh," she said in a small voice. "Well. That solves the mystery, then." An imaginary friend. "Thank you. I'm sorry I bothered you," she said, and hung up the phone.

She studied the letter she still held in her hand, until the script blurred. Noah, too, was blurred when she raised her eyes. "No Lizzie Parks. She was an imaginary friend."

Avoiding him, she went to the love seat, gathered the rest of the letters that had been in the packet, and retied the yarn that held them together.

Noah lowered himself beside her. "She was an unhappy woman."

Paige swore softly and lowered her head. "An imaginary friend."

"Others have them."

"In their late thirties?"

"Sometimes. These letters aren't much different from what many adults write, only they call it a journal. So Mara wrote her journal in letter form, and put a name at the top. It's just a difference in style. That's all."

But Paige was devastated. "An imaginary friend. She must have been that much more lonely that any of us ever imagined."

"That's not your fault, Paige." He drew her close. "You were nearby. She might have taken advantage of you if she'd wanted to. Same with all the other people who liked her so much. But she chose to keep her thoughts to herself."

Paige supposed. "Mara was pulled in two different directions, one dictated by her past, one by her present. To satisfy the first meant repudiating the second, and vice versa. It was a no-win situation. She was bound to fail." She pressed her face to Noah's collarbone and took a shuddering breath. "I feel so very, very, very bad for her."

The telephone rang. Paige didn't move at first. Noah was a comfort. But when the second ring came, her sense of duty took over. "Hello?"

"Dr. Pfeiffer?"

"Yes."

"This is Anthony Perrine, Noah's father."

She glanced at Noah. "Dr. Perrine. How are you?"

"I'm well, but I'm afraid there's a problem. A short time ago, I received a call from Sara's mother. Sara has disappeared. Liv has been trying to reach Noah without any luck. I thought he might be with you."

"He is. Right here." She put the phone to Noah's ear. His hand covered hers there.

"Yes, Dad?"

Paige watched his face grow somber, then angry.

"Liv doesn't *know* how long she's been gone?" He listened. "Swell." To Paige he said, "Liv slept late. She hasn't seen her since last night." To his father he said, "Where has she looked?" He listened, pushing his glasses higher on his nose. "I'll start calling her Mount Court friends. I don't think there are any in the Bay area, but I'll work my way eastward. She could have thumbed, God help her."

The doorbell rang. Paige let Nonny answer it.

"Have her call every one of the old friends that Sara might have contacted while she was there," Noah told his father. "Where would she have gone lugging that huge duffel bag? And why would she have run off that way? Did Liv say they'd been arguing?"

Paige put her ear to the phone but couldn't make out the answer. So she whispered, "Ask if she left any clues—matchbooks, telephone numbers thrown in the wastebasket, bus schedules."

Noah nodded. He held her gaze while he listened to what his father was saying, then he related Paige's suggestions. "Sara wouldn't want to just vanish. She's not—"

"An unhappy child," Paige said into the mouthpiece. "She's adjusted well at Mount Court. She likes it here. If anything—"

"I'd imagine her getting on the first plane out of San Francisco—"

"And flying back here," she finished.

"Hi, guys," came a voice from the door.

Paige and Noah swung around to face Sara, who was grinning from ear to ear.

Noah let out a sigh of relief. While Paige left his side and wrapped her arms around Sara, he told his father, "She just walked in. She looks fine." He cleared his throat. "I'm dying to hear how she got here. Do me a favor and call Liv, Dad? Tell her I'll talk with her another time." He hung up the phone.

Paige was still holding Sara—protecting her, she fancied, from whatever punishment Noah had in mind. Then Noah's arms encircled them both, and she released her breath.

Noah wanted to be angry at Sara but couldn't. She hadn't gone to see a friend; she had come home to him. That meant the world to him. Moreover, when she explained that she had taken a cab to the airport, changed her ticket to a flight one day earlier, and taken another cab first to Mount Court, then to Paige's, he couldn't find much fault. She had used common sense. At no time had she done anything dangerous—thoughtless, perhaps, in that she'd given her mother a scare, but she'd been angry. It seemed that Liv had done little more than spend Thanksgiving Day with Sara. She had a new boyfriend, with whom she spent most of her time. Sara had been very much on her own.

Noah was furious at Liv, though not surprised. She was a selfish woman. He had every intention of telling her so when they spoke.

"She told me to visit my friends," Sara said, holding Sami on her lap, while Noah, Paige, and Nonny sat nearby, "but there wasn't anybody to see. My two closest friends were away, and the others didn't want to see me any more than I wanted to see them. I wanted to say hi to Jeff—he was my stepdad for so long and I have his name, for God's sake—but she forbade it. So there was nothing to do. I figured that I could just as well do nothing here."

Noah saw defiance. And pride. "Another time," he cautioned, because it was one thing if he told Liv off, another if Sara showed disrespect, "tell your mother you're leaving."

"She would have tried to stop me. She would have taken my ticket and my money. She would have locked me in my room."

Noah doubted that.

Sara was staring at him. "You don't believe me."

"Did she ever lock you in your room?"

"Once."

He would have asked when, had her expression not told him. It had been after one of the shoplifting incidents. Sara didn't want him telling Paige and Nonny about those.

So he didn't ask. And her defiance faded. In a more reasonable tone she said, "She would have made me go out with her and Ray, and I didn't want to do that. He's smarmy."

"Smarmy?" Paige asked.

"He fawns all over her. Whatever she says or does is always right. If she decides to marry him, I'm outta there for good."

Noah rather liked the thought of that, except that he felt a moral responsibility to take the high road. "She's still your mother. You don't see her much now that you're living with me, but it would be nice if when you do get together you could be civil to one another."

Sara made a face. "Tell *her* that. She wasn't very civil to me. She kept telling me that something was wrong—either my hair was a mess, or my skin looked lousy, or I was gaining weight."

"You're not gaining weight," Paige said quickly. Eating disorders were the rage among the girls at Mount Court. She didn't want to encourage another.

"I weigh fifteen pounds more than her," Sara said.

"You're also four inches taller," Noah pointed out.

"Which means," Paige added, "that inch by inch you weigh less than she does. You can tell her that next time she mentions it."

Noah grinned at Paige's resourcefulness. It was but another of the things that he loved—like the way she had hugged Sara without recrimination, the way she had put in her two cents when he'd been talking with his father, the way her thoughts had run parallel to his.

Then his smile faded, because he didn't know what would happen if he went to Santa Fe next year and she stayed here.

"Anyway," Sara went on, "I won't be seeing her for a while. Not until spring break in March."

"Aren't you going there for Christmas?" Paige asked with a questioning look at Noah.

He shook his head. "She goes for Thanksgiving and spring break. Summer has yet to be decided."

"So what are you doing over Christmas?" Nonny asked. The gleam in her eye told Noah she had plans.

"You tell me," he invited.

"You'll stay here, of course. We'll have a big tree right in that corner. We'll decorate the house and hang stockings on the mantel, and sing carols in Tucker center with the rest of the townsfolk."

"Me too?" Sara asked.

"Why, yes, you too," Nonny answered.

Noah would have hugged her for the wholehearted way she included Sara in her doings, except that the picture she painted was a bit premature. "Actually," he said, "I was thinking of taking Sara to New York over Christmas to see Rockefeller Center and—"

"New York stinks," Sara cried.

"I agree," Nonny said.

Paige looked at her. "No one asked your opinion, Nonny."

"Well, I gave it anyway. And I'll continue to give it," she said as she rose from her chair, "because I happen to be the senior member of this group"—she went to Sara's side—"which means I've lived the longest and had the most experience—come, Sara—and my experience tells me that we'll all have a far nicer time staying here." She led Sara, who carried Sami, toward the kitchen. "We'll be deciding what to make for supper."

"I'll bring something in," Noah called after them.

"Mexican!" Nonny called back.

"I can't eat Mexican!"

"Then we'll *cook!*"

Noah watched the three of them disappear. He thought of the time Sara spent with his parents. She was comfortable with them. But with Nonny she was different. Nonny was an unexpected gift, part adult, part elf. Sara couldn't resist her.

Or Sami, for that matter. For someone who didn't have previous experience—despite what she had once told Paige—with children, Sara did just fine with Sami. She held her like a pro, played with her like a pro. But then, with little children one didn't need experience, just love.

Noah hadn't thought Sara had so much. She had always been quiet and self-contained, even sullen, yet in this house she smiled, she talked, she participated.

He reached for Paige's hand. "What are you thinking?"

"Same thing you are," she said with a sigh. "You'd think Sami was her sister."

"She could be."

"Yes. Well."

"It's worth considering."

"Fine for you to say. You're not the one who's being asked to give up everything you've spent the whole of your adult life building." She straightened her fingers, but Noah didn't let go.

"Come on, Paige. People have relocated before." He suddenly read more on her face. "But it's not just the relocation, is it? It's the commitment. It terrifies you."

She took a breath and let it out in a high-pitched, "Uh-huh."

Which was another thing he loved about her. She was honest. He didn't necessarily agree with everything she said—certainly in this case he didn't agree—but she said what she felt.

He tried to reason with her. "It doesn't make sense. Your life has commitment written all over it."

"In some spheres, yes."

"Why not in all?"

"Because all's too much to ask."

"So you quit while you're ahead," he suggested with some bitterness. He was hurt that she wasn't willing to take a chance on him, on them.

"That's not it."

"Sure sounds it to me."

"No. I'm just recognizing my limits. I'm trying to avoid failure."

"And in the process you're missing out on the best life has to offer. Being with someone you love is the best kind of commitment imaginable. Lonely people all over the world would give anything for it. Think of your friend Mara."

"I do. All the time."

"Do you think she'd be backing away, like you are?"

"Not fair, Noah."

"True," he said, leaning closer, "but desperate cir- cumstances require desperate measures. You're backing away. Taking the coward's way out. Why? Because your parents treated you like a drag so you think of family life as a drag? Well, what do you think you've had here— you, Nonny, and Sami? It's family life, and it's no drag. Same when Sara and I join you. You enjoy it. You know you do."

She freed her hand and clutched it in her lap. "My life was so simple before. Suddenly you're asking me to be a wife and a mother not once, but twice over, and on top of that you're asking me to abandon my practice and move to Santa Fe."

"That's negotiable," he offered, thinking for sure that he would pique her interest; but she only shot him a look.

"Negotiable? How romantic."

"What I'm saying is that my leaving Tucker isn't a done deed."

"Fine. If you stay here, we can continue on like we are now."

"Which would suit you perfectly well. You could keep on with your work, and play at having a husband and kids, and then when the going gets rough, you could take off, free as a bird."

"I'd never do that."

"Right! So what's the difference if you're married?"

"Precisely? What's the difference if I'm not?"

He started to laugh. He couldn't help it. "Christ, you have a quick mouth. Always could tie me up with words. Right from the start."

"And right from the start you were rigid," she returned. "You got an idea in your mind, like evening study hall, and insisted on it come hell or high water. Good Lord, Noah, you've been through one marriage and failed. Why in the world do you want to try it again?"

"So I can do it right this time."

"And you're sure you will?"

"I think so."

"Well, you have more faith in yourself than I have in me."

"No," he said sadly. "I just want it more, I guess. That's all." Feeling dejected, thinking that if Paige didn't really love him, moving back to Santa Fe and putting everything about Tucker, Vermont, behind him might be the only way he'd survive, he left to join the others in the kitchen.

Paige didn't know what to do. Conflicting thoughts chased each other around in her head, leaving her little peace that night. Loving Noah was brand new. Left to her own devices, she might have worn the knowledge around for a while to see about the comfort of the fit, but he wasn't giving her that luxury. He was pressuring her to make decisions she didn't feel capable of making.

Then, the following afternoon, after she had muddled her way through a day's work, she got a call from Joan Felix that upped the pressure something fierce.

Twenty-one

I think we have one," Joan said.

Paige didn't follow. "One what?"

"Family. For Sami. It's a mother and father who have four biological children and are looking to adopt a fifth. They just moved to Vermont from the Midwest. We had a preliminary meeting with them last Friday. On the surface, they look good. It'll be at least a month before the home study is complete. You've been through that, so you know what it's like."

Paige heard only half of what Joan was saying. An awful thumping inside her drowned out the rest. She caught something about a biological family for Sami, four children wanting to take her west, but the only thing that really registered was an image of Sami's bedroom, suddenly empty and quiet and cold.

"Paige? Are you there?"

"Yes."

"I thought for a minute that we'd gotten cut off."

"I'm sorry." Paige pressed a hand to her stomach. "Would you tell me again? You found a family for Sami?"

She tried to listen this time, but when she hung up the phone, she was feeling nauseated. It was one upheaval in her life too many. She made her way back to the kitchen and opened a can of ginger ale. She was sipping it, willing her stomach to settle and her mind to make sense out of what she'd learned, when Angie slipped in.

She didn't say anything, just leaned against the counter near Paige with a nervous look on her face.

Paige didn't like that look. Not on the all-knowing and confident Angie. "Why do I get the feeling something's happened?" she asked warily.

"Ben and I are going to make it," Angie said.

The words registered. Paige intellectualized them and managed a semienthusiastic, "That's great, Angie," but she knew there was more. Whereas Angie should have looked pleased, she remained nervous.

"But we may be moving."

"Moving?"

"Back to New York."

"Oh, Angie!"

Angie closed her hands around Paige's wrists and, beseechingly, said, "I'm torn, Paige. In so many ways. If I were the only one involved, I'd never even be considering this. I love Tucker. I love you. I love our families. But I'm not the only one involved—much as I may have fooled myself into thinking that for too long a time. There's Ben. And what it boils down to is that he needs to be in the city. He's bored here."

Paige didn't know what to say. She couldn't grasp a future without Angie. From her first conception of the practice, Angie had played a vital role. "But . . . what will you do?"

"I called a friend in Manhattan. He knows of two slots for pediatricians—both slightly upstate, but within easy commuting distance. I may look into them." She paused, expectant in a skeptical sort of way. "What do you think?"

Paige was having trouble thinking, what with her world tipping over again, but she tried. "I think, uh, I think that you can't possibly go, because we need you here, but if that's what's necessary to save your marriage, you'll have to." Angie leaving? Sami being adopted by strangers?

Her stomach was a single large knot.

"Nothing's definite," Angie said. "I may hate both positions, and Ben may decide to work out of

Montpelier, or teach in Hanover, or even commute to New York. But if he wants to go, I can't say no. He tried here. For ten years he did, for my sake, and we all know what happened. So now I'm trying to listen to what he's saying. He's a smart guy. He knew his son. Dougie may only be fourteen, but he's happy at Mount Court. He could either stay at school here or come with us if we move—not that I love the idea of his staying, any more than I love his boarding now. My heart still rebels. My mind sees the merit in it. Dougie needs to breathe. If the values I've spent fourteen years instilling in him haven't taken by now, they never will." She took a quick breath. "I'm trying to look realistically at the future. I haven't done that before." She searched Paige's face. "Say something."

"I can't. You've always known what was best for you."

"No. I thought I did. I thought that what was best for me was automatically best for Ben and Doug, but I was wrong. What's best for me is intricately tied up with what's best for them. They're individuals with individual needs. If I can't help satisfy their needs, then satisfying my own becomes meaningless. My happiness is contingent on theirs, which isn't to say," she added wryly, "that I've become subservient. I won't go anywhere unless I find something that will give me professional pleasure, and Ben agrees with that. But I can't be calling the shots all the time anymore. Some of the time. Not all."

Paige wrapped her arms around Angie.

"Mara missed it," Angie mused. "She wanted happiness, and it eluded her. We couldn't understand that, because we saw so much success in her life, only she saw what we didn't. She saw how easy it was to confuse success for happiness. She saw the potential for more. I want to realize it."

Paige held on tight.

After a minute Angie asked, "Are you all right?"

Paige let out a shaky breath. "They found a family for Sami."

"Oh, Lord." Angie drew back. "Are they taking her now?"

"Not yet. But soon." Paige started to tremble. "I have to leave now."

"Where are you going? Let me come."

"No. I need time. I have to think."

"Can I talk with you later?"

Paige nodded. At least she thought she did, but she wasn't sure if the directions she was giving to her body were being carried out. She felt uncoordinated, her steps uneven as she returned to her office. She dropped her purse twice before finally getting a grip on it, couldn't seem to fit her keys into the ignition of her car, and when she got on the road, she drove for five minutes before looking through the dwindling daylight and wondering where she was headed.

It was with a determined effort that she finally got her bearings. Ten minutes later she drove under Mount Court's curved wrought-iron arch. One minute after that, she pulled up in front of the administration building. Noah's secretary wasn't at her desk, so she went right to his door. He was inside, engrossed in a set of spreadsheets. The cuffs of his white shirt had been turned back, the neck button undone, and his tie loosened. He looked like a man who didn't need an interruption.

She stood at the door, feeling guilty that she had come. Noah had his share of problems with Mount Court. He didn't deserve her problems, too.

But he had said that he loved her. And, given the devastation she was feeling, no one else would do.

He looked up in surprise and came out of his chair. "Paige. I didn't know you were coming." He approached her, frowning. "You look pale." He drew her into the room and closed the door.

"I'm sorry to bother you. I know you're busy—"

"Don't apologize. Never apologize."

"It's been a god-awful afternoon, like everything's unraveling. Angie is talking about moving away, and the adoption agency found a family for Sami." She looked up at him, letting her eyes say all she couldn't put into words.

He rubbed her arms lightly.

"It probably won't happen until after the holidays, but then they'll take her away from me. She'll have two real parents and four siblings. And a nice house, I guess. Joan said they seem like good people." She was suddenly appalled. "But *four* kids? She won't get much attention in a family of seven. She'll just be another kid to wear the hand-me-downs of the ones that came before her. And the family is just moving to Vermont, which means that they don't know people here. They don't have an established support network. And if he's taking a new job, who's to say the job won't fall through? Or that he won't decide he hates it and move somewhere else? Sami can't be moving around all the time. She needs to be able to settle in one place and stay there."

"Did you tell Joan that?" Noah asked.

"No. She took me off guard. I couldn't say much of anything."

"Certainly not that you want to keep Sami yourself."

Paige saw the dare in his eyes. She broke away and went to the window. Beyond it, the campus was covered with snow. The occasional student passed by wearing the wool overcoat that was the covering de rigueur for the winter semester, but otherwise the scene was as bleak as her view of the future.

"It isn't fair," she said, burying her hands in the pockets of her own wool topcoat. "I didn't ask for Sami, but suddenly there she was, and I owed it to Mara to take her. So now, just when I've gotten used to having her, they find a family. Why didn't they find one right away? Why did it have to take three months? I mean, it's not fair to Sami, either. If she were an infant, three months might not be crucial, as long as there was someone to hold her and hug her. But she's no infant, and it isn't just any old someone who's been holding her and hugging her. It's me. It's Nonny. It's you." Of course, he would be leaving, too. And Angie. And even Nonny, if Sami left. *It wasn't fair.*

"I hate change," she cried. "I've always hated change. Most of all, I hate change that happens after you've adapted to the change that you didn't want in the *first* place."

Noah came to lean against the wall where the window ended. In a low voice he said, "I don't think change is the real issue here."

"It's definitely one of them," Paige insisted. "For the first three years of my life my parents dragged me around wherever they went. I never had my own room, never had my own friends, never had much more by way of constancy than a teddy bear, and even that got lost in one of the moves. Finally Nonny put her foot down and took me in. It was another three years before I was willing to spend even a single night away from her house. Stability happens to be very important to me."

Noah crossed his arms over his chest. "The real issue here," he went on as though she hadn't spoken, "is what you want in life. I don't believe—not for one minute—that you took Sami in only because you felt you owed it to Mara. To do something as momentous as that—and to continue doing it, even when it meant that you had to go through all the red tape of being approved as a foster parent—demanded something else. Somewhere deep inside, you liked the thought of having Sami with you. Maybe it was to fill the void that Mara's death left, maybe it was to satisfy your own maternal instincts—"

"I don't have maternal instincts."

"You sure as hell do," he argued. "You may hide behind your profession and call it doctoring, but make no mistake, you mother your patients. You mother Jill. You mother Sara. And you damn well mother Sami. Maternal instincts are as natural to you as doctoring."

"But—"

"It's not just that you've *gotten used* to having Sami. She isn't just a habit. You *love* her. Face it, Paige. You do."

"Of course I love her," Paige admitted. "How could I help but love her? She's a darling child—"

"No, no," he interrupted with a wave, "we're not talking love in the general sense here. You love her like a mother loves her child. You take pride in her accomplishments. You worry when she's sick. You look forward to coming home from work and seeing her. You give her time that you'd otherwise give to yourself, and you don't think twice about it, because that's what mothers do."

"She's been a novelty for me," Paige reasoned. "I've never had a child around the house before."

"And you like it. Admit it."

"She's such a *good* child."

"And you like having her around," he challenged.

"Okay." She couldn't see bickering the point. "I like having her around."

"Only you run into trouble when you think of formalizing the relationship. Just like you run into trouble when you think of formalizing our relationship. You shy away from making formal commitments. So where does that leave you?" he asked. "Ultimately it leaves you alone. Sami will go either to this family or another one. Nonny will go back to her own apartment. I'll go to Santa Fe, and that'll be that."

Paige could picture it. Those very images had been hovering at the periphery of her awareness since Joan had called. No. Longer. They had been hovering since she realized she loved Noah.

His arms were at his sides now, his voice sheathed in steel and reminiscent of the man she had first locked horns with three months before. "Your life will be just as it was before Mara died," he said, "only it won't be as nice as you remembered it being, because you'll be coming home every day to an empty house. You'll be eating dinner alone. You'll be sitting on that love seat of yours, reading Mara's letters for the umpteenth time, and you'll be wondering what Sami is doing, or Nonny, or me. Only we'll all be gone, and there will be no way you'll be able to get us back. So, on top of everything else, you'll be feeling regret. Your nights will be lonely as hell."

"Why are you saying all this?" she cried. She had come for comfort, not torment.

He didn't answer, simply stood with his arms limp, but something about the way he was looking at her caused a tugging inside. His glasses reflected the lights in the room. Behind them, she could swear she saw tears.

More gently he said, "I sometimes see my life that way, busy all day and barren at night. So now I'm looking forty-four in the eye, and I'm wondering where I go from here. I'm thinking that I came to this town expecting nothing. And now suddenly there's something. It's out there waiting to be grabbed, and even if I go for it, it might slip right through my hands. So I'm in the same quandary as you."

She went to him and slid a hand in his. "You aren't just talking about us, are you?"

He shook his head.

"This job?"

He thought for a minute, pursed his lips, shrugged. "I can't separate the two. Does Mount Court excite me because when I go out on an afternoon I know there's a chance I'll bump into you down by the gym, or at the hospital? Is the challenge more meaningful because I can look forward to telling you about it at night?" He looked perplexed. "I didn't ask for this, either, Paige. I didn't want entanglements. I came here expecting to stay for a year and then be gone. Sara and I had a lot to work out, still do. The last thing I needed—wanted— was to fall in love with a married woman."

She was bemused. "I'm not married."

"You are. To the town. To your practice. To the conviction that things were better before." He gave her a sad smile and rapped her hand against his thigh. "You came to me for comfort because you're confused. Well, hell, I'm confused, too. I can't tell you what to do about Sami. It's something only you can decide." His phone rang. "All I know is that you'd better decide quick. I'm no expert in the workings of adoption agencies, but my guess is that once things get moving they may be hard to stop. By the time you make your call, it could be too late. You could lose Sami by default."

And him, Paige thought. She could lose him, too, if she didn't take a stand soon. But there were so many issues involved. Her simple life was totally muddled.

The phone rang again.

"One way or the other," he said in his softest voice yet, "make a decision. Soon. Before the window closes." He released her hand and went to the phone.

Mara had written about that window, about opportunities here and gone, and Noah was right. The call was hers. Either she went for a new life or she returned to the old. One held everything she knew and trusted, the other was filled with unknowns. The old and trusted was safe and secure, and the new—who knew if it would work?

Needing to think through it all, she turned to leave.

"Wait," Noah called, frowning into the phone. "Dr. Pfeiffer is here," he told whoever was on the other end. "We'll be right over." He hung up and reached for his jacket. "Julie Engel is at the infirmary. She passed out in the library. The nurse doesn't like some of the answers she's getting."

Paige grabbed on Julie's problems as an escape from her own. "Like what?" she asked as they hurried out of his office. She was thinking of drugs. The rigid set of Noah's jaw was consistent with that.

"Like this isn't the first time she's passed out," he said. "Like she's been feeling sick for the past week. Mainly in the mornings."

Paige didn't like the sound of that, either. Not drugs. Sex.

Noah held the door and followed her out. Under his breath, as they strode along, he murmured, "This is not what I need. Not now. Not when things are finally starting to look good here. In the whole month of November, the disciplinary problems were petty things—closely missed curfews, a few skipped classes, one boy smoking in the bathroom, and it wasn't even pot. We're making progress, at least I thought we were." He made a sound. "I might have known it would be Julie."

Deirdre and Alicia were in the small outer room of the infirmary. They moved in on Paige the instant she and Noah entered.

"She just fainted dead away."

"Flat out on the floor."

"We got her here as fast as we could."

"I told her to see the nurse last week."

"She's been eating next to nothing."

"Maybe it's the flu."

Paige stopped only long enough to put a comforting hand on each girl's shoulder. "I'll take a look. You both sit and relax."

Julie was lying on the examining table, fully dressed. She had an arm over her eyes.

Paige removed the arm. "How do you feel?"

Julie shot an uneasy glance at Noah, who stood by the door. "I'm okay. I just passed out."

"People don't 'just' pass out. There's always a reason for it." She felt Julie's forehead, but it was comfortably cool. She found the pulse at her wrist. "I understand this isn't the first time it's happened."

"I was just dizzy the other times."

"There's always a reason for dizziness, too. And for morning sickness."

"I said I was sick a few mornings ago," Julie grumbled. "I didn't say I had morning sickness."

Her pulse was fine. "When was your last period?"

Julie darted another glance at Noah. "Does he have to be in here?"

"The answer," Noah said, "concerns me and this school."

Julie gave a high laugh. "Like you were the one who did it?"

Paige caught Noah's eye and motioned toward the waiting room. "We won't be a minute." Noah looked disgusted, but he left. Paige turned back to Julie. "Last period?"

Julie rolled her eyes. "How am I supposed to know? I don't keep track on a calendar."

Paige remained patient. "Was it within the last week?"

"No."

"Within the last two weeks?"

"No."

"Within the last month?"

Julie was slower in answering and then begrudging. "No."

"Within the last *two* months?"

The look Julie gave her was answer enough.

"O-kay," Paige said, helping her sit up. "I think we'll take a ride to my office. I can examine you there."

"I'm all right. Really."

Paige looked her in the eye. "Are you on the pill?"

"Where would I get birth control? My dad would kill me if he ever got a bill for it."

Which pretty much ruled out a diaphragm, too. "Are you sexually active?"

Julie squirmed. "That's an embarrassing question."

"Not for an attractive and often provocative young woman. Let me rephrase it. Are you a virgin?"

"No."

"Have you been with a man within the last three months?"

"I don't keep score."

"Julie."

She looked away. "Yes, not that it concerns you any."

"It concerns me a lot," Paige said, helping her off the table. "It concerns me because, while I don't approve of sexual activity among girls your age, even *more* I don't approve of unsafe sex. You can get birth control without sending a bill to your father. You can get it at my office, or at any clinic. And you can refuse to have sex with a guy unless he's willing to use something."

"Well, if he doesn't happen to have it with him, what do I say?"

"You say *no*." It was as simple as that, but so difficult for teenagers to do. Paige sighed. "I care about you, Julie. I don't want you to be pregnant, but if you are, the sooner you know, the greater your options will be."

Paige drove Julie in her car. Noah followed in his. It wasn't long before the three of them were sitting in Paige's office, with Paige fighting an odd sense of déjà vu. Such a short time ago, it seemed, she was sitting with Jill. Now here was Julie, from a privileged home and in a privileged school, so different from Jill, yet so similar.

"First off, we have to call your father," Noah said. "Any decision you reach has to involve him."

"No, it doesn't. I'm eighteen."

"But you're a student at my school, for which your father pays the tuition. You were in our care when this happened. It's my obligation to tell him."

"He's right," Paige told Julie. "How you and your father decide to handle it from there is your choice, but as Head of Mount Court, Mr. Perrine has to call."

"He'll want to know who the father is," Noah said.

So did Paige. Someone hadn't used a condom. That person had been as shortsighted as Julie. Whoever it was ought to be with her when she faced her father.

Julie sat back on the sofa, crossed one knee over the other, and smoothed tight jeans over long, slender thighs.

"Julie?" Paige prompted.

Julie eyed her mutinously. "I thought you were on my side."

"I am. That's why I want to know. You didn't do this alone. You shouldn't have to be alone in handling it."

Julie said nothing.

Noah leaned forward. Gently he said, "Look. You can stonewall if you want. You don't have to tell us. We understand that you're in an awkward position, but your father may not be as understanding. He's going to want to know who the father is and where we were, that we couldn't stop this from happening."

Julie snorted. "You can't stop things from happening. You don't know half of what goes on in the dorms."

"We know more than you think, but you're right," he said less patiently, and rose. "We can't stop things like this from happening unless we run the place like a prison, which I refuse to do. It isn't fair to those students who do have a sense of responsibility."

Paige, too, rose.

"I'll drive her back," Noah said, looking tired. "Then I'll try her father. We can't do much more until we reach him."

Paige nodded and walked them outside. It was all she could do not to slip her hand through Noah's again. She wanted his warmth. She also wanted to ask if he would come by that night, but she couldn't very well do it with Julie right there. So she simply smiled and waved when they drove off, then headed home.

She was mentally drained, feeling nearly as bad for Noah having to deal with the pregnancy of one of his students and the potential for scandal at Mount Court, as she felt for herself. Her own worries took precedence, though, when she walked into the house. From the kitchen came the sound of Sami's squeals. She followed them and stood for a time, unobserved, at the door.

Sami was in her high chair. Nonny was feeding her. The kitchen was messy in a lived-in sort of way.

Paige tried to imagine coming home to a spotless, quiet, empty house. It was a chilling thought. But the other—the other was unsettling, too. Could she come home to a full house and not feel guilty that she hadn't cooked dinner? Could she just pick up and leave at night when she had emergency calls? Could she simply close her door and shut everyone out when she wanted to be alone?

She gasped when something furry and alive rubbed against her leg.

"Paige," Nonny exclaimed, "come in, come in, there's a little someone here who's anxious to see you."

Paige bent to give kitty a tickle—kitty, who was growing bigger and more affectionate by the day—then went to Sami, who tipped her head back and gave her a saucy grin. "Hi, sweetie. How's my little girl?" Her throat tightened around the words. Sami wasn't hers. Other parents were in the process of staking their claim.

"Tell Mommy what you did today," Nonny urged Sami. "Go on. Tell her."

"What did you do?" Paige managed to ask.

"She took a step," Nonny said proudly. "Just one, before she fell, but considering that three months ago she could barely sit by herself, it's astounding."

"Took a step?" Paige asked Sami. "Let me see." She waited only long enough for Nonny to wipe the food from Sami's face before lifting her out of the high chair. Holding her close, she carried her into the living room, then stood her up at the sofa and moved back.

She held out her arms. "Come here, sweetheart. Walk to Mommy."

Sami plopped down on her seat.

Paige gently stood her up again and moved back. "I want to see. I miss such good things when I'm at work. Show me now, sweetie."

Sami plopped down again, but this time, before Paige could go to her, she crawled to Paige, climbed up on her knees, and held out her arms.

Paige picked her up, acutely aware of the way tiny arms circled her neck. "Oh, sweetie," she whispered, torn to bits and on the verge of tears. "I do love you. But motherhood is an awesome undertaking. Like marriage."

The phone rang. Paige continued to hug Sami, but when it rang again, she reached for it.

"We have a problem," Noah said without prelude. "A *real* problem."

"Another one? I'm not sure I can take it."

"Julie's father is furious. He's flying up in the morning with his lawyer. He says he's suing the school."

Paige thought quickly. "He hasn't got a case. Julie has a history of not following the rules at Mount Court. She has a history of being disciplined. It's not like you all turned the other way and ignored what was going on. Besides, she is eighteen."

"You're right. No case. But he can make enough noise to rake me and my school over the coals. I can take it. I'm not sure the school can. But there's more, Paige. Julie's suddenly saying that the father of her baby is Peter Grace."

"Peter," Paige cried. "That's nonsense!"

"It's what Julie says."

"Well, she's lying," Paige vowed, but the words were no sooner out of her mouth than she thought of the letter Julie had written to Peter, the pictures he claimed he hadn't taken of her, and the ones he had indeed taken, though not of Julie, that had upset Mara so.

"She claims," Noah said, "that he forced her."

"Of course. She'd have to say that. It's the only hope she has of weaseling her way out of this. But it isn't true," Paige insisted, praying she was right.

Noah sighed at the other end of the line. His voice lowered. "I was hoping to drive over and sneak in your window, but I'm thinking I should pick you up at the front door and pay Peter Grace a visit. I have to know his side of the story, and fast. The potential for damage to Mount Court is substantial. So is the potential for damage to your practice."

Paige realized that as he said it. She thought of losing the practice, on top of Angie and Noah and Sami. "What's happening, Noah?" she asked in a wavering voice. "My world is breaking up."

"Not yet, babe. Not yet. Can you be ready in fifteen minutes?"

"Yes—no." She struggled to decide how best to handle Peter. "Let me go alone. Peter tends to get defensive."

"If he's innocent—"

"It doesn't matter. That's just the way he is. He may be angered so by the accusation that he turns around and walks out, which won't accomplish anything at all. I'll go alone, then I'll call you when I get back."

Noah reluctantly agreed. She hung up the phone but sat for a bit holding Sami, who was playing happily with the silver pendant that hung around her neck. "Do you like that?" she asked softly.

"Ma. Ma. Ma. Ma."

"My mother sent it from L.A. a few years ago. She said she knew the artist. Think she did?"

"Fooooo."

"I like it, too. Chloe's a great gift giver. A lousy mother, but a great gift giver. She should have been my rich aunt."

"If she'd been that," Nonny said from the door, "you wouldn't have been my granddaughter, and I wouldn't have led half as rewarding a life."

"You'd have been footloose and fancy free."

Nonny shook her head. "I need to do meaningful things, and the more the better. I've felt younger since I've been here than I have in years."

"You're an angel, doing all this for me. I can't thank you enough."

"Don't you hear what I'm *saying*, Paige? I don't *want* your thanks. I just want you to let me keep on doing what I've been doing. Send me back to that apartment and I'll die in a week."

"Hush! Don't say that!"

"A week," Nonny repeated defiantly. "No more. One week."

Paige rolled her eyes. "Well, I'm not sending you back yet, so you can forget about dying. And right now I need you. I have to make a quick run to Peter's." She gave Sami a hug and felt a tug at her heartstrings when the little girl clung to her sweater. "I'll be back," she said softly. She pried the little fist free and kissed it. "I promise. I'll be back."

Peter didn't answer her knock, but his car was in the driveway, so Paige didn't leave. She let herself in, thinking that if he had been behind the break-in at her house, fair was fair. She went through the first floor calling his name, to no avail.

The basement door was open and the light on. She called again. When he didn't answer, she went down the stairs. He was standing with his back to her, hands on his hips, shirt cuffs rolled back over a handsome maroon sweater. He was looking at a row of photographs that hung drying on the line.

She stepped closer. She wasn't surprised to find that the pictures—one shot, actually, printed at different levels of enlargement—were of Mara, but she would never have guessed at the feeling they captured. Through a smile, a tilt of the head, a softness that Peter's camera had nabbed, it was a Mara she had rarely seen.

"Wow," Paige breathed, momentarily forgetting why she had come.

Peter nodded. "Finally."

She couldn't take her eyes from the prints. One was the echo of another, with no diminishing effect. "They're stunning, Peter."

"Thanks."

"This is how I'd like to remember her."

"Beautiful?"

"At peace."

He studied the prints for another while, before finally letting out a sigh of relief. "I knew what I wanted. I just wasn't sure I'd be able to get it. Negatives can be deceptive. I've probably looked at this one ten times without seeing the potential."

"What made you see it this time?"

He shrugged. "My eyes. They're clearer. And my mind. Working better. Rational, rather than desperate."

"You're at peace with her death?"

"I've accepted it. I'm remembering her life more now. The good things. I feel like my own life is finally aimed right."

He didn't sound to Paige like a man consumed by guilt, or like a man with anything to hide, which surely he would be if he had impregnated Julie Engel. But he certainly did look handsome in his maroon sweater. The color was perfect for him. Then again, maybe it was his acceptance of Mara's death that became him so.

"Can we talk?" she asked quietly.

He looked around in surprise, as though realizing for the first time that she was there.

She led the way back upstairs—it would have been wrong to have said what she had to say in front of Mara—and waited until he had shut the door before saying, "Julie Engel is pregnant."

His head jerked slightly. "Don't know why that surprises me. She was looking for trouble. It was only a matter of time before she found it."

"She's saying you're the father."

His expression spoke of the bizarre. "Me. You're kidding."

"She told her father, who told Noah, who told me."

"Jesus." He dropped his head, then brought it right back up and speared Paige with a look. "Do you believe her?"

"I don't want to. You told me once that there was nothing going on between you."

"It's the God's truth. I never touched the girl. She might have wanted it differently. She might have *fantasized* it differently. But the minute she unbuttoned her shirt, I left. I told you that."

"She says you forced her to have sex."

"Forced? Good God, Paige, if you weren't convinced before, you should be now. Julie Engel is one hot little number. No way would anyone have to force her. My guess is it'd be the other way around."

"Do you have any pictures of her?"

"Not a one. I told you that, too. The pictures I took were in broad daylight in the park by the church. They were innocent shots, supposedly for her stepmother, but when she tried to make it into something more, I was outta there. I exposed what I'd taken. She can't pin anything on me. She doesn't have a shred of proof."

"Unfortunately," Paige cautioned, "the accusation can do the harm, whether there's proof or not."

"I'm innocent until proven guilty."

"In court. On the street, not so. As Head of Mount Court, Noah will have to fight the charge that the school's physician forced himself on a female student. As pediatricians, our group will have to fight the charge that one of us forced himself on a patient. *If* all this gets out. So we have to nip it in the bud, which is why I'm here. Aside from the picture-taking episode, have you been alone with Julie lately?"

"No."

"Has she ever come here?"

"Never."

"When did you see her last?"

"Right before Thanksgiving, at the hospital. She was doing volunteer work."

"She may say she sneaks off to see you at night."

"Well, she doesn't. I've been staying late at the hospital. You can ask the nurses on Three-B."

Paige wondered if he was involved with one of them. Then she thought of Kate Ann Murther and experienced a sudden dawning. It must have shown on her face, because Peter grew defensive.

"There's nothing wrong with my seeing Kate Ann. People jump to judgment about her without a whit of knowledge, but she's a sweet person. Sometimes we talk, sometimes we watch a movie. When she asks about my work, she asks intelligent questions. She's grateful for anything and everything I do, because it's so much more than she's ever had. Here she is, a paraplegic, and she feels good about herself. Because of me. Because I care."

Paige touched his arm. "I think that's wonderful."

"Then why do you look so astounded?"

"Because it makes sense now. You have been different lately. Calmer. More directed."

"Tragedies help you prioritize things. So does a person like Kate Ann. I'm taking on Jamie Cox, because, damn it, he ought to help pay her medical bills, and if he doesn't, I may just marry her and let my insurance pay." He looked momentarily unsure. "I could do worse."

"Much worse," she agreed, feeling a sudden, deep warmth for the man.

He rubbed his palm over his chest, over the fine, hand-loomed maroon wool that Paige had seen remnants of not so many weeks before. "Mara was right. I do sabotage relationships. But I'm comfortable with Kate Ann. I can be me, and she likes it. So I'm thinking more clearly and seeing more clearly." He gestured toward the basement. "Maybe that's what those pictures were about."

"Maybe," Paige said, feeling an odd envy.

"I won't have Julie Engel ruining everything. So. How do I prevent it?"

"We," Paige corrected, because she had a new faith in Peter. "We show up at Noah's office tomorrow when Julie's father does. We bring our own lawyer and threaten to countersue for damages if any are caused. That will give the Engels cause to keep their mouths shut while they weigh their options. And while they're doing that, we try to learn what we can at Mount Court. Julie has friends—"

"*Loyal* friends."

"But they like you, too." She smiled crookedly, having spotted a rose in a bed of thorns. "You're a charmer, Peter. You wink at them, and their little hearts flutter. Just the thing that's gotten you in trouble could get you out. If those friends understand how much damage an unjust accusation will cause you, they may come forward. Julie's been fooling around with someone. Her friends probably won't have witnessed it firsthand, but they'll know something. You'll see."

It sounded right, and easy, and fair. Paige just hoped it would prove so. With everything else closing in around her, she needed something to work.

Twenty-two

Noah stood at his desk at noon the next day, not quite knowing how his life had suddenly become so complex and wondering if he could hold it together. He had been hired as interim Head at Mount Court first and foremost for his managerial skills. He hoped they were good enough.

One thing was for sure. He wasn't quitting. He had done that twelve years ago, when Liv had humiliated him. He had walked away and made a new life, and in the process he had lost Sara. He had no intention of losing her this time.

Nor—despite what her reluctant little mind supposed—did he intend to lose Paige.

And then there was Mount Court. What he had first thought to be a horror of a place had turned out to be something with promise. The best of the faculty were emerging as leaders, shaming the laziest to do more. Same with the kids. First-term grades were higher than they had been in years, and while there were grumbles aplenty about the increased course demands, there were smiles as well. For the first time the students knew what was expected of them. They knew what the rules were, knew what would happen if they broke those rules. The fact that they were thriving was a validation of Noah's approach.

Now along comes Julie Engel, insisting that Peter Grace had raped her. And along comes Julie's father with his lawyer, making grandiose threats. Countering them were Peter Grace and his lawyer, who had, for the time being, at least, gagged the Engels by threatening a countersuit if a smear took place before ample evidence was found. That gave Noah a little time.

"They're here," his secretary said from the door.

He waved a hand. The secretary relayed the gesture and stood aside while four girls entered the room. They were Julie's friends—Alicia, Deirdre, Tia, and Annie. They had called earlier to ask to see him, to his relief. If he had been the one to call them, he would have been accused of tampering with potentially hostile witnesses. Now he was simply the Head of Mount Court being accessible to his students.

He motioned them to sit and perched on the corner of the radiator. "What can I do for you?" he asked, as if he didn't know.

Alicia, the spokeswoman apparent, said, "We heard what happened this morning."

"How?" he asked, as if he didn't know.

"Julie told us. She said she wasn't supposed to, and she made us promise not to do anything, but she's really upset. She said you don't believe her. But we *saw*, Mr. Perrine."

He sat very still. "You saw what?"

"We saw her with Dr. Grace."

"Doing what?"

"They were hugging. It was at the hospital, right in front of everyone."

Noah might have moaned in disgust, if he hadn't had faith in Paige, who had faith in Peter. "What kind of hug was it?"

Alicia looked confused, clearly caught off guard.

"What do you mean?" Deirdre asked.

"Was it a friendly hug?"

"What other kinds are there?"

"There are passionate ones. Or desperate ones. There are relieved ones. And victorious ones."

"They were *wrapped in each other's arms*."

"Uh-huh," Noah acknowledged. "That's how I'd define a hug. What I want to know is what kind you saw."

"It was a *hug*," Alicia insisted, as though that made it all clear.

"Then perhaps there wasn't anything wrong with it," Noah pointed out. "I hugged you—remember, when we all made it across Knife Edge—and no one thought anything amiss. Did you think I was coming on to you?"

Alicia colored. Quickly she said, "No."

"But you're sure that the way Dr. Grace and Julie were hugging suggested they were having an affair. How do you know? What did you see that suggested passion? Did they kiss?"

"Maybe later."

"Did you see them do it?"

"No."

"Did they hold hands when they were drawing apart?"

Alicia sought the others' help, but they remained quiet. "No," she conceded, then added, "They couldn't do that. Everyone was watching."

"They were watching the hug, too. I take it that it was less suggestive than hand holding? Pretty innocent, huh?" When Alicia didn't respond, he said, "Okay. Let's talk about words. Did they say anything to each other at the time of this hug? Make any promises? Set a date for later?"

Tia said, "We didn't hear. We were on our way downstairs."

"Just because we didn't hear anything," Deirdre put in, "doesn't mean it didn't happen."

"Yet you choose to believe that it did," Noah said.

"Because Julie says."

Noah drew in a deep breath and sat straighter. "Well, I say that Julie is in a whole lot of trouble and wants someone to share the heat. So she's fingering Dr. Grace, who is old enough to be her father and, by the way, has no trouble finding women closer to his own age. Why would he be interested in an eighteen-year-old?"

"Men always like younger women."

"Always?"

"A *lot* of the time."

"Are you speaking from personal experience, Deirdre? Has Dr. Grace ever come on to you?"

"No."

"Or you?" he asked Alicia, who quickly shook her head. "Or you?" he asked the other two. There wasn't a single nod.

"Yet you jump at the chance to say that he came on to Julie."

"She said he did."

"And you're her friends, so you're supporting her. That's a fine thing to do, assuming the case is a valid one. If not, your support is ill spent. If she's lying, you won't look so great. You'll be walking around here with egg on your faces, because if she's lying, the other kids will know. They'll know that she was fooling around with another student, or maybe with someone at home during fall break, who just happened to get her pregnant, and chances are they'll know who that boy is. Do you think he'll sit back and let Dr. Grace take the fall for him?"

"He'll get in worse trouble if he comes forward," Annie said, and immediately knew she had blundered. She shot a frightened look at the others, who tried their best to ignore her.

Noah didn't home in on her. If he couldn't get a name from the others, he might seek her out separately, but she was the most vulnerable of the bunch. He wouldn't put her on the spot. Not yet.

"The fact is," he said to the group as a whole, "the deed is done. Julie is pregnant. You girls know; the rest of the school will know before long, and kids will be whispering." He knew how that worked. Boy, did he ever. "My guess is that it'll be the major topic of discussion, second only to where you all will be skiing over Christmas. And there will be speculation. Dr. Grace may seem like a perfect patsy, but he'll be denying her claim. If it comes to a trial, his lawyer will put you girls on the witness stand and ask you the same kinds of questions I asked you before, and you're going to make fools of yourselves. Because one hug, between people who know one another, particularly in this day and age of the sensitive man, does not make an affair. There might have been any number of reasons for that hug, all totally innocent. If any of you saw something else, something more definitive between Julie and Dr. Grace, either at that time or at another time, I'd like to hear about it. I'd also like to hear about relationships she may have with guys here. You can be sure I'll be asking the faculty. They see more than you think."

"Why can't Julie just get an abortion and be done with it?" Tia asked. "Why does *anyone* have to be named?"

"In theory, no one does, though that means Julie has to take the flak alone. In this case, someone has already been named, and that someone stands to lose his practice and his reputation. I want to get at the truth before that happens." He looked from one face to the other. "Any suggestions about who the guilty party really is? Any names Julie might be scribbling in her notebooks? Anyone she might be stealing off to be with in the shack by the pond—you didn't think I knew about that?" he asked in response to the widened eyes. "I was young once. That'd be the place I'd pick if I wanted shelter from the night with my girl." He made a round of the faces again. "No thoughts on who's using the shack now?"

If they had any, they weren't sharing them.

"Let me say one more thing, then," he offered gently. As he saw it, his job included the teaching of values. "You kids have an unwritten code that says you don't rat on each other, and that's commendable, in some circumstances. In others, it isn't at all.

"This is one of those others. I could understand you maintaining a silence if no names had been mentioned. What happened between Julie and this other person was private. If they don't speak up, that's their decision. But we'll probably find out who it was anyway, and the longer it goes on, the harder it will be on that person." He let the thought sink in before adding, "If you all keep your silence and sit by while Dr. Grace's name is smeared, you'll be as guilty as Julie."

He saw one hard swallow, several fidgety fingers, and a pair of eyes that were trying not to blink. Quietly and with disappointment, he said, "If any of you want to talk again, alone or together, I'll be around and glad to listen."

He gave the radiator a pat, rose, and went to the desk. By the time he had focused on the papers there, the girls had left. The timing couldn't have been better. Two minutes later he got a call from the president of the Board of Trustees.

Roger Russell had graduated from Mount Court thirty years before, was a successful businessman in New York, and traveled to Tucker for monthly meetings. He and Noah talked on the phone in between. Noah liked him. He was thoughtful and reasonable, realistic about Mount Court's problems, and anxious to solve them. He was a modifying force for the rest of the board, which was older, more conservative and demanding. If any of those others had been president, Noah might not have taken the job. It was Roger's personal plea that had clinched it.

Now Roger was pleading again. "Tell me that what Clint Engel just told me isn't true."

Noah had known Clint would call him. When parents were paying as much as Mount Court parents were, if they didn't get satisfaction from the Head of the school, they went higher. "I'm not sure what he told you, but the part about his daughter being pregnant is true."

"By the school's doctor?"

"That part isn't true."

"Are you sure?"

"Reasonably. I don't know the man well, but I do know one of his partners, and she *is* vouching for him. Apparently Julie made a play for Peter. She asked him to take pictures of her, and when he refused, she was angry. Now she's pregnant, and she needs someone to blame, hence her revenge. The real father could be one of half a dozen seniors here. She's an active dater."

"Clint is livid. Whether or not charges are brought against the doctor, he blames the school for lax supervision."

"Do you?" Noah asked, wanting to know where he stood.

"Of course not. The school can't take these kids to the toilet, for God's sake, but sex happens there. Sex happens all over the place at boarding schools, except maybe at the few single-sex schools that remain, and even then you never know. So how can we get at the truth?"

"I'll be meeting with the faculty members who are closest to Julie later," Noah said. "They may know who the boy is. Or they may be able to find out. It won't be so bad if it's a student—easy to blame on the irresponsibility of youth, rather than a man the school pays to guard the well-being of the students."

Roger sighed. "We have a serious problem in either case. I tried to calm Clint down, but he's out for blood. I've set up a meeting with him here in the city tomorrow. Our lawyer will come. Between the two of us, we may be able to convince Clint that he's hurting his daughter more than anyone by making a scene."

"He's a volatile man. It's no wonder she had to cry rape. He has her up against a wall."

"He's working on putting us there, too, Noah, and damn it, I don't like that. Mount Court is finally getting its act together. To be set back by one irresponsible girl doesn't seem right."

Noah tried to think positively. "It may come to nothing. She may break down and confess to being involved with someone else, in which case her father will know she was lying. Or someone else may come forward, with the same result. The school is in trouble only if Clint chooses to take us to court."

"Let's hope he doesn't," Roger replied. "For more reasons than one. You've done a remarkable job in three months. I was hoping I could convince you to stay."

In September, Noah wouldn't have considered it. He would have laughed in Roger's face. But things had changed. He might want to stay now. For more reasons than one. "I promised you one year. You'll have that, at least."

"But you've started good programs. I want them continued and more added. If this thing goes to court, that may be impossible. The board will want to distance itself from you and everything you've done, which means regressing to the place we were at before you came. You'll be blamed right along with the doctor. We won't have much of a choice, Noah, if Mount Court is to come out with the least amount of damage."

Noah understood that. He was a realist. Unfortunately, if he left under the cloud of a lawsuit, finding another headship would be hard. He could go back to the foundation, but that wasn't what he wanted.

"I'll let you know what happens tomorrow," Roger concluded. "In the meanwhile, call me if you learn anything. We have to settle this soon, one way or another."

Noah knew precisely what Roger hadn't said. Totally aside from minimizing the damage to Mount Court that would arise from a scandal, there was the matter of hiring a new Head. If Noah wasn't staying, other candidates would have to be interviewed. The time for that was fast approaching.

Noah had no sooner signed off with Roger than he received a call from Walker Gray, a member of the board. He, too, had received a call from Clint Engel, who belonged to his golf club. Walker was far less sympathetic than Roger had been.

"How could this have happened? I thought you were brought in to straighten things out, so now one of our students has been molested by the school doctor. How did it *happen?*"

"She was *allegedly* molested," Noah corrected. "Nothing's been proven. The doctor denies he ever touched the girl in anything but a professional manner."

"Well, he's lying."

"Do you have proof of that?"

"She's *pregnant.*"

Noah let the absurdity of the accusation hang on the line for a minute, during which he made sure his temper was in check. Then he said, "That's no more proof that she was molested by our doctor, than that she was molested by her own father."

"Clint wouldn't touch the girl!"

"Peter Grace claims he wouldn't, either. So who do you believe? The fact is that Julie is a social butterfly. She could have been with any number of boys, either here or at home."

"Do you have *any* control over what happens there?"

Noah defended himself, not only then, but a short time later when another member of the board called and, a short time after that, another. All told that afternoon, he spoke with five board members and four parents. His secretary had just left for the day when the phone rang again, and he nearly let it ring. But he could calm people down. The more of them he talked with, the more heard the rational argument. So he answered the phone.

It was Jim Kehane, his Santa Fe connection. "Just wondering if you've given more thought to coming here next year," he said. "The offer is open. We're starting to set up interviews with other candidates. I'd like to set some up for you. As things stand now, you're our first choice."

Noah wanted to say, "Wait 'til you hear what's been going on here. I may not be your first choice for long." Instead he said, "I'm interested." He had to keep his options open. "What would you like me to do?"

"A résumé is all we need now. A letter or two of recommendation wouldn't hurt, either. The rest will come later. Say, this is good news, Noah. I was worried you'd decide to stay at Mount Court. I take it everything is going well there?"

Noah managed to answer with an ambiguity that didn't compromise him, but he got off the phone as quickly as possible and left the office soon after. He didn't need more phone calls. What he needed was to meet with Julie's dorm parent and faculty adviser.

Paige's last patient of the day was a three-year-old girl, the first child of a couple from lower Tucker. Her parents rarely saw each other; one worked the day shift and one the night so that Emily was never alone. The father, who had brought her in after she had coughed her way through the day, had her dressed in multiple layers against the December cold. None of the layers matched. She looked like a roly-poly rag doll—in Paige's view absolutely precious.

Paige handed the father the prescription she had just written out and lifted the child from the examining table. "Give her the medicine four times a day, but make sure she's eaten something before she takes it. Keep her warm, have her drink as much as she'll take, and call me if you don't see improvement in two days."

As though knowing help was on the way, little Emily was peaceful in Paige's arms. "Such a sweetheart," Paige said with a smile, but the smile grew sad when she thought of how Sami would be at three, and the knot in her stomach reclenched. She was fine when she was working and mentally challenged, but at in-between times like this, brief moments when her mind wandered, she fell back into a melancholy funk.

She hugged Emily and returned her to her father, saw them to the door, and retreated into her office. Peter and Angie joined her there a short time later.

"Any news?" Angie asked Peter.

He shook his head, looking exhausted. Paige suspected he was having as much trouble concentrating as she had.

"Julie's father isn't moving to bring charges yet," he said, "but I don't know how long we can hold him off. She still insists it was me."

"Did she say it to your face?" Angie asked.

"No. I tried to get her to. I asked her outright, there in Perrine's office, but her lawyer cut in and accused me of harassing her. If she continues to point at me, and if no one else comes forward, it's only a matter of time before they go to the cops. They'll indict me for rape, her word against mine." He eyed Paige. "It doesn't look good."

Paige, who was sitting with her fists pressed to her mouth, wanted to disagree, but she couldn't find the words. She was overwhelmed thinking what damage a rape charge would do to Peter, to Mount Court—and to the practice, which was the one single, most solid entity around which the rest of her life revolved. If it fell apart along with everything else, she might just hang in the air for an agonizing minute before shattering on the ground.

"What is Julie doing about the baby?" Angie asked.

"She isn't about to tell me," Peter remarked dryly. "Have you heard anything?"

Paige shook her head. "Her father has taken her back to New York. She'll see an obstetrician there."

"Do you think she'll abort it?" Angie asked.

Paige had no idea.

"Whether she does or not," Peter insisted, "DNA tests will prove that the baby isn't mine. My lawyer is putting a request into writing that if there is an abortion, the fetal tissue should be tested. If they fail to do it, they're destroying evidence. I wish there were as conclusive a test for rape."

"She never complained to anyone," Angie pointed out. "She never showed up with bruises."

He grunted. "She couldn't very well have told Paige that Paige's own partner raped her."

"Sure she could have."

"She'll say she couldn't. She'll stand there in the DA's office, wearing the most sedate clothes she can buy, playing the part of the innocent."

"If no one else ever saw bruises—"

"Don't need bruises. By definition, rape is sex against a woman's will. Bruises aren't required."

"But they would certainly help her prove her case. If she's without proof of force, and if tests show that the baby isn't yours, her case becomes skimpy."

"You underestimate Julie," he argued. "So did I, until she came out with this charge. She's a shrewd little bitch. She'll say that I raped her while she was involved with someone, and that she honestly thought the baby was mine rather than his. Believe me, she'll let the rape charge stand. She's that pissed at me for not being attracted to her." He snorted. "I should be flattered."

"Peter," Angie chided.

He ran a hand along the back of his neck. "She'll never admit that she lied. She's stubborn and proud. She's defiant. And she's terrified of her father." He faced them. "It doesn't look good. It's only a matter of time before word gets out, and once it does, the practice stands to suffer. Maybe I should resign before that happens."

Paige, who had been listening to the give and take in muted dread, dropped her fists and said, "No."

Angie said the same.

"Think about it," Peter invited on a note of self-mockery. "This may be my one most selfless moment in life. You won't get a better offer."

"No."

"No."

"And if I'm indicted and our patients go else-where?"

"Where will they go?" Angie asked. "We're the best around."

"Yeah. The only catch to that line of reasoning is that you'll be hundreds of miles away in New York."

"That's not definite at all."

"But it is definite that Paige will be here. So what do you say, Paige? You're the one who stands to lose most."

"And Cynthia," Angie pointed out. "She's an inno-cent in this mess."

"You're all innocent. I'm the bad guy here. Paige? What do you say?"

Paige was trying to concentrate, but it was hard when things like sadness, fear, and regret interfered. Even more distracting were persistent images—of a school in the desert, of Noah, of Nonny and Sami, of Angie in New York, of Mara decaying on the hillside overlooking town.

Mara would have known what to tell Peter. This was the kind of situation in which she came to life. When she believed in a cause, she fought. She had the strength for it. And Paige?

To her horror, her eyes filled with tears. She tried to hide them by examining her fingers. "I, uh"—she cleared her throat—"I don't think it's fair that this should happen right now. Damn it, it isn't." She took a steadying breath and raised her eyes. "You've gotten your act together, Peter. It's like you found yourself after the accident—with Kate Ann and all—and now you're fighting Jamie Cox like Mara would have done. And you, too, Angie. You don't deserve this now. You didn't turn over and die when things at home got tense. You fought."

"I took a risk of the heart," Angie said. "They're necessary sometimes."

A risk of the heart. Like Mara's deep connect.

Paige's throat started to tighten again. After clearing it, she said, "You won. Things are better at home. Whether or not you move, the choice should be yours. You shouldn't be forced out because our patients are spooked by a lie." She looked from one to the other. They had both come a long way since Mara's death. And she? She was marking time, lacking the courage to act.

"Paige?" Angie queried softly.

Lacking the courage to *make decisions*. But if she waited, she would lose. She would fail. Like Mara.

"I don't want any resignations," she said with abrupt force. "No resignations."

"Would you rather we talk about this later?"

She brushed at the tears in the corners of her eyes and shook her head. "I have to go home to see Sami." Her eyes, damp but steady, met Peter's. "No resignation. We fight."

Angie arrived home to an empty house, which didn't make sense, given the hour. Ben was usually home by then. Especially lately.

Along with their agreement to talk things out, they had agreed to try to coordinate their schedules. Angie would tell him when she would be home from work, and he would make an effort to be there when she arrived. It wasn't quite the spontaneity that they had thrived on in their twenties, but they weren't in their twenties anymore. They were in their forties. Spontaneity was harder to come by—which didn't mean that they couldn't do exciting things, simply that they had to plan more for them.

Ben hadn't told her of any plans that would keep him away from home this late in the day. She was on the verge of worry when she heard his car in the drive. She was at the back door in time to welcome not only Ben, but Dougie.

"What a treat!" She gave both of them hugs, then studied Dougie, who looked vaguely down at the mouth. "Is everything all right?"

"He heard about Peter," Ben explained. "I wanted to get him home for a little while so that we could talk about it."

Angie gave his arm a grateful squeeze. It was the kind of thing she would have done herself, had Ben not accused her of smothering the boy.

She led Dougie to the table and sat him down. "The grapevine works with the speed of light. What is it saying about poor Peter?"

"That he raped Julie. But I don't believe it, Mom. I know Peter. He isn't that kind of guy."

She slipped onto the seat beside him. "Are the kids believing it?"

"Big time. Some of them are getting hyper, and it's not only the girls. They're saying he's a pervert. That he likes kids. That they don't want him getting near them again. I've been telling them that they're nuts, but they won't listen. It's like they love the excitement of this."

Angie shot a look across the table, to where Ben lounged on a chair. "He's very perceptive."

"And disillusioned?" Ben asked.

Angie shared that worry. To Dougie she said, "Don't be too hard on them. They don't know Peter like you do. They're simply reacting against everything that's in the news these days. But you're right to argue in Peter's behalf. He says he's innocent, and I believe him."

"But if none of the kids will let him near them, that means he's out of a job at Mount Court. That's not fair."

"No. It's not. But things may change. All we need is someone coming forward to tell who Julie was really with."

"Someone fathered the baby she's carrying," Ben said. "We need to know who."

Dougie glanced from one to the other. "Don't look at me. I don't know who the guy is. I don't know Julie Engel at all. I'm just telling you what the kids are saying."

"Are they only talking about Peter?" Angie asked. "Aren't they saying anything at all about Julie?"

"My friends don't know her, either, Mom. She's a *senior.*"

"Your mother knows that," Ben said. "She's thinking that if you heard gossip about Peter, you might have heard gossip about Julie."

"No. Just about Peter. I *hate* it when they call him a pervert. He's a friend of ours, and he's your partner. It doesn't say much about you if you're practicing with a pervert."

"Peter is no pervert," Angie vowed. She thought of the letters Paige had found and the tales they told, and felt that Mara wouldn't mind at all if she shared one. "He and Mara were in love. Did you know that?"

Dougie's eyes went wide. "Were they really?"

Angie nodded.

"Then why didn't they get married?"

"They weren't ready to share their feelings with other people, I guess. Maybe they would have in time, if she had lived."

"She would be *furious* if she heard the stories the kids at school are spreading!"

"You're right," Angie admitted.

"She would be right up there defending him," Ben put in. "That's why it's good that you're there. You can do it for her."

"I can't do much," Dougie muttered. "I defend him, but everyone jumps all over me."

"Are you feeling uncomfortable there?"

"All the time? No way. Just when people get going on this."

Angie was suddenly struck by his voice. It was lower than it had been. She couldn't see signs of a beard, but that would come. He was growing up. "You really do like boarding, don't you," she said.

"It's neat."

"What if," she began, shot a look at Ben, then went on, "What if we didn't live so close? Would you be as comfortable?"

Dougie grew guarded. "I don't know. Why do you ask?"

But Angie regretted having mentioned it. She should have waited until she and Ben had talked it out. She should have let Ben take the lead rather than doing it herself. She had barged in out of habit, assuming that what weighed heavily on her mind weighed as heavily on Ben's. She was orchestrating again.

She sent Ben a silent apology, but he didn't seem perturbed. Rather, he picked up the thread of her thought. "She asks because we've been thinking that I need to have more to do in a day. I finish my work early and then don't know what to do with myself. You're at

Mount Court, and your mom is at the office, and I'm bored. So," he said, taking a breath, "there's a possibility that we may move closer to the city."

"What city?" Dougie asked warily.

"New York."

"But that's so far away!"

"Then," Ben went on, sounding perfectly content, "there's the possibility that we won't move." He looked at Angie. "I talked with some folks at Dartmouth earlier today. They liked the idea of my teaching. They liked it a lot."

Angie brightened. "Did they? That's great!"

"It's just in the first stages of talk, but they knew who I was right away. They thought the students would, too. And you were right. I could go the route of either political science or art."

"Hanover isn't New York."

"No. It doesn't have gridlock."

"But I thought you wanted to hang around with the guys in the city room."

"This might be more interesting. Certainly more of a challenge. Assuming it pans out."

"It will." She was confident of it. "You're too good for it not to."

He gave her a shrug and that tiny twist of his lips that curled her stomach. "At any rate, it seems like the thing to try first, before we pick up and relocate. If it doesn't work, then we can think of the other, but moving is the most disruptive of the alternatives. Your stakes here in Tucker are pretty high. It isn't fair to you to rush into anything that involves leaving."

Angie would have hugged him if they'd been alone. Then she caught herself, realized the foolishness of that thinking, and, rounding the table, circled his neck from behind.

"You have a kind father, Dougie," she said by Ben's cheek.

"You have a kind mother," Ben said, smiling. "She was willing to give it all up here for me."

Dougie was looking confused. "Are you guys okay?"

"Definitely," Angie said. "Hey, I have a geat idea. Why don't we stop over at Peter's—" She cut herself off. She was orchestrating again. Old habits died hard.

"Why don't we stop over at Peter's," Ben finished, "so that he can personally assure you that he isn't a pervert, then we'll catch dinner at the Inn before we drop you back at school. Sound good?"

Peter wasn't at home. He was at Tucker General, on Three-B with Kate Ann. They were cleaning out the last of three Chinese food containers—with chopsticks, which Kate Ann had never used before but had gotten the knack of with surprising speed.

"You did good," Peter said with satisfaction.

She blushed. "I was hungry."

"That's because they're working you so hard." He had the physical therapy department bending over backward for her, and while there wasn't any response in her legs, the rest of her was learning to compensate. "But it's good for you, Kate Ann. You know that, don't you?"

She nodded. "I know it."

"Spoken with resignation." He touched her cheek. "What's wrong?"

"Nothing."

"Are you sure?"

She nodded again, but in the next instant she shook her head. She looked suddenly smaller—Kate Ann had a way of shrinking when she was frightened—and her voice followed suit. "They say I can go home soon."

"They're right."

"But my house isn't made for a—for a—"

"It needs to be adapted. That's easy enough to do."

"But I can't afford it."

"We have a good lawyer working on the case."

"But even if he wins, it won't be for a while."

"Right," Peter said. He cleared away the take-out containers and brushed bits of fried rice from the sheets.

Then he sat on the edge of the bed and tried to act casual, as though he had just come up with the idea rather than having mulled it over for days. "I was thinking that I'd adapt my house for it. You could live there."

Her eyes went wide in horror. "Your house? Oh, no! I couldn't!"

"Why not?" he asked.

"Because it's *your* house. You've already done too much."

"Not really. I've led a selfish sort of life."

"You've done *everything* for me."

"And gotten as much out of it myself. You've been an eye opener for me, Kate Ann. You're the first person I've ever really been generous toward."

"But the children you treat—"

"Their parents pay for my services. They owe me a fee, which is pretty much the way I've looked at life since I came back here to practice. People owe me—money, respect, admiration, adoration. I felt it was my due, after everything I went through as a kid. Like it was proof that I was a big, successful guy, even when I didn't feel like a big, successful guy. But you went through the same shit, and you don't feel anyone owes you a thing. That's why it's so nice to give to you. Besides," he said, feeling oddly shy as he took her hand, "I like you. You're a decent, sincere, responsible person."

"But I mess things up."

"So you're not mechanical."

"I'm not good with people."

"You're perfectly good with me. And you were perfectly good with my family on Thanksgiving."

Her eyes were doe sad. "I didn't know what to say."

"You held your own."

"But that was one day. Living in your house would be every day."

He had to smile. Kate Ann could be persistent. She could also be thick, though that was a product of years of believing what people said about her. "Why do you think I've been coming here every night?"

"Because you're in the hospital anyway."

"Wrong. You're the only one I see here at nights. Just think how much easier it would be if I could go home to see you."

"But—"

"But what?"

"You'd want that?"

"I wouldn't be asking if I didn't. Actually," he said, allowing his mind to wander back to the horror of the day, "I may be getting the better part of the deal." He studied her hand, so fragile in his. "You see, I have a problem."

In a rush she said, "Don't apologize I don't expect anything certainly not any kind of feeling."

"But I do feel," he said, and dared to look up. "I like you a lot, Kate Ann."

"But—but—you don't want me around all the time. You love Mara." They had discussed her at length. Peter had told Kate Ann almost everything. Many a night they had talked far after visiting hours were done, which was no sweat on Peter's part. After all, he was a doctor.

"Loved," he said now. "Past tense. Mara is dead. She can't talk to me. She can't make me smile. She's gone, Kate Ann, and maybe I'm wrong. Maybe one part of me will always love her, but it's not the part that's alive and looking toward the future."

"But you need to be with people."

"You are people."

"*Female* people."

"You are female people."

"You know what I mean," she murmured, and looked so dejected that he leaned forward and brushed his lips against her forehead. Her eyes reflected instant shock.

"That's for being so nice," Peter said, and took a deep breath, "and for making me feel good while the rest of my world is about to shatter." Then he told her about Julie.

"She said *that?*"

He nodded. "If she stands by it, my reputation is gone."

"But she can't say it. I saw her put her arms around you that day."

"What day?"

"The day you introduced her to me. You were standing over there at the door and she came up from behind and put her arms around you. You removed them and told her not to do it again."

"You heard that?"

Kate Ann nodded. "Then you brought her in here and suggested that she get me whatever I needed. She wasn't happy."

"No," he said with a sigh of relief. "She wasn't. You really remember that?"

Kate Ann nodded again.

He smiled. "That is good news, Kate Ann. Good news indeed. A little while ago I told Paige and Angie that the practice could topple if Julie has her way. She claims I want her. It's her word against mine, with no proof either way. But if you're willing to testify about what you saw, that's a start." He couldn't stop smiling. Quiet little Kate Ann, mousy little Kate Ann, *his* Kate Ann to the rescue.

He couldn't wait to tell Paige.

Twenty-three

Paige wasn't immediately concerned when she didn't see Nonny's car. Nonny often ran errands with Sami, and though she was usually home before dark, it was dark so early now that the usual changed.

Her concern came when she went into the kitchen and didn't find a note.

Nonny always left notes when she went out.

Paige looked all over, but she didn't see one. Telling herself that it was simply an oversight on Nonny's part, she went into the bedroom to change into jeans.

"Where are they?" she asked kitty, who was scampering about in such excitement that Paige wondered how long she had been alone.

If kitty knew, kitty wasn't telling.

So Paige went back to the kitchen. It was spotless. Aside from the high chair that stood similarly spotless in the corner, it was much as it would have been had Paige lived alone. But she didn't live alone. She lived with Nonny and Sami, and after the upsetting day she'd had, she had to see them. She had to talk with Nonny. And hold Sami.

She called the General Store, but Hollis Weebly hadn't seen them. She tried the bakery, with similar luck. She tried her neighbor, Mrs. Corkell, with whom Nonny had struck up a friendship, but Mrs. Corkell hadn't seen them. She called three of Nonny's friends in West Winter—Sylvia, Helen, and Elisabeth—but Sylvia hadn't seen them, and neither Helen nor Elisabeth was at home.

She sat down on the stairs in the front hall, tossing a scrunched-up paper ball to kitty, who retrieved it, dropped it at her feet, then crouched down in avid anticipation.

"Just you and me," she said, giving the paper another toss and listening for the tiny patter of kitty's paws on the wood floor. It was indeed a tiny patter, a negligible sound in a dead silent house. Just you and me, she thought, and was infinitely glad just then that she wasn't alone.

But that thought led to another—to several, actually. She imagined Nonny taking herself and her things back to West Winter and Sami being taken away to

God only knew where by strangers. She imagined that the house was as quiet as this every night, just kitty and her, having dinner alone, tossing a paper ball back and forth, night after night after night, because Noah would have moved on, too. And Sara. And Angie, who had taken her risk of the heart and won. And Peter, who might lose his case against Julie but had found himself in spite of it. There would be plenty of people left in Tucker to see, none of whom she wanted to see. Not in the same way.

Year after year after year.

She felt a swift shaft of panic, followed by a hollowness so dense that it threatened to swallow her up. She heard words—*nights in my house are silent—dead— barren*—and thought of Mara, up on the hillside, buried six feet under with hopes and dreams that would never be realized. And suddenly she knew what she wanted.

Or what she didn't want.

She didn't want to live in a house that was silent, dead, and barren. She didn't want to be the victim of missed connections. She didn't want Sami raised by someone else. She didn't want Nonny moving back to West Winter. And she didn't want Noah to leave.

She jumped up from the stairs so quickly that kitty squealed in alarm. Snatching her up, she hurried to the phone and punched out Noah's number.

He sounded exhausted, and rightfully so. He had the weight of his own world on his shoulders. But she had to see him. "Can you come over? I can't find Nonny. I'm imagining all kinds of awful things."

"Give me five minutes," he said, and five minutes later he pulled into the driveway. He ran to the door with Sara on his heels.

Without saying a word, Paige wrapped her arms around his neck and held on tightly. It was only after several minutes of his returning her hug that she was able to talk. She told of coming home to a dark house, finding no note, and phoning all around. She told of sitting on the stairs for what seemed like hours.

"It was awful, Noah," she cried from beneath the shelter of his arm. "The house was dead quiet. Just kitty and me. And it used to be just me *alone*—before Mara died—and that was fine. But something's changed. It isn't fine anymore." When he drew her into his arms again, she felt an instant relief. "I don't want to go back."

"Me neither," he whispered.

"I have to grow. I can't keep holding on to the past."

"No kidding."

"But it's scary."

"Most good things are."

Sara cleared her throat. "Am I supposed to be here?"

"Definitely," Noah said in full voice. "You're part of it."

Paige would have reached out for her if she hadn't been loving Noah's hold so much. There was something new in it, something permanent that should have terrified her but didn't.

"Maybe I should go out looking for Nonny," Sara suggested.

"No. We'll call Norman Fitch in a—"

"Yooo-hoooo," came a call from the kitchen. "Anyone home?"

Paige looked up. Swearing softly, she broke away from Noah and, taking Sara in hand, ran toward the kitchen. Nonny was bundled as tightly and brightly as Sami. Neither looked as though there were anything at all wrong.

"Where have you been?" Paige cried. She caught Sami up in one arm and hugged Nonny with the other. "Noah was about to call the police!"

"But I left a note," Nonny said. "Right there on the table. I said I was going to visit Elisabeth. She's baby-sitting her grandchildren while their parents are away."

"There was no note."

"But I did leave it," Nonny insisted.

"I was so worried!"

"We weren't *that* late."

"But it was dark, and the house was empty and still."
Paige looked Nonny in the eye, suddenly excited. "I'm
keeping Sami. For good. Will you stay?"

Nonny's whole face lit up. "I certainly will. Hallelu-
jah, it's about time."

Paige raised a sheepish look to Noah, who was a wall
of warmth by her shoulder. "I guess it is."

Behind his glasses, his eyes were as bright as Nonny's
face.

"Here's Nonny's note," Sara said, coming through
the door, unfolding the paper ball that Paige had been
tossing to kitty.

Paige gawked. "But it was crumpled up on the
floor."

Sara flattened it on the table. Seconds later kitty was
there, trying to paw it off again.

" 'Scuse me," Noah said, taking Sami from Paige and
putting her in Sara's arms. "I have to talk with Paige
alone for a minute."

He had her by the hand and was leading her from
the room before she could protest, and once he had her
in the front hall, pinned to the wall by the weight of his
body, protest was the last thing on her mind. He kissed
her with a thoroughness that blurred her thoughts.
Having made a bundle of momentous decisions in
an incredibly short time, she was feeling relieved of

an awesome burden. Which was ironic. Since being burdened was what she had feared most.

"Did you mean all you said?" he asked.

She was distinctly lightheaded. "I believe so."

"You want me?"

She pushed his glasses higher on the bridge of his nose. "I've always wanted you."

"To marry?"

She nodded.

"What if I have to leave Tucker?"

"I've always wanted to see Santa Fe."

"If things blow up here, Santa Fe might be out of the question, too. I may have to forget teaching."

"You'll have to work somewhere. And I can work anywhere."

"But you love Tucker."

"I love you more." The words flowed from the heart and caused a catch in Noah's breath. He gave her more of his weight. She loved that, too. "Do you remember our first night?" she asked.

"In Mara's yard?"

"I was feeling totally empty. And then you came out and held me, and the emptiness went. Only I'm just now realizing it. Thick-headed of me, huh?"

"We're all thick-headed when it comes to protecting long-held beliefs. I've done the same. In the process I nearly lost my daughter." He dragged in a long, deep, not-wholly-happy breath. "We have something good at Mount Court, Sara and I. Given the choice, I'd take Tucker over Santa Fe, that's how far I've come, but if things blow up, I may not have the choice. I'll be taking the credit for this one, whichever way it goes."

"Then we'd better make sure it goes the way we want," Paige said with a determination that she might have thought had gone to the grave with Mara. But Mara lived—in Peter and Kate Ann, in Angie and Ben, and now in Paige. It was an incredibly good feeling. An incredibly satisfying feeling. An incredibly *empowering* feeling.

"What?" Noah prompted.

But Paige caught sight of Sara at the kitchen door, looking unsure and alone. She held out an arm and waited for her to join them before saying, "Your dad just made the ultimate confession that even if he had other choices, his first one would be to stay on at Mount Court. What do you think?"

Sara shrugged. "Mount Court's okay."

" 'Okay' isn't good enough. We need enthusiasm."

"I *like* it," she said.

"Then you want to stay, too?"

"Yes."

Paige could tell by the smile she was trying to check that she meant it, and she gave a satisfied sigh. "All that's left, then, is to find out who fathered Julie Engel's baby." She looked up at Noah. "How do we do that?"

"Small groups," he said. "The last of the classes are being held before exams. I think I'll visit a few."

"You'll turn everyone against Julie," Sara cried.

"No. I'll say that she's trying to protect someone, but that we need to know who that someone is. I won't be criticizing Julie."

"They'll think you are. They won't talk."

"Do you think they know who it is?" he asked.

"I don't know."

"Do *you* know who it is?"

"You're asking me to betray my friends."

"No. I'm asking if you know who it is."

"Same difference," Sara said. She broke away and returned to the kitchen.

Noah sighed. He looked at Paige. "She's right, isn't she."

Paige ached for them both. "She's in an untenable position, between you and her friends."

"I wouldn't put her there, if I didn't feel so desperate. To come so close, so close to having it all . . ." His voice trailed off. He drew Paige against him, the one in need of comfort now, and Paige gave him her all. It was an honor and a breeze, the farthest thing from a burden that she had ever done in her life.

Noah knew the code of silence kept by students such as those at Mount Court and knew the misery a child could endure if her classmates thought that she had broken it. That was why he concentrated on talking with juniors and seniors rather than sophomores.

He had worked hard building a relationship with Sara. It was young and fragile. He didn't want anything to shatter it.

No one came forward. One day passed, then another and another, and the charges against Peter Grace and Mount Court, though never formalized in any legal way, seemed to gain legitimacy simply because they weren't proven false. Word spread through town. There was a rash of canceled appointments.

Noah talked with the students again. Paige followed up on his talks. They explained what was happening to Peter and what could happen to Mount Court if false charges prevailed. They pushed for the truth, but no matter how often Noah assured the students that they could come to him in confidence, no one came.

Worried parents called. Concerned trustees called. The faculty began murmuring among themselves much as they had at the start of the year. Worst of all, in Noah's book, a distance sprang up between Sara and him.

"She's withdrawing again," he told Paige. "It's happening right before my eyes, and I can't do a damn thing to stop it. When I ask, she says nothing's wrong. But she avoids me."

"Let me talk with her," Paige said, and she did, but with negligible success. "She says she's nervous about exams."

"Do you believe her?"

"She asked me the same thing. I told her I did, that exam period was always a tense time, especially for the first set of finals at a new school. She bought that. Then I asked if the Julie business might be getting her down, too, and she said no. Too quickly."

"What do you think?"

"I think that the kids are talking. Something's up. I've gotten the same feeling from some of the others I've spoken with. They know something, Noah."

The problem was getting it out of them. He wanted it done before Christmas, but with classes ending and exams beginning, he couldn't very well keep up the pressure. Their minds would be turning to studying.

Or so he thought. On the night after the last day of classes, prior to a day set aside solely for studying, he got a call from the MacKenzie dorm parent. "We're having a problem here, Noah," she said. "I think you ought to come over."

"What kind of problem?"

"Arguments. I'm hearing Julie Engel's name, but not much else."

Julie was temporarily out of the picture. Her father had decided to keep her in New York through Christmas. If she had made a decision about the baby, no one knew what it was. Nor did anyone know if she would return to Tucker.

"I'll be right there," Noah said. After phoning Paige with the news, he grabbed his parka and ran through the snow-crusted darkness to MacKenzie.

The group in the lounge was sexually mixed, talking loudly, and oblivious of his arrival. They were sitting in a jumble, squeezed together on chairs, each other's laps, and the floor, as if in a show of solidarity. At first glance he saw sophomores, juniors, and seniors. At second glance he saw Sara. She was standing alone, with her arms wrapped around herself, and looked as though she had been crying. It was all he could do not to rush to her side.

"But that's not our job," one of the girls was arguing. "It's the cops' job."

"The whole point is to learn the truth *before* they have to come in," Sara cried. "No one wants them involved."

"Certainly not the Board of Trustees," came the counterargument, "and certainly not your father. He'd probably be happy if Julie stays in New York forever, like she was never a student here. But she's been here longer than he has, and longer than you have, Sara. You don't have any right to blab. It's none of your business."

"But it's the right thing to do."

"Ratting on friends?"

"He's *not a friend* if he's letting Dr. Grace take the blame for something he didn't do."

Noah's heart was straining at the seams, torn in two directions at once. He couldn't have been more un-happy to find Sara in this position—or more proud. Lest he be accused of eavesdropping and thereby make the situation worse, he cleared his throat and came forward. "I thought you'd all be studying. I take it there's more on your mind than exams."

All heads flew his way.

"It's Sara's fault. She won't let it go."

Noah might have identified the voice, but he didn't bother. He didn't care who was speaking. What he cared about was the content and the fact that such a large group—he guessed there were twenty-five kids in the lounge—had seen fit to join in.

"Besides, it's over," someone else said. "Julie had an abortion."

Noah had figured she would. "Unfortunately," he said, "just because the baby's gone doesn't mean the case is over. The rape charge against Dr. Grace still stands. As far as the scuttlebutt goes, he's the one who made her pregnant." He looked into a sea of stony faces. "We know that she's been involved with three guys here at school." He saw two of them in the group. "I have to tell you, it's a disappointment to me that none of them has come forward. Is each one positive that he didn't father the child?"

"I didn't," Scott Dunby said, looking at his friends defensively. "We went in town together a few times, but we didn't fool around."

"It doesn't matter who did it," came a disgruntled female voice.

"It sure does," Noah returned. "Dr. Grace is being raked over the coals. His practice is already suffering." He saw Paige driving up to the dorm. "In my book, that's not fair."

Someone snickered. "He has a lawyer. He'll survive."

"Are you going to pay those hefty legal fees for him, Hans?" Noah asked the boy who had snickered. "How would you feel if one of the girls in this room—in front of her parents and me—wrongly accused you of rape?" Hans reddened, looked at his friends, snickered again. "How would you feel," Noah went on, "if you knew that if you were convicted, you could go to jail for years?"

"That wouldn't happen. I'm just a kid."

"Well, Dr. Grace isn't. So just imagine yourself in his shoes. Imagine that he goes to court and is convicted.

Imagine his sitting in a jail cell, with his life spoiled, for something he didn't do."

"He could be tried and acquitted."

"Okay. Imagine that. Imagine he goes to trial, is found not guilty, and then tries to pick up his life. Except that half of his patients have gone to other doctors, and even though he's been found not guilty, there are still those people who always wonder. And then there's the matter of the thousands of dollars that he owes his lawyer. All because he was innocent."

"Maybe he really did it," someone said, "so he deserves to suffer."

"Innocent until proven guilty," Noah advised as Paige came through the door. He felt better when she reached his side. "Besides, it isn't only Dr. Grace. He shares a practice with three other doctors."

"It figures you'd stick up for your squeeze," someone said amid murmurs of assent.

"That has nothing to do with this," Noah countered. "This has to do with whoever was involved with Julie."

"You're making *us* feel like the bad guys."

"I'm sorry if that's what I've done, but the situation is urgent. You'll all be leaving for two weeks of vacation soon, and those two weeks are critical. This should be settled before the holidays."

"Do you want us to lie just to get Dr. Grace off the hook?"

"No. I want the truth. If you don't know the truth, don't say anything at all."

"That's what we've been doing, and you won't let it go."

"Because I think some of you know more than you're letting on." He pushed at his glasses. "I've said this before, but I really do see myself as a teacher of values. That's what so much of this fall has been about, and it's why I'm so disappointed now. Those of you who did the Katahdin climb experienced a raw, gut-deep honesty when we crossed Knife Edge. Those of you who've done community service have seen the less fortunate firsthand and known the decency of helping. Those of you who've worked on the house with me have built something from nothing. There's no deceit when you're hammering nails or laying shingles, only hard work and the satisfaction of a job well done." He paused. "So what's happening here?" He looked bewilderedly at the faces before him. "Where's the raw honesty? Where's the decency? Where's the satisfaction?"

There was silence.

"You've all come so far. Why not come even farther?"

"You're trying to get someone in trouble."

"He's trying to get someone *out* of trouble," Sara put in.

"By getting one of us *in* trouble."

"But if Dr. Grace didn't do it," she pleaded.

The group dissolved into murmurs. Noah caught fragments, things like "on their side" and "not one of us," and he burned.

"She very definitely *is* one of you," he said. "If she wasn't, she would have already told me everything you all are hiding."

"I'm going to tell you anyway," Sara declared, looking more furious than he'd ever seen her. Her eyes were flooded, but the rest of her features were hard as steel. "If they want to say I'm not one of them, that's fine, because if this is what they think is right, I don't *want* to be one of them." She turned to Noah. "It was Ron Jordan."

There was a rustle of voices, then a random, "How do *you* know?"

Sara turned on the boy who had asked. "I know because I saw. I saw them in the woods one night."

"Then you broke the rules," he charged. "You're not supposed to go into the woods at night."

"Right," she said, crinkling up her nose in a taunting way, "but we all do it. It was right after fall break. Julie and Ron were out there, and they weren't being quiet. And even if I *hadn't* seen them, I'd have known it was Ron the same way you do. All of you know. Everyone's been talking about it for days." Still angry, she turned to Noah. "I'm saying it was Ron. Do you believe me?"

"I do," he said. Ron Jordan was the one boy on his short list of three who wasn't there. He was also the one several of the faculty had suspected.

Noah went to her at the same time Paige did, but Sara wasn't interested in either of them. She was looking at the others, her body trembling with anger. Tears slipped down her cheeks, but still she said, "It was hard for me coming here in September. I didn't know anyone. Every time I turned around, someone was calling my father names, and I was terrified you'd find out who I was. Then I made friends. And you found out he wasn't so bad. And you found out who I was and liked me anyway. And then this happened." She wiped her nose with her hand. "Well, I don't care if you don't like me anymore. That's your loss. My father's coming here was the best thing that's ever happened to this school. If you're all too selfish to see that, fine. I don't want to be friends with you."

A voice emerged from the crowd, then a face. It was Meredith. "I'm not too selfish," she said, and threw her arms around Sara. "It was Ron," she conceded softly.

Behind her there was a momentary silence. Then Annie Miller and another girl came forward to join them. Timidly Annie said to Noah, "Julie was upset.

I don't think she knew what would happen when she accused Dr. Grace. She wasn't thinking about that."

Three more students gathered around Sara, boys this time. One was Derek Wiggins. "At first, people thought it was me. But when I was with Julie, I always used something. Always. I didn't know who else she'd been with."

Another twosome came forward. "She couldn't believe she was pregnant. She didn't know what to do."

"I know that," Noah said kindly. "And I don't want us standing here criticizing her. She's gone through a lot. As long as I have the truth, I'll leave her alone to recover."

"It was Ron."

"He wanted to come forward, but she swore him to silence."

"He's in big trouble."

Noah shook his head. His anger had gone the way of false accusations overturned. "Ron made a mistake. He owes Julie a call. He owes apologies to her father and, more important, to Dr. Grace. You can be sure I'll be talking with him, but the past is done. The baby is gone. The important thing now is to move on." He felt a hand slip into his, Paige's hand, warm, confident, and committed. He was stunned by the incredible peace he found on her face.

"Tucker?" she asked softly.

He sought out Sara, who was surrounded by friends and smiling now through her tears. Her eyes met his.

"Tucker?" he mouthed.

She nodded.

He looked at Paige and felt a wash of the very same peace that made her face a joy to behold. "Tucker it is."

"Dear Mara," Paige wrote:

Spring has finally come. The sun is appearing earlier rising higher, staying longer. I saw the first of the snowdrops today, vividly green against the last of the melting snow, topped by little white bells just aching to open. They are sweet things, hopeful things, things of promise, as life is now.

In the six months since you left us, much has changed. The least of that is the practice, which continues to thrive and will do so as long as babies are born, toddlers catch colds, and children shove impossibly small foreign objects into their ears. Cynthia Wales is wonderful—young, full of energy, and dedicated to kids. She isn't the crusader that you were. Hell, she isn't you. But then, we knew she wouldn't be. And it's all right. Because we're carrying the ball more now. The three of us. Who survived.

For Angie and Ben, the past few months have been ones of soul-searching and healing. You'd have hated Ben for what he did, but I do believe he hates himself for it, too. Hurtful as it was, his telling Angie about Nora Eaton shocked them both out of complacency. They think about things now that they had taken for granted. They talk more. They do more. Ben has signed on to teach a seminar at Dartmouth next fall, which will give him the intellectual stimulation he needs, and with Doug boarding at Mount Court, he and Angie have more time to devote to themselves. They go off for weekends sometimes, or just for the day—though there are times when I suspect that they are holed up at home not answering the phone. If so, that's good. Angie needs it. And Ben. Men are needy creatures. You knew that long before we did.

Needy. But neither hopeless nor helpless, as Peter has proven. He was devastated when you died, though it took him a while to admit it. He loved you deeply and profoundly. When he came to realize it, he hit rock bottom. Then the old movie house collapsed, and it was like he rose from the debris, a phoenix from the ashes. He is more at peace with himself now and, in that sense, more self-confident, which isn't to say that he'll ever be totally free of the little boy who was the playground pariah, just that he accepts himself more now. He feels better about himself. He takes pride in doing things that are right, things that once upon a time you would have done. He has picked up the banner you left behind and carries it well.

Kate Ann Murther lives with him. You knew she was special, didn't you? Not me. I was as guilty as the rest of the town in overlooking her. Having come to know her now, I find her loyal and determined. She is probably more active in a wheelchair than she ever was before, though that is in part because of Peter. He takes her out—to dinner, a movie, even on a sled in the snow when he's in a photographing mood. He has forced the town to take notice of her, and while he doesn't exactly take her to the Tavern, nor does he go there nightly himself anymore. A few times a week—enough to keep dibs on his booth— that's all. The rest of the nights he's with Kate Ann. Trite as it sounds, she has made his house a home.

As for justice, Jamie Cox is cooked. Ben gave Peter the name of an aggressive lawyer from Montpelier, who is in the process of filing a class action suit against him. By the time the courts are done, Jamie will be persona non grata in Tucker. He'll be powerless. He'll also be stone broke.

And for me, the only way my life could be richer would be if you were here to share it. I have formally adopted Sami, who is such a joy that I shudder to think of her not being mine. You did that, Mara, forced me to be a mother, and if it had never happened, I would have missed out on a kind of fulfillment that being a pediatrician just can't match. Now I have Sara, too. And with a little luck, given the way Noah and I spend our nights, I'm bound to have another.

Nonny says I should have six. Don't ask me why six. But she keeps saying it.

We'll settle for one or two, Noah and I. I'm not sharing him with six. He's too special.

We had a Christmas wedding. It was beautiful. You should have been there, damn it.

She paused to wipe her eyes, then looked up at a wavering image of Sara at the bedroom door. It was Noah's bedroom, in the beautiful brick Tudor at Mount Court that was old but being renovated room by room, and too small but being enlarged that summer. Sara spent as much time here as she did in the dorm. Paige suspected that she would live with them full-time come fall. She was starved for the kind of family life she had never really had.

"What are you writing?" she asked.

Embarrassed, Paige looked at the paper. She thought of fibbing, then thought again. Sara needed the truth. So she sighed and said, "It's a letter to Mara. I want her to know what's happened. And thank her."

When Sara might have said that she was crazy, that Mara was dead and couldn't read any letter, she didn't. Rather, she came to Paige's side, close, and said softly, "You still miss her."

"Yes. I always will." Her eyes filled again. She wiped them and sniffed, then took the tissue Sara whipped from the box on the nightstand.

"Want me to send Dad in?"

Paige smiled through her tears. "No. I'm almost done. I'll be out soon."

Sara nodded. She started for the door but turned back. "Can I get you anything?"

"No, sweetheart. Just be out there when I finish." She watched Sara leave, thinking how much of a friend the girl had become. Paige loved talking with her, shopping with her, teasing Noah with her. She was as sensitive— and warm—and communicative—as her father when the chip on her shoulder slipped, which it was doing more and more often. Pretty soon it would be a thing of the past.

Like Mara. But no. Not like Mara. Mara would never be a thing of the past. Not in the deepest, most meaningful sense.

"You left us too soon," Paige wrote,

but your leaving taught us much, which is some consolation for missing you. You etched your initials on our lives. We are changed forever, for having known you and, yes, for having lived through your death.

I think of you often.

Dear friend and healer. Once loved. Never forgotten.

HARPER LUXE

THE NEW LUXURY IN READING

We hope you enjoyed reading
our new, comfortable print size and found it
an experience you would like to repeat.

Well – you're in luck!

HarperLuxe offers the finest in fiction and
nonfiction books in this same larger print size and
paperback format. Light and easy to read, HarperLuxe
paperbacks are for book lovers who want to see
what they are reading without the strain.

For a full listing of titles and
new releases to come, please visit our website:

www.HarperLuxe.com